THE
MISTS
FROM BEYOND

THE
MISTS
FROM BEYOND

edited by

Robert Weinberg,
Stefan R. Dziemianowicz,
and Martin H. Greenberg

A ROC BOOK

ROC
Published by the Penguin Group
Penguin Books USA Inc., 375 Hudson Street, New York, New York 10014, U.S.A.
Penguin Books Ltd, 27 Wrights Lane, London W8 5TZ, England
Penguin Books Australia Ltd, Ringwood, Victoria, Australia
Penguin Books Canada Ltd, 10 Alcorn Avenue, Toronto, Ontario, Canada M4V 3B2
Penguin Books (N.Z.) Ltd, 182–190 Wairau Road, Auckland 10, New Zealand

Penguin Books Ltd, Registered Offices: Harmondsworth, Middlesex, England

First published by Roc, an imprint of Dutton Signet,
a division of Penguin Books USA Inc.

First Printing, September, 1993
10 9 8 7 6 5 4 3 2 1

LIBRARY OF CONGRESS CATALOGING IN PUBLICATION DATA:
The Mists from beyond / edited by Robert Weinberg, Stefan
  Dziemianowicz, and Martin H. Greenberg.
      p.   cm.
  ISBN 0-451-45239-9
  1. Ghost stories, American.   2. Ghost stories, English.
I. Weinberg, Robert E.   II. Dziemianowicz, Stefan R.
III. Greenberg, Martin Harry.
PS648.G48M57   1993
813'.0873308—dc20   93-17483
                                                              CIP

Printed in the United States of America
Set in Benguiat and Times Roman

Contents

Introduction

In the 1920s, people with an interest in supernatural fiction found it fashionable to proclaim the ghost story "dead." This may have been more a matter of wishful thinking than informed observation.

In the preceding century, the ghost story had virtually defined the tale of supernatural horror, to the extent that even weird tales that did *not* employ ghosts were described, for want of a more appropriate designation, as "ghost" or "spook" stories. Probably more ghost stories were written during the Victorian era, and probably more writers wrote them, than any time since; not only the authors of penny dreadful novels and stories in the popular fiction weeklies, but distinguished men and women of letters like Oscar Wilde, Charlotte Perkins-Gilman, H. G. Wells, Elizabeth Gaskell, and especially Henry James, whose *Turn of the Screw* (1898) is the best example of how highly the ghost story was regarded as a vehicle for the literate imagination.

By the turn of the century, hundreds of ghost stories were in print and employing ghosts in a variety of roles that ranged from agents of supernatural dread to reassuring manifestations of the afterlife. Several writers, including Joseph Sheridan Le Fanu and M. R. James, had established guidelines for the writing of ghostly tales and were associated almost exclusively with the ghost story tradition. Small wonder, then, that by the time the First World War had introduced the world to horrors that superseded any conceivable on the printed page, the ghost story seemed outmoded, overdeveloped, and exhausted of potential.

The Mists from Beyond is proof to the contrary. Seventeen of its twenty stories were written in the half-century between 1941 and 1992, by a variety of American and British male and female writers. Some first appeared in the popular "pulp" fiction magazines, others in prestigious mainstream journals such as *Esquire* and *Woman's Home Companion,* and still others in original anthologies and single author collections. They were written not only by horror writers, but by mystery, suspense, science fiction, and children's writers. At least two represent their authors' only forays into the macabre. Collectively, they offer conclusive evidence that rumors of the ghost story's demise have been greatly exaggerated.

But they also show something more. In their modernity and distinctness from their nineteenth-century predecessors, they show why the ghost story endures from generation to generation. As discerning readers know, most ghost stories are not about ghosts. Rather, the ghost—like the vampire, the werewolf, the zombie, and other brethren in the supernatural fraternity—is a particular symbol writers use to express fundamental human fears regarding death and the Unknown. Although writers shape and adapt such symbols to fit the particular needs of their era, the concerns they embody transcend any one time or place and defy efforts to deny or repress them. It seems safe to assume that as long as human beings harbor doubts about the purpose of life, the possibility of an afterlife, and the proof of the soul's existence, that the ghost story has a secure niche in our literary heritage.

The four classic stories reprinted here show the variety of uses to which ghosts were put in the Victorian era. Charles Dickens's "The Trial for Murder" (1865) and Ambrose Bierce's "The Middle Toe of the Right Foot" (1891) are both tales of retribution from beyond the grave. Where Dickens sustains the ambiguity of his ghost's existence by suggesting that the entire episode may be the fantasy of a guilty mind, Bierce leaves no doubt for his readers that supernatural forces have redressed an injustice that mortals are incapable of rectifying. In Bram Stoker's "The Judge's House" (1914) the ghost is a simple avatar of Evil, while in Edith Wharton's "Afterward" (1910) it is portrayed more symbolically as an unnatural persistence of the past into the present. These four traditional roles of the ghost—as the specter of a haunted conscience, the moral arbiter, the monster indifferent to human concerns, and the symbol of the inexplicable—are also the foundation on which most of the modern ghost stories are built.

Probably the most traditional of the modern stories is Graham Greene's "A Little Place off the Edgware Road," as fine an example as one is likely to find of how there is no subject too strange or intangible for the modern short story. In contrast, there is Joyce Carol Oates's "Night-Side" (1977), which deliberately employs a nineteenth-century setting and William James's Victorian theories of religious experience to discuss a very contemporary crisis of faith. Oates's story and Shirley Jackson's "The Daemon Lover" (1949) are two outstanding examples of how contemporary writers have used the ghost story to explore the psychology of characters trapped in situations of emotional and spiritual duress.

Modern writers continue to present the ghost as a violation of the natural order, but not always with the intention of frightening readers. Robert Bloch's "The Man Who Collected Poe" (1951) and David Morrell's "But at My Back I Will Always Hear" (1983) introduce their terrifying wraiths only during their climaxes, and thus differ markedly from John D. MacDonald's "The Legend of Joe Lee" (1966) where the intrusion of the supernatural upon the natural symbolizes the differences between the younger and older generations, Madeleine L'Engle's "Poor Little Saturday" (1956) in which the supernatural represents a sense of childish wonder that has been leached from the adult world, and John Updike's "The Indian" (1966) which wryly suggests that it is the present, rather than the ghosts of the past, that is the real violation.

Updike's story is just one of several in which writers explore the humorous potential of the ghost story, using the incongruity of the supernatural in the modern world to reflect on the foibles of human nature. Donald E. Westlake's "This Is Death" (1977) and Clive Barker's "Confessions of a (Pornographer's) Shroud" (1984) use spiritual intervention to transform such grim subject matter as suicide and homicide into grist for burlesque comedy, while Harlan Ellison's "Laugh Track" (1984) and Philip José Farmer's "The Making of Revelation, Part I" (1980) are social satires that compare the irrationality of the supernatural to the extravagances of the popular entertainment industry.

For other writers, the ghost story is the only tool possible for addressing social concerns too complex and unwieldy to be dealt with through a purely realistic approach. Fritz Leiber's "Smoke Ghost" (1941) and Ray Bradbury's "The Crowd" (1943) still read as fresh today as they did half a century ago, in part because the questions they raise about urban life and social behavior remain unresolved. Both Davis Grubb in "Cry Havoc" (1976) and Peter Straub in "The Ghost Village" (1992) use the immortal ghost to address the timeless theme of war, but where Grubb approaches his theme abstractly and with clear didactic intentions, Straub finds in a particular experience within the Vietnam War the perfect analogue for how an encounter with the supernatural strips us of all certainties regarding ourselves and our world.

In *The Mists from Beyond,* readers will find ghosts that not only walk by day, but that are exposed to harsh realities inimical to their existence: the cynicism of the contemporary urbanite, the valuelessness of the consumer culture, the physicality of war and street violence, the laughter of disbelief. That they are not so easily exorcised only reinforces the suspicion that ultimately the ghosts of fiction are reflections of the things we fear in ourselves. Thus, a word of caution before delving into the stories that follow: it may be true that what you can't see can't hurt you—but these are ghosts of substance.

—Stefan R. Dziemianowicz
New York, 1993

The Trial for Murder

Charles Dickens

As one of the leading novelists of his age, Charles Dickens (1812–1870) helped legitimize the literary use of horror and the supernatural in such novels as *The Pickwick Papers* (1837), *Bleak House* (1853), and the unfinished *Mystery of Edwin Drood* (1870). Dickens also popularized the idea of the Christmas ghost story, and wrote the definitive tale in this subgenre, "A Christmas Carol." "To Be Taken with a Grain of Salt" (sometimes published as "The Trial for Murder"), which appeared in the 1865 Christmas issue of his magazine *All the Year Round,* is an uncharacteristically dour Dickens tale and an artful blend of supernatural and psychological horror.

I have always noticed a prevalent want of courage, even among persons of superior intelligence and culture, as to imparting their own psychological experiences when those have been of a strange sort. Almost all men are afraid that what they could relate in such wise would find no parallel or response in a listener's internal life, and might be suspected or laughed at. A truthful traveller, who should have seen some extraordinary creature in the likeness of a sea-serpent, would have no fear of mentioning it; but the same traveller, having had some singular presentiment, impulse, vagary of thought, vision (so-called), dream, or other remarkable mental impression, would hesitate considerably before he would own to it. To this reticence I attribute much of the obscurity in which such subjects are involved. We do not habitually communicate our experiences of these subjective things as we do our experiences of objective creation. The consequence is, that the general stock of experience in this regard

11

appears exceptional, and really is so, in respect of being miserably imperfect.

In what I am going to relate, I have no intention of setting
up, opposing, or supporting, any theory whatever. I know the
history of the bookseller in Berlin. I have studied the case of the
wife of a late Astronomer Royal as related by Sir David Brewster, and I have followed the minutest details of a much more
remarkable case of spectral illusion occurring within my private
circle of friends. It may be necessary to state as to this last, that
the sufferer (a lady) was in no degree, however distant, related
to me. A mistaken assumption on that head might suggest an
explanation of a part of my own case—but only a part—which
would be wholly without foundation. It cannot be referred to my
inheritance of any developed peculiarity, nor had I ever before
any at all similar experience, nor have I ever had any at all
similar experience since.

It does not signify how many years ago, or how few, a certain
murder was committed in England, which attracted great attention. We hear more than enough of murderers as they rise in
succession to their atrocious eminence, and I would bury the
memory of this particular brute, if I could, as his body was buried, in Newgate Jail. I purposely abstain from giving any direct
clue to the criminal's individuality.

When the murder was first discovered, no suspicion fell—or I
ought rather to say, for I cannot be too precise in my facts, it
was nowhere publicly hinted that any suspicion fell—on the man
who was afterwards brought to trial. As no reference was at that
time made to him in the newspapers, it is obviously impossible
that any description of him can at that time have been given
in the newspapers. It is essential that this fact be remembered.

Unfolding at breakfast my morning paper, containing the account of that first discovery, I found it to be deeply interesting,
and I read it with close attention. I read it twice, if not three
times. The discovery had been made in a bedroom, and, when
I laid down the paper, I was aware of a flash—rush, flow—I do
not know what to call it, no word I can find is satisfactorily
descriptive, in which I seemed to see that bedroom passing
through my room, like a picture impossibly painted on a running
river. Though almost instantaneous in its passing, it was perfectly

clear; so clear that I distinctly, and with a sense of relief, observed the absence of the dead body from the bed.

It was in no romantic place that I had this curious sensation, but in chambers in Piccadilly, very near to the corner of St. James's Street. It was entirely new to me. I was in my easy-chair at the moment, and the sensation was accompanied with a peculiar shiver which started the chair from its position. (But it is to be noted that the chair ran easily on castors.) I went to one of the windows (there are two in the room, and the room is on the second floor) to refresh my eyes with the moving objects down in Piccadilly. It was a bright autumn morning, and the street was sparkling and cheerful. The wind was high. As I looked out, it brought down from the park a quantity of fallen leaves, which a gust took, and whirled into a spiral pillar. As the pillar fell and the leaves dispersed, I saw two men on the opposite side of the way, going from west to east. They were one behind the other. The foremost man often looked back over his shoulder. The second man followed him, at a distance of some thirty paces, with his right hand menacingly raised. First, the singularity and steadiness of this threatening gesture in so public a thoroughfare attracted my attention; and next, the more remarkable circumstance that nobody heeded it. Both men threaded their way among the other passengers with a smoothness hardly consistent even with the action of walking on a pavement; and no single creature, that I could see, gave them place, touched them, or looked after them. In passing before my windows, they both stared up at me. I saw their two faces very distinctly, and I knew that I could recognise them anywhere. Not that I had consciously noticed anything very remarkable in either face, except that the man who went first had an unusually lowering appearance, and that the face of the man who followed him was of the colour of impure wax.

I am a bachelor, and my valet and his wife constitute my whole establishment. My occupation is in a certain branch bank, and I wish that my duties as head of a department were as light as they are popularly supposed to be. They kept me in town that autumn, when I stood in need of change. I was not ill, but I was not well. My reader is to make the most that can be reasonably made of my feeling jaded, having a depressing sense upon me of a monotonous life, and being "slightly dyspeptic." I am assured by my renowned doctor that my real state of health at that time justifies no stronger description, and I quote his own from his written answers to my request for it.

As the circumstances of the murder, gradually unravelling, took stronger and stronger possession of the public mind, I kept them away from mine by knowing as little about them as was possible in the midst of the universal excitement. But I knew that a verdict of wilful murder had been found against the suspected murderer, and that he had been committed to Newgate for trial. I also knew that his trial had been postponed over one Sessions of the Central Criminal Court, on the ground of general prejudice and want of time for the preparation of the defence. I may further have known, but I believe I did not, when, or about when, the Sessions to which his trial stood postponed would come on.

My sitting-room, bedroom, and dressing-room are all on one floor. With the last there is no communication but through the bedroom. True, there is a door in it, once communicating with the staircase; but a part of the fitting of my bath has been—and had then been for some years—fixed across it. At the same period, and as a part of the same arrangement, the door had been nailed up and canvased over.

I was standing in my bedroom late one night, giving some directions to my servant before he went to bed. My face was towards the only available door of communication with the dressing-room, and it was closed. My servant's back was towards that door. While I was speaking to him, I saw it open, and a man look in, who very earnestly and mysteriously beckoned to me. That man was the man who had gone second of the two along Piccadilly, and whose face was of the colour of impure wax.

The figure, having beckoned, drew back, and closed the door. With no longer pause than was made by my crossing the bedroom, I opened the dressing-room door, and looked in. I had a lighted candle already in my hand. I felt no inward expectation of seeing the figure in the dressing-room, and I did not see it there.

Conscious that my servant stood amazed, I turned round to him, and said, "Derrick, could you believe that in my cool senses I fancied I saw a———"

As I there laid my hand upon his breast, with a sudden start he trembled violently, and said, "O Lord, yes, sir! A dead man beckoning!"

Now I do not believe that this John Derrick, my trusty and attached servant for more than twenty years, had any impression whatever of having seen any such figure, until I touched him. The change in him was so startling, when I touched him, that I fully believe he derived his impression in some occult manner from me at that instant.

I bade John Derrick bring some brandy, and I gave him a dram, and was glad to take one myself. Of what had preceded that night's phenomenon, I told him not a single word. Reflecting on it, I was absolutely certain that I had never seen that face before, except on the one occasion in Piccadilly. Comparing its expression when beckoning at the door with its expression when it had stared up at me as I stood at my window, I came to the conclusion that on the first occasion it had sought to fasten itself upon my memory, and that on the second occasion it had made sure of being immediately remembered.

I was not very comfortable that night, though I felt a certainty difficult to explain, that the figure would not return. At daylight I fell into a heavy sleep, from which I was awakened by John Derrick's coming to my bedside with a paper in his hand.

This paper, it appeared, had been the subject of an altercation at the door between its bearer and my servant. It was a summons to me to serve upon a jury at the forthcoming Sessions at the Central Criminal Court at the Old Bailey. I had never before been summoned on such a jury, as John Derrick well knew. He believed—I am not certain at this hour whether with reason or otherwise—that that class of jurors were customarily chosen on a lower qualification than mine, and he had at first refused to accept the summons. The man who served it had taken the matter very coolly. He had said that my attendance or nonattendance was nothing to him; there the summons was; and I should deal with it at my own peril, and not at his.

For a day or two I was undecided whether to respond to this call, or take no notice of it. I was not conscious of the slightest mysterious bias, influence, or attraction, one way or other. Of that I am as strictly sure as of every other statement that I make here. Ultimately I decided, as a break in the monotony of my life, that I would go.

The appointed morning was a raw morning in the month of November. There was a dense brown fog in Piccadilly, and it became positively black and in the last degree oppressive east of Temple Bar. I found the passages and staircases of the court-house flaringly lighted with gas, and the court itself similarly illuminated. I *think* that, until I was conducted by officers into the old court and saw its crowded state, I did not know that the murderer was to be tried that day. I *think* that, until I was so helped into the old court with considerable difficulty, I did not know into which of the two courts sitting my summons would take me. But this must not be received as a positive assertion, for I am not completely satisfied in my mind on either point.

I took my seat in the place appropriated to jurors in waiting, and I looked about the court as well as I could through the cloud of fog and breath that was heavy in it. I noticed the black vapour hanging like a murky curtain outside the great windows, and I noticed the stifled sound of wheels on the straw or tan that was littered in the street; also, the hum of the people gathered there, which a shrill whistle, or a louder song or hail than the rest, occasionally pierced. Soon afterwards the judges, two in number, entered, and took their seats. The buzz in the court was awfully hushed. The direction was given to put the murderer to the bar. He appeared there. And in that same instant I recognised in him the first of the two men who had gone down Piccadilly.

If my name had been called then, I doubt if I could have answered it audibly. But it was called about sixth or eighth in the panel, and I was by that time able to say, "Here!" Now, observe. As I stepped into the box, the prisoner, who had been looking on attentively, but with no sign of concern, became violently agitated, and beckoned to his attorney. The prisoner's wish to challenge me was so manifest, that it occasioned a pause, during which the attorney, with his hand upon the dock, whispered with his client, and shook his head. I afterwards had it from that gentleman, that the prisoner's first affrighted words to him were, "At all hazards, challenge that man!" But that, as he would give no reason for it, and admitted that he had not even known my name until he heard it called and I appeared, it was not done.

Both on the ground already explained, that I wish to avoid reviving the unwholesome memory of that murderer, and also because a detailed account of his long trial is by no means indispensable to my narrative, I shall confine myself closely to such incidents in the ten days and nights during which we, the jury, were kept together, as directly bear on my own curious personal experience. It is in that, and not in the murderer, that I seek to interest my reader. It is to that, and not to a page of the Newgate Calendar, that I beg attention.

I was chosen foreman of the jury. On the second morning of the trial, after evidence had been taken for two hours (I heard the church clocks strike), happening to cast my eyes over my brother jurymen, I found an inexplicable difficulty in counting them. I counted them several times, yet always with the same difficulty. In short, I made them one too many.

I touched the brother juryman whose place was next me, and I whispered to him, "Oblige me by counting us."

He looked surprised by the request, but turned his head and counted. "Why," says he, suddenly, "we are Thirt———; but no, it's not possible. No. We are twelve."

According to my counting that day, we were always right in detail, but in the gross we were always one too many. There was no appearance—no figure—to account for it; but I had now an inward foreshadowing of the figure that was surely coming.

The jury were housed at the London Tavern. We all slept in one large room on separate tables, and we were constantly in the charge and under the eye of the officer sworn to hold us in safekeeping. I see no reason for suppressing the real name of that officer. He was intelligent, highly polite, and obliging, and (I was glad to hear) much respected in the City. He had an agreeable presence, good eyes, enviable black whiskers, and a fine sonorous voice. His name was Mr. Harker.

When we turned into our twelve beds at night, Mr. Harker's bed was drawn across the door. On the night of the second day, not being disposed to lie down, and seeing Mr. Harker sitting on his bed, I went and sat beside him, and offered him a pinch of snuff. As Mr. Harker's hand touched mine in taking it from my box, a peculiar shiver crossed him, and he said, "Who is this?"

Following Mr. Harker's eyes, and looking along the room, I

saw again the figure I expected—the second of the two men who
had gone down Piccadilly. I rose, and advanced a few steps;
then stopped, and looked round at Mr. Harker. He was quite
unconcerned, laughed, and said in a pleasant way, "I thought
for a moment we had a thirteenth juryman, without a bed. But
I see it is the moonlight."

Making no revelation to Mr. Harker, but inviting him to take
a walk with me to the end of the room, I watched what the
figure did. It stood for a few moments by the bedside of each of
my eleven brother jurymen, close to the pillow. It always went
to the right-hand side of the bed, and always passed out crossing
the foot of the next bed. It seemed, from the action of the head,
merely to look down pensively at each recumbent figure. It took
no notice of me, or of my bed, which was that nearest to Mr.
Harker's. It seemed to go out where the moonlight came in,
through a high window, as by an aerial flight of stairs.

Next morning at breakfast, it appeared that everybody present
had dreamed of the murdered man last night, except myself and
Mr. Harker.

I now felt as convinced that the second man who had gone
down Piccadilly was the murdered man (so to speak), as if it had
been borne into my comprehension by his immediate testimony.
But even this took place, and in a manner for which I was not
at all prepared.

On the fifth day of the trial, when the case for the prosecution
was drawing to a close, a miniature of the murdered man, missing
from his bedroom upon the discovery of the deed, and afterwards
found in a hiding-place where the murderer had been seen digging, was put in evidence. Having been identified by the witness
under examination, it was handed up to the bench, and thence
handed down to be inspected by the jury. As an officer in a
black gown was making his way with it across to me, the figure
of the second man who had gone down Piccadilly impetuously
started from the crowd, caught the miniature from the officer,
and gave it to me with his own hands, at the same time saying,
in a low and hollow tone—before I saw the miniature, which was
in a locket—"I was younger then, and my face was not then
drained of blood." It also came between me and the brother
juryman to whom I would have given the miniature, and between
him and the brother juryman to whom he would have given it,

and so passed it on through the whole of our number, and back into my possession. Not one of them, however, detected this.

At table, and generally when we were shut up together in Mr. Harker's custody, we had from the first naturally discussed the day's proceedings a good deal. On that fifth day, the case for the prosecution being closed, and we having that side of the question in a completed shape before us, our discussion was more animated and serious. Among our number was a vestryman—the densest idiot I have ever seen at large—who met the plainest evidence with the most preposterous objections, and who was sided with by two flabby parochial parasites; all the three impanelled from a district so delivered over to fever that they ought to have been upon their own trial for five hundred murders. When these mischievous blockheads were at their loudest, which was towards midnight, while some of us were already preparing for bed, I again saw the murdered man. He stood grimly behind them, beckoning to me. On my going towards them, and striking into the conversation, he immediately retired. This was the beginning of a separate series of appearances, confined to that long room in which *we* were confined. Whenever a knot of my brother jurymen laid their heads together, I saw the head of the murdered man among theirs. Whenever their comparison of notes was going against him, he would solemnly and irresistibly beckon to me.

It will be borne in mind that down to the production of the miniature, on the fifth day of the trial, I had never seen the appearance in court. Three changes occurred now that we entered on the case for the defence. Two of them I will mention together, first. The figure was now in court continually, and it never there addressed itself to me, but always to the person who was speaking at the time. For instance: the throat of the murdered man had been cut straight across. In the opening speech for the defence, it was suggested that the deceased might have cut his own throat. At that very moment, the figure, with its throat in the dreadful condition referred to (this it had concealed before), stood at the speaker's elbow, motioning across and across its windpipe, now with the right hand, now with the left, vigorously suggesting to the speaker himself the impossibility of such a wound having been self-inflicted by either hand. For another instance: a witness to character, a woman, deposed to the prisoner's being the most amiable of mankind. The figure in that instant stood on the floor before her, looking her full in the face, and pointing out the prisoner's evil countenance with an extended arm and an outstretched finger.

The third change now to be added impressed me strongly as the most marked and striking of all. I do not theorise upon it; I accurately state it, and there leave it. Although the appearance was not itself perceived by those whom it addressed, its coming close to such persons was invariably attended by some trepidation or disturbance on their part. It seemed to me as if it were prevented, by laws to which I was not amenable, from fully revealing itself to others, and yet as if it could invisibly, dumbly, and darkly overshadow their minds. When the leading counsel for the defence suggested that hypothesis of suicide, and the figure stood at the learned gentleman's elbow, frightfully sawing at its severed throat, it is undeniable that the counsel faltered in his speech, lost for a few seconds the thread of his ingenious discourse, wiped his forehead with his handkerchief, and turned extremely pale. When the witness to character was confronted by the appearance, her eyes most certainly did follow the direction of its pointed finger, and rest in great hesitation and trouble upon the prisoner's face. Two additional illustrations will suffice. On the eighth day of the trial, after the pause which was every day made early in the afternoon for a few minutes' rest and refreshment, I came back into court with the rest of the jury some little time before the return of the judges. Standing up in the box and looking about me, I thought the figure was not there, until, chancing to raise my eyes to the gallery, I saw it bending forward, and leaning over a very decent woman, as if to assure itself whether the judges had resumed their seats or not. Immediately afterwards that woman screamed, fainted, and was carried out. So with the venerable, sagacious, and patient judge who conducted the trial. When the case was over, and he settled himself and his papers to sum up, the murdered man, entering by the judges' door, advanced to his Lordship's desk, and looked eagerly over his shoulder at the pages of his notes which he was turning. A change came over his Lordship's face; his hand stopped; the peculiar shiver, that I knew so well, passed over him; he faltered, "Excuse me, gentlemen, for a few moments. I am somewhat oppressed by the vitiated air;" and did not recover until he had drunk a glass of water.

Through all the monotony of six of those interminable ten days—the same judges and others on the bench, the same murderer in the dock, the same lawyers at the table, the same tones of question and answer rising to the roof of the court, the same scratching of the judge's pen, the same ushers going in and out, the same lights kindled at the same hour when there had been any natural light of day, the same foggy curtain outside the great windows when it was foggy, the same rain pattering and dripping when it was rainy, the same footmarks and turnkeys and prisoner day after day on the same sawdust, the same keys locking and unlocking the same heavy doors—through all the wearisome monotony which made me feel as if I had been foreman of the jury for a vast period of time, and Piccadilly had flourished coevally with Babylon, the murdered man never lost one trace of his distinctness in my eyes, nor was he at any moment less distinct than anybody else. I must not omit, as a matter of fact, that I never once saw the appearance which I call by the name of the murdered man look at the murderer. Again and again I wondered, "Why does he not?" But he never did.

Nor did he look at me, after the production of the miniature, until the last closing minutes of the trial arrived. We retired to consider, at seven minutes before ten at night. The idiotic vestryman and his two parochial parasites gave us so much trouble that we twice returned into court to beg to have certain extracts from the judge's notes re-read. Nine of us had not the smallest doubt about those passages, neither, I believe, had any one in the court; the dunder-headed triumvirate, however, having no idea but obstruction, disputed them for that very reason. At length we prevailed, and finally the jury returned into court at ten minutes past twelve.

The murdered man at that time stood directly opposite the jury-box, on the other side of the court. As I took my place, his eyes rested on me with great attention; he seemed satisfied, and slowly shook a great grey veil, which he carried on his arm for the first time, over his head and whole form. As I gave in our verdict, "Guilty," the veil collapsed, all was gone, and his place was empty.

The murderer, being asked by the judge, according to usage,

whether he had anything to say before sentence of death should be passed upon him, indistinctly muttered something which was described in the leading newspapers of the following day as "a few rambling, incoherent, and half-audible words, in which he was understood to complain that he had not had a fair trial, because the foreman of the jury was prepossessed against him." The remarkable declaration that he really made was this: "My Lord, I knew I was a doomed man, when the foreman of my jury came into the box. My Lord, I knew he would never let me off, because before I was taken, he somehow got to my bedside in the night, woke me, and put a rope round my neck."

The Middle Toe
of the Right Foot

Ambrose Bierce

Between 1872 and his disappearance in Mexico in 1913, Ambrose Bierce (1842–1913?) wrote newspaper columns, humorous sketches, essays, short fiction, and some of the most pointed social satire of the day. Bierce's bitter Civil War experiences and tragic life gave the stories in his two principal fiction collections, *Tales of Soldiers and Civilians* (1891) and *Can Such Things Be?* (1893), a cynical edge. "The Middle Toe of the Right Foot" is a regional haunted house story, but more appropriately for Bierce it is also a tale of harsh frontier justice.

I

It is well-known that the old Manton house is haunted. In all the rural district near about, and even in the town of Marshall, a mile away, not one person of unbiased mind entertains a doubt of it; incredulity is confined to those opinionated persons who will be called "cranks" as soon as the useful word shall have penetrated the intellectual demesne of the Marshall *Advance*. The evidence that the house is haunted is of two kinds: the testimony of disinterested witnesses who have had ocular proof, and that of the house itself. The former may be disregarded and ruled out on any of the various grounds of objection which may be urged against it by the ingenious; but facts within the observation of all are material and controlling.

In the first place, the Manton house has been unoccupied by mortals for more than ten years, and with its outbuildings is slowly falling into decay—a circumstance which in itself the judi-

23

cious will hardly venture to ignore. It stands a little way off the loneliest reach of the Marshall and Harriston road, in an opening which was once a farm and is still disfigured with strips of rotting fence and half covered with brambles overrunning a stony and sterile soil long unacquainted with the plow. The house itself is in tolerably good condition, though badly weather-stained and in dire need of attention from the glazier, the smaller male population of the region having attested in the manner of its kind its disapproval of dwelling without dwellers. It is two stories in height, nearly square, its front pierced by a single doorway flanked on each side by a window boarded up to the very top. Corresponding windows above, not protected, serve to admit light and rain to the rooms of the upper floor. Grass and weeds grow pretty rankly all about, and a few shade trees, somewhat the worse for wind, and leaning all in one direction, seem to be making a concerted effort to run away. In short, as the Marshall town humorist explained in the columns of the *Advance,* "the proposition that the Manton house is badly haunted is the only logical conclusion from the premises." The fact that in this dwelling Mr. Manton thought it expedient one night some ten years ago to rise and cut the throats of his wife and two small children, removing at once to another part of the country, has no doubt done its share in directing public attention to the fitness of the place for supernatural phenomena.

To this house, one summer evening, came four men in a wagon. Three of them promptly alighted, and the one who had been driving hitched the team to the only remaining post of what had been a fence. The fourth remained seated in the wagon. "Come," said one of his companions, approaching him, while the others moved away in the direction of the dwelling—"this is the place."

The man addressed did not move. "By God!" he said harshly, "this is a trick, and it looks to me as if you were in it."

"Perhaps I am," the other said, looking him straight in the face and speaking in a tone which had something of contempt in it. "You will remember, however, that the choice of place was with your own assent left to the other side. Of course if you are afraid of spooks—"

"I am afraid of nothing," the man interrupted with another oath, and sprang to the ground. The two then joined the others at the door, which one of them had already opened with some difficulty, caused by rust of lock and hinge. All entered. Inside it was dark, but the man who had unlocked the door produced a candle and matches and made a light. He then unlocked a door on their right as they stood in the passage. This gave them entrance to a large, square room that the candle but dimly lighted. The floor had a thick carpeting of dust, which partly muffled their footfalls. Cobwebs were in the angles of the walls and depended from the ceiling like strips of rotting lace, making undulatory movements in the disturbed air. The room had two windows in adjoining sides, but from neither could anything be seen except the rough inner surfaces of boards a few inches from the glass. There was no fireplace, no furniture; there was nothing: besides the cobwebs and the dust, the four men were the only objects there which were not a part of the structure.

Strange enough they looked in the yellow light of the candle. The one who had so reluctantly alighted was especially spectacular—he might have been called sensational. He was of middle age, heavily built, deep chested and broad shouldered. Looking at his figure, one would have said that he had a giant's strength; at his features, that he would use it like a giant. He was clean shaven, his hair rather closely cropped and gray. His low forehead was seamed with wrinkles above the eyes, and over the nose these became vertical. The heavy black brows followed the same law, saved from meeting only by an upward turn at what would otherwise have been the point of contact. Deeply sunken beneath these, glowed in the obscure light a pair of eyes of uncertain color, but obviously enough too small. There was something forbidding in their expression, which was not bettered by the cruel mouth and wide jaw. The nose was well enough, as noses go; one does not expect much of noses. All that was sinister in the man's face seemed accentuated by an unnatural pallor—he appeared altogether bloodless.

The appearance of the other men was sufficiently commonplace: they were such persons as one meets and forgets that he met. All were younger than the man described, between whom and the eldest of the others, who stood apart, there was apparently no kindly feeling. They avoided looking at each other.

"Gentlemen," said the man holding the candle and keys, "I believe everything is right. Are you ready, Mr. Rosser?"

The man standing apart from the group bowed and smiled.

"And you, Mr. Grossmith?"

The heavy man bowed and scowled.

"You will be pleased to remove your outer clothing."

Their hats, coats, waistcoats and neckwear were soon removed and thrown outside the door, in the passage. The man with the candle now nodded, and the fourth man—he who had urged Grossmith to leave the wagon—produced from the pocket of his overcoat two long, murderous-looking bowie-knives, which he drew now from their leather scabbards.

"They are exactly alike," he said, presenting one to each of the two principals—for by this time the dullest observer would have understood the nature of this meeting. It was to be a duel to the death.

Each combatant took a knife, examined it critically near the candle and tested the strength of blade and handle across his lifted knee. Their persons were then searched in turn, each by the second of the other.

"If it is agreeable to you, Mr. Grossmith," said the man holding the light, "you will place yourself in that corner."

He indicated the angle of the room farthest from the door, whither Grossmith retired, his second parting from him with a grasp of the hand which had nothing of cordiality in it. In the angle nearest the door Mr. Rosser stationed himself, and after a whispered consultation his second left him, joining the other near the door. At that moment the candle was suddenly extinguished, leaving all in profound darkness. This may have been done by a draught from the opened door; whatever the cause, the effect was startling.

"Gentlemen," said a voice which sounded strangely unfamiliar in the altered condition affecting the relations of the senses— "gentlemen, you will not move until you hear the closing of the outer door."

A sound of trampling ensued, then the closing of the inner door; and finally the outer one closed with a concussion which shook the entire building.

A few minutes afterward a belated farmer's boy met a light wagon which was being driven furiously toward the town of Marshall. He declared that behind the two figures on the front seat stood a third, with its hands upon the bowed shoulders of the others, who appeared to struggle vainly to free themselves from its grasp. This figure, unlike the others, was clad in white, and had undoubtedly boarded the wagon as it passed the haunted house. As the lad could boast a considerable former experience with the supernatural thereabouts his word had the weight justly due in the testimony of an expert. The story (in connection with the next day's events) eventually appeared in the *Advance,* with some slight literary embellishments and a concluding intimation that the gentlemen referred to would be allowed the use of the paper's columns for their version of the night's adventure. But the privilege remained without a claimant.

II

The events that led up to this "duel in the dark" were simple enough. One evening three young men of the town of Marshall were sitting in a quiet corner of the porch of the village hotel, smoking and discussing such matters as three educated young men of a Southern village would naturally find interesting. Their names were King, Sancher and Rosser. At a little distance, within easy hearing, but taking no part in the conversation, sat a fourth. He was a stranger to the others. They merely knew that on his arrival by the stage-coach that afternoon he had written in the hotel register the name Robert Grossmith. He had not been observed to speak to anyone except the hotel clerk. He seemed, indeed, singularly fond of his own company—or, as the *personnel* of the *Advance* expressed it, "grossly addicted to evil associations." But then it should be said in justice to the stranger that the *personnel* was himself of a too convivial disposition fairly to judge one differently gifted, and had, moreover, experienced a slight rebuff in an effort at an "interview."

"I hate any kind of deformity in a woman," said King, "whether natural or—acquired. I have a theory that any physical defect has its correlative mental and moral defect."

"I infer, then," said Rosser, gravely, "that a lady lacking the moral advantage of a nose would find the struggle to become Mrs. King an arduous enterprise."

"Of course you may put it that way" was the reply; "but, seriously, I once threw over a most charming girl on learning quite accidentally that she had suffered amputation of a toe. My conduct was brutal if you like, but if I had married that girl I should have been miserable for life and should have made her so."

"Whereas," said Sancher, with a light laugh, "by marrying a gentleman of more liberal views she escaped with a parted throat."

"Ah, you know to whom I refer. Yes, she married Manton, but I don't know about his liberality; I'm not sure but he cut her throat because he discovered that she lacked that excellent thing in woman, the middle toe of the right foot."

"Look at that chap!" said Rosser in a low voice, his eyes fixed upon the stranger.

That chap was obviously listening intently to the conversation.

"Damn his impudence!" muttered King—"what ought we to do?"

"That's an easy one," Rosser replied, rising. "Sir," he continued, addressing the stranger, "I think it would be better if you would remove your chair to the other end of the veranda. The presence of gentlemen is evidently an unfamiliar situation to you."

The man sprang to his feet and strode forward with clenched hands, his face white with rage. All were now standing. Sancher stepped between the belligerents.

"You are hasty and unjust," he said to Rosser; "this gentleman has done nothing to deserve such language."

But Rosser would not withdraw a word. By the custom of the country and the time there could be but one outcome to the quarrel.

"I demand the satisfaction due to a gentleman," said the stranger, who had become more calm. "I have not an acquaintance in this region. Perhaps you, sir," bowing to Sancher, "will be kind enough to represent me in this matter."

Sancher accepted the trust—somewhat reluctantly it must be confessed, for the man's appearance and manner were not at all to his liking. King, who during the colloquy had hardly removed his eyes from the stranger's face and had not spoken a word, consented with a nod to act for Rosser, and the upshot of it was that, the principals having retired, a meeting was arranged for the next evening. The nature of the arrangements has been already disclosed. The duel with knives in a dark room was once a commoner feature of Southwestern life than it is likely to be again. How thin a veneering of "chivalry" covered the essential brutality of the code under which such encounters were possible we shall see.

III

In the blaze of a midsummer noonday the old Manton house was hardly true to its traditions. It was of the earth, earthy. The sunshine caressed it warmly and affectionately, with evident disregard of its bad reputation. The grass greening all the expanse in its front seemed to grow, not rankly, but with a natural and joyous exuberance, and the weeds blossomed quite like plants. Full of charming lights and shadows and populous with pleasant-voiced birds, the neglected shade trees no longer struggled to run away, but bent reverently beneath their burdens of sun and song. Even in the glassless upper windows was an expression of peace and contentment, due to the light within. Over the stony fields the visible heat danced with a lively tremor incompatible with the gravity which is an attribute of the supernatural.

Such was the aspect under which the place presented itself to Sheriff Adams and two other men who had come out from Marshall to look at it. One of these men was Mr. King, the sheriff's deputy; the other, whose name was Brewer, was a brother of the late Mrs. Manton. Under a beneficent law of the State relating to property which has been for a certain period abandoned by an owner whose residence cannot be ascertained, the sheriff was legal custodian of the Manton farm and appurtenances thereunto belonging. His present visit was in mere perfunctory compliance with some order of a court in which Mr. Brewer had an action to get possession of the property as heir to his deceased sister. By a mere coincidence, the visit was made on the day after the night that Deputy King had unlocked the house for another and very different purpose. His presence now was not of his own choosing: he had been ordered to accompany his superior and at the moment could think of nothing more prudent than simulated alacrity in obedience to the command.

Carelessly opening the front door, which to his surprise was not locked, the sheriff was amazed to see, lying on the floor of the passage into which it opened, a confused heap of men's apparel. Examination showed it to consist of two hats, and the same number of coats, waistcoats and scarves, all in a remarkably good state of preservation, albeit somewhat defiled by the dust in which they lay. Mr. Brewer was equally astonished, but Mr. King's emotion is not of record. With a new and lively interest in his own actions the sheriff now unlatched and pushed open a door on the right, and the three entered. The room was apparently vacant—no; as their eyes became accustomed to the dimmer light something was visible in the farthest angle of the wall. It was a human figure—that of a man crouching close in the corner. Something in the attitude made the intruders halt when they had barely passed the threshold. The figure more and more clearly defined itself. The man was upon one knee, his back in the angle of the wall, his shoulders elevated to the level of his ears, his hands before his face, palms outward, the fingers spread and crooked like claws; the white face turned upward on the retracted neck had an expression of unutterable fright, the mouth half open, the eyes incredibly expanded. He was stone dead. Yet, with the exception of a bowie-knife, which had evidently fallen from his own hand, not another object was in the room.

In the thick dust that covered the floor were some confused footprints near the door and along the wall through which it opened. Along one of the adjoining walls, too, past the boarded-up windows, was the trail made by the man himself in reaching his corner. Instinctively in approaching the body the three men followed that trail. The sheriff grasped one of the outthrown arms; it was as rigid as iron, and the application of a gentle force rocked the entire body without altering the relation of its parts. Brewer, pale with excitement, gazed intently into the distorted face. "God of mercy!" he suddenly cried, "it is Manton!"

"You are right," said King, with an evident attempt at calmness: "I knew Manton. He then wore a full beard and his hair long, but this is he."

He might have added: "I recognized him when he challenged Rosser. I told Rosser and Sancher who he was before we played him this horrible trick. When Rosser left this dark room at our heels, forgetting his outer clothing in the excitement, and driving away with us in his shirtsleeves—all through the discreditable proceedings we knew whom we were dealing with, murderer and coward that he was!"

But nothing of this did Mr. King say. With his better light he was trying to penetrate the mystery of the man's death. That he had not once moved from the corner where he had been stationed; that his posture was that of neither attack nor defense; that he had dropped his weapon; that he had obviously perished of sheer horror of something that he *saw*—these were circumstances which Mr. King's disturbed intelligence could not rightly comprehend.

Groping in intellectual darkness for a clew to his maze of doubt, his gaze, directed mechanically downward in the way of one who ponders momentous matters, fell upon something which, there, in the light of day and in the presence of living companions, affected him with terror. In the dust of years that lay thick upon the floor—leading from the door by which they had entered, straight across the room to within a yard of Manton's crouching corpse—were three parallel lines of footprints—light but definite impressions of bare feet, the outer ones those of small children, the inner a woman's. From the point at which they ended they did not return; they pointed all one way. Brewer, who had observed them at the same moment, was leaning forward in an attitude of rapt attention, horribly pale.

"Look at that!" he cried, pointing with both hands at the nearest print of the woman's right foot, where she had apparently stopped and stood. "The middle toe is missing—it was Gertrude!"

Gertrude was the late Mrs. Manton, sister to Mr. Brewer.

The Judge's House

Bram Stoker

Bram Stoker (1847–1912) spent most of his adult life as the business manager of actor Henry Irving, but he is destined to be remembered as the author of *Dracula,* the most famous of all vampire stories. Stoker's other work in the horror genre includes the novels *The Jewel of the Seven Stars* (1903), *The Lady of the Shroud* (1909), *The Lair of the White Worm* (1911), and the posthumously published collection, *Dracula's Guest* (1914). "The Judge's House" is taken from the latter and shows the influence of Stoker's Irish countryman Joseph Sheridan Le Fanu, particularly Le Fanu's classic "Mr. Justice Harbottle."

When the time for his examination drew near Malcolm Malcolmson made up his mind to go somewhere to read by himself. He feared the attractions of the seaside, and also he feared completely rural isolation, for of old he knew its charms, and so he determined to find some unpretentious little town where there would be nothing to distract him. He refrained from asking suggestions from any of his friends, for he argued that each would recommend some place of which he had knowledge, and where he had already acquaintances. As Malcolmson wished to avoid friends he had no wish to encumber himself with the attention of friends' friends, and so he determined to look out for a place for himself. He packed a portmanteau with some clothes and all the books he required, and then took ticket for the first name on the local time-table which he did not know.

When at the end of three hours' journey he alighted at Benchurch, he felt satisfied that he had so far obliterated his tracks as to be sure of having a peaceful opportunity of pursuing

his studies. He went straight to the one inn which the sleepy
little place contained, and put up for the night. Benchurch was
a market town, and once in three weeks was crowded to excess,
but for the remainder of the twenty-one days it was as attractive
as a desert. Malcolmson looked around the day after his arrival
to try to find quarters more isolated than even so quiet an inn
as "The Good Traveller" afforded. There was only one place
which took his fancy, and it certainly satisfied his wildest ideas
regarding quiet; in fact, quiet was not the proper word to apply
to it—desolation was the only term conveying any suitable idea
of its isolation. It was an old rambling, heavy-built house of the
Jacobean style, with heavy gables and windows, unusually small,
and set higher than was customary in such houses, and was surrounded with a high brick wall massively built. Indeed, on examination, it looked more like a ´fortified house than an ordinary
dwelling. But all these things pleased Malcolmson. "Here," he
thought, "is the very spot I have been looking for, and if I can
get opportunity of using it I shall be happy." His joy was increased when he realised beyond doubt that it was not at present
inhabited.

From the post-office he got the name of the agent, who was
rarely surprised at the application to rent a part of the old house.
Mr. Carnford, the local lawyer and agent, was a genial old gentleman, and frankly confessed his delight at anyone being willing
to live in the house.

"To tell you the truth," said he, "I should be only too happy,
on behalf of the owners, to let anyone have the house rent free
for a term of years if only to accustom the people here to see it
inhabited. It has been so long empty that some kind of absurd
prejudice has grown up about it, and this can be best put down
by its occupation—if only," he added with a sly glance at Malcolmson, "by a scholar like yourself, who wants its quiet for a
time."

Malcolmson thought it needless to ask the agent about the
"absurd prejudice"; he knew he would get more information, if
he should require it, on that subject from other quarters. He
paid his three months' rent, got a receipt, and the name of an
old woman who would probably undertake to "do" for him, and
came away with the keys in his pocket. He then went to the
landlady of the inn, who was a cheerful and most kindly person,

and asked her advice as to such stores and provisions as he would be likely to require. She threw up her hands in amazement when he told her where he was going to settle himself.

"Not in the Judge's House!" she said, and grew pale as she spoke. He explained the locality of the house, saying that he did not know its name. When he had finished she answered:

"Aye, sure enough—sure enough the very place! It is the Judge's House sure enough." He asked her to tell him about the place, why so called, and what there was against it. She told him that it was so called locally because it had been many years before—how long she could not say, as she was herself from another part of the country, but she thought it must have been a hundred years or more—the abode of a judge who was held in great terror on account of his harsh sentences and his hostility to prisoners at Assizes. As to what there was against the house itself she could not tell. She had often asked, but no one could inform her; but there was a general feeling that there was *something*, and for her own part she would not take all the money in Drinkwater's Bank and stay in the house an hour by herself. Then she apologised to Malcolmson for her disturbing talk.

"It is too bad of me, sir, and you—and a young gentleman, too—if you will pardon me saying it, going to live there all alone. If you were my boy—and you'll excuse me for saying it—you wouldn't sleep there a night, not if I had to go there myself and pull the big alarm bell that's on the roof!" The good creature was so manifestly in earnest, and was so kindly in her intentions, that Malcolmson, although amused, was touched. He told her kindly how much he appreciated her interest in him, and added:

"But, my dear Mrs. Witham, indeed you need not be concerned about me! A man who is reading for the Mathematical Tripos has too much to think of to be disturbed by any of these mysterious 'somethings,' and his work is of too exact and prosaic a kind to allow of his having any corner in his mind for mysteries of any kind. Harmonical Progression, Permutations and Combinations, and Elliptic Functions have sufficient mysteries for me!" Mrs. Witham kindly undertook to see after his commissions, and he went himself to look for the old woman who had been recommended to him. When he returned to the Judge's House with her, after an interval of a couple of hours, he found Mrs. Witham herself waiting with several men and boys carrying parcels, and an upholsterer's man with a bed in a car, for she said, though tables and chairs might be all very well, a bed that hadn't been aired for mayhap fifty years was not proper for young bones to lie on. She was evidently curious to see the inside of the house; and though manifestly so afraid of the "somethings" that at the slightest sound she clutched on to Malcolmson, whom she never left for a moment, went over the whole place.

After his examination of the house, Malcolmson decided to take up his abode in the great dining-room, which was big enough to serve for all his requirements; and Mrs. Witham, with the aid of the charwoman, Mrs. Dempster, proceeded to arrange matters. When the hampers were brought in and unpacked, Malcolmson saw that with much kind forethought she had sent from her own kitchen sufficient provisions to last for a few days. Before going she expressed all sorts of kind wishes; and at the door turned and said:

"And perhaps, sir, as the room is big and draughty it might be well to have one of those big screens put round your bed at night—though, truth to tell, I would die myself if I were to be so shut in with all kinds of—of 'things,' that put their heads round the sides, or over the top, and look on me!" The image which she had called up was too much for her nerves, and she fled incontinently.

Mrs. Dempster sniffed in a superior manner as the landlady disappeared, and remarked that for her own part she wasn't afraid of all the bogies in the kingdom.

"I'll tell you what it is, sir," she said; "bogies is all kinds and sorts of things—except bogies! Rats and mice, and beetles; and creaky doors, and loose slates, and broken panes, and stiff drawer handles, that stay out when you pull them and then fall down in the middle of the night. Look at the wainscot of the room! It is old—hundreds of years old! Do you think there's no rats and beetles there! And do you imagine, sir, that you won't see none of them? Rats is bogies, I tell you, and bogies is rats; and don't you get to think anything else!"

"Mrs. Dempster," said Malcolmson gravely, making her a polite bow, "you know more than a Senior Wrangler! And let me say, that, as a mark of esteem for your indubitable soundness of head and heart, I shall, when I go, give you possession of this house, and let you stay here by yourself for the last two months of my tenancy, for four weeks will serve my purpose."

"Thank you kindly, sir!" she answered, "but I couldn't sleep away from home a night. I am in Greenhow's Charity, and if I slept a night away from my rooms I should lose all I have got to live on. The rules is very strict; and there's too many watching for a vacancy for me to run any risks in the matter. Only for that, sir, I'd gladly come here and attend on you altogether during your stay."

"My good woman," said Malcolmson hastily, "I have come here on purpose to obtain solitude; and believe me that I am grateful to the late Greenhow for having so organised his admirable charity—whatever it is—that I am perforce denied the opportunity of suffering from such a form of temptation! Saint Anthony himself could not be more rigid on the point!"

The old woman laughed harshly. "Ah, you young gentlemen," she said, "you don't fear for naught; and belike you'll get all the solitude you want here." She set to work with her cleaning; and by nightfall, when Malcolmson returned from his walk—he always had one of his books to study as he walked—he found the room swept and tidied, a fire burning in the old hearth, the lamp lit, and the table spread for supper with Mrs. Witham's excellent fare. "This is comfort, indeed," he said, as he rubbed his hands.

When he had finished his supper, and lifted the tray to the other end of the great oak dining-table, he got out his books again, put fresh wood on the fire, trimmed his lamp, and set himself down to a spell of real hard work. He went on without pause till about eleven o'clock, when he knocked off for a bit to fix his fire and lamp, and to make himself a cup of tea. He had always been a tea-drinker, and during his college life had sat late at work and had taken tea late. The rest was a great luxury to him, and he enjoyed it with a sense of delicious, voluptuous ease. The renewed fire leaped and sparkled, and threw quaint shadows through the great old room; and as he sipped his hot tea he revelled in the sense of isolation from his kind. Then it was that he began to notice for the first time what a noise the rats were making.

"Surely," he thought, "they cannot have been at it all the time I was reading. Had they been, I must have noticed it!" Presently, when the noise increased, he satisfied himself that it was really new. It was evident that at first the rats had been frightened at the presence of a stranger, and the light of fire and lamp; but that as the time went on they had grown bolder and were now disporting themselves as was their wont.

How busy they were! and hark to the strange noises! Up and down behind the old wainscot, over the ceiling and under the floor they raced, and gnawed, and scratched! Malcolmson smiled to himself as he recalled to mind the saying of Mrs. Dempster, "Bogies is rats, and rats is bogies!" The tea began to have its effect of intellectual and nervous stimulus, he saw with joy another long spell of work to be done before the night was past, and in the sense of security which it gave him, he allowed himself the luxury of a good look round the room. He took his lamp in one hand, and went all around, wondering that so quaint and beautiful an old house had been so long neglected. The carving of the oak on the panels of the wainscot was fine, and on and round the doors and windows it was beautiful and of rare merit. There were some old pictures on the walls, but they were coated so thick with dust and dirt that he could not distinguish any detail of them, though he held his lamp as high as he could over his head. Here and there as he went round he saw some crack or hole blocked for a moment by the face of a rat with its bright eyes glittering in the light, but in an instant it was gone, and a squeak and a scamper followed. The thing that most struck him, however, was the rope of the great alarm bell on the roof, which hung down in a corner of the room on the right-hand side of the fireplace. He pulled up close to the hearth a great high-backed carved oak chair, and sat down to his last cup of tea. When this was done he made up the fire, and went back to his work, sitting at the corner of the table, having the fire to his left. For a little while the rats disturbed him somewhat with their perpetual scampering, but he got accustomed to the noise as one does to the ticking of a clock or to the roar of moving water; and he became so immersed in his work that everything in the world, except the problem which he was trying to solve, passed away from him.

He suddenly looked up, his problem was still unsolved, and there was in the air that sense of the hour before the dawn, which is so dread to doubtful life. The noise of the rats had ceased. Indeed it seemed to him that it must have ceased but lately and that it was the sudden cessation which had disturbed him. The fire had fallen low, but still it threw out a deep red glow. As he looked he started in spite of his *sang froid*.

There on the great high-backed carved oak chair by the right side of the fireplace sat an enormous rat, steadily glaring at him with baleful eyes. He made a motion to it as though to hunt it away, but it did not stir. Then he made the motion of throwing something. Still it did not stir, but showed its great white teeth angrily, and its cruel eyes shone in the lamplight with an added vindictiveness.

Malcolmson felt amazed, and seizing the poker from the hearth ran at it to kill it. Before, however, he could strike it, the rat, with a squeak that sounded like the concentration of hate, jumped upon the floor, and, running up the rope of the alarm bell, disappeared in the darkness beyond the range of the green-shaded lamp. Instantly, strange to say, the noisy scampering of the rats in the wainscot began again.

By this time Malcolmson's mind was quite off the problem; and as a shrill cock-crow outside told him of the approach of morning, he went to bed and to sleep.

He slept so sound that he was not even waked by Mrs. Dempster coming in to make up his room. It was only when she had tidied up the place and got his breakfast ready and tapped on the screen which closed in his bed that he woke. He was a little tired still after his night's hard work, but a strong cup of tea soon freshened him up and, taking his book, he went out for his morning walk, bringing with him a few sandwiches lest he should not care to return till dinnertime. He found a quiet walk between high elms some way outside the town, and here he spent the greater part of the day studying his Laplace. On his return he looked in to see Mrs. Witham and to thank her for her kindness. When she saw him coming through the diamond-paned bay window of her sanctum she came out to meet him and asked him in. She looked at him searchingly and shook her head as she said:

"You must not overdo it, sir. You are paler this morning than you should be. Too late hours and too hard work on the brain isn't good for any man! But tell me, sir, how did you pass the night? Well, I hope? But my heart! sir, I was glad when Mrs. Dempster told me this morning that you were all right and sleeping sound when she went in."

"Oh, I was all right," he answered smiling, "the 'somethings' didn't worry me, as yet. Only the rats; and they had a circus, I tell you, all over the place. There was one wicked-looking old devil that sat up on my own chair by the fire, and wouldn't go till I took the poker to him, and then he ran up the rope of the alarm bell and got to somewhere up the wall or the ceiling—I couldn't see where, it was so dark."

"Mercy on us," said Mrs. Witham, "an old devil, and sitting on a chair by the fireside! Take care, sir! take care! There's many a true word spoken in jest."

"How do you mean? Pon my word I don't understand."

"An old devil! The old devil, perhaps. There! sir, you needn't laugh," for Malcolmson had broken into a hearty peal. "You young folks thinks it easy to laugh at things that makes older ones shudder. Never mind, sir! never mind! Please God, you'll laugh all the time. It's what I wish you myself!" and the good lady beamed all over in sympathy with his enjoyment, her fears gone for a moment.

"Oh, forgive me!" said Malcolmson presently. "Don't think me rude; but the idea was too much for me—that the old devil himself was on the chair last night!" And at the thought he laughed again. Then he went home to dinner.

This evening the scampering of the rats began earlier; indeed it had been going on before his arrival, and only ceased whilst his presence by its freshness disturbed them. After dinner he sat by the fire for a while and had a smoke; and then, having cleared his table, began to work as before. Tonight the rats disturbed him more than they had done on the previous night. How they scampered up and down and under and over! How they squeaked, and scratched, and gnawed! How they, getting bolder by degrees, came to the mouths of their holes and to the chinks and cracks and crannies in the wainscoting till their eyes shone like tiny lamps as the firelight rose and fell. But to him, now doubtless accustomed to them, their eyes were not wicked; only their playfulness touched him. Sometimes the boldest of them made sallies out on the floor or along the mouldings of the wainscot. Now and again as they disturbed him Malcolmson made a sound to frighten them, smiting the table with his hand or giving a fierce "Hsh, hsh," so that they fled straightway to their holes.

And so the early part of the night wore on; and despite the noise Malcolmson got more and more immersed in his work.

All at once he stopped, as on the previous night, being overcome by a sudden sense of silence. There was not the faintest sound of gnaw, or scratch, or squeak. The silence was as of the grave. He remembered the odd occurrence of the previous night, and instinctively he looked at the chair standing close by the fireside. And then a very odd sensation thrilled through him.

There, on the great old high-backed carved oak chair beside the fireplace sat the same enormous rat, steadily glaring at him with baleful eyes.

Instinctively he took the nearest thing to his hand, a book of logarithms, and flung it at it. The book was badly aimed and the rat did not stir, so again the poker performance of the previous night was repeated; and again the rat, being closely pursued, fled up the rope of the alarm bell. Strangely too, the departure of this rat was instantly followed by the renewal of the noise made by the general rat community. On this occasion, as on the previous one, Malcolmson could not see at what part of the room the rat disappeared, for the green shade of his lamp left the upper part of the room in darkness, and the fire had burned low.

On looking at his watch he found it was close on midnight; and, not sorry for the *divertissement,* he made up his fire and made himself his nightly pot of tea. He had got through a good spell of work, and thought himself entitled to a cigarette; and so he sat on the great oak chair before the fire and enjoyed it. Whilst smoking he began to think that he would like to know where the rat disappeared to, for he had certain ideas for the morrow not entirely disconnected with a rat-trap. Accordingly he lit another lamp and placed it so that it would shine well into the right-hand corner of the wall by the fireplace. Then he got all the books he had with him, and placed them handy to throw at the vermin. Finally he lifted the rope of the alarm bell and placed the end of it on the table, fixing the extreme end under the lamp. As he handled it he could not help noticing how pliable it was, especially for so strong a rope, and one not in use. "You could hang a man with it," he thought to himself. When his preparations were made he looked around, and said complacently:

"There now, my friend, I think we shall learn something of you this time!" He began his work again, and though as before somewhat disturbed at first by the noise of the rats, soon lost himself in his propositions and problems.

Again he was called to his immediate surroundings suddenly. This time it might not have been the sudden silence only which took his attention; there was a slight movement of the rope, and the lamp moved. Without stirring, he looked to see if his pile of books was within range, and then cast his eye along the rope. As he looked he saw the great rat drop from the rope on the oak armchair and sit there glaring at him. He raised a book in his right hand, and taking careful aim, flung it at the rat. The latter, with a quick movement, sprang aside and dodged the missile. He then took another book, and a third, and flung them one after another at the rat, but each time unsuccessfully. At last, as he stood with a book poised in his hand to throw, the rat squeaked and seemed afraid. This made Malcolmson more than ever eager to strike, and the book flew and struck the rat a resounding blow. It gave a terrified squeak, and turning on his pursuer a look of terrible malevolence, ran up the chair-back and made a great jump to the rope of the alarm bell and ran up it like lightning. The lamp rocked under the sudden strain, but it was a heavy one and did not topple over. Malcolmson kept his eyes on the rat, and saw it by the light of the second lamp leap to a moulding of the wainscot and disappear through a hole in one of the great pictures which hung on the wall, obscured and invisible through its coating of dirt and dust.

"I shall look up my friend's habitation in the morning," said the student, as he went over to collect his books. "The third picture from the fireplace; I shall not forget." He picked up the books one by one, commenting on them as he lifted them. "*Conic Sections* he does not mind, nor *Cycloidal Oscillations,* nor the *Principia,* nor *Quaternions,* nor *Thermodynamics.* Now for the book that fetched him!" Malcolmson took it up and looked at it. As he did so he started, a sudden pallor overspread his face. He looked round uneasily and shivered slightly, as he murmured to himself:

"The Bible my mother gave me! What an odd coincidence." He sat down to work again, and the rats in the wainscot renewed their gambols. They did not disturb him, however; somehow their presence gave him a sense of companionship. But he could not attend to his work, and after striving to master the subject on which he was engaged gave it up in despair, and went to bed as the first streak of dawn stole in through the eastern window.

He slept heavily but uneasily, and dreamed much; and when Mrs. Dempster woke him late in the morning he seemed ill at ease, and for a few minutes did not seem to realise exactly where he was. His first request rather surprised the servant.

"Mrs. Dempster, when I am out today I wish you would get the steps and dust or wash those pictures—specially that one the third from the fireplace—I want to see what they are."

Late in the afternoon Malcolmson worked at his books in the shaded walk, and the cheerfulness of the previous day came back to him as the day wore on, and he found that his reading was progressing well. He had worked out to a satisfactory conclusion all the problems which had as yet baffled him, and it was in a state of jubilation that he paid a visit to Mrs. Witham at "The Good Traveller." He found a stranger in the cosy sitting-room with the landlady, who was introduced to him as Dr. Thornhill. She was not quite at ease, and this, combined with the doctor's plunging at once into a series of questions, made Malcolmson come to the conclusion that his presence was not an accident, so without preliminary he said:

"Dr. Thornhill, I shall with pleasure answer you any question you may choose to ask me if you will answer me one question first."

The doctor seemed surprised, but he smiled and answered at once, "Done! What is it?"

"Did Mrs. Witham ask you to come here and see me and advise me?"

Dr. Thornhill for a moment was taken aback, and Mrs. Witham got fiery red and turned away; but the doctor was a frank and ready man, and he answered at once and openly.

"She did: but she didn't intend you to know it. I suppose it was my clumsy haste that made you suspect. She told me that she did not like the idea of your being in that house all by yourself, and that she thought you took too much strong tea. In fact, she wants me to advise you if possible to give up the tea and the very late hours. I was a keen student in my time, so I suppose I may take the liberty of a college man, and without offence, advise you not quite as a stranger."

Malcolmson with a bright smile held out his hand. "Shake! as they say in America," he said. "I must thank you for your kindness and Mrs. Witham too, and your kindness deserves a return on my part. I promise to take no more strong tea—no tea at all till you let me—and I shall go to bed tonight at one o'clock at latest. Will that do?"

"Capital," said the doctor. "Now tell us all that you noticed in the old house," and so Malcolmson then and there told in minute detail all that had happened in the last two nights. He was interrupted every now and then by some exclamation from Mrs. Witham, till finally when he told of the episode of the Bible the landlady's pent-up emotions found vent in a shriek; and it was not till a stiff glass of brandy and water had been administered that she grew composed again. Dr. Thornhill listened with a face of growing gravity, and when the narrative was complete and Mrs. Witham had been restored he asked:

"The rat always went up the rope of the alarm bell?"

"Always."

"I suppose you know," said the doctor after a pause, "what the rope is?"

"No!"

"It is," said the doctor slowly, "the very rope which the hangman used for all the victims of the Judge's judicial rancour!" Here he was interrupted by another scream from Mrs. Witham, and steps had to be taken for her recovery. Malcolmson having looked at his watch, and found that it was close to his dinner hour, had gone home before her complete recovery.

When Mrs. Witham was herself again she almost assailed the doctor with angry questions as to what he meant by putting such horrible ideas into the poor young man's mind. "He has quite enough there already to upset him," she added. Dr. Thornhill replied:

"My dear madam, I had a distinct purpose in it! I wanted to draw his attention to the bell rope, and to fix it there. It may be that he is in a highly overwrought state, and has been studying too much, although I am bound to say that he seems as sound and healthy a young man, mentally and bodily, as ever I saw—but then the rats—and that suggestion of the devil." The doctor shook his head and went on. "I would have offered to go and stay the first night with him but that I felt sure it would have been a cause of offence. He may get in the night some strange

fright or hallucination; and if he does I want him to pull that
rope. All alone as he is it will give us warning, and we may reach
him in time to be of service. I shall be sitting up pretty late
tonight and shall keep my ears open. Do not be alarmed if
Benchurch gets a surprise before morning.''

"Oh, Doctor, what do you mean? What do you mean?''

"I mean this; that possibly—nay, more probably—we shall
hear the great alarm bell from the Judge's House tonight,'' and
the doctor made about as effective an exit as could be thought
of.

When Malcolmson arrived home he found that it was a little
after his usual time, and Mrs. Dempster had gone away—the
rules of Greenhow's Charity were not to be neglected. He was
glad to see that the place was bright and tidy with a cheerful fire
and a well-trimmed lamp. The evening was colder than might
have been expected in April, and a heavy wind was blowing with
such rapidly increasing strength that there was every promise of
a storm during the night. For a few minutes after his entrance
the noise of the rats ceased; but so soon as they became accustomed to his presence they began again. He was glad to hear
them, for he felt once more the feeling of companionship in their
noise, and his mind ran back to the strange fact that they only
ceased to manifest themselves when that other—the great rat
with the baleful eyes—came upon the scene. The reading-lamp
only was lit and its green shade kept the ceiling and the upper
part of the room in darkness, so that the cheerful light from the
hearth spreading over the floor and shining on the white cloth
laid over the end of the table was warm and cheery. Malcolmson
sat down to his dinner with a good appetite and a buoyant spirit.
After his dinner and a cigarette he sat steadily down to work,
determined not to let anything disturb him, for he remembered
his promise to the doctor, and made up his mind to make the
best of the time at his disposal.

For an hour or so he worked all right, and then his thoughts
began to wander from his books. The actual circumstances
around him, the calls on his physical attention, and his nervous
susceptibility were not to be denied. By this time the wind had
become a gale, and the gale a storm. The old house, solid though
it was, seemed to shake to its foundations, and the storm roared
and raged through its many chimneys and its queer old gables,

producing strange, unearthly sounds in the empty rooms and corridors. Even the great alarm bell on the roof must have felt the force of the wind, for the rope rose and fell slightly, as though the bell were moved a little from time to time, and the limber rope fell on the oak floor with a hard and hollow sound.

As Malcolmson listened to it he bethought himself of the doctor's words, "It is the rope which the hangman used for the victims of the Judge's judicial rancour," and he went over to the corner of the fireplace and took it in his hand to look at it. There seemed a sort of deadly interest in it, and as he stood there he lost himself for a moment in speculation as to who these victims were, and the grim wish of the Judge to have such a ghastly relic ever under his eyes. As he stood there the swaying of the bell on the roof still lifted the rope now and again; but presently there came a new sensation—a sort of tremor in the rope, as though something was moving along it.

Looking up instinctively Malcolmson saw the great rat coming slowly down towards him, glaring at him steadily. He dropped the rope and started back with a muttered curse, and the rat turning ran up the rope again and disappeared, and at the same instant Malcolmson became conscious that the noise of the rats, which had ceased for a while, began again.

All this set him thinking, and it occurred to him that he had not investigated the lair of the rat or looked at the pictures, as he had intended. He lit the other lamp without the shade, and, holding it up went and stood opposite the third picture from the fireplace on the right-hand side where he had seen the rat disappear on the previous night.

At the first glance he started back so suddenly that he almost dropped the lamp, and a deadly pallor overspread his face. His knees shook, and heavy drops of sweat came on his forehead, and he trembled like an aspen. But he was young and plucky, and pulled himself together, and after the pause of a few seconds stepped forward again, raised the lamp, and examined the picture which had been dusted and washed, and now stood out clearly.

It was of a judge dressed in his robes of scarlet and ermine. His face was strong and merciless, evil, crafty, and vindictive, with a sensual mouth, hooked nose of ruddy colour, and shaped like the beak of a bird of prey. The rest of the face was of a cadaverous colour. The eyes were of peculiar brilliance and with a terribly malignant expression. As he looked at them, Malcolmson grew cold, for he saw there the very counterpart of the eyes of the great rat. The lamp almost fell from his hand, he saw the rat with its baleful eyes peering out through the hole in the corner of the picture, and noted the sudden cessation of the noise of the other rats. However, he pulled himself together, and went on with his examination of the picture.

The Judge was seated in a great high-backed carved oak chair, on the right-hand side of a great stone fireplace where, in the corner, a rope hung down from the ceiling, its end lying coiled on the floor. With a feeling of something like horror, Malcolmson recognised the scene of the room as it stood, and gazed around him in an awestruck manner as though he expected to find some strange presence behind him. Then he looked over to the corner of the fireplace—and with a loud cry he let the lamp fall from his hand.

There, in the Judge's arm-chair, with the rope hanging behind, sat the rat with the Judge's baleful eyes, now intensified and with a fiendish leer. Save for the howling of the storm without there was silence.

The fallen lamp recalled Malcolmson to himself. Fortunately it was of metal, and so the oil was not spilt. However, the practical need of attending to it settled at once his nervous apprehensions. When he had turned it out, he wiped his brow and thought for a moment.

"This will not do," he said to himself. "If I go on like this I shall become a crazy fool. This must stop! I promised the doctor I would not take tea. Faith, he was pretty right! My nerves must have been getting into a queer state. Funny I did not notice it. I never felt better in my life. However, it is all right now, and I shall not be such a fool again."

Then he mixed himself a good stiff glass of brandy and water and resolutely sat down to his work.

It was nearly an hour when he looked up from his book, disturbed by the sudden stillness. Without, the wind howled and roared louder than ever, and the rain drove in sheets against the windows, beating like hail on the glass; but within there was no sound whatever save the echo of the wind as it roared in the great chimney, and now and then a hiss as a few raindrops found their way down the chimney in a lull of the storm. The fire had fallen low and had ceased to flame, though it threw out a red glow. Malcolmson listened attentively, and presently heard a thin, squeaking noise, very faint. It came from the corner of the room where the rope hung down, and he thought it was the creaking of the rope on the floor as the swaying of the bell raised and lowered it. Looking up, however, he saw in the dim light the great rat clinging to the rope and gnawing it. The rope was already nearly gnawed through—he could see the lighter colour where the strands were laid bare. As he looked the job was completed, and the severed end of the rope fell clattering on the oaken floor, whilst for an instant the great rat remained like a knob or tassel at the end of the rope, which now began to sway to and fro. Malcolmson felt for a moment another pang of terror as he thought that now the possibility of calling the outer world to his assistance was cut off, but an intense anger took its place, and seizing the book he was reading he hurled it at the rat. The blow was well aimed, but before the missile could reach him the rat dropped off and struck the floor with a soft thud. Malcolmson instantly rushed over towards him, but it darted away and disappeared in the darkness of the shadows of the room. Malcolmson felt that his work was over for the night, and determined then and there to vary the monotony of the proceedings by a hunt for the rat, and took off the green shade of the lamp so as to insure a wider spreading light. As he did so the gloom of the upper part of the room was relieved, and in the new flood of light, great by comparison with the previous darkness, the pictures on the wall stood out boldly. From where he stood, Malcolmson saw right opposite to him the third picture on the wall from the right of the fireplace. He rubbed his eyes in surprise, and then a great fear began to come upon him.

In the centre of the picture was a great irregular patch of brown canvas, as fresh as when it was stretched on the frame. The background was as before, with chair and chimney-corner and rope, but the figure of the Judge had disappeared.

Malcolmson, almost in a chill of horror, turned slowly round, and then he began to shake and tremble like a man in a palsy. His strength seemed to have left him, and he was incapable of action or movement, hardly even of thought. He could only see and hear.

There, on the great high-backed carved oak chair sat the Judge in his robes of scarlet and ermine, with his baleful eyes glaring vindictively, and a smile of triumph on the resolute, cruel mouth, as he lifted with his hands a *black cap*. Malcolmson felt as if the blood was running from his heart, as one does in moments of prolonged suspense. There was a singing in his ears. Without, he could hear the roar and howl of the tempest, and through it, swept on the storm, came the striking of midnight by the great chimes in the market place. He stood for a space of time that seemed to him endless still as a statue, and with wide-open, horror-struck eyes, breathless. As the clock struck, so the smile of triumph on the Judge's face intensified, and at the last stroke of midnight he placed the black cap on his head.

Slowly and deliberately the Judge rose from his chair and picked up the piece of the rope of the alarm bell which lay on the floor, drew it through his hands as if he enjoyed its touch, and then deliberately began to knot one end of it, fashioning it into a noose. This he tightened and tested with his foot, pulling hard at it till he was satisfied and then making a running noose of it, which he held in his hand. Then he began to move along the table on the opposite side to Malcolmson keeping his eyes on him until he had passed him, when with a quick movement he stood in front of the door. Malcolmson then began to feel that he was trapped, and tried to think of what he should do. There was some fascination in the Judge's eyes, which he never took off him, and he had, perforce, to look. He saw the Judge approach—still keeping between him and the door—and raise the noose and throw it towards him as if to entangle him. With a great effort he made a quick movement to one side, and saw the rope fall beside him, and heard it strike the oaken floor. Again the Judge raised the noose and tried to ensnare him, ever keeping his baleful eyes fixed on him, and each time by a mighty effort the student just managed to evade it. So this went on for many times, the Judge seeming never discouraged nor discomposed at failure, but playing as a cat does with a mouse. At last in despair, which had reached its climax, Malcolmson cast a quick glance round him. The lamp seemed to have blazed up, and there was a fairly good light in the room. At the many rat-holes and in the chinks and crannies of the wainscot he saw the rats' eyes; and this aspect, that was purely physical, gave him a gleam of comfort. He looked around and saw that the rope of the great alarm bell was laden with rats. Every inch of it was covered with them, and more and more were pouring through the small circular hole in the ceiling whence it emerged, so that with their weight the bell was beginning to sway.

Hark! it had swayed till the clapper had touched the bell. The sound was but a tiny one, but the bell was only beginning to sway, and it would increase.

At the sound the Judge, who had been keeping his eyes fixed on Malcolmson, looked up, and a scowl of diabolical anger overspread his face. His eyes fairly glowed like hot coals, and he stamped his foot with a sound that seemed to make the house shake. A dreadful peal of thunder broke overhead as he raised the rope again, whilst the rats kept running up and down the rope as though working against time. This time, instead of throwing it, he drew close to his victim, and held open the noose as he approached. As he came closer there seemed something paralysing in his very presence, and Malcolmson stood rigid as a corpse. He felt the Judge's icy fingers touch his throat as he adjusted the rope. The noose tightened—tightened. Then the Judge, taking the rigid form of the student in his arms, carried him over and placed him standing in the oak chair, and stepping up beside him, put his hand up and caught the end of the swaying rope of the alarm bell. As he raised his hand the rats fled squeaking, and disappeared through the hole in the ceiling. Taking the end of the noose which was round Malcolmson's neck he tied it to the hanging-bell rope, and then descending pulled away the chair.

When the alarm bell of the Judge's House began to sound a crowd soon assembled. Lights and torches of various kinds appeared, and soon a silent crowd was hurrying to the spot. They knocked loudly at the door, but there was no reply. Then they burst in the door, and poured into the great dining-room, the doctor at the head.

There at the end of the rope of the great alarm bell hung the body of the student, and on the face of the Judge in the picture was a malignant smile.

Afterward

Edith Wharton

In her time Edith Wharton (1862–1937) was recognized as an author of four novels, including *The House of Mirth* (1905), *Ethan Frome* (1911), *The Custom of the Country* (1913), and the Pulitzer Prize–winning *The Age of Innocence* (1920). The sense of nostalgia for the past that pervades her work can also be found in her supernatural stories, which were collected into the landmark volume *Ghosts* in 1937. More than 80 years after it first saw publication, "Afterward" remains one of the most perfectly orchestrated ghost stories in the English language.

"Oh, there *is* one, of course, but you'll never know it."

The assertion, laughingly flung out six months earlier in a bright June garden, came back to Mary Boyne with a new perception of its significance as she stood, in the December dusk, waiting for the lamps to be brought into the library.

The words had been spoken by their friend Alida Stair, as they sat at tea on her lawn at Pangbourne, in reference to the very house of which the library in question was the central, the pivotal "feature." Mary Boyne and her husband, in quest of a country place in one of the southern or southwestern counties, had, on their arrival in England, carried their problem straight to Alida Stair, who had successfully solved it in her own case; but it was not until they had rejected, almost capriciously, several practical and judicious suggestions that she threw out: "Well, there's Lyng, in Dorsetshire. It belongs to Hugo's cousins, and you can get it for a song."

The reason she gave for its being obtainable on these terms— its remoteness from a station, its lack of electric light, hot water pipes, and other vulgar necessities—were exactly those pleading in its favor with two romantic Americans perversely in search of the economic drawbacks which were associated, in their tradition, with unusual architectural felicities.

"I should never believe I was living in an old house unless I was thoroughly uncomfortable," Ned Boyne, the more extravagant of the two, had jocosely insisted; "the least hint of convenience would make me think it had been bought out of an exhibition, with the pieces numbered, and set up again." And they had proceeded to enumerate, with humorous precision, their various doubts and demands, refusing to believe that the house their cousin recommended was *really* Tudor till they learned it had no heating system, or that the village church was literally in the grounds till she assured them of the deplorable uncertainty of the water supply.

"It's too uncomfortable to be true!" Edward Boyne had continued to exult as the avowal of each disadvantage was successively wrung from her; but he had cut short his rhapsody to ask, with a relapse to distrust: "And the ghost? You've been concealing from us the fact that there is no ghost!"

Mary, at the moment, had laughed with him, yet almost with her laugh, being possessed of several sets of independent perceptions, had been struck by a note of flatness in Alida's answering hilarity.

"Oh, Dorsetshire's full of ghosts, you know."

"Yes, yes; but that won't do. I don't want to have to drive ten miles to see somebody else's ghost. I want one of my own on the premises. *Is* there a ghost at Lyng?"

His rejoinder had made Alida laugh again, and it was then that she had flung back tantalizing: "Oh, there *is* one, of course, but you'll never know it."

"Never know it?" Boyne pulled her up. "But what in the world constitutes a ghost except the fact of its being known for one?"

"I can't say. But that's the story."

"That there's a ghost, that nobody knows it's a ghost?"

"Well—not till afterward, at any rate."

"Till afterward?"

"Not till long long afterward."

"But if it's once been identified as an unearthly visitant, why hasn't it *signalement* been handed down in the family? How has it managed to preserve its incognito?"

Alida could only shake her head. "Don't ask me. But it has."

"And then suddenly"—Mary spoke up as if from cavernous depths of divination—"suddenly, long afterward, one says to one's self *'That was it?'* "

She was startled at the sepulchral sound with which her question fell on the banter of the other two, and she saw the shadow of the same surprise flit across Alida's pupils. "I suppose so. One just has to wait."

"Oh, hang waiting!" Ned broke in. "Life's too short for a ghost who can only be enjoyed in retrospect. Can't we do better than that, Mary?"

But it turned out that in the event they were not destined to, for within three months of their conversation with Mrs. Stair they were settled at Lyng, and the life they had yearned for, to the point of planning it in advance in all its daily details, had actually begun for them.

It was to sit, in the thick December dusk, by just such a wide-hooded fireplace, under just such black oak rafters, with the sense that beyond the mullioned panes the downs were darkened to a deeper solitude: it was for the ultimate indulgence of such sensations that Mary Boyne, abruptly exiled from New York by her husband's business, had endured for nearly fourteen years the soul-deadening ugliness of a Middle Western town, and that Boyne had ground on doggedly at his engineering till, with a suddenness that still made her blink, the prodigious windfall of the Blue Star Mine had put them at a stroke in possession of life and the leisure to taste it. They had never for a moment meant their new state to be one of idleness; but they meant to give themselves only to harmonious activities. She had her vision of painting and gardening (against a background of grey walls), he dreamed of the production of his long-planned book on the "Economic Basis of Culture"; and with such absorbing work ahead no existence could be too sequestered: they could not get far enough from the world, or plunge deep enough into the past.

Dorsetshire had attracted them from the first by an air of remoteness out of all proportion to its geographical position. But to the Boynes it was one of the ever-recurring wonders of the whole incredibly compressed island—a nest of counties, as they put it—that for the production of its effects so little of a given quality went so far: that so few miles made a distance, and so short a distance a difference.

"It's that," Ned had once enthusiastically explained, "that give such depth to their effects, such relief to their contrasts. They've been able to lay the butter so thick on every delicious mouthful."

The butter had certainly been laid on thick at Lyng: the old house hidden under a shoulder of the downs had almost all the finer marks of commerce with a protracted past. The mere fact that it was neither large nor exceptional made it, to the Boynes, abound the more completely in its special charm—the charm of having been for centuries a deep dim reservoir of life. The life had probably not been of the most vivid order: for long periods, no doubt, it had fallen as noiselessly into the past as the quiet drizzle of autumn fell, hour after hour, into the fish pond between the yews; but these backwaters of existence sometimes breed, in their sluggish depths, strange acuities of emotion, and Mary Boyne had felt from the first the mysterious stir of intenser memories.

The feeling had never been stronger than on this particular afternoon when, waiting in the library for the lamps to come, she rose from her seat and stood among the shadows of the hearth. Her husband had gone off, after luncheon, for one of his long tramps on the downs. She had noticed of late that he preferred to go alone; and, in the tried security of their personal relations, had been driven to conclude that his book was bothering him, and that he needed the afternoons to turn over in solitude the problems left from the morning's work. Certainly the book was not going as smoothly as she had thought it would, and there were lines of perplexity between his eyes such as had never been there in his engineering days. He had often, then, looked fagged to the verge of illness, but the native demon of worry had never branded his brow. Yet the few pages he had so far read to her—the introduction, and a summary of the opening chapter—showed a firm hold on his subject, and an increasing confidence in his powers.

The fact threw her into deeper perplexity, since, now that he had done with business and its disturbing contingencies, the one other possible source of anxiety was eliminated. Unless it were his health, then? But physically he had gained since they had come to Dorsetshire, grown robuster, ruddier and fresher eyed. It was only within the last week that she had felt in him the undefiable change which made her restless in his absence, and as tongue-tied in his presence as though it were *she* who had a secret to keep from him!

The thought that there *was* a secret somewhere between them struck her with a sudden rap of wonder, and she looked about her down the long room.

"Can it be the house?" she mused.

The room itself might have been full of secrets. They seemed to be piling themselves up, as evening fell, like the layers and layers of velvet shadow dropping from the low ceiling, the rows of books, the smoke-blurred sculpture of the hearth.

"Why, of course—the house is haunted!" she reflected.

The ghost—Alida's imperceptible ghost—after figuring largely in the banter of their first month or two at Lyng, had been gradually left aside as too ineffectual for imaginative use. Mary had, indeed, as became the tenant of a haunted house, made the customary inquiries among her rural neighbors, but beyond a vague "They do say so, Ma'am," the villagers had nothing to impart. The elusive specter had apparently never had sufficient identity for a legend to crystallize about it, and after a time the Boynes had set the matter down to their profit-and-loss account, agreeing that Lyng was one of the few houses good enough in itself to dispense with supernatural enhancements.

"And I suppose, poor ineffectual demon, that's why it beats its beautiful wings in vain in the void," Mary had laughingly concluded.

"Or, rather," Ned answered in the same strain, "why, amid so much that's ghostly, it can never affirm its separate existence as *the* ghost." And thereupon their invisible housemate had finally dropped out of their references, which were numerous enough to make them soon unaware of the loss.

Now, as she stood on the hearth, the subject of their earlier curiosity revived in her with a new sense of its meaning—a sense gradually acquired through daily contact with the scene of the lurking mystery. It was the house itself, of course, that possessed the ghost-seeing faculty, that communed visually but secretly with its own past; if one could only get into close enough communion with the house, one might surprise its secret, and acquire the ghost sight on one's own account. Perhaps, in his long hours in this very room, where she never trespassed till the afternoon, her husband *had* acquired it already, and was silently carrying about the weight of whatever it had revealed to him. Mary was too well versed in the code of the spectral world not to know that one could not talk about the ghosts one saw: to do so was almost as great a breach of taste as to name a lady in a club. But this explanation did not really satisfy her. "What, after all, except for the fun of the shudder," she reflected, "would he really care for any of their old ghosts?" And thence she was thrown back once more on the fundamental dilemma: the fact that one's greater or less susceptibility to spectral influences had no particular bearing on the case, since, when one *did* see a ghost at Lyng, one did not know it.

"Not till long afterward," Alida Stair had said. Well, supposing Ned *had* seen one when they first came, and had known only within the last week what had happened to him? More and more under the spell of the hour, she threw back her thoughts to the early days of their tenancy, but as first only to recall a lively confusion of unpacking, settling, arranging of books, and calling to each other from remote corners of the house as, treasure after treasure, it revealed itself to them. It was in this particular connection that she presently recalled a certain soft afternoon of the previous October, when, passing from the first rapturous flurry of exploration to a detailed inspection of the old house, she had pressed (like a novel heroine) a panel that opened on a flight of corkscrew stairs leading to a flat ledge of the roof—the roof which, from below, seemed to slope away on all sides too abruptly for any but practiced feet to scale.

The view from this hidden coign was enchanting, and she had flown down to snatch Ned from his papers and give him the freedom of her discovery. She remembered still how, standing at her side, he had passed his arm about her while their gaze flew to the long tossed horizon line of the downs, and then dropped contentedly back to trace the arabesque of yew hedges about the fish pond, and the shadow of the cedar on the lawn.

"And now the other way," he had said, turning her about within his arm; and closely pressed to him, she had absorbed, like some long satisfying draught, the picture of the grey-walled court, the squat lions on the gates, and the lime avenue reaching up to the highroad under the downs.

It was just then, while they gazed and held each other, that she had felt his arm relax, and heard a sharp "Hullo!" that made her turn to glance at him.

Distinctly, yes, she now recalled that she had seen, as she glanced, a shadow of anxiety, of perplexity, rather, fall across his face; and, following his eyes, had beheld the figure of a man—a man in loose greyish clothes, as it appeared to her—who was sauntering down the lime avenue to the court with the doubtful gait of a stranger who seeks his way. Her shortsighted eyes had given her but a blurred impression of slightness and greyishness, with something foreign, or at least unlocal, in the cut of the figure or its dress; but her husband had apparently seen more— seen enough to make him push past her with a hasty "Wait!" and dash down the stairs without pausing to give her a hand.

A slight tendency to dizziness obliged her, after a provisional clutch at the chimney against which they had been leaning, to follow him first more cautiously; and when she had reached the landing she paused again, for a less definite reason, leaning over the banister to strain her eyes through the silence of the brown sun-flecked depths. She lingered there till, somewhere in those depths, she heard the closing of a door; then, mechanically im- pelled, she went down the shallow flights of steps till she reached the lower hall.

The front door stood open on the sunlight of the court, and hall and court were empty. The library door was open, too, and after listening in vain for any sound of voices within, she crossed the threshold, and found her husband alone, vaguely fingering the papers on his desk.

He looked up, as if surprised at her entrance, but the shadow of anxiety had passed from his face, leaving it even, as she fan- cied, a little brighter and clearer than usual.

"What was it? Who was it?" she asked.

"Who?" he repeated, with the surprise still all on his side.

"The man we saw coming toward the house."

He seemed to reflect. "The man? Why, I thought I saw Peters; I dashed after him to say a word about the stable drains, but he had disappeared before I could get down."

"Disappeared? But he seemed to be walking so slowly when we saw him."

Boyne shrugged his shoulders. "So I thought; but he must have got up steam in the interval. What do you say to our trying a scramble up Meldon Steep before sunset?"

That was all. At the time the occurrence had been less than nothing, had, indeed, been immediately obliterated by the magic of their first vision from Meldon Steep, a height which they had dreamed of climbing ever since they had first seen its bare spine rising above the roof of Lyng. Doubtless it was the mere fact of the other incident's having occurred on the very day of their ascent to Meldon that had kept it stored away in the fold of memory from which it now emerged; for in itself it had no mark of the portentous. At the moment there could have been nothing more natural than that Ned should dash himself from the roof in the pursuit of dilatory tradesmen. It was the period when they were always on the watch for one or the other of the specialists employed about the place; always lying in wait for them, and rushing out at them with questions, reproaches or reminders. And certainly in the distance the grey figure had looked like Peters.

Yet now, as she reviewed the scene, she felt her husband's explanation of it to have been invalidated by the look of anxiety on his face. Why had the familiar appearance of Peters made him anxious? Why, above all, if it was of such prime necessity to confer with him on the subject of the stable drains, had the failure to find him produced such a look of relief? Mary could not say that any one of these questions had occurred to her at the time, yet, from the promptness with which they now marshalled themselves at her summons, she had a sense that they must all along have been there, waiting their hour.

II

Weary with her thoughts, she moved to the window. The library was now quite dark, and she was surprised to see how much faint light the outer world still held.

As she peered out into it across the court, a figure shaped itself far down the perspective of bare limes: it looked a mere blot of deeper grey in the greyness, and for an instant, as it moved toward her, her heart thumped to the thought "It's the ghost!"

She had time, in that long instant, to feel suddenly that the man of whom, two months earlier, she had had a distant vision from the roof, was now, at his predestined hour, about to reveal himself as *not* having been Peters, and her spirit sank under the impending fear of the disclosure. But almost with the next tick of the clock the figure, gaining substance and character, showed itself even to her weak sight as her husband's; and she turned to meet him, as he entered, with the confession of her folly.

"It's really too absurd," she laughed out, "but I never *can* remember!"

"Remember what?" Boyne questioned as they drew together.

"That when one sees the Lyng ghost one never knows it."

Her hand was on his sleeve, and he kept it there, but with no response in his gesture or in the lines of his preoccupied face.

"Did you think you'd seen it?" he asked, after an appreciable interval.

"Why, I actually took *you* for it, my dear, in my mad determination to spot it!"

"Me—just now?" His arm dropped away, and he turned from her with a faint echo of her laugh. "Really, dearest, you'd better give it up, if that's the best you can do."

"Oh, yes, I give it up. Have *you*?" she asked, turning around on him abruptly.

The parlormaid had entered with letters and a lamp, and the light struck up into Boyne's face as he bent above the tray she presented.

"Have *you*!" Mary perversely insisted, when the servant had disappeared on her errand of illumination.

"Have I what?" he rejoined absently, the light bringing out the sharp stamp of worry between his brows as he turned over the letters.

"Given up trying to see the ghost." Her heart beat a little at the experiment she was making.

Her husband, laying his letters aside, moved away into the shadow of the hearth.

"I never tried," he said, tearing open the wrapper of a newspaper.

"Well, of course," Mary persisted, "the exasperating thing is that there's no use trying, since one can't be sure till so long afterward."

He was unfolding the paper as if he had hardly heard her; but after a pause, during which the sheets rustled spasmodically between his hands, he looked up to ask, "Have you any idea *how long?*"

Mary had sunk into a low chair beside the fireplace. From her seat she glanced over, startled, at her husband's profile, which was projected against the circle of lamplight.

"No; none. Have *you?*" she retorted, repeating her former phrase with an added stress of intention.

Boyne crumpled the paper into a bunch, and then, inconsequently, turned back with it toward the lamp.

"Lord, no! I only meant," he exclaimed, with a faint tinge of impatience, "is there any legend, any tradition, as to that?"

"Not that I know of," she answered; but the impulse to add "What makes you ask?" was checked by the reappearance of the parlormaid, with tea and a second lamp.

With the dispersal of shadows, and the repetition of the daily domestic office, Mary Boyne felt herself less oppressed by that sense of something mutely imminent which had darkened her afternoon. For a few moments she gave herself to the details of her task, and when she looked up from it she was struck to the point of bewilderment by the change in her husband's face. He had seated himself near the farther lamp, and was absorbed in the perusal of his letters; but was it something he had found in them, or merely the shifting of her own point of view, that had restored his features to their normal aspect? The longer she looked the more definitely the change affirmed itself. The lines of tension had vanished, and such traces of fatigue as lingered were of the kind easily attributable to steady mental effort. He glanced up, as if drawn by her gaze, and met her eyes with a smile.

"I'm dying for my tea, you know; and here's a letter for you," he said.

She took the letter he held out in exchange for the cup she proffered him, and, returning to her seat, broke the seal with the languid gesture of the reader whose interests are all enclosed in the circle of one cherished presence.

Her next conscious motion was that of starting to her feet, the letter falling to them as she rose, while she held out to her husband a newspaper clipping.

"Ned! What's this? What does it mean?"

He had risen at the same instant, almost as if hearing her cry before she uttered it; and for a perceptible space of time he and she studied each other, like adversaries watching for an advantage, across the space between her chair and his desk.

"What's what? You fairly made me jump!" Boyne said at length, moving toward her with a sudden half-exasperated laugh. The shadow of apprehension was on his face again, not now a look of fixed foreboding, but a shifting vigilance of lips and eyes that gave her the sense of his feeling himself invisibly surrounded.

Her hand shook so that she could hardly give him the clipping. "This article—from the *Waukesha Sentinel*—that a man named Elwell has brought suit against you—that there was something wrong about the Blue Star Mine. I can't understand more than half."

They continued to face each other as she spoke, and to her astonishment she saw that her words had the almost immediate effect of dissipating the strained watchfulness of his look.

"Oh, *that!*" He glanced down the printed slip, and then folded it with the gesture of one who handles something harmless and familiar. "What's the matter with you this afternoon, Mary? I thought you'd got bad news."

She stood before him with her undefinable terror subsiding slowly under the reassurance of his tone.

"You knew about this, then—it's all right?"

"Certainly I knew about it; and it's all right."

"But what *is* it? I don't understand. What does this man accuse you of?"

"Pretty nearly every crime in the calendar." Boyne had tossed the clipping down, and thrown himself into an armchair near the fire. "Do you want to hear the story? It's not particularly interesting—just a squabble over interests in the Blue Star."

"But who is this Elwell? I don't know the name."

"Oh, he's a fellow I put into it—gave him a hand up. I told you all about him at the time."

"I daresay. I must have forgotten." Vainly she strained back among her memories. "But if you helped him, why does he make this return?"

"Probably some shyster lawyer got hold of him and talked him over. It's all rather technical and complicated. I thought that kind of thing bored you."

His wife felt a sting of compunction. Theoretically, she deprecated the American wife's detachment from her husband's professional interests, but in practice she had always found it difficult to fix her attention on Boyne's report of the transactions in which his varied interests involved him. Besides, she had felt during their years of exile, that, in a community where the amenities of living could be obtained only at the cost of efforts, as arduous as her husband's professional labors, such brief leisure as he and she could command should be used as an escape from immediate preoccupations, a flight to the life they always dreamed of living. Once or twice, now that this new life had actually drawn its magic circle about them, she had asked herself if she had done right; but hitherto such conjectures had been no more than the retrospective excursions of an active fancy. Now, for the first time, it startled her a little to find how little she knew of the material foundation on which her happiness was built.

She glanced at her husband, and was again reassured by the composure of his face; yet she felt the need of more definite grounds for her reassurance.

"But doesn't this suit worry you? Why have you never spoken to me about it?"

He answered both questions at once. "I didn't speak of it at first because it *did* worry me—annoyed me, rather. But it's all ancient history now. Your correspondent must have got hold of a back number of the *Sentinel.*"

She felt a quick thrill of relief. "You mean it's over? He's lost his case?"

There was a just perceptible delay in Boyne's reply. "The suit's been withdrawn—that's all."

But she persisted, as if to exonerate herself from the inward charge of being too easily put off. "Withdrawn it because he saw he had no chance?"

"Oh, he had no chance," Boyne answered.

She was still struggling with a dimly felt perplexity at the back of her thoughts.

"How long ago was it withdrawn?"

He paused, as if with a slight return to his former uncertainty. "I've just had the news now; but I've been expecting it."

"Just now—in one of your letters?"

"Yes; in one of my letters."

She made no answer, and was aware only, after a short interval of waiting, that he had risen, and, strolling across the room, had placed himself on the sofa at her side. She felt him, as he did so, pass an arm about her, she felt his hand seek hers and clasp it, and turning slowly, drawn by the warmth of his cheek, she met his smiling eyes.

"It's all right—it's all right?" she questioned, through the flood of her dissolving doubts; and "I give you my word it was never righter!" he laughed back at her, holding her close.

III

One of the strangest things she was afterward to recall out of all the next day's strangeness was the sudden and complete recovery of her sense of security.

It was in the air when she woke in her low-ceiled, dusky room; it went with her downstairs to the breakfast table, flashed out at her from the fire, and reduplicated itself from the flanks of the urn and the sturdy flutings of the Georgian teapot. It was as if in some roundabout way, all her diffused fears of the previous day, with their moment of sharp concentration about the newspaper article—as if this dim questioning of the future, and startled return upon the past, had between them liquidated the arrears of some haunting moral obligation. If she had indeed been careless of her husband's affairs, it was, her new state seemed to prove, because her faith in him instinctively justified such carelessness; and his right to her faith had now affirmed itself in the very face of menace and suspicion. She had never seen him more untroubled, more naturally and unconsciously himself, than after the cross-examination to which she had subjected him: it was almost as if he had been aware of her doubts, and had wanted the air cleared as much as she did.

It was as clear, thank heaven, as the bright outer light that surprised her almost with a touch of summer when she issued from the house for her daily round of the gardens. She had left

Boyne at his desk, indulging herself, as she passed the library door, by a last peep at his quiet face, where he bent, pipe in mouth, above his papers; and now she had her own morning's task to perform. The task involved, on such charmed winter days, almost as much happy loitering about the different quarters of her domain as if spring were already at work there. There were such endless possibilities still before her, such opportunities to bring out the latent graces of the old place, without a single irreverent touch of alteration, that the winter was all too short to plan what spring and autumn executed. And her recovered sense of safety gave, on this particular morning, a peculiar zest to her progress through the sweet still place. She went first to the kitchen garden, where the espaliered pear trees drew complicated patterns on the walls, and pigeons were fluttering and preening about the silvery-slated roof of their cot. There was something wrong about the piping of the hothouse, and she was expecting an authority from Dorchester, who was to drive out between trains and make a diagnosis of the boiler. But when she dipped into the damp heat of the greenhouses, among the spiced scents and waxy pinks and reds of old-fashioned exotics—even the flora of Lyng was in the note!—she learned that the great man had not arrived, and, the day being too rare to waste in an artificial atmosphere, she came out again and paced along the springy turf of the bowling green to the gardens behind the house. At their farther end rose a grass terrace, looking across the fish pond and yew hedges to the long house front with its twisted chimney stacks and blue roof angles all drenched in the pale gold moisture of the air.

Seen thus, across the level tracery of the gardens, it sent her, from open windows and hospitably smoking chimneys, the look of some warm human presence, of a mind slowly ripened on a sunny wall of experience. She had never before had such a sense of her intimacy with it, such a conviction that its secrets were all beneficent, kept, as they said to children, "for one's good," such a trust in its power to gather up her life and Ned's into the harmonious pattern of the long long story it sat there weaving in the sun.

She heard steps behind her, and turned, expecting to see the gardener accompanied by the engineer from Dorchester. But only one figure was in sight, that of a youngish slightly built man, who, for reasons she could not on the spot have given, did not remotely resemble her notion of an authority on hothouse boilers. The newcomer, on seeing her, lifted his hat, and paused with the air of a gentleman—perhaps a traveler—who wishes to make it known that his intrusion is involuntary. Lyng occasionally attracted the more cultivated traveler, and Mary half expected to see the stranger dissemble a camera, or justify his presence by producing it. But he made no gesture of any sort, and after a moment she asked, in a tone responding to the courteous hesitation of his attitude: "Is there anyone you wish to see?"

"I came to see Mr. Boyne," he answered. His intonation, rather than his accent, was faintly American, and Mary, at the note, looked at him more closely. The brim of his soft felt hat cast a shade on his face, which, thus obscured, wore to her shortsighted gaze a look of seriousness, as of a person arriving on business, and civilly but firmly aware of his rights.

Past experience had made her equally sensible to such claims; but she was jealous of her husband's morning hours, and doubtful of his having given anyone the right to intrude on them.

"Have you an appointment with my husband?" she asked.

The visitor hesitated, as if unprepared for the question.

"I think he expects me," he replied.

It was Mary's turn to hesitate. "You see this is his time for work: he never sees anyone in the morning."

He looked at her a moment without answering; then, as if accepting her decision, he began to move away. As he turned, Mary saw him pause and glance up at the peaceful house front. Something in his air suggested weariness and disappointment, the dejection of the traveler who has come from far off and whose hours are limited by the timetable. It occurred to her that if this were the case her refusal might have made his errand vain, and a sense of compunction caused her to hasten after him.

"May I ask if you have come a long way?"

He gave her the same grave look. "Yes—I have come a long way."

"Then, if you'll go to the house, no doubt my husband will see you now. You'll find him in the library."

She did not know why she had added the last phrase, except from a vague impulse to atone for her previous inhospitality. The visitor seemed about to express his thanks, but her attention was distracted by the approach of the gardener with a companion who bore all the marks of being the expert from Dorchester.

"This way," she said, waving the stranger to the house; and an instant later she had forgotten him in the absorption of her meeting with the boiler maker.

The encounter led to such far-reaching results that the engineer ended by finding it expedient to ignore his train, and Mary was beguiled into spending the remainder of the morning in absorbed confabulation among the flower pots. When the colloquy ended, she was surprised to find that it was nearly luncheon time, and she half expected, as she hurried back to the house, to see her husband coming out to meet her. But she found no one in the court but an undergardener raking the gravel, and the hall, when she entered it, was so silent that she guessed Boyne to be still at work.

Not wishing to disturb him, she turned into the drawing room, and there, at her writing table, lost herself in renewed calculations of the outlay to which the morning's conference had pledged her. The fact that she could permit herself such follies had not yet lost its novelty; and somehow, in contrast to the vague fears of the previous days, it now seemed an element of her recovered security, of the sense that, as Ned had said, things in general had never been "righter."

She was still luxuriating in a lavish play of figures when the parlormaid, from the threshold, roused her with an inquiry as to the expediency of serving luncheon. It was one of their jokes that Trimmle announced luncheon as if she were divulging a state secret, and Mary, intent upon her papers, merely murmured an absent-minded assent.

She felt Trimmle wavering doubtfully on the threshold, as if in rebuke of such unconsidered assent; then her retreating steps sounded down the passage, and Mary, pushing away her papers, crossed the hall and went to the library door. It was still closed, and she wavered in her turn, disliking to disturb her husband, yet anxious that he should not exceed his usual measure of work. As she stood there, balancing her impulses, Trimmle returned with the announcement of luncheon, and Mary, thus impelled, opened the library door.

Boyne was not at his desk, and she peered about her, expecting to discover him before the bookshelves, somewhere down the length of the room; but her call brought no response, and gradually it became clear to her that he was not there.

She turned back to the parlormaid.

"Mr. Boyne must be upstairs. Please tell him that luncheon is ready."

Trimmle appeared to hesitate between the obvious duty of obedience and an equally obvious conviction of the foolishness of the injunction laid on her. The struggle resulted in her saying: "If you please, Madam, Mr. Boyne's not upstairs."

"Not in his room? Are you sure?"

"I'm sure, Madam."

Mary consulted the clock. "Where is he, then?"

"He's gone out," Trimmle announced, with the superior air of one who has respectfully waited for the question that a well-ordered mind would have put first.

Mary's conjecture had been right, then. Boyne must have gone to the gardens to meet her, and since she had missed him, it was clear that he had taken the shorter way by the south door, instead of going round to the court. She crossed the hall to the French window opening directly on the yew garden, but the parlormaid, after another moment of inner conflict, decided to bring out: "Please, Madam, Mr. Boyne didn't go that way."

Mary turned back. "Where *did* he go? And when?"

"He went out of the front door, up the drive, Madam." It was a matter of principle with Trimmle never to answer more than one question at a time.

"Up the drive? At this hour?" Mary went to the door herself, and glanced across the court through the tunnel of bare limes. But its perspective was as empty as when she had scanned it on entering.

"Did Mr. Boyne leave no message?"

Trimmle seemed to surrender herself to a last struggle with the forces of chaos.

"No, Madam. He just went out with the gentleman."

"The gentleman? What gentleman?" Mary wheeled about, as if to front this new factor.

"The gentleman who called, Madam," said Trimmle resignedly.

"When did a gentleman call? Do explain yourself, Trimmle!"

Only the fact that Mary was very hungry, and that she wanted to consult her husband about the greenhouses, would have caused her to lay so unusual an injunction on her attendant; and even now she was detached enough to note in Trimmle's eye the dawning defiance of the respectful subordinate who has been pressed too hard.

"I couldn't exactly say the hour, Madam, because I didn't let the gentleman in," she replied, with an air of discreetly ignoring the irregularity of her mistress's course.

"You didn't let him in?"

"No, Madam. When the bell rang I was dressing, and Agnes—"

"Go and ask Agnes, then," said Mary.

Trimmle still wore her look of patient magnanimity. "Agnes would not know, Madam, for she had unfortunately burnt her hand in trimming the wick of the new lamp from town"—Trimmle, as Mary was aware, had always been opposed to the new lamp—"and so Mrs. Dockett sent the kitchenmaid instead."

Mary looked again at the clock. "It's after two! Go and ask the kitchenmaid if Mr. Boyne left any word."

She went into luncheon without waiting, and Trimmle presently brought her there the kitchenmaid's statement that the gentleman had called about eleven o'clock, and that Mr. Boyne had gone out with him without leaving any message. The kitchenmaid did not even know the caller's name, for he had written it on a slip of paper, which he had folded and handed to her, with the injunction to deliver it at once to Mr. Boyne.

Mary finished her luncheon, still wondering, and when it was over, and Trimmle had brought the coffee to the drawing room, her wonder had deepened to a first faint tinge of disquietude. It was unlike Boyne to absent himself without explanation at so unwonted an hour, and the difficulty of identifying the visitor whose summons he had apparently obeyed made his disappearance the more unaccountable. Mary Boyne's experience as the wife of a busy engineer, subject to sudden calls and compelled to keep irregular hours, had trained her to the philosophic acceptance of surprises; but since Boyne's withdrawal from business he had adopted a Benedictine regularity of life. As if to make up for the dispersed and agitated years, with their "stand-up" lunches, and dinners rattled down to the joltings of the dining cars, he cultivated the last refinements of punctuality and monotony, discouraging his wife's fancy for the unexpected, and declaring that to a delicate taste there were infinite gradations of pleasure in the recurrences of habit.

Still, since no life can completely defend itself from the unforeseen, it was evident that all Boyne's precautions would sooner or later prove unavailable, and Mary concluded that he had cut short a tiresome visit by walking with his caller to the station, or at least accompanying him for part of the way.

This conclusion relieved her from further preoccupation, and she went out herself to take up her conference with the gardener. Thence she walked to the village post office, a mile or so away; and when she turned toward home the early twilight was setting in.

She had taken a footpath across the downs, and as Boyne, meanwhile, had probably returned from the station by the high-road, there was little likelihood of their meeting. She felt sure, however, of his having reached the house before her; so sure that, when she entered it herself, without even pausing to inquire of Trimmle, she made directly for the library. But the library was still empty, and with an unwonted exactness of visual memory she observed that the papers on her husband's desk lay precisely as they had lain when she had gone in to call him to luncheon.

Then of a sudden she was seized by a vague dread of the unknown. She had closed the door behind her on entering, and as she stood alone in the long silent room, her dread seemed to take shape and sound, to be there breathing and lurking among the shadows. Her shortsighted eyes strained through them, half-discerning an actual presence, something aloof, that watched and knew; and in the recoil from the intangible presence she threw herself on the bell rope and gave it a sharp pull.

The sharp summons brought Trimmle in precipitately with a lamp, and Mary breathed again at this sobering reappearance of the usual.

"You may bring tea if Mr. Boyne is in," she said, to justify her ring.

"Very well, Madam. But Mr. Boyne is not in," said Trimmle, putting down the lamp.

"Not in? You mean he's come back and gone out again?"

"No, Madam. He's never been back."

The dread stirred again, and Mary knew that now it had her fast.

"Not since he went out with—the gentleman?"

"Not since he went out with the gentleman."

"But who *was* the gentleman?" Mary insisted, with the shrill note of someone trying to be heard through a confusion of noises.

"That I couldn't say, Madam." Trimmle, standing there by the lamp, seemed suddenly to grow less round and rosy, as though eclipsed by the same creeping shade of apprehension.

"But the kitchenmaid knows—wasn't it the kitchenmaid who let him in?"

"She doesn't know either, Madam, for he wrote his name on a folded paper."

Mary, through her agitation, was aware that they were both designating the unknown visitor by a vague pronoun, instead of the conventional formula which, till then, had kept their allusions within the bounds of conformity. And at the same moment her mind caught at the suggestion of the folded paper.

"But he must have a name! Where's the paper?"

She moved to the desk, and began to turn over the documents that littered it. The first that caught her eye was an unfinished letter in her husband's hand, with his pen lying across it, as though dropped there at a sudden summons.

"My dear Parvis"—who was Parvis?—"I have just received your letter announcing Elwell's death, and while I suppose there is now no further risk of trouble, it might be safer—"

She tossed the sheet aside, and continued her search; but no folded paper was discoverable among the letters and pages of manuscript which had been swept together in a heap, as if by a hurried or a startled gesture.

"But the kitchenmaid *saw* him. Send her here," she commanded, wondering at her dullness in not thinking sooner of so simple a solution.

Trimmle vanished in a flash, as if thankful to be out of the room, and when she reappeared, conducting the agitated underling, Mary had regained her self-possession, and had her questions ready.

The gentleman was a stranger, yes—that she understood. But what had he said? And, above all, what had he looked like? The first question was easily enough answered, for the disconcerting reason that he had said so little—had merely asked for Mr. Boyne, and scribbling something on a bit of paper, had requested that it should at once be carried in to him.

"Then you don't know what he wrote? You're not sure it *was* his name?"

The kitchenmaid was not sure, but supposed it was, since he had written it in answer to her inquiry as to whom she should announce.

"And when you carried the paper in to Mr. Boyne, what did he say?"

The kitchenmaid did not think that Mr. Boyne had said anything, but she could not be sure, for just as she had handed him the paper and he was opening it, she had become aware that the visitor had followed her into the library, and she had slipped out, leaving the two gentlemen together.

"But then, if you left them in the library, how do you know that they went out of the house?"

This question plunged the witness into a momentary inarticulateness, from which she was rescued by Trimmle, who, by means of ingenious circumlocutions, elicited the statement that before she could cross the hall to the back passage she had heard the two gentlemen behind her, and had seen them go out of the front door together.

"Then, if you saw the strange gentleman twice, you must be able to tell me what he looked like."

But with this final challenge to her powers of expression it became clear that the limit of the kitchenmaid's endurance had been reached. The obligation of going to the front door to "show in" a visitor was in itself so subversive of the fundamental order of things that it had thrown her faculties into hopeless disarray, and she could only stammer out, after various panting efforts: "His hat, mum, was different-like as you might say—"

"Different? How different?" Mary flashed out, her own mind, in the same instant, leaping back to an image left on it that morning, and then lost under layers of subsequent impressions.

"His hat had a wide brim, you mean, and his face was pale— a youngish face?" Mary pressed her, with a white-lipped intensity of interrogation. But if the kitchenmaid found any adequate answer to this challenge, it was swept away for her listener down the rushing current of her own convictions. The stranger—the stranger in the garden! Why had Mary not thought of him before? She needed no one now to tell her that it was he who had called for her husband and gone away with him. But who was he, and why had Boyne obeyed him?

IV

It leaped out at her suddenly, like a grin out of the dark, that they had often called England so little—"such a confoundedly hard place to get lost in."

A confoundedly hard place to get lost in! That had been her husband's phrase. And now, with the whole machinery of official investigation sweeping its flashlights from shore to shore, and across the dividing straits; now, with Boyne's name blazing from the walls of every town and village, his portrait (how that wrung her!) hawked up and down the country like the image of a hunted criminal; now the little compact populous island so policed, surveyed and administered, revealed itself as a Sphinxlike guardian of abysmal mysteries, staring back into his wife's anguished eyes as if with the wicked joy of knowing something they would never know!

In the fortnight since Boyne's disappearance there had been no word of him, no trace of his movements. Even the usual misleading reports that raise expectancy in tortured bosoms had been few and fleeting. No one but the kitchenmaid had seen Boyne leave the house, and no one else had seen "the gentleman" who accompanied him. All inquiries in the neighborhood failed to elicit the memory of a stranger's presence that day in the neighborhood of Lyng. And no one had met Edward Boyne, either alone or in company, in any of the neighboring villages, or on the road across the downs, or at either of the local railway stations. The sunny English noon had swallowed him as completely as if he had gone out into Cimmerian night.

Mary, while every official means of investigation was working at its highest pressure, had ransacked her husband's papers for any trace of antecedent complications, of entanglements or obligations unknown to her, that might throw a ray into the darkness. But if any such had existed in the background of Boyne's life, they had vanished like the slip of paper on which the visitor had written his name. There remained no possible thread of guidance except—if it were indeed an exception—the letter which Boyne had apparently been in the act of writing when he received his mysterious summons. That letter, read and reread by his wife, and submitted by her to the police, yielded little enough to feed conjecture.

"I have just heard of Elwell's death, and while I suppose there is now no further risk of trouble, it might be safer—" That was all. The "risk of trouble" was easily explained by the newspaper clipping which had apprised Mary of the suit brought against her husband by one of his associates in the Blue Star enterprise. The only new information conveyed by the letter was the fact of its showing Boyne, when he wrote it, to be still apprehensive of the results of the suit, though he had told his wife that it had been withdrawn, and though the letter itself proved that the plaintiff was dead. It took several days of cabling to fix the identity of the "Parvis" to whom the fragment was addressed, but even after these inquiries had shown him to be a Waukesha lawyer, no new facts concerning the Elwell suit were elicited. He appeared to have had no direct concern in it, but to have been conversant with the facts merely as an acquaintance, and possible intermediary; and he declared himself unable to guess with what object Boyne intended to seek his assistance.

This negative information, sole fruit of the first fortnight's search, was not increased by a jot during the slow weeks that followed. Mary knew that the investigations were still being carried on, but she had a vague sense of their gradually slackening, as the actual march of time seemed to slacken. It was as though the days, flying horror-struck from the shrouded image of the one inscrutable day, gained assurance as the distance lengthened, till at last they fell back into their normal gait. And so with the human imaginations at work on the dark event. No doubt it occupied them still, but week by week and hour by hour it grew less absorbing, took up less space, was slowly but inevitably crowded out of the foreground of consciousness by the new problems perpetually bubbling up from the cloudy caldron of human experience.

Even Mary Boyne's consciousness gradually felt the same lowering of velocity. It still swayed with the incessant oscillations of conjecture; but they were slower, more rhythmical in their beat. There were even moments of weariness when, like the victim of some poison which leaves the brain clear, but holds the body motionless, she saw herself domesticated with the horror, accepting its perpetual presence as one of the fixed conditions of life.

These moments lengthened into hours and days, till she passed into a phase of stolid acquiescence. She watched the routine of daily life with the incurious eye of a savage on whom the meaningless processes of civilization make but the faintest impression. She had come to regard herself as part of the routine, a spoke of the wheel, revolving with its motion; she felt almost like the furniture of the room in which she sat, an insensate object to be dusted and pushed about with the chairs and tables. And this deepening apathy held her fast at Lyng, in spite of the entreaties of friends and the usual medical recommendation of "change." Her friends supposed that her refusal to move was inspired by the belief that her husband would one day return to the spot from which he had vanished, and a beautiful legend grew up about this imaginary state of waiting. But in reality she had no such belief: the depths of anguish enclosing her were no longer lighted by flashes of hope. She was sure that Boyne would never come back, that he had gone out of her sight as completely as if Death itself had waited that day on the threshold. She had even renounced, one by one, the various theories as to his disappearance which had been advanced by the press, the police, and her own agonized imagination. In sheer lassitude her mind turned from these alternatives of horror, and sank back into the blank fact that he was gone.

No, she would never know what had become of him—no one would ever know. But the house *knew;* the library in which she spent her long lonely evenings knew. For it was here that the last scene had been enacted, here that the stranger had come, and spoken the word which had caused Boyne to rise and follow him. The floor she trod had felt his tread; the books on the shelves had seen his face; and there were moments when the intense consciousness of the old dusky walls seemed about to break out into some audible revelation of their secret. But the revelation never came, and she knew it would never come. Lyng was not one of the garrulous old houses that betray the secrets entrusted to them. Its very legend proved that it had always been the mute accomplice, the incorruptible custodian, of the mysteries it had surprised. And Mary Boyne, sitting face-to-face with its silence, felt the futility of seeking to break it by any human means.

V

"I don't say it *wasn't* straight, and yet I don't say it *was* straight. It was business."

Mary, at the words, lifted her head with a start, and looked intently at the speaker.

When, half an hour before, a card with "Mr. Parvis" on it had been brought up to her, she had been immediately aware that the name had been a part of her consciousness ever since she had read it at the head of Boyne's unfinished letter. In the library she had found awaiting her a small sallow man with a bald head and gold eyeglasses, and it sent a tremor through her to know that this was the person to whom her husband's last known thought had been directed.

Parvis, civilly, but without vain preamble—in the manner of a man who has his watch in his hand—had set forth the object of his visit. He had "run over" to England on business, and finding himself in the neighborhood of Dorchester, had not wished to leave it without paying his respects to Mrs. Boyne; and without asking her, if the occasion offered, what she meant to do about Bob Elwell's family.

The words touched the spring of some obscure dread in Mary's bosom. Did her visitor, after all, know what Boyne had meant by his unfinished phrase? She asked for an elucidation of his question, and noticed at once that he seemed surprised at her continued ignorance of the subject. Was it possible that she really knew as little as she said?

"I know nothing—you must tell me," she faltered out; and her visitor thereupon proceeded to unfold his story. It threw, even to her confused perceptions, and imperfectly initiated vision, a lurid glare on the whole hazy episode of the Blue Star Mine. Her husband had made his money in that brilliant speculation at the cost of "getting ahead" of someone less alert to seize the chance; and the victim of his ingenuity was young Robert Elwell, who had "put him on" to the Blue Star scheme.

Parvis, at Mary's first cry, had thrown her a sobering glance through his impartial glasses.

"Bob Elwell wasn't smart enough, that's all; if he had been, he might have turned round and served Boyne the same way. It's the kind of thing that happens every day in business. I guess it's what the scientists call the survival of the fittest—see?" said Mr. Parvis, evidently pleased with the aptness of his analogy.

Mary felt a physical shrinking from the next question she tried to frame: it was as though the words on her lips had a taste that nauseated her.

"But then—you accused my husband of doing something dishonorable?"

Mr. Parvis surveyed the question dispassionately. "Oh, no, I don't. I don't even say it wasn't straight." He glanced up and down the long lines of books, as if one of them might have supplied him with the definition he sought. "I don't say it *wasn't* straight, and yet I don't say it *was* straight. It was business." After all, no definition in his category could be more comprehensive than that.

Mary sat staring at him with a look of terror. He seemed to her like the indifferent emissary of some evil power.

"But Mr. Elwell's lawyers apparently did not take your view, since I suppose the suit was withdrawn by their advice."

"Oh, yes; they knew he hadn't a leg to stand on, technically. It was when they advised him to withdraw the suit that he got desperate. You see, he'd borrowed most of the money he lost in the Blue Star, and he was up a tree. That's why he shot himself when they told him he had no show."

The horror was sweeping over Mary in great deafening waves.

"He shot himself? He killed himself because of *that*?"

"Well, he didn't kill himself, exactly. He dragged on two months before he died." Parvis emitted the statement as unemotionally as a gramophone grinding out its record.

"You mean that he tried to kill himself, and failed? And tried again?"

"Oh, he didn't have to *try* again," said Parvis grimly.

They sat opposite each other in silence, he swinging his eyeglasses thoughtfully about his finger, she, motionless, her arms stretched along her knees in an attitude of rigid tension.

"But if you knew all this," she began at length, hardly able to force her voice above a whisper, "how is it that when I wrote you at the time of my husband's disappearance you said you didn't understand his letter?"

Parvis received this without perceptible embarrassment: "Why, I didn't understand it—strictly speaking. And it wasn't the time to talk about it, if I had. The Elwell business was settled when the suit was withdrawn. Nothing I could have told you would have helped you to find your husband."

Mary continued to scrutinize him. "Then why are you telling me now?"

Still Parvis did not hesitate. "Well, to begin with, I supposed you knew more than you appear to—I mean about the circumstances of Elwell's death. And then people are talking of it now; the whole matter's been raked up again. And I thought if you didn't know you ought to."

She remained silent, and he continued: "You see, it's only come out lately what a bad state Elwell's affairs were in. His wife's a proud woman, and she fought on as long as she could, going out to work, and taking sewing at home when she got too sick—something with the heart, I believe. But she had his mother to look after, and the children, and she broke down under it, and finally had to ask for help. That called attention to the case, and the papers took it up, and a subscription was started. Everybody out there liked Bob Elwell, and most of the prominent names in the place are down on the list, and people began to wonder why—"

Parvis broke off to fumble in an inner pocket. "Here," he continued, "here's an account of the whole thing from the *Sentinel*—a little sensational, of course. But I guess you'd better look it over."

He held out a newspaper to Mary, who unfolded it slowly, remembering, as she did so, the evening when, in that same room, the perusal of a clipping from the *Sentinel* had first shaken the depths of her security.

As she opened the paper, her eyes, shrinking from the glaring headlines, "Widow of Boyne's Victim Forced to Appeal for Aid," ran down the column of text to two portraits inserted in it. The first was her husband's, taken from a photograph made the year they had come to England. It was the picture of him that she liked best, the one that stood on the writing table upstairs in her bedroom. As the eyes in the photograph met hers, she felt it would be impossible to read what was said of him, and closed her lids with the sharpness of the pain.

"I thought if you felt disposed to put your name down—" she heard Parvis continue.

She opened her eyes with an effort, and they fell on the other portrait. It was that of a youngish man, slightly built, with features somewhat blurred by the shadow of a projecting hat brim. Where had she seen that outline before? She stared at it confusedly, her heart hammering in her ears. Then she gave a cry.

"This is the man—the man who came for my husband!"

She heard Parvis start to his feet, and was dimly aware that she had slipped backward into the corner of the sofa, and that he was bending above her in alarm. She straightened herself, and reached out for the paper, which she had dropped.

"It's the man! I should know him anywhere!" she persisted in a voice that sounded to her own ears like a scream.

Parvis's answer seemed to come to her from far off, down endless fog-muffled windings.

"Mrs. Boyne, you're not very well. Shall I call somebody? Shall I get a glass of water?"

"No, no, no!" She threw herself toward him, her hand frantically clutching the newspaper. "I tell you, it's the man! I *know* him! He spoke to me in the garden!"

Parvis took the journal from her, directing his glasses to the portrait. "It can't be, Mrs. Boyne. It's Robert Elwell."

"Robert Elwell?" Her white stare seemed to travel into space. "Then it was Robert Elwell who came for him."

"Came for Boyne? The day he went away from here?" Parvis's voice dropped as hers rose. He bent over, laying a fraternal hand on her, as if to coax her gently back into her seat. "Why, Elwell was dead! Don't you remember?"

Mary sat with her eyes fixed on the picture, unconscious of what he was saying.

"Don't you remember Boyne's unfinished letter to me—the one you found on his desk that day? It was written just after he'd heard of Elwell's death." She noticed an odd shake in Parvis's unemotional voice. "Surely you remember!" he urged her.

Yes, she remembered: that was the profoundest horror of it. Elwell had died the day before her husband's disappearance; and this was Elwell's portrait; and it was the portrait of the man who had spoken to her in the garden. She lifted her head and looked slowly about the library. The library could have borne witness that it was also the portrait of the man who had come in that day to call Boyne from his unfinished letter. Through the misty surgings of her brain she heard the faint boom of half-forgotten words—words spoken by Alida Stair on the lawn at Pangbourne before Boyne and his wife had ever seen the house at Lyng, or had imagined that they might one day live there.

"This was the man who spoke to me," she repeated.

She looked again at Parvis. He was trying to conceal his disturbance under what he probably imagined to be an expression of indulgent commiseration; but the edges of his lips were blue. "He thinks me mad; but I'm not mad," she reflected; and suddenly there flashed upon her a way of justifying her strange affirmation.

She sat quiet, controlling the quiver of her lips, and waiting till she could trust her voice; then she said, looking straight at Parvis: "Will you answer me one question, please? When was it that Robert Elwell tried to kill himself?"

"When—when?" Parvis stammered.

"Yes; the date. Please try to remember."

She saw that he was growing still more afraid of her. "I have a reason," she insisted.

"Yes, yes. Only I can't remember. About two months before, I should say."

"I want the date," she repeated.

Parvis picked up the newspaper. "We might see here," he said, still humoring her. He ran his eyes down the page. "Here it is. Last October—the—"

She caught the words from him. "The 20th, wasn't it?" With a sharp look at her, he verified. "Yes, the 20th. Then you *did* know?"

"I know now." Her gaze continued to travel past him. "Sunday, the 20th—that was the day he came first."

Parvis's voice was almost inaudible. "Came *here* first?"

"Yes."

"You saw him twice, then?"

"Yes, twice." She just breathed it at him. "He came first on the 20th of October. I remember the date because it was the day

we went up Meldon Steep for the first time." She felt a faint
gasp of inward laughter at the thought that but for that she might
have forgotten.

Parvis continued to scrutinize her, as if trying to intercept her
gaze.

"We saw him from the roof," she went on. "He came down
the lime avenue toward the house. He was dressed just as he is
in that picture. My husband saw him first. He was frightened,
and ran down ahead of me; but there was no one there. He had
vanished."

"Elwell had vanished?" Parvis faltered.

"Yes." Their two whispers seemed to grope for each other. "I
couldn't think what had happened. I see now. He *tried* to come
then; but he wasn't dead enough—he couldn't reach us. He had
to wait for two months to die; and then he came back again—
and Ned went with him."

She nodded at Parvis with the look of triumph of a child who
has worked out a difficult puzzle. But suddenly she lifted her
hands with a desperate gesture, pressing them to her temples.

"Oh, my God! I sent him to Ned—I told him where to go! I
sent him to this room!" she screamed.

She felt the walls of books rush toward her, like inward falling
ruins; and she heard Parvis, a long way off, through the ruins,
crying to her, and struggling to get at her. But she was numb to
his touch, she did not know what he was saying. Through the
tumult she heard but one clear note, the voice of Alida Stair,
speaking on the lawn at Pangbourne.

"You won't know till afterward," it said. "You won't know
till long, long afterward."

Smoke Ghost

Fritz Leiber

A six-time winner of science fiction's Hugo Award and two-time recipient of the World Fantasy Award, Fritz Leiber (1910–1992) is one of the few authors to make an indelible impact on the fields of science fiction, fantasy, *and* horror. Through novels like *Conjure Wife* (1943), which explained witchcraft as a form of higher mathematics, and *Gather, Darkness!* (1943), in which scientists of a post-apocalyptic future masquerade as religious mystics, he helped to modernize many themes of classic fantasy. In "Smoke Ghost" (1941), a forerunner of his urban horror classics *You're All Alone* (1950) and *Our Lady of Darkness* (1977), Leiber found a home for horror's oldest supernatural entity in the contemporary city.

M iss Millick wondered just what had happened to Mr. Wran. He kept making the strangest remarks when she took dictation. Just this morning he had quickly turned around and asked, "Have you ever seen a ghost, Miss Millick?" And she had tittered nervously and replied, "When I was a girl there was a thing in white that used to come out of the closet in the attic bedroom when I slept there, and moan. Of course it was just my imagination. I was frightened of lots of things." And he had said, "I don't mean that kind of ghost. I mean a ghost from the world today, with the soot of the factories on its face and the pounding of machinery in its soul. The kind that would haunt coal yards and slip around at night through deserted office buildings like this one. A real ghost. Not something out of books." And she hadn't known what to say.

He'd never been like this before. Of course he might be joking, but it didn't sound that way. Vaguely Miss Millick wondered whether he mightn't be seeking some sort of sympathy from her. Of course, Mr. Wran was married and had a little child, but that didn't prevent her from having daydreams. The daydreams were not very exciting, still they helped fill up her mind. But now he was asking her another of those unprecedented questions.

"Have you ever thought what a ghost of our times would look like, Miss Millick? Just picture it. A smoky composite face with the hungry anxiety of the unemployed, the neurotic restlessness of the person without purpose, the jerky tension of the high-pressure metropolitan worker, the uneasy resentment of the striker, the callous opportunism of the scab, the aggressive whine of the panhandler, the inhibited terror of the bombed civilian, and a thousand other twisted emotional patterns. Each one overlying and yet blending with the other, like a pile of semi-transparent masks?"

Miss Millick gave a little self-conscious shiver and said, "That would be terrible. What an awful thing to think of."

She peered furtively across the desk. She remembered having heard that there had been something impressively abnormal about Mr. Wran's childhood, but she couldn't recall what it was. If only she could do something—laugh at his mood or ask him what was really wrong. She shifted the extra pencils in her left hand and mechanically traced over some of the shorthand curlicues in her notebook.

"Yet, that's just what such a ghost or vitalized projection would look like, Miss Millick," he continued, smiling in a tight way. "It would grow out of the real world. It would reflect the tangled, sordid, vicious things. All the loose ends. And it would be very grimy. I don't think it would seem white or wispy, or favor graveyards. It wouldn't moan. But it would mutter unintelligibly, and twitch at your sleeve. Like a sick, surly ape. What would such a thing want from a person, Miss Millick? Sacrifice? Worship? Or just fear? What could you do to stop it from troubling you?"

Miss Millick giggled nervously. There was an expression beyond her powers of definition in Mr. Wran's ordinary, flat-cheeked, thirtyish face, silhouetted against the dusty window. He turned away and stared out into the gray downtown atmosphere that rolled in from the railroad yards and the mills. When he spoke again his voice sounded far away.

"Of course, being immaterial, it couldn't hurt you physically— at first. You'd have to be peculiarly sensitive to see it, or be aware of it at all. But it would begin to influence your actions. Make you do this. Stop you from doing that. Although only a projection, it would gradually get its hooks into the world of things as they are. Might even get control of suitably vacuous minds. Then it could hurt whomever it wanted."

Miss Millick squirmed and read back her shorthand, like the books said you should do when there was a pause. She became aware of the failing light and wished Mr. Wran would ask her to turn on the overhead. She felt scratchy, as if soot were sifting down onto her skin.

"It's a rotten world, Miss Millick," said Mr. Wran, talking at the window. "Fit for another morbid growth of superstition. It's time the ghosts, or whatever you call them, took over and began a rule of fear. They'd be no worse than men."

"But"—Miss Millick's diaphragm jerked, making her titter inanely—"of course, there aren't any such things as ghosts."

Mr. Wran turned around.

"Of course there aren't, Miss Millick," he said in a loud, patronizing voice, as if she had been doing the talking rather than he. "Science and common sense and psychiatry all go to prove it."

She hung her head and might even have blushed if she hadn't felt so all at sea. Her leg muscles twitched, making her stand up, although she hadn't intended to. She aimlessly rubbed her hand along the edge of the desk.

"Why, Mr. Wran, look what I got off your desk," she said, showing him a heavy smudge. There was a note of clumsily playful reproof in her voice. "No wonder the copy I bring you always gets so black. Somebody ought to talk to those scrubwomen. They're skimping on your room."

She wished he would make some normal joking reply. But instead he drew back and his face hardened.

"Well, to get back," he rapped out harshly, and began to dictate.

When she was gone, he jumped up, dabbed his finger experimentally at the smudged part of the desk, frowned worriedly at the almost inky smears. He jerked open a drawer, snatched out a rag, hastily swabbed off the desk, crumpled the rag into a ball and tossed it back. There were three or four other rags in the drawer, each impregnated with soot.

Then he went over to the window and peered out anxiously through the dusk, his eyes searching the panorama of roofs, fixing on each chimney and water tank.

"It's a neurosis. Must be. Compulsions. Hallucinations," he muttered to himself in a tired, distraught voice that would have made Miss Millick gasp. "It's that damned mental abnormality cropping up in a new form. Can't be any other explanation. But it's so damned real. Even the soot. Good thing I'm seeing the psychiatrist. I don't think I could force myself to get on the elevated tonight." His voice trailed off, he rubbed his eyes, and his memory automatically started to grind.

It had all begun on the elevated. There was a particular little sea of roofs he had grown into the habit of glancing at just as the packed car carrying him homeward lurched around a turn. A dingy, melancholy little world of tar-paper, tarred gravel, and smoky brick. Rusty tin chimneys with odd conical hats suggested abandoned listening posts. There was a washed-out advertisement of some ancient patent medicine on the nearest wall. Superficially it was like ten thousand other drab city roofs. But he always saw it around dusk, either in the smoky half-light, or tinged with red by the flat rays of a dirty sunset, or covered by ghostly windblown white sheets of rain-splash, or patched with blackish snow; and it seemed unusually bleak and suggestive; almost beautifully ugly though in no sense picturesque; dreary, but meaningful. Unconsciously it came to symbolize for Catesby Wran certain disagreeable aspects of the frustrated, frightened century in which he lived, the jangled century of hate and heavy industry and total wars. The quick daily glance into the half darkness became an integral part of his life. Oddly, he never saw it in the morning, for it was then his habit to sit on the other side of the car, his head buried in the paper.

One evening toward winter he noticed what seemed to be a shapeless black sack lying on the third roof from the tracks. He did not think about it. It merely registered as an addition to the well-known scene and his memory stored away the impression for further reference. Next evening, however, he decided he had been mistaken in one detail. The object was a roof nearer than he had thought. Its color and texture, and the grimy stains around it, suggested that it was filled with coal dust, which was hardly reasonable. Then, too, the following evening it seemed to have been blown against a rusty ventilator by the wind—which could hardly have happened if it were at all heavy. Perhaps it was filled with leaves. Catesby was surprised to find himself anticipating his next daily glance with a minor note of apprehension. There was something unwholesome in the posture of the thing that stuck in his mind—a bulge in the sacking that suggested a misshaped head peering around the ventilator. And his apprehension was justified, for that evening the thing was on the nearest roof, though on the farther side, looking as if it had just flopped down over the low brick parapet.

Next evening the sack was gone. Catesby was annoyed at the momentary feeling of relief that went through him, because the whole matter seemed too unimportant to warrant feelings of any sort. What difference did it make if his imagination had played tricks on him, and he'd fancied that the object was slowly crawling and hitching itself closer across the roofs? That was the way any normal imagination worked. He deliberately chose to disregard the fact that there were reasons for thinking his imagination was by no means a normal one. As he walked home from the elevated, however, he found himself wondering whether the sack was really gone. He seemed to recall a vague, smudgy trail leading across the gravel to the nearer side of the roof, which was masked by a parapet. For an instant an unpleasant picture formed in his mind—that of an inky, humped creature crouched behind the parapet, waiting.

The next time he felt the familiar grating lurch of the car, he caught himself trying not to look out. That angered him. He turned his head quickly. When he turned it back, his compact face was definitely pale. There had been only time for a fleeting rearward glance at the escaping roof. Had he actually seen in silhouette the upper part of a head of some sort peering over the parapet? Nonsense, he told himself. And even if he had seen something, there were a thousand explanations which did not involve the supernatural or even true hallucination. Tomorrow he would take a good look and clear up the whole matter. If necessary, he would visit the roof personally, though he hardly

knew where to find it and disliked in any case the idea of pamper-
ing a silly fear.

He did not relish the walk home from the elevated that evening, and visions of the thing disturbed his dreams, and were in
and out of his mind all next day at the office. It was then that
he first began to relieve his nerves by making jokingly serious
remarks about the supernatural to Miss Millick, who seemed
properly mystified. It was on the same day, too, that he became
aware of a growing antipathy to grime and soot. Everything he
touched seemed gritty, and he found himself mopping and wiping
at his desk like an old lady with a morbid fear of germs. He
reasoned that there was no real change in his office, and that
he'd just now become sensitive to the dirt that had always been
there, but there was no denying an increasing nervousness. Long
before the car reached the curve, he was straining his eyes
through the murky twilight, determined to take in every detail.

Afterward he realized he must have given a muffled cry of
some sort, for the man beside him looked at him curiously, the
woman ahead gave him an unfavorable stare. Conscious of his
own pallor and uncontrollable trembling, he stared back at them
hungrily, trying to regain the feeling of security he had completely lost. They were the usual reassuringly wooden-faced people everyone rides home with on the elevated. But suppose he
had pointed out to one of them what he had seen—that sodden,
distorted face of sacking and coal dust, that boneless paw which
waved back and forth, unmistakably in his direction, as if re-
minding him of a future appointment—he involuntarily shut his
eyes tight. His thoughts were racing ahead to tomorrow evening.
He pictured this same windowed oblong of light and packed humanity surging around the curve—then an opaque monstrous
form leaping out from the roof in a parabolic swoop—an unmen-
tionable face pressed close against the window, smearing it with
wet coal dust—huge paws fumbling sloppily at the glass—

Somehow he managed to turn off his wife's anxious inquiries.
Next morning he reached a decision and made an appointment
for that evening with a psychiatrist a friend had told him about.
It cost him a considerable effort, for Catesby had a well-grounded
distaste for anything dealing with psychological abnormality. Visiting a psychiatrist meant raking up an episode in his past which
he had never fully described even to his wife. Once he had made

the decision, however, he felt considerably relieved. The psychiatrist, he told himself, would clear everything up. He could almost fancy him saying, "Merely a bad case of nerves. However, you must consult the occulist whose name I'm writing down for you, and you must take two of these pills in water every four hours," and so on. It was almost comforting, and made the coming revelation he would have to make seem less painful.

But as the smoky dusk rolled in, his nervousness had returned and he had let his joking mystification of Miss Millick run away with him until he had realized he wasn't frightening anyone but himself.

He would have to keep his imagination under better control, he told himself, as he continued to peer out restlessly at the massive, murky shapes of the downtown office buildings. Why, he had spent the whole afternoon building up a kind of neo-medieval cosmology of superstition. It wouldn't do. He realized then that he had been standing at the window much longer than he'd thought, for the glass panel in the door was dark and there was no noise coming from the outer office. Miss Millick and the rest must have gone home.

It was then he made the discovery that there would have been no special reason for dreading the swing around the curve that night. It was, as it happened, a horrible discovery. For, on the shadowed roof across the street and four stories below, he saw the thing huddle and roll across the gravel and, after one upward look of recognition, merge into the blackness beneath the water tank.

As he hurriedly collected his things and made for the elevator, fighting the panicky impulse to run, he began to think of hallucination and mild psychosis as very desirable conditions. For better or for worse, he pinned all his hopes on the psychiatrist.

"So you find yourself growing nervous and . . . er . . . jumpy, as you put it," said Dr. Trevethick, smiling with dignified geniality. "Do you notice any more definite physical symptoms? Pain? Headache? Indigestion?"

Catesby shook his head and wet his lips. "I'm especially nervous while riding in the elevated," he muttered swiftly.

"I see. We'll discuss that more fully. But I'd like you first to tell me about something you mentioned earlier. You said there was something about your childhood that might predispose you to nervous ailments. As you know, the early years are critical ones in the development of an individual's behavior pattern."

Catesby studied the yellow reflections of frosted globes in the dark surface of the desk. The palm of his left hand aimlessly rubbed the thick nap of the armchair. After a while he raised his head and looked straight into the doctor's small brown eyes.

"From perhaps my third to my ninth year," he began, choosing the words with care, "I was what you might call a sensory prodigy."

The doctor's expression did not change. "Yes?" he inquired politely.

"What I mean is that I was supposed to be able to see through walls, read letters through envelopes and books through their covers, fence and play Ping-Pong blindfolded, find things that were buried, read thoughts." The words tumbled out.

"And could you?" The doctor's voice was toneless.

"I don't know. I don't suppose so," answered Catesby, long-lost emotions flooding back into his voice. "It's all confused now. I thought I could, but then they were always encouraging me. My mother . . . was . . . well . . . interested in psychic phenomena. I was . . . exhibited. I seem to remember seeing things other people couldn't. As if most opaque objects were transparent. But I was very young. I didn't have any scientific criteria for judgment."

He was reliving it now. The darkened rooms. The earnest assemblages of gawking, prying adults. Himself alone on a little platform, lost in a straight-backed wooden chair. The black silk handkerchief over his eyes. His mother's coaxing, insistent questions. The whispers. The gasps. His own hate of the whole business, mixed with hunger for the adulation of adults. Then the scientists from the university, the experiments, the big test. The reality of those memories engulfed him and momentarily made him forget the reason why he was disclosing them to a stranger.

"Do I understand that your mother tried to make use of you as a medium for communicating with the . . . er . . . other world?"

Catesby nodded eagerly.

"She tried to, but she couldn't. When it came to getting in touch with the dead, I was a complete failure. All I could do— or thought I could do—was see real, existing, three-dimensional objects beyond the vision of normal people. Objects anyone could have seen except for distance, obstruction, or darkness. It was always a disappointment to Mother."

He could hear her sweetish, patient voice saying, "Try again, dear, just this once. Katie was your aunt. She loved you. Try to hear what she's saying." And he had answered, "I can see a woman in a blue dress standing on the other side of Dick's house." And she had replied, "Yes, I know, dear. But that's not Katie. Katie's a spirit. Try again. Just this once, dear." The doctor's voice gently jarred him back into the softly gleaming office.

"You mentioned scientific criteria for judgment, Mr. Wran. As far as you know, did anyone ever try to apply them to you?"

Catesby's nod was emphatic.

"They did. When I was eight, two young psychologists from the university got interested in me. I guess they did it for a joke at first, and I remember being very determined to show them I amounted to something. Even now I seem to recall how the note of polite superiority and amused sarcasm drained out of their voices. I suppose they decided at first that it was very clever trickery, but somehow they persuaded Mother to let them try me out under controlled conditions. There were lots of tests that seemed very businesslike after Mother's slipshod little exhibitions. They found I was clairvoyant—or so they thought. I got worked up and on edge. They were going to demonstrate my supernormal sensory powers to the university psychology faculty. For the first time, I began to worry about whether I'd come through. Perhaps they kept me going at too hard a pace, I don't know. At any rate, when the test came, I couldn't do a thing. Everything became opaque. I got desperate and made things up out of my imagination. I lied. In the end I failed utterly, and I believe the two young psychologists got into a lot of hot water as a result."

He could hear the brusque, bearded man saying, "You've been taken in by a child, Flaxman, a mere child. I'm greatly disturbed. You've put yourself on the same plane as common charlatans. Gentlemen, I ask you to banish from your minds this whole sorry episode. It must never be referred to." He winced at the recollection of his feeling of guilt. But at the same time he was beginning to feel exhilarated and almost lighthearted. Unburdening his long-repressed memories had altered his whole view-point. The episodes on the elevated began to take on what seemed their proper proportions as merely the bizarre workings of overwrought nerves and an overly suggestible mind. The doctor, he anticipated confidently, would disentangle the obscure subconscious causes, whatever they might be. And the whole business would be finished off quickly, just as his childhood experience—which was beginning to seem a little ridiculous now—had been finished off.

"From that day on," he continued, "I never exhibited a trace of my supposed powers. My mother was frantic and tried to sue the university. I had something like a nervous breakdown. Then the divorce was granted, and my father got custody of me. He did his best to make me forget it. We went on long outdoor vacations and did a lot of athletics, associated with normal matter-of-fact people. I went to business college eventually. I'm in advertising now. But," Catesby paused, "now that I'm having nervous symptoms, I've wondered if there mightn't be a connection. It's not a question of whether I was really clairvoyant or not. Very likely my mother taught me a lot of unconscious deceptions, good enough to fool even young psychology instructors. But don't you think it may have some important bearing on my present condition?"

For several moments the doctor regarded him with a professional frown. Then he said quietly, "And is there some . . . er . . . more specific connection between your experiences then and now? Do you by any chance find that you are once again beginning to . . . er . . . see things?"

Catesby swallowed. He had felt an increasing eagerness to unburden himself of his fears, but it was not easy to make a beginning, and the doctor's shrewd question rattled him. He forced himself to concentrate. The thing he thought he had seen on the roof loomed up before his inner eye with unexpected vividness. Yet it did not frighten him. He groped for words.

Then he saw that the doctor was not looking at him but over his shoulder. Color was draining out of the doctor's face and his eyes did not seem so small. Then the doctor sprang to his feet, walked past Catesby, threw up the window and peered into the darkness.

As Catesby rose, the doctor slammed down the window and

said in a voice whose smoothness was marred by a slight, persistent gasping, "I hope I haven't alarmed you. I saw the face of . . . er . . . a Negro prowler on the fire escape. I must have frightened him, for he seems to have gotten out of sight in a hurry. Don't give it another thought. Doctors are frequently bothered by *voyeurs* . . . er . . . Peeping Toms."

"A Negro?" asked Catesby, moistening his lips.

The doctor laughed nervously. "I imagine so, though my first odd impression was that it was a white man in black face. You see, the color didn't seem to have any brown in it. It was dead-black."

Catesby moved toward the window. There were smudges on the glass. "It's quite all right, Mr. Wran." The doctor's voice had acquired a sharp note in impatience, as if he were trying hard to reassume his professional authority. "Let's continue our conversation. I was asking you if you were"—he made a face—"seeing things."

Catesby's whirling thoughts slowed down and locked into place. "No, I'm not seeing anything that other people don't see, too. And I think I'd better go now. I've been keeping you too long." He disregarded the doctor's halfhearted gesture of denial. "I'll phone you about the physical examination. In a way you've already taken a big load off my mind." He smiled woodenly. "Good night, Dr. Trevethick."

Catesby Wran's mental state was a peculiar one. His eyes searched every angular shadow, he glanced sideways down each chasm-like alley and barren basement passageway, and kept stealing looks at the irregular line of the roofs, yet he was hardly conscious of where he was going. He pushed away the thoughts that came into his mind, and kept moving. He became aware of a slight sense of security as he turned into a lighted street where there were people and high buildings and blinking signs. After a while he found himself in the dim lobby of the structure that housed his office. Then he realized why he couldn't go home, why he daren't go home—after what had happened at the office of Dr. Trevethick.

"Hello, Mr. Wran," said the night elevator man, a burly figure in overalls, sliding open the grille-work door to the old-fashioned cage. "I didn't know you were working nights now, too."

Catesby stepped in automatically. "Sudden rush of orders," he murmured inanely. "Some stuff that has to be gotten out."

The cage creaked to a stop at the top floor. "Be working very late, Mr. Wran?"

He nodded vaguely, watched the car slide out of sight, found his keys, swiftly crossed the outer office, and entered his own. His hand went out to the light switch, but then the thought occurred to him that the two lighted windows, standing out against the dark bulk of the building, would indicate his whereabouts and serve as a goal toward which something could crawl and climb. He moved his chair so that the back was against the wall and sat down in the semidarkness. He did not remove his overcoat.

For a long time he sat there motionless, listening to his own breathing and the faraway sounds from the streets below: the thin metallic surge of the crosstown streetcar, the farther one of the elevated, faint, lonely cries and honkings, indistinct rumblings. Words he had spoken to Miss Millick in nervous jest came back to him with the bitter taste of truth. He found himself unable to reason critically or connectedly, but by their own volition thoughts rose up into his mind and gyrated slowly and rearranged themselves with the inevitable movement of planets.

Gradually his mental picture of the world was transformed. No longer a world of material atoms and empty spaces, but a world in which the bodiless existed and moved according to its own obscure laws or unpredictable impulses. The new picture illuminated with dreadful clarity certain general facts which had always bewildered and troubled him and from which he had tried to hide: the inevitability of hate and war, the diabolically timed mischances which wreck the best of human intentions, the walls of willful misunderstanding that divide one man from another, the eternal vitality of cruelty and ignorance and greed. They seemed appropriate now, necessary parts of the picture. And superstition only a kind of wisdom.

Then his thoughts returned to himself and the question he had asked Miss Millick, "What would such a thing want from a person? Sacrifices? Worship, or just fear? What could you do to stop it from troubling you?" It had become a practical question.

With an explosive jangle, the phone began to ring. "Cate, I've been trying everywhere to get you," said his wife. "I never thought you'd be at the office. What are you doing? I've been worried."

He said something about work.

"You'll be home right away?" came the faint anxious question. "I'm a little frightened. Ronny just had a scare. It woke him up. He kept pointing to the window saying, 'Black man, black man.' Of course it's something he dreamed. But I'm frightened. You will be home? What's that, dear? Can't you hear me?"

"I will. Right away," he said. Then he was out of the office, buzzing the night bell and peering down the shaft.

He saw it peering up the shaft at him from the deep shadows three floors below, the sacking face pressed against the iron grille-work. It started up the stair at a shockingly swift, shambling gait, vanishing temporarily from sight as it swung into the second corridor below.

Catesby clawed at the door to the office, realized he had not locked it, pushed it in, slammed and locked it behind him, retreated to the other side of the room, cowered between the filing cases and the wall. His teeth were clicking. He heard the groan of the rising cage. A silhouette darkened the frosted glass of the door, blotting out part of the grotesque reverse of the company name. After a little the door opened.

The big-globed overhead light flared on and, standing inside the door, her hand on the switch, was Miss Millick.

"Why, Mr. Wran," she stammered vacuously, "I didn't know you were here. I'd just come in to do some extra typing after the movie. I didn't . . . but the lights weren't on. What were you—"

He stared at her. He wanted to shout in relief, grab hold of her, talk rapidly. He realized he was grinning hysterically.

"Why, Mr. Wran, what's happened to you?" she asked embarrassedly, ending with a stupid titter. "Are you feeling sick? Isn't there something I can do for you?"

He shook his head jerkily and managed to say, "No, I'm just leaving. I was doing some extra work myself."

"But you *look* sick," she insisted, and walked over toward him. He inconsequentially realized she must have stepped in mud, for her high-heeled shoes left neat black prints.

"Yes, I'm sure you must be sick. You're so terribly pale."

She sounded like an enthusiastic, incompetent nurse. Her face brightened with a sudden inspiration. "I've got something in my bag that'll fix you up right away," she said. "It's for indigestion."

She fumbled at her stuffed oblong purse. He noticed that she was absentmindedly holding it shut with one hand while she tried to open it with the other. Then, under his very eyes, he saw her bend back the thick prongs of metal locking the purse as if they were tinfoil, or as if her fingers had become a pair of steel pliers.

Instantly his memory recited the words he had spoken to Miss Millick that afternoon. "It couldn't hurt you physically—at first . . . gradually get its hooks into the world . . . might even get control of suitably vacuous minds. Then it could hurt whomever it wanted." A sickish, cold feeling grew inside him. He began to edge toward the door.

But Miss Millick hurried ahead of him.

"You don't have to wait, Fred," she called. "Mr. Wran's decided to stay a while longer."

The door to the cage shut with a mechanical rattle. The cage creaked. Then she turned around in the door.

"Why, Mr. Wran," she gurgled reproachfully, "I just couldn't think of letting you go home now. I'm sure you're terribly unwell. Why, you might collapse in the street. You've just got to stay here until you feel different."

The creaking died away. He stood in the center of the office, motionless. His eyes traced the coal-black course of Miss Millick's footprints to where she stood blocking the door. Then a sound that was almost a scream was wrenched out of him, for it seemed to him that the blackness was creeping up her legs under the thin stockings.

"Why, Mr. Wran," she said, "you're acting as if you were crazy. You must lie down for a while. Here, I'll help you off with your coat."

The nauseously idiotic and rasping note was the same; only it had been intensified. As she came toward him he turned and ran through the storeroom, clattered a key desperately at the lock of the second door to the corridor.

"Why, Mr. Wran," he heard her call, "are you having some kind of a fit? You must let me help you."

The door came open and he plunged out into the corridor and up the stairs immediately ahead. It was only when he reached the top that he realized the heavy steel door in front of him led to the roof. He jerked up the catch.

"Why, Mr. Wran, you mustn't run away. I'm coming after you."

Then he was out on the gritty gravel of the roof. The night sky was clouded and murky, with a faint pinkish glow from the neon signs. From the distant mills rose a ghostly spurt of flame. He ran to the edge. The street lights glared dizzily upward. Two men were tiny round blobs of hat and shoulders. He swung around.

The thing was in the doorway. The voice was no longer solicitous but moronically playful, each sentence ending in a titter.

"Why, Mr. Wran, why have you come up here? We're all alone. Just think, I might push you off."

The thing came slowly toward him. He moved back until his heels touched the low parapet. Without knowing why, or what he was going to do, he dropped to his knees. He dared not look at the face as it came nearer, a focus for the worst in the world, a gathering point for poisons from everywhere. Then the lucidity of terror took possession of his mind, and words formed on his lips.

"I will obey you. You are my god," he said. "You have supreme power over man and his animals and his machines. You rule this city and all others. I recognize that."

Again the titter, closer. "Why, Mr. Wran, you never talked like this before. Do you mean it?"

"The world is yours to do with as you will, save or tear to pieces," he answered fawningly, the words automatically fitting themselves together in vaguely liturgical patterns. "I recognize that. I will praise, I will sacrifice. In smoke and soot I will worship you for ever."

The voice did not answer. He looked up. There was only Miss Millick, deathly pale and swaying drunkenly. Her eyes were closed. He caught her as she wobbled toward him. His knees gave way under the added weight and they sank down together on the edge of the roof.

After a while she began to twitch. Small noises came from her throat and her eyelids edged open.

"Come on, we'll go downstairs," he murmured jerkily, trying to draw her up. "You're feeling bad."

"I'm terribly dizzy," she whispered. "I must have fainted, I didn't eat enough. And then I'm so nervous lately, about the war and everything, I guess. Why, we're on the roof! Did you bring me up here to get some air? Or did I come up without knowing it? I'm awfully foolish. I used to walk in my sleep, my mother said."

As he helped her down the stairs, she turned and looked at him. "Why, Mr. Wran," she said, faintly, "you've got a big black smudge on your forehead. Here, let me get it off for you." Weakly she rubbed at it with her handkerchief. She started to sway again and he steadied her.

"No, I'll be all right," she said. "Only I feel cold. What happened, Mr. Wran? Did I have some sort of fainting spell?"

He told her it was something like that.

Later, riding home in the empty elevated car, he wondered how long he would be safe from the thing. It was a purely practical problem. He had no way of knowing, but instinct told him he had satisfied the brute for some time. Would it want more when it came again? Time enough to answer that question when it arose. It might be hard, he realized, to keep out of an insane asylum. With Helen and Ronny to protect, as well as himself, he would have to be careful and tight-lipped. He began to speculate as to how many other men and women had seen the thing or things like it.

The elevated slowed and lurched in a familiar fashion. He looked at the roofs near the curve. They seemed very ordinary, as if what made them impressive had gone away for a while.

The Crowd

Ray Bradbury

Ray Bradbury is renowned for introducing science fiction into the literary mainstream through novels like *The Martian Chronicles* (1950) and *Fahrenheit 451* (1953), and for blurring the boundary between fantasy and autobiography in *Dandelion Wine* (1957), *Death Is a Lonely Business* (1985), *A Graveyard for Lunatics* (1990) and *Green Shadows, White Whale* (1992). "The Crowd" is taken from his first book, *Dark Carnival* (1947), a collection of weird tales that transformed simple childhood fears into overwhelming horrors, invested the most mundane elements of daily life with supernatural dread—and changed the course of modern horror fiction.

After the accident, the crowd gathered swiftly. A ring of faces looking down at Spallner, stirring, shifting, gaping. Where they all came from, he did not know. He had heard their hard heels clattering over the asphalt of the street, heard their shouts and tiny squeals and curses as they saw the new motor car crumpled against the brick wall.

Blood was trickling from a gash on his brow. It swam across his face and he had trouble breathing. And yet he was strangely calm. He couldn't understand why.

He should be afraid of dying, but death was farthest from his thoughts. He was looking at the crowd that bent over him; a good two dozen people, jammed one in back of the other, looking down, looking down.

There was something in the expression on their faces. He could tell that he wouldn't die.

He could tell by their expressions . . .

Someone, far back, said, "Is he dead?"

Someone else replied, "No. He's not dead. He's not going to die. He'll be all right."

Naturally. Of course he wasn't going to die. They wouldn't let him. He could read it in their faces, that he would be all right.

The wheels of the car, turned up to the sky, were still spinning dizzily. He heard them whirring, slowing. There was something about the wheels, too. Something.

Gasoline crawled on the asphalt, mixed with blood. Feet moved.

"All right; break it up in there, break it up!" A thick Irish voice shouted its way through the crowd. Blue-serge legs appeared. A red Irish face peered down. "You okay, son?"

Spallner nodded his head weakly. "I'll—I'll be all right." A swallowing pause. "Ambulance?"

"Be here any minute now. You just take it easy."

Spallner did take it easy. He rested back against a coat somebody had thoughtfully slipped under his head. He had time to listen and look and smell.

He looked at the faces. A cordon of questioning, shifting faces. What sort of people were they, where were they from, what did they do?

He examined each one. First, a man's face; thin, bright, alert and pale, staring at him; continually swallowing and wetting his lips as if he were hypnotized.

Beside him stood a small-boned woman with red hair and too much powder on her face. She was a calcimined wren with a high, hysterical voice. She wrung a handkerchief with her thin fingers.

Behind the officer, a little boy with freckles wavered. Tears streamed down his ruddy cheeks. He was barefooted, his eyes were scrouged up tight and he kept opening them and blinking them and closing them again.

A siren split the night wide open at the seams. The crowd craned its neck, as if it were all on a marionette string, activated by one silent will.

A sort of fear raced through Spallner then. The crowd twisted back, to gaze at him. Faces. There was something suggestive about them. Something he could not quite catch with his mind. What was it . . . ?

Other faces. An old man with a face like a bleached apricot, bald and whimpering in his throat. A young woman whose hands were twitching all by themselves at her sides, as if they did not belong to her. A high school student, pimpled-faced, who kept drawing back from the blood, but who always returned, curious, to look again. He couldn't help himself.

Where had they all come from?

So strange, thought Spallner, how a crowd gathers after an accident. Instantly, with the speed of Mercury, they materialized; young, old, glib and sour and frightened and calm. They came running for blocks, out of side-streets and out of alleys and out of houses and hotels and out of cabs and street cars and busses. They came quickly. It was impossible that so many people could gather in one place at once.

They came as to the call of Gabriel.

The ambulance shrieked up, and the siren bubbled to a moan, then into silence. White uniforms took the plunge into the throng, wedged a trail through with a carrier.

"What is it?"

The officer told them. The crowd watched and listened. Effectively, the internes shifted Spallner onto the carrier, hoisted him and slid him into the ambulance.

One of the internes hopped in, slammed the doors shut. Through the square glass windows a few faces of the crowd still stared.

There was something wrong with the crowd. Something far worse than what had happened to Spallner. He felt uneasiness in his stomach.

Engines roared to life. The ambulance started. It pulled away from the curb, from the crumpled wreck, the blood and gas, away from the crowd.

The crowd that always came so fast. So strangely fast. To form a circle. A circle; like a ring of—

Vultures . . . ?

Blackness enveloped Spallner. It clipped off everything.

He saw the wheel spinning in his brain as he came to his senses. One wheel. Four wheels. Spinning, spinning and whirring with a relentlessly whining song. Around and around and around again.

He knew it was wrong. Something wrong with the wheels or

the whole scene and setup. A vague wrongness which he could not quite fathom. But the auto wheels spun, his brain spun with them, and faces, the faces of the crowd, hurtled in mad dervish fashion at the core of the wheels.

Out of the spiraling nebula came sunlight, a doctor, his voice, his quiet, gentle face and a thin warm hand taking Spallner's pulse.

Things cleared into crystal sharpness. Spallner discovered the hospital room, with its exact germicidal odor, and a nurse standing behind the doctor.

"There you are," said the doctor as Spallner's eyes fluttered open. "How do you feel?"

The wheels had rolled away, taking the crowd and the nausea with them.

Spallner tried a weak smile. "Fine—I guess." His head was bandaged. Everything else was intact, under cover.

"I'm Doctor Melchior."

"Something's wrong, Doctor. Something's wrong—"

"I should say so. The accident—"

"No, no. I'm trying to think." Spallner lifted himself from the pillow, only to be gently pressed back by Melchior's hands.

"You can think just as well lying down, Mr. Spallner. Now, tell me what's wrong. Something about the accident?"

"In a way. Something about a wheel and a crowd." Spallner shook his head and winced. "Ah, don't mind me, I'm crazy." He bit his lips and looked at the physician. "If I tell you something, will you promise not to commit me to an insane asylum?"

"I promise. What is it?"

Spallner had to force it out, and he seemed embarrased. "It was the crowd, Doctor Melchior. The crowd last night—I—I didn't *like* it."

Days of sunshine followed. Five of them. Doctor Melchior told him his stay at the hospital was almost over.

"You're lucky, Mr. Spallner. If that gash on your brow had been an eighth of an inch deeper—"

"There's something I'd like to know. Accidents do things to people, don't they?"

"What sort of things?"

"Up here," replied Spallner. He touched his head. "Doesn't it wreck your time sense?"

"Sometimes. It all depends."

"One minute seems like an hour or maybe an hour seems like a minute. Right?"

The physician nodded. "Panic often does that."

"Well—here's how it was. I was driving down a perfectly deserted street. Hitting about sixty. And then the blow-out. I jumped the curb, hit the wall. It was pretty awful. I was shocked, I know, but I still remember lots of things. Mostly, the crowd.

"It got there too *quick,* Doctor. The crowd got there too quick. About thirty seconds after the smash they were all there, standing over me and staring at me. . . . It's not right they should have run that fast, so late at night . . ."

Clearing his throat, Melchior raised his hand. "You can answer your own problem. Your senses, temporarily warped, also threw a bend into time. What you thought was twenty seconds, was, in reality maybe five or six minutes. That's a normal time for a crowd to gather."

Spallner fell silent. In his mind he saw the crowd again. And—and the wheels—all of them—spinning around. He jerked.

"Doctor, I've got it. I know! It's impossible to twist the order of things completely if I was conscious all the way through! And I *was*! I remember; the wheels of the car. They were still spinning when the crowd got there. They were still spinning!"

Melchior said nothing, but frowned.

"I'm positive of that!" exclaimed Spallner. "The wheels were spinning, and spinning fast! You know yourself that the wheels of a car at a certain angle won't spin fast for a very long time. Friction'd cut it down immediately.

"That's what it is, I swear it. I saw them bending over me and then I heard the wheels singing around and around. I looked and saw them!"

The physician rose quietly and stood over his patient. "I've seen patients like you before. You're reshuffling your memories to fit a pattern you thought up. You want them to fit the pattern, and they do. You need a few more sedatives, young man. And, later, when you get out of the hospital, try a visit to a psychiatrist. He'll help you weed out your mind—"

"The street was empty, Doctor Melchior. Not a soul in sight.

And there's one other thing. It was the look on the crowd's faces. Something that told me I wouldn't die. . . .''

"You're suffering from shock," said Melchior.

Released from the hospital, the first thing Spallner did was call a taxi.

"I'm recovering from an accident," he told the driver. "If I don't ride now, and ride fast, I'll never drive again. Take me home at nothing under forty."

He climbed into the taxi and they were off. He was afraid at first. Calmness and confidence returned slowly as they hurtled homeward, and he finally began to worry, instead, about the night of the accident. About the wheels and the crowd.

Halfway home, traffic thickened.

The cabbie twisted his chunky slab of face around and growled. "Shall I detour? Looks like a wreck up ahead."

"Yes, detour. I— No. No, on the other hand, cabbie—pull ahead. Let's—let's take a look."

The cabbie grunted. "Okay—it's your dough; if it's blood you want." The taxi weaved in and out among parked cars. Sirens were wailing, police cars drove up. "Los Angeles is one helluva town ta drive in," snorted the cabbie.

He honked his horn, angled out the window, yelling, "Get that flea-trap outa the way, klunk—get goin'!" The cab swerved into a notch and idled. "Have ta hold it a sec," explained the cabbie. He turned, wiping his brow. "Funny, ain't it, how a crowd gathers when there's 'n accident?"

Spallner started. He saw his fingers tremble on his knee, and then he looked at the cabbie and he said, "Have you noticed that, too?"

The cabbie nodded profoundly. "Sure. You find that no matter what happens. A babe pulls a faint on the corner of Wilshire and LaBrea and in five minutes you got a mob big enough they need a convention permit." The cabbie snorted. "Bunch of morbid guys. What they call 'em?—sadists? Maybe they're curious, I dunno. Anyway, they come runnin' as if it was their own relative got beaned. Crazy."

Spallner sat very quietly, digesting all this. It was a fact. It could be corroborated at any accident. A fire, or a wreck or an explosion. People appeared as if by magic. It all seemed a bit fantastic.

Gingerly, Spallner advanced the subject a step further. "Ever seen an accident late at night?"

"Yeah. Don't make no difference, though. There's always a crowd—"

With that, the cabbie shifted gears and plowed out around a street car. The wreck came to view. Two cars interlocked smashingly, fenders severed and gashed, both of them snarled into the cowcatcher of the streetcar. A body lay on the sidewalk. You knew there was a body there even if you couldn't see it. Because of the crowd.

The crowd with its back toward Spallner. With its back toward him. Spallner opened the window and almost started to yell. But he didn't have the nerve.

He didn't have the nerve.

He was afraid to see their *faces*. . . .

At the dinner table, alone, Spallner took another glass of port and pulled it down. His butler came in and cleared away the dishes. Pausing at the door, watching Spallner take his fourth glass, he cleared his throat warningly.

Spallner laughed. "It's all right, Mac. I'll stay sober."

"But, sir—so soon after the hospital."

"I *need* it."

"Yes, sir. Anything else?"

"Nnn-no—yes. Yes, there is, Mac. I've got a hunch. I want some newspapers, a lot of them. Buy every paper printed recently."

"How far back shall I go, sir?"

"Spread it out. Buy one paper every other week for the last two years. And buy *all* the papers for the last month." Spallner poured more wine. "I'm going to the office for a brief check-up. I'll drop you at the newspaper plant and pick you up later."

"May I ask what you want these papers for, sir?"

"What for?" Spallner put the wine to his lips and savored it. "I—I'm looking up some pictures of some old friends. Yes, that's it. Some old friends."

Spallner drove a new car downtown. He talked and laughed again with his partner, Morgan, up in his private office. This continued for half an hour. All the while they were talking, at the back of his brain a small watch ticked, a watch that never needed winding. It was the memory of a few little things.

"I seem to have a penchant for accidents these days," said Spallner. "I got out of the hospital this morning and the first thing on the way home, I detoured around one."

"Things run in cycles," said Morgan absentmindedly.

They went on talking for half an hour more, until there was a hard, blunt metal noise, a grinding and rending from the street. Overlooking the intersection from the fourth floor, both Spallner and Morgan had a good view of an accident in birth.

A truck and a cream-colored Cadillac.

"What'd I tell you?" exclaimed Morgan. "Cycles."

A great bond of ice closed in on Spallner as he stood there, looking at his watch, at the small second hand. One, two, three, four, five seconds—people running—eight, nine, ten, eleven, twelve—from all over people came running—fifteen, sixteen, seventeen and more people and more cars and more blowing of horns. Spallner shook uncontrollably. He couldn't stop shaking. He was afraid.

The crowd gathered so fast.

Spallner kept looking down. He saw a woman's body sprawled a few moments before the cordon of curious people ate it up. He was frozen and shaking and afraid. He kept swallowing hard.

Morgan noticed. "You'd better sit down, old man. You look lousy."

"I'm all right. I'm all right. Let me alone. I'm all right. Can—can you see those people down there? I wish we were closer. I wish—"

He strained his eyes to see. The faces were all a blur. He tried to concentrate on one or two of them, but the crowd was jostling and mixing, he couldn't draw a bead on any one face.

Once he thought he saw a red-haired woman. He couldn't be positive.

"Have you a pair of binoculars, Morgan?"

"What in hell for?"

"I want to take a look."

"Sorry. Not here. Now, look, this isn't good at all for you. You're pale, you're shaking—"

Spallner tautened himself with an effort and turned. "Will you come along, Morgan? And hurry."

"What's the rush? Where're you going?"

Spallner thrust the door aside, hurried out. Morgan paced after him to the elevator. They waited. Spallner impatiently. "If only I'm there in time."

"Time for what?"

"Don't mind me—I'm insane. Here we are. Come on."

Elevator doors sliced open, shut behind them, the floor sank, stratas of offices whipped past them. Street floor. Doors opened. Spallner strode out, his head bursting into a fiery ache, the scarred brow throbbing.

The street. Confusion. Spallner vaulted across the mental confusion of the intersection, his dark eyes probing, prodding, demanding.

Momentarily, he glimpsed a face in the crowd. The face of a red-haired woman with too much powder on her face.

"There, Morgan, there! Did you see her?"

"Who?"

"Damn it; she's gone! The crowd closed in!"

He plunged through bodies, legs, elbows, startled faces, rough voices. The little red-haired woman had been about halfway through. Evidently she had seen him coming. She was gone.

Another recognizable face! A little boy with freckles who was crying. But there are many little boys in the world. They have freckles. And they cry. And anyway, it was no use; this little boy ran off just before Spallner reached him, slipped into nothing.

"Is she dead?" someone asked. "Is she dead?"

That voice. It sounded so very, very familiar. Where had he heard it before?

"She's dying," someone else replied. "She'll be dead before the ambulance arrives. They shouldn't have moved her. They shouldn't have moved her."

All of the faces in the crowd seemed vaguely familiar. Spallner brushed through them, seeking, hoping; afraid and alert.

"Hey, Mister, stop your pushing!"

"Who you shoving, buddy?"

All different faces, though. He couldn't be sure of any of them.

The siren was whining as he elbowed back out to Morgan, who caught him as he staggered and almost dropped.

"God, Spallner, you look awful. Better get some rest, quick. Why in hell'd you come down?"

"I don't know. I really don't. They moved, Morgan, someone moved her. You should never move a traffic victim. It kills them. It kills them."

"Yeah. That's the way with people. The dumb saps."

"I haven't much to go on," said Spallner. "As far as ordinary logic goes, anyway." He arranged newspaper clippings carefully. Side by side he placed them. Finished, he motioned at them.

"Take a squint at these, Morgan. See what you think."

Morgan squinted, and then winced impatiently. "What's gotten into you?" he complained. "Ever since your accident you act as if every traffic scramble was part of your life. What's the idea of all these clippings of motor car crackups, all these photos?"

"It's not the cars, Morgan," Spallner said quietly. "It's the crowd that gathers after the accident. Look at it. Look at the faces. Compare one picture with another."

"This is silly."

"Here. This accident in the Wilshire District. Compare it to this one in Hollywood. No resemblance. But now, let's align it with another snapped in the Wilshire District ten years ago."

He pointed. "This woman. She's in both pictures. She's the same woman, wouldn't you say so?"

"Ye-ess. I'd say she was. But what has that to do with your phobia about accidents?"

"Simply this; these pictures were taken ten years apart. And the accidents occurred about three miles from each other."

"So what? This woman happened coincidentally to be there."

"Once, maybe. But eight times over a period of ten years, no. Look." He dealt out six more pictures, each dated about a year apart. "She's in *all* of them!"

"Maybe she's perverted."

"She's more than that. I don't know what. There are two other points. How does she *happen* to be there so quickly at each accident? And why does she wear the same clothes in pictures taken over a ten-year period?"

"That's right. She is, isn't she?"

"And, last of all, she was standing over *me* the night of the accident a week ago!"

Spallner made a file, putting pictures and duplicates into the file. He marked crayon rings around familiar faces. This done, he had evidence that almost convinced the skeptic, Morgan.

"What," asked Morgan, "does this all add up to?"

"I don't know what it adds up to, except that there's a universal law about accidents. *Crowds gather.* They *always* gather. And people, just like you and I, have wondered from time to time, from time immemorial, why they gathered so quickly. *I* know the answer. Here it is!"

He flung the clippings down. "It frightens me. I don't know how to figure it!"

"These people—mightn't they be thrill-hunters, perverted sensationalists with a carnal lust for blood and morbidity?"

Spallner shrugged. He sifted the papers through and through. "Does that explain their being at all the accidents? Notice that they stick to one territory. An accident in Hollywood will bring out one group of faces. An accident in Huntington Park another. But there's a norm for faces, a certain percentage appear at each accident."

Morgan gaped. "They're not *all* the same faces, are they?"

"Of course not. Accidents draw *normal* people, too, in the course of time. But *these,* I find, are always the *first* ones there!"

"Who are they? What do they want? You keep hinting and never telling. Good Lord, you must have some idea. You've scared yourself, and now you've got me jumping."

"I don't know. I've tried questioning them, tried even getting *to* them. Someone always gets in my way, or trips me. I'm always too late. They slip into the crowd and vanish. They get away. The crowd offers protection to some of its members. They see me coming!"

"Sounds like some sort of clique."

"It is. I don't know *what* you'd call them. They have one thing in common, I know. They always show up together. At a fire or an explosion or on the sidelines of a war, at any public demonstration of this thing called death. Vultures, hyenas or saints, I don't know which. I just don't know. But I'm going to the police about it. It's gone on long enough. One of them shifted that woman's body two days ago on Seventh Street. They shouldn't have moved her. They shouldn't have interfered. It killed her."

His eyes narrowed.

"Oh, I just happened to think of it . . ."

"What?"

"Maybe they *wanted* her dead."

Busy stuffing a briefcase full of his clippings, Spallner shivered. "I'm going down to the police station now. Come along?"

"I have an appointment with the wife."

"Oh, yes. I forgot. See you later, then."

"Give my regards to the cops. Think they'll believe you?"

"Oh, they'll believe me all right. Good night."

Wilshire Boulevard was dimmed out because of the war restrictions. Huge billboards and neon lights were darkened, streetlights themselves had been enfeebled to a sickly illumination.

Spallner took it slow and easy driving downtown.

"I want to get there alive," he told himself.

Driving depends on two things. Your car and the others. Other cars do quick, fatal things. A huge freight truck just ahead of Spallner suddenly threw on its air-brakes.

It stopped too suddenly.

Spallner shouted, jammed his brakes. Ramming, his new car crashed into the rear of the truck. The windshield hammered back into Spallner's face. His body was forced back and forth in several lightning jerks. Then all motion stopped, all noise stopped and only pain filled the night.

After a long silence, horns began to honk. Somebody screamed. Traffic jolted to shrieking standstills. The car had not turned over this time.

But there was a crowd.

Spallner struggled to climb out of the car. His heart bounded, his lungs caved in and out, wheezing horribly. The car door cracked open and he slipped, fell down onto his face and lay there bleeding.

"You're a lucky man, Mr. Spallner. If that gash had been an eighth of an inch deeper . . ."

"Never move a traffic victim. You might kill him. . . ."

His head was bleeding thick red blood.

And the crowd gathered out of nowhere.

He tried to move, and he realized something was *wrong* with
his spine. He hadn't felt much. But it was hurt. He couldn't
move. He didn't dare move.

He couldn't speak. He opened his mouth. Nothing came out
but gagging.

Someone said, "Give me a hand. We'll roll him over and lift
him into a comfortable position."

"No! No!" Spallner's brain burst apart in a scream. "Don't
move me! You idiots, you'll kill me if you move me! You'll kill
me. Don't!"

But he could not say any of this. He could only think it.

Hands touched him, grasped him. They started to lift him. He
cried out and nausea overtook him. They straightened him out
into a ramrod of horrible agony. Two men did it. One of them
who was thin, bright, alert and pale, who stared at Spallner and
kept wetting his lips as if he were hypnotized; and another man
who was old and wrinkled like an apricot.

He had seen their faces before.

A familiar voice said, "Is—is he dead?"

Another voice, a memorable voice replied, "No. Not yet. But
he will be before the ambulance gets here."

"It's all a mad plot! Like every accident!" cried Spallner hysterically at the solid wall of faces. They were all around him, the
judges and jurors, the faces he had seen before.

The freckled boy.

The red-haired woman.

The girl with the arms that twitched at her sides all by
themselves.

"I know what you're here for! You're here just like you're at
all accidents! To make sure that the right ones live and the right
ones die! That's why you lifted me. You knew it would kill me!
You knew I'd live if you left me alone!

"And that's the way it's always been since time began, when
crowds gather. You can get away with murder easier this way.
You can cover up, saying you didn't know it was dangerous to
move a hurt man!"

He gaped at them. "Who are you? Where do you come from
and how do you get here so soon? You're the crowd that's always
in the way, using up valuable air that a dying man's lungs need,

using up the space he needs to lie in, alone, tramping on people to make sure they die, that's you! I know all of you!"

Faces. The high school student with the pimpled face. The old man. The red-haired woman.

Someone picked up the briefcase. "Whose is this?" they asked.

"It's mine! It's evidence against you all."

Green eyes, inverted over him. Upside down, green eyes staring at him from under a slouch hat.

Faces.

Somewhere a siren wailed. The ambulance was coming.

But, looking at the faces, the construction and cast and form of the faces, Spallner knew it was too late.

He read it in their faces. They *knew*.

Spallner tried to speak. A few fragments got out.

"It—looks as if I'd join you now. I—I guess I'm a member of the band, now."

He smiled wanly. "Just—just remember—remember one thing—" He chuckled painfully. "At—at the next accident—whenever it is—tonight or tomorrow or next week. It's I who will be the *first one there*! You'll find me when you all arrive."

He closed his eyes then, and waited for the coroner.

A Little Place
off the
Edgware Road

Graham Greene

One tends to associate Graham Greene (1904–1991), author of
Brighton Rock (1938), *The Ministry of Fear* (1943), and *The Third
Man* (1950), more with suspense than supernatural fiction. But
these novels, along with his one genuine excursion into the supernatural, *The End of the Affair* (1951), are all linked by questions of good and evil, and faith and skepticism, that preoccupied
Greene's imagination for more than half a century. In addition to
being a novelist, essayist, and critic, Greene was also one of
the best writers of short fiction in the twentieth century, as proved
by "A Little Place off the Edgware Road" (1947), a perfect short
story that just happens to end on a note of unrelenting horror.

Craven came up past the Achilles statue in the thin summer
rain. It was only just after lighting-up time, but already the
cars were lined up all the way to the Marble Arch, and the sharp
acquisitive faces peered out ready for a good time with anything
possible which came along. Craven went bitterly by with the
collar of his mackintosh tight round his throat: it was one of his
bad days.

All the way up the park he was reminded of passion, but you
needed money for love. All that a poor man could get was lust.
Love needed a good suit, a car, a flat somewhere, or a good
hotel. It needed to be wrapped in cellophane. He was aware all

the time of the stringy tie beneath the mackintosh, and the frayed sleeves: he carried his body about with him like something he hated. (There were moments of happiness in the British Museum reading-room, but the body called him back.) He bore, as his only sentiment, the memory of ugly deeds committed on park chairs. People talked as if the body died too soon—that wasn't the trouble, to Craven, at all. The body kept alive—and through the glittering tinselly rain, on his way to a rostrum, passed a little man in a black suit carrying a banner, "The Body shall rise again." He remembered a dream he had three times woken trembling from: he had been alone in the huge dark cavernous burying ground of all the world. Every grave was connected to another under the ground: the globe was honeycombed for the sake of the dead, and on each occasion of dreaming he had discovered anew the horrifying fact that the body doesn't decay. There are no worms and dissolution. Under the ground the world was littered with masses of dead flesh ready to rise again with their warts and boils and eruptions. He had lain in bed and remembered—as "tidings of great joy"—that the body after all was corrupt.

He came up into the Edgware Road walking fast—the Guardsmen were out in couples, great languid elongated beasts—the bodies like worms in their tight trousers. He hated them, and hated his hatred because he knew what it was, envy. He was aware that every one of them had a better body than himself: indigestion creased his stomach: he felt sure that his breath was foul—but who could he ask? Sometimes he secretly touched himself here and there with scent: it was one of his ugliest secrets. Why should he be asked to believe in the resurrection of this body he wanted to forget? Sometimes he prayed at night (a hint of religious belief was lodged in his breast like a worm in a nut) that *his* body at any rate should never rise again.

He knew all the side streets round the Edgware Road only too well: when a mood was on, he simply walked until he tired, squinting at his own image in the windows of Salmon & Gluckstein and the ABCs. So he noticed at once the posters outside the disused theatre in Culpar Road. They were not unusual, for sometimes Barclays Bank Dramatic Society would hire the place for an evening—or an obscure film would be tradeshown there. The theatre had been built in 1920 by an optimist who thought the cheapness of the site would more than counter-balance its disadvantages of lying a mile outside the conventional theatre zone. But no play had ever succeeded, and it was soon left to gather rat-holes and spiderwebs. The covering of the seats was never renewed, and all that ever happened to the place was the temporary false life of an amateur play or a trade show.

Craven stopped and read—there were still optimists it appeared, even in 1939, for nobody but the blindest optimist could hope to make money out of the place as "The Home of the Silent Film." The first season of "primitives" was announced (a high-brow phrase): there would never be a second. Well, the seats were cheap, and it was perhaps worth a shilling to him, now that he was tired, to get in somewhere out of the rain. Craven bought a ticket and went in to the darkness of the stalls.

In the dead darkness a piano tinkled something monotonously recalling Mendelssohn: he sat down in a gangway seat, and could immediately feel the emptiness all round him. No, there would never be another season. On the screen a large woman in a kind of toga wrung her hands, then wobbled with curious jerky movements towards a couch. There she sat and stared out like a sheep-dog distractedly through her loose and black and stringy hair. Sometimes she seemed to dissolve altogether into dots and flashes and wiggly lines. A sub-title said, "Pompilia betrayed by her beloved Augustus seeks an end to her troubles."

Craven began at last to see—a dim waste of stalls. There were not twenty people in the place—a few couples whispering with their heads touching, and a number of lonely men like himself wearing the same uniform of the cheap mackintosh. They lay about at intervals like corpses—and again Craven's obsession returned: the tooth-ache of horror. He thought miserably—I am going mad: other people don't feel like this. Even a disused theatre reminded him of those interminable caverns where the bodies were waiting for resurrection.

"A slave to his passion Augustus calls for yet more wine."

A gross middle-aged Teutonic actor lay on an elbow with his arm round a large woman in a shift. The Spring Song tinkled ineptly on, and the screen flickered like indigestion. Somebody felt his way through the darkness, scrabbling past Craven's knees—a small man: Craven experienced the unpleasant feeling of a large beard brushing his mouth. Then there was a long sigh

as the newcomer found the next chair, and on the screen events
had moved with such rapidity that Pompilia had already stabbed
herself—or so Craven supposed—and lay still and buxom among
her weeping slaves.

A low breathless voice sighed out close to Craven's ear:
"What's happened? Is she asleep?"

"No. Dead."

"Murdered?" the voice asked with a keen interest.

"I don't think so. Stabbed herself."

Nobody said "Hush": nobody was enough interested to object
to a voice: they drooped among the empty chairs in attitudes of
weary inattention.

The film wasn't nearly over yet: there were children somehow
to be considered: was it all going on to a second generation? But
the small bearded man in the next seat seemed to be interested
only in Pompilia's death. The fact that he had come in at that
moment apparently fascinated him. Craven heard the word "coincidence" twice, and he went on talking to himself about it in
low out-of-breath tones. "Absurd when you come to think of it,"
and then "no blood at all." Craven didn't listen: he sat with his
hands clasped between his knees, facing the fact as he had faced
it so often before, that he was in danger of going mad. He had
to pull himself up, take a holiday, see a doctor (God knew what
infection moved in his veins). He became aware that his bearded
neighbour had addressed him directly. "What?" he asked impatiently, "what did you say?"

"There would be more blood than you can imagine."

"What are you talking about?"

When the man spoke to him, he sprayed him with damp
breath. There was a little bubble in his speech like an impedi-
ment. He said, "When you murder a man . . ."

"This was a woman," Craven said impatiently.

"That wouldn't make any difference."

"And it's got nothing to do with murder anyway."

"That doesn't signify." They seemed to have got into an absurd and meaningless wrangle in the dark.

"I know, you see," the little bearded man said in a tone of
enormous conceit.

"Know what?"

"About such things," he said with guarded ambiguity.

Craven turned and tried to see him clearly. Was he mad? Was this a warning of what he might become—babbling incomprehensibly to strangers in cinemas? He thought, By God, no, trying to see: I'll be sane yet. I *will* be sane. He could make out nothing but a small black hump of body. The man was talking to himself again. He said, "Talk. Such talk. They'll say it was all for fifty pounds. But that's a lie. Reasons and reasons. They always take the first reason. Never look behind. Thirty years of reasons. Such simpletons," he added again in that tone of breathless and unbounded conceit. So this was madness. So long as he could realize that, he must be sane himself—relatively speaking. Not so sane perhaps as the seekers in the park or the Guardsmen in the Edgware Road, but saner than this. It was like a message of encouragement as the piano tinkled on.

Then again the little man turned and sprayed him. "Killed herself, you say? But who's to know that? It's not a mere question of what hand holds the knife." He laid a hand suddenly and confidingly on Craven's: it was damp and sticky. Craven said with horror as a possible meaning came to him: "What are you talking about?"

"I know," the little man said. "A man in my position gets to know almost everything."

"What is your position?" Craven said, feeling the sticky hand on his, trying to make up his mind whether he was being hysterical or not—after all, there were a dozen explanations—it might be treacle.

"A pretty desperate one *you'd* say." Sometimes the voice almost died in the throat altogether. Something incomprehensible had happened on the screen—take your eyes from these early pictures for a moment and the plot had proceeded on at such a pace . . . Only the actors moved slowly and jerkily. A young woman in a nightdress seemed to be weeping in the arms of a Roman centurion: Craven hadn't seen either of them before. *"I am not afraid of death, Lucius—in your arms."*

The little man began to titter—knowingly. He was talking to himself again. It would have been easy to ignore him altogether if it had not been for those sticky hands which he now removed: he seemed to be fumbling at the seat in front of him. His head had a habit of lolling suddenly sideways—like an idiot child's. He said distinctly and irrelevantly: "Bayswater Tragedy."

"What was that?" Craven said sharply. He had seen those words on a poster before he entered the park.

"What?"

"About the tragedy."

"To think they call Cullen Mews Bayswater." Suddenly the little man began to cough—turning his face towards Craven and coughing right at him: it was like vindictiveness. The voice said brokenly, "Let me see. My umbrella." He was getting up.

"You didn't have an umbrella."

"My umbrella," he repeated, "My—" and seemed to lose the word altogether. He went scrabbling out past Craven's knees.

Craven let him go, but before he had reached the billowy dusty curtains of the Exit the screen went blank and bright—the film had broken, and somebody immediately turned up one dirt-choked chandelier above the circle. It shone down just enough for Craven to see the smear on his hands. This wasn't hysteria: this was a fact. He wasn't mad: he had sat next to a madman who in some mews— what was the name Colon, Collin . . . Craven jumped up and made his own way out: the black curtain flapped in his mouth. But he was too late: the man had gone and there were three turnings to choose from. He chose instead a telephone-box and dialled with an odd sense for him of sanity and decision 999.

It didn't take two minutes to get the right department. They were interested and very kind. Yes, there had been a murder in a mews—Cullen Mews. A man's neck had been cut from ear to ear with a bread knife—a horrid crime. He began to tell them how he had sat next the murderer in a cinema: it couldn't be anyone else: there was blood now on his hands—and he remembered with repulsion as he spoke the damp beard. There must have been a terrible lot of blood. But the voice from the Yard interrupted him. "Oh no," it was saying, "we have the murderer—no doubt of it at all. It's the body that's disappeared."

Craven put down the receiver. He said to himself aloud, "Why should this happen to *me*? Why to *me*?" He was back in the horror of his dream—the squalid darkening street outside was only one of the innumerable tunnels connecting grave to grave where the imperishable bodies lay. He said, "It was a dream, a dream," and leaning forward he saw in the mirror above the telephone his own face sprinkled by tiny drops of blood like dew from a scent-spray. He began to scream, "I won't go mad. I won't go mad. I'm sane. I won't go mad." Presently a little crowd began to collect, and soon a policeman came.

The Daemon Lover

Shirley Jackson

In her 1959 novel *The Haunting of Hill House* (filmed by Robert Wise as *The Haunting*), Shirley Jackson (1919–1965) created a brilliant psychological study comparing the repressed psyche to a haunted house. Her short fiction, collected into *The Lottery; or, The Adventures of James Harris* (1949) and *Come Along With Me* (1968), further explored the boundary between the supernatural and the psychologically aberrant. "The Daemon Lover" is quintessential Jackson, a simple tale of misunderstanding that becomes increasingly mired in the inexplicable.

She had not slept well; from one-thirty, when Jamie left and she went lingeringly to bed, until seven, when she at last allowed herself to get up and make coffee, she had slept fitfully, stirring awake to open her eyes and look into the half-darkness, remembering over and over, slipping again into a feverish dream. She spent almost an hour over her coffee—they were to have a real breakfast on the way—and then, unless she wanted to dress early, had nothing to do. She washed her coffee cup and made the bed, looking carefully over the clothes she planned to wear, worried unnecessarily, at the window, over whether it would be a fine day. She sat down to read, thought that she might write a letter to her sister instead, and began, in her finest handwriting. "Dearest Anne, by the time you get this I will be married. Doesn't it sound funny? I can hardly believe it myself, but when I tell you how it happened, you'll see it's even stranger than that. . . ."

Sitting, pen in hand, she hesitated over what to say next, read

116

the lines already written, and tore up the letter. She went to the window and saw that it was undeniably a fine day. It occurred to her that perhaps she ought not to wear the blue silk dress; it was too plain, almost severe, and she wanted to be soft, feminine. Anxiously she pulled through the dresses in the closet, and hesitated over a print she had worn the summer before; it was too young for her, and it had a ruffled neck, and it was very early in the year for a print dress, but still. . . .

She hung the two dresses side by side on the outside of the closet door and opened the glass doors carefully closed upon the small closet that was her kitchenette. She turned on the burner under the coffeepot, and went to the window; it was sunny. When the coffeepot began to crackle she came back and poured herself coffee, into a clean cup. I'll have a headache if I don't get some solid food soon, she thought, all this coffee, smoking too much, no real breakfast. A headache on her wedding day; she went and got the tin box of aspirin from the bathroom closet and slipped it into her blue pocketbook. She'd have to change to a brown pocketbook if she wore the print dress, and the only brown pocketbook she had was shabby. Helplessly, she stood looking from the blue pocketbook to the print dress, and then put the pocketbook down and went and got her coffee and sat down near the window, drinking her coffee, and looking carefully around the one-room apartment. They planned to come back here tonight and everything must be correct. With sudden horror she realized that she had forgotten to put clean sheets on the bed; the laundry was freshly back and she took clean sheets and pillow cases from the top shelf of the closet and stripped the bed, working quickly to avoid thinking consciously of why she was changing the sheets. The bed was a studio bed, with a cover to make it look like a couch, and when it was finished no one would have known she had just put clean sheets on it. She took the old sheets and pillow cases into the bathroom and stuffed them down into the hamper, and put the bathroom towels in the hamper too, and clean towels on the bathroom racks. Her coffee was cold when she came back to it, but she drank it anyway.

When she looked at the clock, finally, and saw that it was after nine, she began at last to hurry. She took a bath, and used one of the clean towels, which she put into the hamper and replaced with a clean one. She dressed carefully, all her underwear fresh and most of it new; she put everything she had worn the day before, including her nightgown, into the hamper. When she was ready for her dress, she hesitated before the closet door. The blue dress was certainly decent, and clean, and fairly becoming, but she had worn it several times with Jamie, and there was nothing about it which made it special for a wedding day. The print dress was overly pretty, and new to Jamie, and yet wearing such a print this early in the year was certainly rushing the season. Finally she thought, This is my wedding day, I can dress as I please, and she took the print dress down from the hanger. When she slipped it on over her head it felt fresh and light, but when she looked at herself in the mirror she remembered that the ruffles around the neck did not show her throat to any great advantage, and the wide swinging skirt looked irresistibly made for a girl, for someone who would run freely, dance, swing it with her hips when she walked. Looking at herself in the mirror she thought with revulsion, It's as though I was trying to make myself look prettier than I am, just for him; he'll think I want to look younger because he's marrying me; and she tore the print dress off so quickly that a seam under the arm ripped. In the old blue dress she felt comfortable and familiar, but unexciting. It isn't what you're wearing that matters, she told herself firmly, and turned in dismay to the closet to see if there might be anything else. There was nothing even remotely suitable for her marrying Jamie, and for a minute she thought of going out quickly to some little shop nearby, to get a dress. Then she saw that it was close on ten, and she had no time for more than her hair and her make-up. Her hair was easy, pulled back into a knot at the nape of her neck, but her make-up was another delicate balance between looking as well as possible, and deceiving as little. She could not try to disguise the sallowness of her skin, or the lines around her eyes, today, when it might look as though she were only doing it for her wedding, and yet she could not bear the thought of Jamie's bringing to marriage anyone who looked haggard and lined. You're thirty-four years old after *all,* she told herself cruelly in the bathroom mirror. Thirty, it said on the license.

It was two minutes after ten; she was not satisfied with her clothes, her face, her apartment. She heated the coffee again and sat down in the chair by the window. Can't do anything more now, she thought, no sense trying to improve anything the last minute.

Reconciled, settled, she tried to think of Jamie and could not see his face clearly, or hear his voice. It's always that way with someone you love, she thought, and let her mind slip past today and tomorrow, into the farther future, when Jamie was established with his writing and she had given up her job, the golden house-in-the-country future they had been preparing for the last week. "I used to be a wonderful cook," she had promised Jamie, "with a little time and practice I could remember how to make angel-food cake. And fried chicken," she said, knowing how the words would stay in Jamie's mind, half-tenderly. "And Hollandaise sauce."

Ten-thirty. She stood up and went purposefully to the phone. She dialed, and waited, and the girl's metallic voice said, ". . . the time will be exactly ten-twenty-nine." Half-consciously she set her clock back a minute; she was remembering her own voice saying last night, in the doorway: "Ten o'clock then. I'll be ready. Is it really *true*?"

And Jamie laughing down the hallway.

By eleven o'clock she had sewed up the ripped seam in the print dress and put her sewing-box away carefully in the closet. With the print dress on, she was sitting by the window, drinking another cup of coffee. I could have taken more time over my dressing after all, she thought; but by now it was so late he might come any minute, and she did not dare try to repair anything without starting all over. There was nothing to eat in the apartment except the food she had carefully stocked up for their life beginning together: the unopened package of bacon, the dozen eggs in their box, the unopened bread and the unopened butter; they were for breakfast tomorrow. She thought of running downstairs to the drugstore for something to eat, leaving a note on the door. Then she decided to wait a little longer.

By eleven-thirty she was so dizzy and weak that she had to go downstairs. If Jamie had had a phone she would have called him then. Instead, she opened her desk and wrote a note: "Jamie, have gone downstairs to the drugstore. Back in five minutes." Her pen leaked onto her fingers and she went into the bathroom and washed, using a clean towel which she replaced. She tacked the note on the door, surveyed the apartment once more to make sure that everything was perfect, and closed the door without locking it, in case he should come.

In the drugstore she found that there was nothing she wanted to eat except more coffee, and she left it half-finished because she suddenly realized that Jamie was probably upstairs waiting and impatient, anxious to get started.

But upstairs everything was prepared and quiet, as she had left it, her note unread on the door, the air in the apartment a little stale from too many cigarettes. She opened the window and sat down next to it until she realized that she had been asleep and it was twenty minutes to one.

Now, suddenly, she was frightened. Waking without preparation into the room of waiting and readiness, everything clean and untouched since ten o'clock, she was frightened, and felt an urgent need to hurry. She got up from the chair and almost ran across the room to the bathroom, dashed cold water on her face, and used a clean towel; this time she put the towel carelessly back on the rack without changing it; time enough for that later. Hatless, still in the print dress with a coat thrown on over it, the wrong blue pocketbook with the aspirin inside in her hand, she locked the apartment door behind her, no note this time, and ran down the stairs. She caught a taxi on the corner and gave the driver Jamie's address.

It was no distance at all; she could have walked it if she had not been so weak, but in the taxi she suddenly realized how imprudent it would be to drive brazenly up to Jamie's door, demanding him. She asked the driver, therefore, to let her off at a corner near Jamie's address and, after paying him, waited till he drove away before she started to walk down the block. She had never been here before; the building was pleasant and old, and Jamie's name was not on any of the mailboxes in the vestibule, nor on the doorbells. She checked the address; it was right, and finally she rang the bell marked "Superintendent." After a minute or two the door buzzer rang and she opened the door and went into the dark hall where she hesitated until a door at the end opened and someone said, "Yes?"

She knew at the same moment that she had no idea what to ask, so she moved forward toward the figure waiting against the light of the open doorway. When she was very near, the figure said, "Yes?" again and she saw that it was a man in his shirt-sleeves, unable to see her any more clearly than she could see him.

With sudden courage she said, "I'm trying to get in touch with someone who lives in this building and I can't find the name outside."

"What's the name you wanted?" the man asked, and she realized she would have to answer.

"James Harris," she said. "Harris."

The man was silent for a minute and then he said, "Harris." He turned around to the room inside the lighted doorway and said, "Margie, come here a minute."

"What now?" a voice said from inside, and after a wait long enough for someone to get out of a comfortable chair a woman joined him in the doorway, regarding the dark hall. "Lady here," the man said. "Lady looking for a guy name of Harris, lives here. Anyone in the building?"

"No," the woman said. Her voice sounded amused. "No men named Harris here."

"Sorry," the man said. He started to close the door. "You got the wrong house, lady," he said, and added in a lower voice, "or the wrong guy," and he and the woman laughed.

When the door was almost shut and she was alone in the dark hall she said to the thin lighted crack still showing, "But he *does* live here; I know it."

"Look," the woman said, opening the door again a little, "it happens all the time."

"Please don't make any mistake," she said, and her voice was very dignified, with thirty-four years of accumulated pride. "I'm afraid you don't understand."

"What did he look like?" the woman said wearily, the door still only part open.

"He's rather tall, and fair. He wears a blue suit very often. He's a writer."

"No," the woman said, and then, "Could he have lived on the third floor?"

"I'm not sure."

"There was a fellow," the woman said reflectively. "He wore

a blue suit a lot, lived on the third floor for a while. The Roysters lent him their apartment while they were visiting her folks upstate."

"That might be it; I thought, though. . . ."

"This one wore a blue suit mostly, but I don't know how tall he was," the woman said. "He stayed there about a month."

"A month ago is when—"

"You ask the Roysters," the woman said. "They come back this morning. Apartment 3B."

The door closed, definitely. The hall was very dark and the stairs looked darker.

On the second floor there was a little light from a skylight far above. The apartment doors lined up, four on the floor, uncommunicative and silent. There was a bottle of milk outside 2C.

On the third floor, she waited for a minute. There was the sound of music beyond the door of 3B, and she could hear voices. Finally she knocked, and knocked again. The door was opened and the music swept out at her, an early afternoon symphony broadcast. "How do you do," she said politely to this woman in the doorway. "Mrs. Royster?"

"That's right." The woman was wearing a housecoat and last night's make-up.

"I wonder if I might talk to you for a minute?"

"Sure," Mrs. Royster said, not moving.

"About Mr. Harris."

"*What* Mr. Harris?" Mrs. Royster said flatly.

"Mr. James Harris. The gentleman who borrowed your apartment."

"O Lord," Mrs. Royster said. She seemed to open her eyes for the first time. "What'd he do?"

"Nothing. I'm just trying to get in touch with him."

"O Lord," Mrs. Royster said again. Then she opened the door wider and said, "Come in," and then, "Ralph!"

Inside, the apartment was still full of music, and there were suitcases half unpacked on the couch, on the chairs, on the floor. A table in the corner was spread with the remains of a meal, and the young man sitting there, for a minute resembling Jamie, got up and came across the room.

"What about it?" he said.

"Mr. Royster," she said. It was difficult to talk against the music. "The superintendent downstairs told me that this was where Mr. James Harris has been living."

"Sure," he said. "If that was his name."

"I thought you lent him the apartment," she said, surprised.

"*I* don't know anything about him," Mr. Royster said. "He's one of Dottie's friends."

"Not *my* friends," Mrs. Royster said. "No friend of mine." She had gone over to the table and was spreading peanut butter on a piece of bread. She took a bite and said thickly, waving the bread and peanut butter at her husband, "Not *my* friend."

"You picked him up at one of those damn meetings," Mr. Royster said. He shoved a suitcase off the chair next to the radio and sat down, picking up a magazine from the floor next to him. "I never said more'n ten words to him."

"You said it was okay to lend him the place," Mrs. Royster said before she took another bite. "You never said a word against him, after *all*."

"*I* don't say anything about *your* friends," Mr. Royster said.

"If he'd of been a friend of mine you would have said *plenty,* believe me," Mrs. Royster said darkly. She took another bite and said, "Believe me, he would have said *plenty*."

"That's all I want to hear," Mr. Royster said, over the top of the magazine. "No more, now."

"You see," Mrs. Royster pointed the bread and peanut butter at her husband. "That's the way it is, day and night."

There was silence except for the music bellowing out of the radio next to Mr. Royster, and then she said, in a voice she hardly trusted to be heard over the radio noise, "Has he gone, then?"

"Who?" Mrs. Royster demanded, looking up from the peanut butter jar.

"Mr. James Harris."

"Him? He must've left this morning, before we got back. No sign of him anywhere."

"Gone?"

"Everything was fine, though, perfectly fine. I told you," she said to Mr. Royster, "I told you he'd take care of everything fine. I can always tell."

"You were lucky," Mr. Royster said.

"Not a thing out of place," Mrs. Royster said. She waved her bread and peanut butter inclusively. "Everything just the way we left it," she said.

"Do you know where he is now?"

"Not the slightest idea," Mrs. Royster said cheerfully. "But, like I said, he left everything fine. Why?" she asked suddenly. "You looking for *him*?"

"It's very important."

"I'm sorry he's not here," Mrs. Royster said. She stepped forward politely when she saw her visitor turn toward the door.

"Maybe the super saw him," Mr. Royster said into the magazine.

When the door was closed behind her the hall was dark again, but the sound of the radio was deadened. She was halfway down the first flight of stairs when the door was opened and Mrs. Royster shouted down the stairwell, "If I see him I'll tell him you were looking for him."

What can I do? she thought, out on the street again. It was impossible to go home, not with Jamie somewhere between here and there. She stood on the sidewalk so long that a woman, leaning out of a window across the way, turned and called to someone inside to come see. Finally, on an impulse, she went into the small delicatessen next door to the apartment house, on the side that led to her own apartment. There was a small man reading a newspaper, leaning against the counter; when she came in he looked up and came down inside the counter to meet her.

Over the glass case of cold meats and cheese she said, timidly, "I'm trying to get in touch with a man who lived in the apartment house next door, and I just wondered if you know him."

"Whyn't you ask the people there?" the man said, his eyes narrow, inspecting her.

It's because I'm not buying anything, she thought, and she said, "I'm sorry. I asked them, but they don't know anything about him. They think he left this morning."

"I don't know what you want *me* to do," he said, moving a little back toward his newspaper. "I'm not here to keep track of guys going in and out next door."

She said quickly, "I thought you might have noticed, that's all. He would have been coming past here, a little before ten o'clock. He was rather tall, and he usually wore a blue suit."

"Now how many men in blue suits go past here every day,

lady?" the man demanded. "You think I got nothing to do but—"

"I'm sorry," she said. She heard him say, "For God's sake," as she went out the door.

As she walked toward the corner, she thought, he must have come this way, it's the way he'd go to get to my house, it's the only way for him to walk. She tried to think of Jamie: where would he have crossed the street? What sort of person was he actually—would he cross in front of his own apartment house, at random in the middle of the block, at the corner?

On the corner was a newsstand; they might have seen him there. She hurried on and waited while a man bought a paper and a woman asked directions. When the newsstand man looked at her she said, "Can you possibly tell me if a rather tall young man in a blue suit went past here this morning around ten o'clock?" When the man only looked at her, his eyes wide and his mouth a little open, she thought, he thinks it's a joke, or a trick, and she said urgently, "It's very important, please believe me. I'm not teasing you."

"*Look,* lady," the man began, and she said eagerly, "He's a writer. He might have bought magazines here."

"What you want him for?" the man asked. He looked at her, smiling, and she realized that there was another man waiting in back of her and the newsdealer's smile included him. "Never mind," she said, but the newsdealer said, "Listen, maybe he did come by here." His smile was knowing and his eyes shifted over her shoulder to the man in back of her. She was suddenly horribly aware of her over-young print dress, and pulled her coat around her quickly. The newsdealer said, with vast thoughtfulness, "Now I don't know for sure, mind you, but there might have been someone like your gentleman friend coming by this morning."

"About ten?"

"About ten," the newsdealer agreed. "Tall fellow, blue suit. I wouldn't be at all surprised."

"Which way did he go?" she said eagerly. "Uptown?"

"Uptown," the newsdealer said, nodding. "He went uptown. That's just exactly it. What can I do for you, sir?"

She stepped back, holding her coat around her. The man who had been standing behind her looked at her over his shoulder and then he and the newsdealer looked at one another. She wondered for a minute whether or not to tip the newsdealer but when both men began to laugh she moved hurriedly on across the street.

Uptown, she thought, that's right, and she started up the avenue, thinking: He wouldn't have to cross the avenue, just go up six blocks and turn down my street, so long as he started uptown. About a block farther on she passed a florist's shop; there was a wedding display in the window and she thought, This is my wedding day after all, he might have gotten flowers to bring me, and she went inside. The florist came out of the back of the shop, smiling and sleek, and she said, before he could speak, so that he wouldn't have a chance to think she was buying anything: "It's *terribly* important that I get in touch with a gentleman who may have stopped in here to buy flowers this morning. *Terribly* important."

She stopped for breath, and the florist said, "Yes, what sort of flowers were they?"

"I don't know," she said, surprised. "He never—" She stopped and said, "He was a rather tall young man, in a blue suit. It was about ten o'clock."

"I see," the florist said. "Well, *really,* I'm afraid . . ."

"But it's *so* important," she said. "He may have been in a hurry," she added helpfully.

"Well," the florist said. He smiled genially, showing all his small teeth. "For a *lady,*" he said. He went to a stand and opened a large book. "Where were they to be sent?" he asked.

"Why," she said, "I don't think he'd have sent them. You see, he was coming—that is, he'd *bring* them."

"Madam," the florist said; he was offended. His smile became deprecatory, and he went on, "Really, you must realize that unless I have *something* to go on. . . ."

"*Please* try to remember," she begged. "He was tall, and had a blue suit, and it was about ten this morning."

The florist closed his eyes, one finger to his mouth, and thought deeply. Then he shook his head. "I simply *can't,*" he said.

"Thank you," she said despondently, and started for the door, when the florist said, in a shrill, excited voice, "Wait! Wait just a moment, madam." She turned and the florist, thinking again, said finally, "Chrysanthemums?" He looked at her inquiringly.

"Oh, *no*," she said; her voice shook a little and she waited for a minute before she went on. "Not for an occasion like this, I'm sure."

The florist tightened his lips and looked away coldly. "Well, of *course* I don't know the *occasion*," he said, "but I'm almost certain that the gentleman you were inquiring for came in this morning and purchased chrysanthemums. No delivery."

"You're *sure*?" she asked.

"Positive," the florist said emphatically. "That was absolutely the man." He smiled brilliantly, and she smiled back and said, "Well, thank you very much."

He escorted her to the door. "Nice corsage?" he said, as they went through the shop. "Red roses? Gardenias?"

"It was very kind of you to help me," she said at the door.

"Ladies always look their best in flowers," he said, bending his head toward her. "Orchids, perhaps?"

"No, thank you," she said, and he said, "I hope you find your young man," and gave it a nasty sound.

Going on up the street she thought, Everyone thinks it's so *funny*: and she pulled her coat tighter around her, so that only the ruffle around the bottom of the print dress was showing.

There was a policeman on the corner, and she thought, Why don't I go to the police—you go to the police for a missing person. And then thought, What a fool I'd look like. She had a quick picture of herself standing in a police station, saying, "Yes, we were going to be married today, but he didn't come," and the policemen, three or four of them standing around listening, looking at her, at the print dress, at her too-bright make-up, smiling at one another. She couldn't tell them any more than that, could not say, "Yes, it looks silly, doesn't it, me all dressed up and trying to find the young man who promised to marry me, but what about all of it you don't know? I have more than this, more than you can see: talent, perhaps, and humor of a sort, and I'm a lady and I have pride and affection and delicacy and a certain clear view of life that might make a man satisfied and productive and happy; there's more than you think when you look at me."

The police were obviously impossible, leaving out Jamie and

what he might think when he heard she'd set the police after him. "No, no," she said aloud, hurrying her steps, and someone passing stopped and looked after her.

On the coming corner—she was three blocks from her own street—was a shoeshine stand, an old man sitting almost asleep in one of the chairs. She stopped in front of him and waited, and after a minute he opened his eyes and smiled at her.

"Look," she said, the words coming before she thought of them, "I'm sorry to bother you, but I'm looking for a young man who came up this way about ten this morning, did you see him?" And she began her description, "Tall, blue suit, carrying a bunch of flowers?"

The old man began to nod before she was finished. "I saw him," he said. "Friend of yours?"

"Yes," she said, and smiled back involuntarily.

The old man blinked his eyes and said, "I remember I thought, You're going to see your girl, young fellow. They all go to see their girls," he said, and shook his head tolerantly.

"Which way did he go? Straight on up the avenue?"

"That's right," the old man said. "Got a shine, had his flowers, all dressed up, in an awful hurry. You got a girl, I thought."

"Thank you," she said, fumbling in her pocket for her loose change.

"She sure must of been glad to see him, the way he looked," the old man said.

"Thank you," she said again, and brought her hand empty from her pocket.

For the first time she was really sure he would be waiting for her, and she hurried up the three blocks, the skirt of the print dress swinging under her coat, and turned into her own block. From the corner she could not see her own windows, could not see Jamie looking out, waiting for her, and going down the block she was almost running to get to him. Her key trembled in her fingers at the downstairs door, and as she glanced into the drugstore she thought of her panic, drinking coffee there this morning, and almost laughed. At her own door she could wait no longer, but began to say, "Jamie, I'm here, I was so worried," even before the door was open.

Her own apartment was waiting for her, silent, barren, afternoon shadows lengthening from the window. For a minute she

saw only the empty coffee cup, thought, He has been here waiting, before she recognized it as her own, left from the morning.
She looked all over the room, into the closet, into the bathroom.

"I never saw him," the clerk in the drugstore said. "I know
because I would of noticed the flowers. No one like that's been
in."

The old man at the shoeshine stand woke up again to see her
standing in front of him. "Hello again," he said, and smiled.

"Are you *sure*?" she demanded. "Did he go on up the
avenue?"

"I watched him," the old man said, dignified against her tone.
"I thought, There's a young man's got a girl, and I watched him
right into the house."

"What house?" she said remotely.

"Right there," the old man said. He leaned forward to point.
"The next block. With his flowers and his shine and going to see
his girl. Right into her house."

"Which one?" she said.

"About the middle of the block," the old man said. He looked
at her with suspicion, and said, "What you trying to do,
anyway?"

She almost ran, without stopping to say "Thank you." Up on
the next block she walked quickly, searching the houses from the
outside to see if Jamie looked from a window, listening to hear
his laughter somewhere inside.

A woman was sitting in front of one of the houses, pushing a
baby carriage monotonously back and forth the length of her
arm. The baby inside slept, moving back and forth.

The question was fluent, by now, "I'm sorry, but did you see
a young man go into one of these houses about ten this morning?
He was tall, wearing a blue suit, carrying a bunch of flowers."

A boy about twelve stopped to listen, turning intently from
one to the other, occasionally glancing at the baby.

"Listen," the woman said tiredly, "the kid has his bath at ten.
Would I see strange men walking around? I ask you."

"Big bunch of flowers?" the boy asked, pulling at her coat.
"Big bunch of flowers? I seen him, missus."

She looked down and the boy grinned insolently at her.
"Which house did he go in?" she asked wearily.

"You gonna divorce him?" the boy asked insistently.

"That's not nice to ask the lady," the woman rocking the carriage said.

"Listen," the boy said, "I seen him. He went in there." He pointed to the house next door. "I followed him," the boy said. "He give me a quarter." The boy dropped his voice to a growl, and said, " 'This is a big day for me, kid,' he says. Give me a quarter."

She gave him a dollar bill. "Where?" she said.

"Top floor," the boy said. "I followed him till he give me the quarter. Way to the top." He backed up the sidewalk, out of reach, with the dollar bill. "You gonna divorce him?" he asked again.

"Was he carrying flowers?"

"Yeah," the boy said. He began to screech. "You gonna divorce him, missus? You got something on him?" He went careening down the street, howling, "She's got something on the poor guy," and the woman rocking the baby laughed.

The street door of the apartment house was unlocked; there were no bells in the outer vestibule, and no lists of names. The stairs were narrow and dirty; there were two doors on the top floor. The front one was the right one; there was a crumpled florist's paper on the floor outside the door, and a knotted paper ribbon, like a clue, like the final clue in the paper-chase.

She knocked, and thought she heard voices inside, and she thought, suddenly, with terror, What shall I say if Jamie is there, if he comes to the door? The voices seemed suddenly still. She knocked again and there was silence, except for something that might have been laughter far away. He could have seen me from the window, she thought, it's the front apartment and that little boy made a dreadful noise. She waited, and knocked again, but there was silence.

Finally she went to the other door on the floor, and knocked. The door swung open beneath her hand and she saw the empty attic room, bare lath on the walls, floorboards unpainted. She stepped just inside, looking around; the room was filled with bags of plaster, piles of old newspapers, a broken trunk. There was a noise which she suddenly realized was a rat, and then she saw it, sitting very close to her, near the wall, its evil face alert, bright eyes watching her. She stumbled in her haste to be out with the door closed, and the skirt of the print dress caught and tore.

She knew there was someone inside the other apartment, because she was sure she could hear low voices and sometimes laughter. She came back many times, every day for the first week. She came on her way to work, in the mornings; in the evenings, on her way to dinner alone, but no matter how often or how firmly she knocked, no one ever came to the door.

The Man Who
Collected Poe

Robert Bloch

The stories Robert Bloch (1917–   ) gathered for his first collection, *The Opener of the Way* (1945), show the strong influence of American horror writer H. P. Lovecraft. But Bloch's
suspense novels, which include *The Scarf* (1947), *The Kidnap-
per* (1954), *Firebug* (1961), *Night of the Ripper* (1984), and of
course *Psycho* (1959) and its sequels *Psycho II* (1982) and *Psycho House* (1989), show the influence of Edgar Allan Poe, father
of the psychological horror story. In "The Man Who Collected
Poe" (1951), Bloch resurrects the spirit of Poe figuratively, to
show how eagerly some Poe enthusiasts might do so literally.

D uring the whole of a dull, dark, and soundless day in the
autumn of the year, when the clouds hung oppressively low
in the heavens, I had been passing alone, by automobile, through
a singularly dreary tract of country, and at length found myself,
as the shades of the evening drew on, within view of my
destination.

I looked upon the scene before me—upon the mere house,
and the simple landscape features of the domain—upon the bleak
walls—upon the vacant eye-like windows—decayed trees—with
a feeling of utter confusion commingled with dismay. For it
seemed to me as though I had visited this scene once before, or
read of it, perhaps, in some frequently rescanned tale. And yet
assuredly it could not be, for only three days had passed since I
had made the acquaintance of Launcelot Canning and received
an invitation to visit him at his Maryland residence.

The circumstances under which I met Canning were simple; I happened to attend a bibliophilic meeting in Washington and was introduced to him by a mutual friend. Casual conversation gave place to absorbed and interested discussion when he discovered my preoccupation with works of fantasy. Upon learning that I was traveling upon a vacation with no set itinerary, Canning urged me to become his guest for a day and to examine, at my leisure, his unusual display of memorabilia.

"I feel, from our conversation, that we have much in common," he told me. "For you see, sir, in my love of fantasy I bow to no man. It is a taste I have perhaps inherited from my father and from his father before him, together with their considerable acquisitions in the genre. No doubt you would be gratified with what I am prepared to show you, for in all due modesty, I beg to style myself the world's leading collector of the works of Edgar Allan Poe."

I confess that his invitation as such did not enthrall me, for I hold no brief for the literary hero-worshiper or the scholarly collector as a type. I own to a more than passing interest in the tales of Poe, but my interest does not extend to the point of ferreting out the exact date upon which Mr. Poe first decided to raise a moustache, nor would I be unduly intrigued by the opportunity to examine several hairs preserved from that hirsute appendage.

So it was rather the person and personality of Launcelot Canning himself which caused me to accept his proffered hospitality. For the man who proposed to become my host might have himself stepped from the pages of a Poe tale. His speech, as I have endeavored to indicate, was characterized by a courtly rodomontade so often exemplified in Poe's heroes—and beyond certainty, his appearance bore out the resemblance.

Launcelot Canning had the cadaverousness of complexion, the large, liquid, luminous eye, the thin, curved lips, the delicately modeled nose, finely molded chin, and dark, web-like hair of a typical Poe protagonist.

It was this phenomenon which promoted my acceptance and led me to journey to his Maryland estate, which, as I now perceived, in itself manifested a Poe-etic quality of its own, intrinsic in the images of the gray sedge, the ghastly tree-stems, and the vacant and eye-like windows of the mansion of gloom. All that was lacking was a tarn and a moat—and as I prepared to enter the dwelling I half-expected to encounter therein the carved ceilings, the somber tapestries, the ebon floors and the phantasmagoric armorial trophies so vividly described by the author of *Tales of the Grotesque and Arabesque*.

Nor upon entering Launcelot Canning's home was I too greatly disappointed in my expectations. True to both the atmospheric quality of the decrepit mansion and to my own fanciful presentiments, the door was opened in response to my knock by a valet who conducted me, in silence, through dark and intricate passages to the study of his master.

The room in which I found myself was very large and lofty. The windows were long, narrow, and pointed, and at so vast a distance from the black oaken floor as to be altogether inaccessible from within. Feeble gleams of encrimsoned light made their way through the trellised panes, and served to render sufficiently distinct the more prominent objects around; the eye, however, struggled in vain to reach the remoter angles of the chamber or the recesses of the vaulted and fretted ceiling. Dark draperies hung upon the walls. The general furniture was profuse, comfortless, antique, and tattered. Many books and musical instruments lay scattered about, but failed to give any vitality to the scene.

Instead they rendered more distinct that peculiar quality of quasi-recollection; it was as though I found myself once again, after a protracted absence, in a familiar setting. I had read, I had imagined, I had dreamed, or I had actually beheld this setting before.

Upon my entrance, Launcelot Canning arose from a sofa on which he had been lying at full length, and greeted me with a vivacious warmth which had much in it, I at first thought, of an overdone cordiality.

Yet his tone, as he spoke of the object of my visit, of his earnest desire to see me, and of the solace he expected me to afford him in a mutual discussion of our interests, soon alleviated my initial misapprehension.

Launcelot Canning welcomed me with the rapt enthusiasm of the born collector—and I came to realize that he was indeed just that. For the Poe collection he shortly proposed to unveil before me was actually his birthright.

Initially, he disclosed, the nucleus of the present accumulation had begun with his grandfather, Christopher Canning, a respected merchant of Baltimore. Almost eighty years ago he had been one of the leading patrons of the arts in his community and as such was partially instrumental in arranging for the removal of Poe's body to the southeastern corner of the Presbyterian Cemetery at Fayette and Green streets, where a suitable monument might be erected. This even occurred in the year 1875, and it was a few years prior to that time that Canning laid the foundation of the Poe collection.

"Thanks to his zeal," his grandson informed me, "I am today the fortunate possessor of a copy of virtually every existing specimen of Poe's published works. If you will step over here"—and he led me to a remote corner of the vaulted study, past the dark draperies, to a bookshelf which rose remotely to the shadowy ceiling—"I shall be pleased to corroborate that claim. Here is a copy of *Al Aaraaf, Tamerlane and other Poems* in the 1829 edition, and here is the still earlier *Tamerlane and other Poems* of 1827. The Boston edition, which, as you doubtless know, is valued today at fifteen thousand dollars. I can assure you that Grandfather Canning parted with no such sum in order to gain possession of this rarity."

He displayed the volumes with an air of commingled pride and cupidity which is ofttimes characteristic of the collector and is by no means to be confused with either literary snobbery or ordinary greed. Realizing this, I remained patient as he exhibited further treasures—copies of the *Philadelphia Saturday Courier* containing early tales, bound volumes of *The Messenger* during the period of Poe's editorship, *Graham's Magazine,* editions of the *New York Sun* and the *New York Mirror* boasting, respectively, of "The Balloon Hoax" and "The Raven," and files of *The Gentleman's Magazine.* Ascending a short library ladder, he handed down to me the Lea and Blanchard edition of *Tales of the Grotesque and Arabesque,* the *Conchologist's First Book,* the Putnam *Eureka,* and, finally, the little paper booklet, published in 1843 and sold for twelve and a half cents, entitled *The Prose Romances of Edgar A. Poe*; an insignificant trifle containing two tales which is valued by present-day collectors at fifty thousand dollars.

Canning informed me of this last fact, and, indeed, kept up a running commentary upon each item he presented. There was no doubt that he was a Poe scholar as well as a Poe collector, and his words informed tattered specimens of the *Broadway Journal* and *Godey's Lady's Book* with a singular fascination not necessarily inherent in the flimsy sheets or their contents.

"I owe a great debt to Grandfather Canning's obsession," he observed, descending the ladder and joining me before the bookshelves. "It is not altogether a breach of confidence to admit that his interest in Poe did reach the point of an obsession, and perhaps eventually of an absolute mania. The knowledge, alas, is public property, I fear.

"In the early seventies he built this house, and I am quite sure that you have been observant enough to note that it in itself is almost a replica of a typical Poe-esque mansion. This was his study, and it was here that he was wont to pore over the books, the letters, and the numerous mementos of Poe's life.

"What prompted a retired merchant to devote himself so fanatically to the pursuit of a hobby, I cannot say. Let it suffice that he virtually withdrew from the world and from all other normal interests. He conducted a voluminous and lengthy correspondence with aging men and women who had known Poe in their lifetime—made pilgrimages to Fordham, sent his agents to West Point, to England and Scotland, to virtually every locale in which Poe had set foot during his lifetime. He acquired letters and souvenirs as gifts, he bought them, and—I fear—stole them, if no other means of acquisition proved feasible."

Launcelot Canning smiled and nodded. "Does all this sound strange to you? I confess that once I, too, found it almost incredible, a fragment of romance. Now, after years spent here, I have lost my own objectivity."

"Yes, it is strange," I replied. "But are you quite sure that there was not some obscure personal reason for your grandfather's interest? Had he met Poe as a boy, or been closely associated with one of his friends? Was there, perhaps, a distant, undisclosed relationship?"

At the mention of the last word, Canning started visibly, and a tremor of agitation overspread his countenance.

"Ah!" he exclaimed. "There you voice my own inmost conviction. A relationship—assuredly there must have been one—I am morally, instinctively certain that Grandfather Canning felt or knew himself to be linked to Edgar Poe by ties of blood. Nothing else could account for his strong initial interest, his continuing defense of Poe in the literary controversies of the day, and his final melancholy lapse into a world of delusion and illusion.

"Yet he never voiced a statement or put an allegation upon paper—and I have searched the collection of letters in vain for the slightest clue.

"It is curious that you so promptly divine a suspicion held not only by myself but by my father. He was only a child at the time of my Grandfather Canning's death, but the attendant circumstances left a profound impression upon his sensitive nature. Although he was immediately removed from this house to the home of his mother's people in Baltimore, he lost no time in returning upon assuming his inheritance in early manhood.

"Fortunately being in possession of a considerable income, he was able to devote his entire lifetime to further research. The name of Arthur Canning is still well-known in the world of literary criticism, but for some reason he preferred to pursue his scholarly examination of Poe's career in privacy. I believe this preference was dictated by an inner sensibility; that he was endeavoring to unearth some information which would prove his father's, his, and for that matter, my own, kinship to Edgar Poe."

"You say your father was also a collector?" I prompted.

"A statement I am prepared to substantiate," replied my host, as he led me to yet another corner of the shadow-shrouded study. "But first, if you would accept a glass of wine?"

He filled, not glasses, but veritable beakers from a large carafe, and we toasted one another in silent appreciation. It is perhaps unnecessary for me to observe that the wine was a fine old amontillado.

"Now, then," said Launcelot Canning. "My father's special province in Poe research consisted of the accumulation and study of letters."

Opening a series of large trays or drawers beneath the bookshelves, he drew out file after file of glassined folios, and for the space of the next half-hour I examined Edgar Poe's correspondence—letters to Henry Herring, to Dr. Snodgrass, Sarah Shelton, James P. Moss, Elizabeth Poe—missives to Mrs. Rockwood, Helen Whitman, Anne Lynch, John Pendleton Kennedy—notes to Mrs. Richmond, to John Allan, to Annie, to his brother,

Henry—a profusion of documents, a veritable epistolary cornucopia.

During the course of my perusal my host took occasion to refill our beakers with wine, and the heady draught began to take effect—for we had not eaten, and I own I gave no thought to food, so absorbed was I in the yellowed pages illumining Poe's past.

Here was wit, erudition, literary criticism; here were the muddled, maudlin outpourings of a mind gone in drink and despair; here was the draft of a projected story, the fragments of a poem; here was a pitiful cry for deliverance and a paean to living beauty; here was a dignified response to a dunning letter and an editorial pronunciamento to an admirer; here was love, hate, pride, anger, celestial serenity, abject penitence, authority, wonder, resolution, indecision, joy, and soul-sickening melancholia.

Here was the gifted elocutionist, the stammering drunkard, the adoring husband, the frantic lover, the proud editor, the indigent pauper, the grandiose dreamer, the shabby realist, the scientific inquirer, the gullible metaphysician, the dependent stepson, the free and untrammeled spirit, the hack, the poet, the enigma that was Edgar Allan Poe.

Again the beakers were filled and emptied.

I drank deeply with my lips, and with my eyes more deeply still.

For the first time the true enthusiasm of Launcelot Canning was communicated to my own sensibilities—I divined the eternal fascination found in a consideration of Poe the writer and Poe the man; he who wrote Tragedy, lived Tragedy, was Tragedy; he who penned Mystery, lived and died in Mystery, and who today looms on the literary scene as Mystery incarnate.

And Mystery Poe remained, despite Arthur Canning's careful study of the letters. "My father learned nothing," my host confided, "even though he assembled, as you see here, a collection to delight the heart of a Mabbott or a Quinn. So his search ranged further. By this time I was old enough to share both his interest and his inquiries. Come," and he led me to an ornate chest which rested beneath the windows against the west wall of the study.

Kneeling, he unlocked the repository, and then drew forth, in rapid and marvelous succession, a series of objects each of which boasted of intimate connection with Poe's life.

There were souvenirs of his youth and his schooling abroad—a book he had used during his sojourn at West Point—mementos of his days as a theatrical critic in the form of playbills, a pen used during his editorial period, a fan once owned by his girl-wife, Virginia, a brooch of Mrs. Clemm's; a profusion of objects including such diverse articles as a cravat-stock and—curiously enough—Poe's battered and tarnished flute.

Again we drank, and I own the wine was potent. Canning's countenance remained cadaverously wan—but, moreover, there was a species of mad hilarity in his eye—an evident restrained hysteria in his whole demeanor. At length, from the scattered heap of curiosa, I happened to draw forth and examine a little box of no remarkable character, whereupon I was constrained to inquire its history and what part it had played in the life of Poe.

"In the *life* of Poe?" A visible tremor convulsed the features of my host, then rapidly passed in transformation to a grimace, a rictus of amusement. "This little box—and you will note how, by some fateful design or contrived coincidence it bears a resemblance to the box he himself conceived of and described in his tale 'Berenice'—this little box is concerned with his death, rather than his life. It is, in fact, the selfsame box my grandfather Christopher Canning clutched to his bosom when they found him down there."

Again the tremor, again the grimace. "But stay, I have not yet told you of the details. Perhaps you would be interested in seeing the spot where Christopher Canning was stricken; I have already told you of his madness, but I did no more than hint at the character of his delusions. You have been patient with me, and more than patient. Your understanding shall be rewarded, for I perceive you can be fully entrusted with the facts."

What further revelations Canning was prepared to make I could not say, but his manner was such as to inspire a vague disquiet and trepidation in my breast.

Upon perceiving my unease he laughed shortly and laid a hand upon my shoulder. "Come, this should interest you as an *aficionado* of fantasy," he said. "But first, another drink to speed our journey."

He poured, we drank, and then he led the way from that

vaulted chamber, down the silent halls, down the staircase, and into the lowest recesses of the building until we reached what resembled a donjon-keep, its floor and the interior of a long archway carefully sheathed in copper. We paused before a door of massive iron. Again I felt in the aspect of this scene an element evocative of recognition or recollection.

Canning's intoxication was such that he misinterpreted, or chose to misinterpret, my reaction.

"You need not be afraid," he assured me. "Nothing has happened down here since that day, almost seventy years ago, when his servants discovered him stretched out before this door, the little box clutched to his bosom; collapsed, and in a state of delirium from which he never emerged. For six months he lingered, a hopeless maniac—raving as wildly from the very moment of his discovery as at the moment he died—babbling his visions of the giant horse, the fissured house collapsing into the tarn, the black cat, the pit, the pendulum, the raven on the pallid bust, the beating heart, the pearly teeth, and the nearly liquid mass of loathsome—of detestable putridity from which a voice emanated.

"Nor was that all he babbled," Canning confided, and here his voice sank to a whisper that reverberated through the copper-sheathed hall and against the iron door. "He hinted other things far worse than fantasy; of a ghastly reality surpassing all of the phantasms of Poe.

"For the first time my father and the servants learned the purpose of the room he had built beyond this iron door, and learned too what Christopher Canning had done to establish his title as the world's foremost collector of Poe.

"For he babbled again of Poe's death, thirty years earlier, in 1849—of the burial in the Presbyterian cemetery—and of the removal of the coffin in 1874 to the corner where the monument was raised. As I told you, and as was known then, my grandfather had played a public part in instigating that removal. But now we learned of the private part—learned that there was a monument and a grave, but no coffin in the earth beneath Poe's alleged resting place. The coffin now rested in the secret room at the end of this passage. That is why the room, the house itself, had been built.

"I tell you, he had stolen the body of Edgar Allan Poe—and

as he shrieked aloud in his final madness, did not this indeed make him the greatest collector of Poe?

"His ultimate intent was never divined, but my father made one significant discovery—the little box clutched to Christopher Canning's bosom contained a portion of the crumbled bones, the veritable dust that was all that remained of Poe's corpse."

My host shuddered and turned away. He led me back along that hall of horror, up the stairs, into the study. Silently, he filled our beakers and I drank as hastily, as deeply, as desperately as he.

"What could my father do? To own the truth was to create a public scandal. He chose instead to keep silence; to devote his own life to study in retirement.

"Naturally the shock affected him profoundly; to my knowledge he never entered the room beyond the iron door, and, indeed, I did not know of the room or its contents until the hour of his death—and it was not until some years later that I myself found the key among his effects.

"But find the key I did, and the story was immediately and completely corroborated. Today I am the greatest collector of Poe—for he lies in the keep below, my eternal trophy!"

This time I poured the wine. As I did so, I noted for the first time the imminence of a storm; the impetuous fury of its gusts shaking the casements, and the echoes of its thunder rolling and rumbling down the time-corroded corridors of the old house.

The wild, overstrained vivacity with which my host hearkened, or apparently hearkened, to these sounds did nothing to reassure me—for his recent revelation led me to suspect his sanity.

That the body of Edgar Allan Poe had been stolen—that this mansion had been built to house it—that it was indeed enshrined in a crypt below—that grandsire, son, and grandson had dwelt here alone, apart, enslaved to a sepulchral secret—was beyond sane belief.

And yet, surrounded now by the night and the storm, in a setting torn from Poe's own frenzied fancies, I could not be sure. Here the past was still alive, the very spirit of Poe's tales breathed forth its corruption upon the scene.

As thunder boomed, Launcelot Canning took up Poe's flute, and, whether in defiance of the storm without or as a mocking accompaniment, he played; blowing upon it with drunken persistence, with eerie atonality, with nerve-shattering shrillness. To the shrieking of that infernal instrument the thunder added a braying counterpoint.

Uneasy, uncertain, and unnerved, I retreated into the shadows of the bookshelves at the farther end of the room, and idly scanned the titles of a row of ancient tomes. Here was the *Chiromancy* of Robert Flud, the *Directorium Inquisitorium,* a rare and curious book in quarto Gothic that was the manual of a forgotten church; and betwixt and between the volumes of pseudo-scientific inquiry, theological speculation, and sundry incunabula, I found titles that arrested and appalled me. *De Vermis Mysteriis* and the *Liber Eibon,* treatises on demonology, on witchcraft, on sorcery moldered in crumbling bindings. The books were old, but the books were not dusty. They had been read—

"Read them?" It was as though Canning divined my inmost thoughts. He had put aside his flute and now approached me, tittering as though in continued drunken defiance of the storm. Odd echoes and boomings now sounded through the long halls of the house, and curious grating sounds threatened to drown out his words and his laughter.

"Read them?" said Canning. "I study them. Yes, I have gone beyond grandfather and father, too. It was I who procured the books that held the key, and it was I who found the key. A key more difficult to discover, and more important, than the key to the vaults below. I often wonder if Poe himself had access to these selfsame tomes, knew the selfsame secrets. The secrets of the grave and what lies beyond, and what can be summoned forth if one but holds the key."

He stumbled away and returned with wine. "Drink," he said. "Drink to the night and the storm."

I brushed the proffered glass aside. "Enough," I said. "I must be on my way."

Was it fancy or did I find fear frozen on his features? Canning clutched my arm and cried, "No, stay with me! This is no night on which to be alone; I swear I cannot abide the thought of being alone, I can bear to be alone no more!"

His incoherent babble mingled with the thunder and the echoes; I drew back and confronted him. "Control yourself," I counseled. "Confess that this is a hoax, an elaborate imposture arranged to please your fancy."

"Hoax? Imposture? Stay, and I shall prove to you beyond all doubt"—and so saying, Launcelot Canning stooped and opened a small drawer set in the wall beneath and beside the bookshelves. "This should repay you for your interest in my story, and in Poe," he murmured. "Know that you are the first other person than myself to glimpse these treasures."

He handed me a sheaf of manuscripts on plain white paper; documents written in ink curiously similar to that I had noted while perusing Poe's letters. Pages were clipped together in groups, and for a moment I scanned titles alone.

" 'The Worm of Midnight,' by Edgar Poe," I read, aloud. " 'The Crypt,' " I breathed. And here, " 'The Further Adventures of Arthur Gordon Pym ' "—and in my agitation I came close to dropping the precious pages. "Are these what they appear to be—the unpublished tales of Poe?"

My host bowed.

"Unpublished, undiscovered, unknown, save to me—and to you."

"But this cannot be," I protested. "Surely there would have been a mention of them somewhere, in Poe's own letters or those of his contemporaries. There would have been a clue, an indication, somewhere, someplace, somehow."

Thunder mingled with my words, and thunder echoed in Canning's shouted reply.

"You dare to presume an imposture? Then compare!" He stooped again and brought out a glassined folio of letters. "Here—is this not the veritable script of Edgar Poe? Look at the calligraphy of the letter, then at the manuscripts. Can you say they are not penned by the selfsame hand?"

I looked at the handwriting, wondered at the possibilities of a monomaniac's forgery. Could Launcelot Canning, a victim of mental disorder, thus painstakingly simulate Poe's hand?

"Read, then!" Canning screamed through the thunder. "Read, and dare to say that these tales were written by any other than Edgar Poe, whose genius defies the corruption of Time and the Conqueror Worm!"

I read but a line or two, holding the topmost manuscript close to eyes that strained beneath wavering candlelight; but even in the flickering illumination I noted that which told me the only, the incontestable truth. For the paper, the curiously *unyellowed* paper, bore a visible watermark; the name of a firm of well-known modern stationers, and the date—1949.

Putting the sheaf aside, I endeavored to compose myself as I moved away from Launcelot Canning. For now I knew the truth; knew that one hundred years after Poe's death a semblance of his spirit still lived in the distorted and disordered soul of Canning. Incarnation, reincarnation, call it what you will; Canning was, in his own irrational mind, Edgar Allan Poe.

Stifled and dull echoes of thunder from a remote portion of the mansion now commingled with the soundless seething of my own inner turmoil, as I turned and rashly addressed my host.

"Confess!" I cried. "Is it not true that you have written these tales, fancying yourself the embodiment of Poe? Is it not true that you suffer from a singular delusion born of solitude and everlasting brooding upon the past; that you have reached a stage characterized by the conviction that Poe still lives on in your own person?"

A strong shudder came over him and a sickly smile quivered about his lips as he replied. "Fool! I say to you that I have spoken the truth. Can you doubt the evidence of your senses? This house is real, the Poe collection exists, and the stories exist—they exist, I swear, as truly as the body lying in the crypt below!"

I took up the little box from the table and removed the lid. "Not so," I answered. "You said your grandfather was found with this box clutched to his breast, before the door of the vault, and that it contained Poe's dust. Yet you cannot escape the fact that the box is empty." I faced him furiously. "Admit it, the story is a fabrication, a romance. Poe's body does not lie beneath this house, nor are these his unpublished works, written during his lifetime and concealed."

"True enough," Canning's smile was ghastly beyond belief. "The dust is gone because I took it and used it—because in the works of wizardry I found the formulae, the arcana whereby I could raise the flesh, re-create the body from the essential salts of the grave. Poe does not *lie* beneath this house—he *lives*! And the tales are *his posthumous works*!"

Accented by thunder, his words crashed against my consciousness.

"That was the end-all and the be-all of my planning, of my

studies, of my work, of my life! To raise, by sorcery, the veritable spirit of Edgar Poe from the grave—reclothed and animate in flesh—set him to dwell and dream and do his work again in the private chambers I built in the vaults below—and this I have done! To steal a corpse is but a ghoulish prank; mine is the achievement of true genius!"

The distinct, hollow, metallic, and clangorous yet apparently muffled reverberation accompanying his words caused him to turn in his seat and face the door of the study, so that I could not see the workings of his countenance—nor could he read my own reaction to his ravings.

His words came but faintly to my ears through the thunder that now shook the house in a relentless grip; the wind rattling the casements and flickering the candle flame from the great silver candelabra sent a soaring sighing in an anguished accompaniment to his speech.

"I would show him to you, but I dare not; for he hates me as he hates life. I have locked him in the vault, alone, for the resurrected have no need of food or drink. And he sits there, pen moving over paper, endlessly moving, endlessly pouring out the evil essence of all he guessed and hinted at in life and which he learned in death.

"Do you not see the tragic pity of my plight? I sought to raise his spirit from the dead, to give the world anew of his genius— and yet these tales, these works, are filled and fraught with a terror not to be endured. They cannot be shown to the world, he cannot be shown to the world; in bringing back the dead I have brought back the fruits of death!"

Echoes sounded anew as I moved toward the door—moved, I confess, to flee this accursed house and its accursed owner.

Canning clutched my hand, my arm, my shoulder. "You cannot go!" he shouted above the storm. "I spoke of his escaping, but did you not guess? Did you not hear it through the thunder— the grating of the door?"

I pushed him aside and he blundered backward, upsetting the candelabra, so that flames licked now across the carpeting.

"Wait!" he cried. "Have you not heard his footstep on the stair? *Madman, I tell you that he now stands without the door!*"

A rush of wind, a roar of flame, a shroud of smoke rose all

about us. Throwing open the huge, antique panels to which Canning pointed, I staggered into the hall.

I speak of wind, of flame, of smoke—enough to obscure all vision. I speak of Canning's screams, and of thunder loud enough to drown all sound. I speak of terror born of loathing and of desperation enough to shatter all my sanity.

Despite these things, I can never erase from my consciousness that which I beheld as I fled past the doorway and down the hall.

There without the doors there *did* stand a lofty and enshrouded figure; a figure all too familiar, with pallid features, high, domed forehead, moustache set above a mouth. My glimpse lasted but an instant, an instant during which the man—the corpse—the apparition—the hallucination, call it what you will—moved forward into the chamber and clasped Canning to his breast in an unbreakable embrace. Together, the two figures tottered toward the flames, which now rose to blot out vision forevermore.

From that chamber, and from that mansion, I fled aghast. The storm was still abroad in all its wrath, and now fire came to claim the house of Canning for its own.

Suddenly there shot along the path before me a wild light, and I turned to see whence a gleam so unusual could have issued—but it was only the flames, rising in supernatural splendor to consume the mansion, and the secrets, of the man who collected Poe.

Poor Little Saturday

Madeleine L'Engle

Madeleine L'Engle's (1918–   ) adult novels include her first book, *The Small Rain* (1945), and its sequel, *A Severed Wasp* (1983). However, she is best known for her children's books, including the science fantasy *A Wrinkle in Time* (1962), *A Wind in the Door* (1973), and *A Swiftly Tilting Planet* (1980). "Poor Little Saturday" offers a child's eye view of the supernatural that renders ghosts and other fantastic beings more wistful than frightening.

The witch woman lived in a deserted, boarded-up plantation house, and nobody knew about her but me. Nobody in the nosey little town in south Georgia where I lived when I was a boy knew that if you walked down the dusty main street to where the post office ended it, and then turned left and followed that road a piece until you got to the rusty iron gates of the drive to the plantation house, you could find goings-on would make your eyes pop out. It was just luck that I found out. Or maybe it wasn't luck at all. Maybe the witch woman wanted me to find out because of Alexandra. But now I wish I hadn't because the witch woman and Alexandra are gone forever and it's much worse than if I'd never known them.

Nobody'd lived in the plantation house since the Civil War when Colonel Londermaine was killed and Alexandra Londermaine, his beautiful young wife, hung herself on the chandelier in the ballroom. A while before I was born some northerners bought it but after a few years they stopped coming and people said it was because the house was haunted. Every few years a gang of boys or men would set out to explore the house but

147

nobody ever found anything, and it was so well boarded up it was hard to force an entrance, so by and by the town lost interest in it. No one climbed the wall and wandered around the grounds except me.

I used to go there often during the summer because I had bad spells of malaria when sometimes I couldn't bear to lie on the iron bedstead in my room with the flies buzzing around my face, or out on the hammock on the porch with the screams and laughter of the other kids as they played torturing my ears. My aching head made it impossible for me to read, and I would drag myself down the road, scuffling my bare sunburned toes in the dust, wearing the tattered straw hat that was supposed to protect me from the heat of the sun, shivering and sweating by turns. Sometimes it would seem hours before I got to the iron gates near which the brick wall was lowest. Often I would have to lie panting on the tall prickly grass for minutes until I gathered strength to scale the wall and drop down on the other side.

But once inside the grounds it seemed cooler. One funny thing about my chills was that I didn't seem to shiver nearly as much when I could keep cool as I did at home where even the walls and the floors, if you touched them, were hot. The grounds were filled with live oaks that had grown up unchecked everywhere and afforded an almost continuous green shade. The ground was covered with ferns which were soft and cool to lie on, and when I flung myself down on my back and looked up, the roof of leaves was so thick that sometimes I couldn't see the sky at all. The sun that managed to filter through lost its bright pitiless glare and came in soft yellow shafts that didn't burn you when they touched you.

One afternoon, a scorcher early in September, which is usually our hottest month (and by then you're fagged out by the heat anyhow), I set out for the plantation. The heat lay coiled and shimmering on the road. When you looked at anything through it, it was like looking through a defective pane of glass. The dirt road was so hot that it burned even through my callused feet and as I walked clouds of dust rose in front of me and mixed with the shimmying of the heat. I thought I'd never make the plantation. Sweat was running into my eyes, but it was cold sweat, and I was shivering so that my teeth chattered as I walked.

When I managed finally to fling myself down on my soft green bed of ferns inside the grounds I was seized with one of the worst chills I'd ever had in spite of the fact that my mother had given me an extra dose of quinine that morning and some 666 malaria medicine to boot. I shut my eyes tight and clutched the ferns with my hands and teeth to wait until the chill had passed, when I heard a soft voice call:

"Boy."

I thought at first I was delirious, because sometimes I got light-headed when my bad attacks came on; only then I remembered that when I was delirious I didn't know it; all the strange things I saw and heard seemed perfectly natural. So when the voice said, "Boy," again, as soft and clear as the mockingbird at sunrise, I opened my eyes.

Kneeling near me on the ferns was a girl. She must have been about a year younger than I. I was almost sixteen so I guess she was fourteen or fifteen. She was dressed in a blue and white gingham dress; her face was very pale, but the kind of paleness that's supposed to be, not the sickly pale kind that was like mine showing even under the tan. Her eyes were big and very blue. Her hair was dark brown and she wore it parted in the middle in two heavy braids that were swinging in front of her shoulders as she peered into my face.

"You don't feel well, do you?" she asked. There was no trace of concern or worry in her voice. Just scientific interest.

I shook my head. "No," I whispered, almost afraid that if I talked she would vanish, because I had never seen anyone here before, and I thought that maybe I was dying because I felt so awful, and I thought maybe that gave me the power to see the ghost. But the girl in blue and white checked gingham seemed as I watched her to be good flesh and blood.

"You'd better come with me," she said. "She'll make you all right."

"Who's she?"

"Oh—just Her," she said.

My chill had begun to recede by now, so when she got up off her knees, I scrambled up, too. When she stood up her dress showed a white ruffled petticoat underneath it, and bits of green moss had left patterns on her knees and I didn't think that would happen to the knees of a ghost, so I followed her as she led the way towards the house. She did not go up the sagging, half-rotted steps which led to the veranda about whose white pillars wisteria vines climbed in wild profusion, but went around to the side of the house where there were slanting doors to a cellar. The sun and rain had long since blistered and washed off the paint, but the doors looked clean and were free of the bits of bark from the eucalyptus tree which leaned nearby and which had dropped its bits of dusty peel on either side; so I knew that these cellar stairs must frequently be used.

The girl opened the cellar doors. "You go down first," she said. I went down the cellar steps which were stone, and cool against my bare feet. As she followed me she closed the cellar doors after her and as I reached the bottom of the stairs we were in pitch darkness. I began to be very frightened until her soft voice came out of the black.

"Boy, where are you?"

"Right here."

"You'd better take my hand. You might stumble."

We reached out and found each other's hands in the darkness. Her fingers were long and cool and they closed firmly around mine. She moved with authority as though she knew her way with the familiarity born of custom.

"Poor Sat's all in the dark," she said, "but he likes it that way. He likes to sleep for weeks at a time. Sometimes he snores awfully. Sat, darling!" she called gently. A soft, bubbly, blowing sound came in answer, and she laughed happily. "Oh, Sat, you are sweet!" she said, and the bubbly sound came again. Then the girl pulled at my hand and we came out into a huge and dusty kitchen. Iron skillets, pots and pans, were still hanging on either side of the huge stove, and there was a rolling pin and a bowl of flour on the marble topped table in the middle of the room. The girl took a lighted candle off the shelf.

"I'm going to make cookies," she said as she saw me looking at the flour and the rolling pin. She slipped her hand out of mine. "Come along." She began to walk more rapidly. We left the kitchen, crossed the hall, went through the dining room, its old mahogany table thick with dust although sheets covered the pictures on the walls. Then we went into the ballroom. The mirrors lining the walls were spotted and discolored; against one wall was a single delicate gold chair, its seat cushioned with pale

rose and silver woven silk; it seemed extraordinarily well preserved. From the ceiling hung the huge chandelier from which
Alexandra Londermaine had hung herself, its prisms catching
and breaking up into a hundred colors the flickering of the candle
and the few shafts of light that managed to slide in through the
boarded-up windows. As we crossed the ballroom the girl began
to dance by herself, gracefully, lightly, so that her full blue and
white checked gingham skirts flew out around her. She looked
at herself with pleasure in the old mirrors as she danced, the
candle flaring and guttering in her right hand.

"You've stopped shaking. Now what will I tell Her?" she said
as we started to climb the broad mahogany staircase. It was very
dark so she took my hand again, and before we had reached the
top of the stairs I obliged her by being seized by another chill.
She felt my trembling fingers with satisfaction. "Oh, you've
started again. That's good." She slid open one of the huge double
doors at the head of the stairs.

As I looked in to what once must have been Colonel Londermaine's study I thought that surely what I saw was a scene in a
dream or a vision in delirium. Seated at the huge table in the
center of the room was the most extraordinary woman I had ever
seen. I felt that she must be very beautiful, although she would
never have fulfilled any of the standards of beauty set by our
town. Even though she was seated I felt that she must be im-
mensely tall. Piled up on the table in front of her were several
huge volumes, and her finger was marking the place in the open
one in front of her, but she was not reading. She was leaning
back in the carved chair, her head resting against a piece of blue
and gold embroidered silk that was flung across the chair back,
one hand gently stroking a fawn that lay sleeping in her lap. Her
eyes were closed and somehow I couldn't imagine what color
they would be. It wouldn't have surprised me if they had been
shining amber or the deep purple of her velvet robe. She had a
great quantity of hair, the color of mahogany in firelight, which
was cut quite short and seemed to be blown wildly about her
head like flame. Under her closed eyes were deep shadows, and
lines of pain about her mouth. Otherwise there were no marks
of age on her face but I would not have been surprised to learn
that she was any age in the world—a hundred, or twenty-five.

Her mouth was large and mobile and she was singing something in a deep, rich voice. Two cats, one black, one white, were coiled up, each on a book, and as we opened the doors a leopard stood up quietly beside her, but did not snarl or move. It simply stood there and waited, watching us.

The girl nudged me and held her finger to her lips to warn me to be quiet, but I would not have spoken—could not, anyhow, my teeth were chattering so from my chill which I had completely forgotten, so fascinated was I by this woman sitting back with her head against the embroidered silk, soft deep sounds coming out of her throat. At last these sounds resolved themselves into words, and we listened to her as she sang. The cats slept indifferently, but the leopard listened, too:

> I sit high in my ivory tower,
>   The heavy curtains drawn.
> I've many a strange and lustrous
>   flower,
>   A leopard and a fawn
>
> Together sleeping by my chair
>   And strange birds softly winging,
> And ever pleasant to my ear
>   Twelve maidens' voices singing.
>
> Here is my magic maps' array,
>   My mystic circle's flame.
> With symbol's art He lets me play,
>   The unknown my domain,
>
> And as I sit here in my dream
>   I see myself awake,
> Hearing a torn and bloody scream,
>   Feeling my castle shake . . .

Her song wasn't finished but she opened her eyes and looked at us. Now that his mistress knew we were here the leopard seemed ready to spring and devour me at one gulp, but she put her hand on his sapphire-studded collar to restrain him.

"Well, Alexandra," she said, "who have we here?"

The girl, who still held my hand in her long, cool fingers, answered, "It's a boy."

"So I see. Where did you find him?"

The voice sent shivers up and down my spine.

"In the fern bed. He was shaking. See? He's shaking now. Is he having a fit?" Alexandra's voice was filled with pleased interest.

"Come here, boy," the woman said.

As I didn't move, Alexandra gave me a push, and I advanced slowly. As I came near, the woman pulled one of the leopard's ears gently, saying, "Lie down, Thammuz." The beast obeyed, flinging itself at her feet. She held her hand out to me as I approached the table. If Alexandra's fingers felt firm and cool, hers had the strength of the ocean and the coolness of jade. She looked at me for a long time and I saw that her eyes were deep blue, much bluer than Alexandra's, so dark as to be almost black. When she spoke again her voice was warm and tender: "You're burning up with fever. One of the malaria bugs?" I nodded. "Well, we'll fix that for you."

When she stood and put the sleeping faun down by the leopard, she was not as tall as I had expected her to be; nevertheless she gave an impression of great height. Several of the bookshelves in one corner were emptied of books and filled with various shaped bottles and retorts. Nearby was a large skeleton. There was an acid stained washbasin, too; that whole section of the room looked like part of a chemist's or physicist's laboratory. She selected from among the bottles a small amber-colored one, and poured a drop of the liquid it contained into a glass of water. As the drop hit the water there was a loud hiss and clouds of dense smoke arose. When it had drifted away she handed the glass to me and said, "Drink. Drink, my boy!"

My hand was trembling so that I could scarcely hold the glass. Seeing this, she took it from me and held it to my lips.

"What is it?" I asked.

"Drink it," she said, pressing the rim of the glass against my teeth. On the first swallow I started to choke and would have pushed the stuff away, but she forced the rest of the burning liquid down my throat. My whole body felt on fire. I felt flame flickering in every vein and the room and everything in it swirled around. When I had regained my equilibrium to a certain extent I managed to gasp out again, "What is it?"

She smiled and answered,

"Nine peacocks' hearts, four
    bats' tongues,
A pinch of moondust and a
    hummingbird's lungs."

Then I asked a question I would never have dared ask if it hadn't been that I was still half drunk from the potion I had swallowed, "Are you a witch?"

She smiled again, and answered, "I make it my profession."

Since she hadn't struck me down with a flash of lightning, I went on. "Do you ride a broomstick?"

This time she laughed. "I can when I like."

"Is it—is it very hard?"

"Rather like a bucking bronco at first, but I've always been a good horsewoman, and now I can manage very nicely. I've finally progressed to sidesaddle, though I still feel safer astride. I always rode my horse astride. Still, the best witches ride sidesaddle, so . . . Now run along home. Alexandra has lessons to study and I must work. Can you hold your tongue or must I make you forget?"

"I can hold my tongue."

She looked at me and her eyes burnt into me like the potion she had given me to drink. "Yes, I think you can," she said. "Come back tomorrow if you like. Thammuz will show you out."

The leopard rose and led the way to the door. As I hesitated, unwilling to tear myself away, it came back and pulled gently but firmly on my trouser leg.

"Good-bye, boy," the witch woman said. "And you won't have any more chills and fever."

"Good-bye," I answered. I didn't say thank you. I didn't say good-bye to Alexandra. I followed the leopard out.

She let me come every day. I think she must have been lonely. After all I was the only thing there with a life apart from hers. And in the long run the only reason I have had a life of my own is because of her. I am as much a creation of the witch woman's as Thammuz the leopard was, or the two cats, Ashtaroth and Orus (it wasn't until many years after the last day I saw the witch woman that I learned that those were the names of the fallen angels).

She did cure my malaria, too. My parents and the townspeople thought that I had outgrown it. I grew angry when they talked about it so lightly and wanted to tell them that it was the witch woman, but I knew that if ever I breathed a word about her I would be eternally damned. Mama thought we should write a testimonial letter to the 666 Malaria Medicine people, and maybe they'd send us a couple of dollars.

Alexandra and I became very good friends. She was a strange, aloof creature. She liked me to watch her while she danced alone in the ballroom or played on an imaginary harp—though sometimes I fancied I could hear the music. One day she took me into the drawing room and uncovered a portrait that was hung between two of the long boarded-up windows. Then she stepped back and held her candle high so as to throw the best light on the picture. It might have been a picture of Alexandra herself, or Alexandra as she might be in five years.

"That's my mother," she said. "Alexandra Londermaine."

As far as I knew from the tales that went about town, Alexandra Londermaine had given birth to only one child, and that stillborn, before she had hung herself on the chandelier in the ballroom—and anyhow, any child of hers would have been Alexandra's mother or grandmother. But I didn't say anything because when Alexandra got angry she became ferocious like one of the cats, and was given to leaping on me, scratching and biting. I looked at the portrait long and silently.

"You see, she has on a ring like mine," Alexandra said, holding out her left hand, on the fourth finger of which was the most beautiful sapphire and diamond ring I had ever seen, or rather, that I could ever have imagined, for it was a ring apart from any owned by even the most wealthy of the townsfolk. Then I realized that Alexandra had brought me in here and unveiled the portrait simply that she might show me the ring to better advantage, for she had never worn a ring before.

"Where did you get it?"

"Oh, she got it for me last night."

"Alexandra," I asked suddenly, "how long have you been here?"

"Oh, a while."

"But how long?"

"Oh, I don't remember."

"But you must remember."

"I don't. I just came—like Poor Sat."

"'Who's Poor Sat?" I asked, thinking for the first time of whoever it was that had made the gentle bubbly noises at Alexandra the day she found me in the fern bed.

"Why, we've never shown you Sat, have we!" she exclaimed. "I'm sure it's all right, but we'd better ask Her first."

So we went to the witch woman's room and knocked. Thammuz pulled the door open with his strong teeth and the witch woman looked up from some sort of experiment she was making with test tubes and retorts. The fawn, as usual, lay sleeping near her feet. "Well?" she said.

"Is it all right if I take him to see Poor Little Saturday?" Alexandra asked her.

"Yes, I suppose so," she answered. "But no teasing," and turned her back to us and bent again over her test tubes as Thammuz nosed us out of the room.

We went down to the cellar. Alexandra lit a lamp and took me back to the corner furthest from the doors, where there was a stall. In the stall was a two-humped camel. I couldn't help laughing as I looked at him because he grinned at Alexandra so foolishly, displaying all his huge buck teeth and blowing bubbles through them.

"She said we weren't to tease him," Alexandra said severely, rubbing her cheek against the preposterous splotchy hair that seemed to be coming out, leaving bald pink spots of skin on his long nose.

"But what—" I started.

"She rides him sometimes." Alexandra held out her hand while he nuzzled against it, scratching his rubbery lips against the diamond and sapphire of her ring. "Mostly She talks to him. She says he is very wise. He goes up to Her room sometimes and they talk and talk. I can't understand a word they say. She says it's Hindustani and Arabic. Sometimes I can remember little bits of it, like *iderow, sorcabatcha,* and *anna bihed bech.* She says I can learn to speak with them when I finish learning French and Greek."

Poor Little Saturday was rolling his eyes in delight as Alexandra scratched behind his ears. "Why is he called Poor Little Saturday?" I asked.

Alexandra spoke with a ring of pride in her voice. "I named him. She let me."

"But why did you name him that?"

"Because he came last winter on the Saturday that was the shortest day of the year, and it rained all day so it got light later and dark earlier than it would have if it had been nice, so it really didn't have as much of itself as it should, and I felt so sorry for it I thought maybe it would feel better if we named him after it . . . She thought it was a nice name!" she turned on me suddenly.

"Oh, it is! It's a fine name!" I said quickly, smiling to myself as I realized how much greater was this compassion of Alexandra's for a day than any she might have for a human being. "How did She get him?" I asked.

"Oh, he just came."

"What do you mean?"

"She wanted him so he came. From the desert."

"He *walked!*"

"Yes. And swam part of the way. She met him at the beach and flew him here on the broomstick. You should have seen him. She was still all wet and looked so funny. She gave him hot coffee with things in it."

"What things?"

"Oh, just things."

Then the witch woman's voice came from behind us. "Well, children?"

It was the first time I had seen her out of her room. Thammuz was at her right heel, the fawn at her left. The cats, Ashtaroth and Orus, had evidently stayed upstairs. "Would you like to ride Saturday?" she asked me.

Speechless, I nodded. She put her hand against the wall and a portion of it slid down into the earth so that Poor Little Saturday was free to go out. "She's sweet, isn't she?" the witch woman asked me, looking affectionately at the strange, bumpy-kneed, splay-footed creature. "Her grandmother was very good to me in Egypt once. Besides, I love camel's milk."

"But Alexandra said she was a he!" I exclaimed.

"Alexandra's the kind of woman to whom all animals are he except cats, and all cats are she. As a matter of fact, Ashtaroth and Orus are she, but it wouldn't make any difference to Alexandra if they weren't. Go on out, Saturday. Come on!"

Saturday backed out, bumping her bulging knees and ankles against her stall, and stood under a live oak tree. "Down," the witch woman said. Saturday leered at me and didn't move. "Down, sorcabatcha!" the witch woman commanded, and Saturday obediently got down on her knees. I clambered up onto her, and before I had managed to get at all settled she rose with such a jerky motion that I knocked my chin against her front hump and nearly bit my tongue off. Round and round Saturday danced while I clung wildly to her front hump and the witch woman and Alexandra rolled on the ground with laughter. I felt as though I were on a very unseaworthy vessel on the high seas, and it wasn't long before I felt violently seasick as Saturday pranced among the live oak trees, sneezing delicately.

At last the witch woman called out, "Enough!" and Saturday stopped in her traces, nearly throwing me, and kneeling laboriously. "It was mean to tease you," the witch woman said, pulling my nose gently. "You may come sit in my room with me for a while if you like."

There was nothing I liked better than to sit in the witch woman's room and to watch her while she studied from her books, worked out strange looking mathematical problems, argued with the zodiac, or conducted complicated experiments with her test tubes and retorts, sometimes filling the room with sulphurous odors or flooding it with red or blue light. Only once was I afraid of her, and that was when she danced with the skeleton in the corner. She had the room flooded with a strange red glow and I almost thought I could see the flesh covering the bones of the skeleton as they danced together like lovers. I think she had forgotten that I was sitting there, half hidden in the wing chair, because when they had finished dancing and the skeleton stood in the corner again, his bones shining and polished, devoid of any living trappings, she stood with her forehead against one of the deep red velvet curtains that covered the boarded-up windows and tears streamed down her cheeks. Then she went back to her test tubes and worked feverishly. She never alluded to the incident and neither did I.

As winter drew on she let me spend more and more time in

the room. Once I gathered up courage enough to ask her about herself, but I got precious little satisfaction.

"Well, then, are you maybe one of the northerners who bought the place?"

"Let's leave it at that, boy. We'll say that's who I am. Did you know that my skeleton was old Colonel Londermaine? Not so old, as a matter of fact; he was only thirty-seven when he was killed at the battle of Bunker Hill—or am I getting him confused with his great-grandfather. Rudolph Londermaine? Anyhow he was only thirty-seven, and a fine figure of a man, and Alexandra only thirty when she hung herself for love of him on the chandelier in the ballroom. Did you know that the fat man with the red mustaches has been trying to cheat your father? His cow will give sour milk for seven days. Run along now and talk to Alexandra. She's lonely."

When the winter had turned to spring and the camellias and azaleas and Cape Jessamine had given way to the more lush blooms of early May, I kissed Alexandra for the first time, very clumsily. The next evening when I managed to get away from the chores at home and hurried out to the plantation, she gave me her sapphire and diamond ring which she had swung for me on a narrow bit of turquoise satin. "It will keep us both safe," she said, "if you wear it always. And then when we're older we can get married and you can give it back to me. Only you mustn't let anyone see it, ever, ever, or She'd be very angry."

I was afraid to take the ring but when I demurred Alexandra grew furious and started kicking and biting and I had to give in.

Summer was almost over before my father discovered the ring hanging about my neck. I fought like a witch boy to keep him from pulling out the narrow ribbon and seeing the ring, and indeed the ring seemed to give me added strength and I had grown, in any case, much stronger during the winter than I had ever been in my life. But my father was still stronger than I, and he pulled it out. He looked at it in dead silence for a moment and then the storm broke. That was the famous Londermaine ring that had disappeared the night Alexandra Londermaine hung herself. That ring was worth a fortune. Where had I got it?

No one believed me when I said I had found it in the grounds near the house—I chose the grounds because I didn't want anybody to think I had been in the house or indeed that I was able to get in. I don't know why they didn't believe me; it still seems quite logical to me that I might have found it buried among the ferns.

It had been a long, dull year, and the men of the town were all bored. They took me and forced me to swallow quantities of corn liquor until I didn't know what I was saying or doing. When they had finished with me I didn't even manage to reach home before I was violently sick and then I was in my mother's arms and she was weeping over me. It was morning before I was able to slip away to the plantation house. I ran pounding up the mahogany stairs to the witch woman's room and opened the heavy sliding doors without knocking. She stood in the center of the room in her purple robe, her arms around Alexandra who was weeping bitterly. Overnight the room had completely changed. The skeleton of Colonel Londermaine was gone, and books filled the shelves in the corner of the room that had been her laboratory. Cobwebs were everywhere, and broken glass lay on the floor; dust was inches thick on her worktable. There was no sign of Thammuz, Ashtaroth or Orus, or the fawn, but four birds were flying about her, beating their wings against her hair.

She did not look at me or in any way acknowledge my presence. Her arm about Alexandra, she led her out of the room and to the drawing room where the portrait hung. The birds followed, flying around and around them. Alexandra had stopped weeping now. Her face was very proud and pale and if she saw me miserably trailing behind them she gave no notice. When the witch woman stood in front of the portrait the sheet fell from it. She raised her arm; there was a great cloud of smoke; the smell of sulphur filled my nostrils, and when the smoke was gone, Alexandra was gone, too. Only the portrait was there, the fourth finger of the left hand now bearing no ring. The witch woman raised her hand again and the sheet lifted itself up and covered the portrait. Then she went, with the birds, slowly back to what had once been her room, and still I tailed after, frightened as I had never been before in my life, or have been since.

She stood without moving in the center of the room for a long time. At last she turned and spoke to me.

"Well, boy, where is the ring?"

"They have it."

"They made you drunk, didn't they?"

"Yes."

"I was afraid something like this would happen when I gave Alexandra the ring. But it doesn't matter . . . I'm tired . . ." She drew her hand wearily across her forehead.

"Did I—did I tell them everything?"

"You did."

"I—I didn't know."

"I know you didn't know, boy."

"Do you hate me now?"

"No, boy, I don't hate you."

"Do you have to go away?"

"Yes."

"I bowed my head. "I'm so sorry . . ."

She smiled slightly. "The sands of time . . . Cities crumble and rise and will crumble again and breath dies down and blows once more . . ."

The birds flew madly about her head, pulling at her hair, calling into her ears. Downstairs we could hear a loud pounding, and then the crack of boards being pulled away from a window.

"Go, boy," she said to me. I stood rooted, motionless, unable to move. "GO!" she commanded, giving me a mighty push so that I stumbled out of the room. They were waiting for me by the cellar doors and caught me as I climbed out. I had to stand there and watch when they came out with her. But it wasn't the witch woman, my witch woman. It was *their* idea of a witch woman, someone thousands of years old, a disheveled old creature in rusty black, with long wisps of gray hair, a hooked nose, and four wiry black hairs springing out of the mole on her chin. Behind her flew the four birds and suddenly they went up, up, into the sky, directly in the path of the sun until they were lost in its burning glare.

Two of the men stood holding her tightly, although she wasn't struggling, but standing there, very quiet, while the others searched the house, searched it in vain. Then as a group of them went down into the cellar I remembered, and by a flicker of the old light in the witch woman's eyes I could see that she remembered, too. Poor Little Saturday had been forgotten. Out she came, prancing absurdly up the cellar steps, her rubbery lips stretched back over her gigantic teeth, her eyes bulging with terror. When she saw the witch woman, her lord and master, held captive by two dirty, insensitive men, she let out a shriek and began to kick and lunge wildly, biting, screaming with the bloodcurdling, heartrending screams that only a camel can make. One of the men fell to the ground, holding a leg in which the bone had snapped from one of Saturday's kicks. The others scattered in terror, leaving the witch woman standing on the veranda supporting herself by clinging to one of the huge wisteria vines that curled around the columns. Saturday clambered up onto the veranda, and knelt while she flung herself between the two humps. Then off they ran, Saturday still screaming, her knees knocking together, the ground shaking as she pounded along. Down from the sun plummeted the four birds and flew after them.

Up and down I danced, waving my arms, shouting wildly until Saturday and the witch woman and the birds were lost in a cloud of dust, while the man with the broken leg lay moaning on the ground beside me.

The Indian

John Updike

John Updike's (1932–   ) Pulitzer Prize-winning quartet of novels about aging businessman Rabbit Angstrom, *Rabbit Run*
(1960), *Rabbit Redux* (1971), *Rabbit Is Rich* (1981), and *Rabbit
at Rest* (1990), have been hailed as a definitive chronicle of life
in postwar America. His other works include *The Witches of
Eastwick* (1984), which examines the battle of the sexes in terms
of the supernatural, *Roger's Version* (1986), a reinterpretation of
Hawthorne's *The Scarlet Letter,* and numerous collections of
short fiction, essays, poetry, and criticism. "The Indian," like
much of his work, is concerned with the chasm separating America's historical past from its present.

The town, in New England, of Tarbox, restrained from em-
bracing the sea by a margin of tawny salt marshes, locates
its downtown four miles inland up the Musquenomenee River,
which ceases to be tidal at the waterfall of the old hosiery mill,
now given over to the manufacture of plastic toys. It was to the
mouth of this river, in May of 1634, that the small party of
seventeen men, led by the younger son of the governor of the
Massachusetts Bay Colony—Jeremiah Tarbox being only his second in command—came in three rough skiffs with the purpose
of establishing amid such an unpossessed abundance of salt hay
a pastoral plantation. This, with God's forbearance, they did.
They furled their sails and slowly rowed, each boat being
equipped with four oarlocks, in search of firm land, through
marshes that must appear, now that their grass is no longer har-
vested by men driving horses shod in great wooden discs, much
the same today as they did then—though undoubtedly the natural

abundance of ducks, cranes, otter, and deer has been somewhat diminished. Tarbox himself, in his invaluable diary, notes that the squealing of the livestock in the third skiff attracted a great cloud of "protesting sea-fowl." The first houses (not one of which still stands, the oldest in town dating, in at least its central timbers and fireplace, from 1642) were strung along the base of the rise of firm land called Near Hill, which, with its companion Far Hill, a mile away, in effect bounds the densely populated section of the present township. In winter the population of Tarbox numbers something less than seven thousand; in summer the figure may be closer to nine thousand. The width of the river mouth and its sheltered advantage within Tarbox Bay seemed to promise the makings of a port to rival Boston; but in spite of repeated dredging operations the river has proved incorrigibly silty, and its shallow winding channels, rendered especially fickle where the fresh water of the river most powerfully clashes with the restless saline influx of the tide, frustrate all but pleasure craft. These Chris-Craft and Kit-Kats, skimming seaward through the exhilarating avenues of wild hay, in the early morning may pass, as the fluttering rust-colored horizon abruptly yields to the steely blue monotone of the open water, a few dour clammers in hip boots patiently harrowing the tidewater floor. The intent posture of their silhouettes distinguishes them from the few bathers who have drifted down from the dying campfires by whose side they have dozed and sung and drunk away a night on the beach— one of the finest and least spoiled, it should be said, on the North Atlantic coast. Picturesque as Millet's gleaners, their torsos doubled like playing cards in the rosy mirror of the dawn-stilled sea, these sparse representatives of the clamming industry, founded in the eighteen-eighties by an immigration of Greeks and continually harassed by the industrial pollution upriver, exploit the sole vein of profit left in the name of old Musquenomenee. This shadowy chief broke the bread of peace with the son of the Governor, and within a year both were dead. The body of the one was returned to Boston to lie in the Kings Chapel graveyard; the body of the other is supposedly buried, presumably upright, somewhere in the woods on the side of Far Hill where even now no houses have intruded, though the tract is rumored to have been sold to a divider.

Until the postwar arrival of Boston commuters, still much of a minority, Tarbox lived (discounting the summer people, who came and went in the marshes each year like the migrations of mallards) as a town apart. A kind of curse has kept its peace. The handmade-lace industry, which reached its peak just before the American Revolution, was destroyed by the industrial revolution; the textile mills, never numerous, were finally emptied by the industrialization of the South. They have been succeeded by a scattering of small enterprises, electronic in the main, which have staved off decisive depression.

Viewed from the spur of Near Hill where the fifth edifice, now called Congregationalist, of the religious society incorporated in 1635 on this identical spot thrusts its spire into the sky, and into a hundred colored postcards purchasable at all four local drugstores—viewed from this eminence, the business district makes a neat and prosperous impression. This is especially true at Christmastime, when colored lights are strung from pole to pole, and at the height of summer, when girls in shorts and bathing suits decorate the pavements. A one-hour parking limit is enforced during business hours, but the traffic is congested only during the evening homeward exodus: A stoplight has never been thought quite necessary. A new Woolworth's with a noble façade of corrugated laminated Fiberglas has been erected on the site of a burned-out tenement. If the building which it vacated across the street went begging nearly a year for a tenant, and if some other properties along the street nervously change hands and wares now and then, nevertheless there is not that staring stretch of blank shop windows which desolates the larger mill towns to the north and west. Two hardware stores confront each other without apparent rancor; three banks vie in promoting solvency; several luncheonettes withstand waves of factory workers and high-school students; and a small proud army of *petit-bour-geois* knights—realtors and lawyers and jewellers—parades up and down in clothes that would not look quaint on Madison Avenue. The explosive thrust of superhighways through the land has sprinkled on the town a cosmopolitan garnish; one resourceful divorcée has made a good thing of selling unabashedly smart women's clothes and Scandinavian kitchen accessories, and, next door, a foolish young matron nostalgic for Vassar has opened a

combination paperback bookstore and art gallery, so that now
the Tarbox town derelict, in sneaking with his cherry-red face
and tot of rye from the liquor store to his home above the shoe-
repair nook, must walk a garish gantlet of abstract paintings by
a minister's wife from Gloucester. Indeed, the whole street is
laid open to an accusatory chorus of brightly packaged titles by
Freud, Camus, and those others through whose masterworks our
civilization moves toward its dark climax. Strange to say, so viru-
lent is the spread of modern culture, some of these same titles
can be had, seventy-five cents cheaper, in the homely old maga-
zine-and-newspaper store in the middle of the block. Here, sitting
stoically on the spines of the radiator behind the large left-hand
window, the Indian can often be seen.

He sits in this window for hours at a time, politely waving to
any passerby who happens to glance his way. It is hard always
to avoid his eye, his form is so unexpected, perched on the radiator above cards of pipes and pyramids of Prince Albert tins and
fanned copies of *True* and *Male* and *Sport*. He looks, behind
glass, somewhat shadowy and thin, but outdoors he is solid
enough. During other hours he takes up a station by Leonard's
Pharmaceutical on the corner. There is a splintered telephone
pole here that he leans against when he wearies of leaning against
the brick wall. Occasionally he even sits upon the fire hydrant
as if upon a campstool, arms folded, legs crossed, gazing across
at the renovations on the face of Poirier's Liquor Mart. In cold
or wet weather he may sit inside the drugstore, expertly pro-
longing a coffee at the counter, running his tobacco-dyed finger-
tip around and around the rim of the cup as he watches the
steam fade. There are other spots—untenanted doorways, the
benches halfway up the hill, idle chairs in the barbershops—
where he loiters, and indeed there cannot be a square foot of
the downtown pavement where he has not at some time or other
paused; but these two spots, the window of the news store and
the wall of the drugstore, are his essential habitat.

It is difficult to discover anything about him. He wears a plaid
lumberjack shirt with a gray turtleneck sweater underneath, and
chino pants olive rather than khaki in color, and remarkably
white tennis sneakers. He smokes and drinks coffee, so he must
have some income, but he does not, apparently, work. Inquiry

reveals that now and then he is employed—during the last Christmas rush he was seen carrying baskets of Hong Kong shirts and Italian crèche elements through the aisles of the five-and-ten—but he soon is fired or quits, and the word "lazy," given somehow more than its usual force of disapproval, sticks in the mind, as if this is the clue. Disconcertingly, he knows your name. Even though you are a young mutual-fund analyst newly bought into a neo-saltbox on the beach road and downtown on a Saturday morning to rent a wallpaper steamer, he smiles if he catches your eye, lifts his hand lightly, and says, "Good morning, Mr.——," supplying your name. Yet his own name is impossible to learn. The simplest fact about a person, identity's very seed, is in his case utterly hidden. It can be determined, by matching consistencies of hearsay, that he lives in that tall, speckle-shingled, disreputable hotel overlooking the atrophied railroad tracks, just down from the Amvets, where shuffling Polish widowers and one-night-in-town salesmen hang out, and in whose bar, evidently, money can be wagered and women may be approached. But his name, whether it is given to you as Tugwell or Frisbee or Wigglesworth, even if it were always the same name would be in its almost parodic Yankeeness incredible. "But he's an Indian!"

The face of your informant—say, the chunky Irish dictator of the School Building Needs Committee, a dentist—undergoes a faint rapt transformation. His voice assumes its habitual whisper of extravagant discretion. "Don't go around saying that. He doesn't like it. He prides himself on being a typical run-down Yankee."

But he *is* an Indian. This is, alone, certain. Who but a savage would have such an immense capacity for repose? His cheekbones, his never-faded skin, the delicate little jut of his scowl, the drooping triangularity of his eye sockets, the way his vertically lined face takes the light, the lusterless black of his hair are all so profoundly Indian that the imagination, surprised by his silhouette as he sits on the hydrant gazing across at the changing face of the liquor store, effortlessly plants a feather at the back of his head. His air of waiting, of gazing; the softness of his motions; the odd sense of proprietorship and ease that envelops him; the good humor that makes his vigil gently dreadful—all these are totally foreign to the shambling shy-eyes and moist

lower lip of the failed Yankee. His age and status are too peculiar. He is surely older than forty and younger than sixty—but *is*
this sure? And, though he greets everyone by name with a light
wave of his hand, the conversation never passes beyond a greet-
ing, and even in the news store, when the political contention
and convivial obscenity literally drive housewives away from the
door, he does not seem to participate. He witnesses, and now
and then offers in a gravelly voice a debated piece of town history, but he does not participate.

It is caring that makes mysteries. As you grow indifferent, they
lift. You live longer in the town, season follows season, the half-
naked urban people arrive on the beach, multiply, and like leaves
fall away again, and you have ceased to identify with them. The
marshes turn green and withdraw through gold into brown, and
their indolent, untouched, enduring existence penetrates your
fibre. You find you must drive down toward the beach once a
week or it is like a week without love. The ice cakes pile up
along the banks of the tidal inlets like the rubble of ruined temples. You begin to meet, without seeking them out, the vestigial
people: the unmarried daughters of vanished mill owners, the
retired high-school teachers, the senile deacons in their unheated
seventeenth-century houses with attics full of old church records
in spidery brown ink. You enter, by way of an elderly babysitter, a world where at least they speak of him as "the Indian."
An appalling snicker materializes in the darkness on the front
seat beside you as you drive dear Mrs. Knowlton home to her
shuttered house on a back road. "If you knew what they say,
Mister, if you knew what they say." And at last, as when in a
woods you break through miles of underbrush into a clearing,
you stand up surprised, taking a deep breath of the obvious,
agreeing with the trees that of course this is the case. Anybody
who is anybody knew all along. The mystery lifts, with some
impatience, here, in Miss Horne's low-ceilinged front parlor,
which smells of warm fireplace ashes and of peppermint balls
kept ready in red-tinted knobbed glass goblets for whatever
openmouthed children might dare to come visit such a very
old lady, all bent double like a little gripping rose clump, Miss
Horne, a fable in her lifetime. Her father had been the sixth
minister before the present one (whom she does *not* care for)
at the First Church, and *his* father the next but one before

him. There had been a Horne among those first seventeen
men. Well—where was she?—yes, the Indian. The Indian had
been loitering—waiting, if you prefer—in the center of town
when she was a tiny girl in gingham. And he is no older now
than he was then.

The Legend of Joe Lee

John D. MacDonald

John D. MacDonald (1916–1986) is best known as a writer of crime and detective fiction and most closely associated with the hard-boiled detective Travis Magee, hero of more than 20 novels written between 1964 and 1985. Few readers are aware that MacDonald wrote fantasy and science fiction such as the novels *Wine of the Dreamers* (1951), *Ballroom of the Skies* (1952), *The Girl, the Gold Watch, and Everything* (1962), and the short fiction collected into *Other Worlds, Other Times* (1979). "The Legend of Joe Lee" is an unusual story in which the ghost is both a literal presence and a metaphor for the spirit of the age.

"Tonight," Sergeant Lazeer said, "we get him for sure."

We were in a dank office in the Afaloosa County Courthouse in the flat wetlands of south central Florida. I had come over from Lauderdale on the half chance of a human interest story that would tie in with the series we were doing on the teen-age war against the square world of the adult.

He called me over to the table where he had the county map spread out. The two other troopers moved in beside me. "It's a full moon night and he'll be out for sure," Lazeer said, "and what we're fixing to do is bottle him on just the right stretch, where he got no way off it, no old back country roads he knows like the shape of his own fist. And here we got it." He put brackets at either end of a string-straight road.

Trooper McCollum said softly, "That there, Mister, is a eighteen-mile straight, and we cruised it slow, and you turn on off it you're in the deep ditch and the black mud and the 'gator water."

Lazeer said, "We stake out both ends, hid back good with lights out. We got radio contact, so when he comes whistling in either end, we got him bottled."

He looked up at me as though expecting an opinion, and I said, "I don't know a thing about road blocks, Sergeant, but it looks as if you could trap him."

"You ride with me, Mister, and we'll get you a story."

"There's one thing you haven't explained, Sergeant. You said you know who the boy is. Why don't you just pick him up at home?"

The other trooper Frank Gaiders said, "Because that fool kid ain't been home since he started this crazy business five-six months ago. His name is Joe Lee Cuddard, from over to Lasco City. His folks don't know where he is, and don't much care, him and that Farris girl he was running with, so we figure the pair of them is off in the piney woods someplace, holed up in some abandoned shack, coming out at night for kicks, making fools of us."

"Up till now, boy," Lazeer said. "Up till tonight. Tonight is the end."

"But when you've met up with him on the highway," I asked, "you haven't been able to catch him?"

The three big, weathered men looked at each other with slow, sad amusement, and McCollum sighed, "I come the closest. The way these cars are beefed up as interceptors, they can do a dead honest hundred and twenty. I saw him across the flats, booming to where the two road forks come together up ahead, so I floored it and I was flat out when the roads joined, and not over fifty yards behind him. In two minutes he had me by a mile, and in four minutes it was near two, and then he was gone. That comes to a hundred and fifty, my guess."

I showed my astonishment. "What the hell does he drive?"

Lazeer opened the table drawer and fumbled around in it and pulled out a tattered copy of a hot-rodder magazine. He opened it to a page where readers had sent in pictures of their cars. It didn't look like anything I had ever seen. Most of it seemed to be bare frame, with a big chromed engine. There was a teardrop-shaped passenger compartment mounted between the big rear wheels, bigger than the front wheels, and there was a tail-fin

arrangement that swept up and out and then curved back so that
the high rear ends of the fins almost met.

"That engine," Frank Gaiders said, "it's a '61 Pontiac, the big
one he bought wrecked and fixed up, with blowers and special
cams and every damn thing. Put the rest of it together himself.
You can see in the letter there, he calls it a C.M. Special. C.M.
is for Clarissa May, that Farris girl he took off with. I saw that
thing just one time, oh, seven, eight months ago, right after he
got it all finished. We got this magazine from his daddy. I saw
it at the Amoco gas in Lasco City. You could near give it a
ticket standing still. Strawberry flake paint it says in the letter.
Damnedest thing, bright strawberry with little like gold flakes in
it, then covered with maybe seventeen coats of lacquer, all
rubbed down so you look down into that paint like it was six
inches deep. Headlights all the hell over the front of it and big
taillights all over the back, and shiny pipes sticking out. Near
two year he worked on it. Big racing flats like the drag strip kids
use over to the airport."

I looked at the coarse screen picture of the boy standing beside
the car, hands on his hips, looking very young, very ordinary,
slightly self-conscious.

"It wouldn't spoil anything for you, would it," I asked, "if I
went and talked to his people, just for background?"

" 'Long as you say nothing about what we're fixing to do,"
Lazeer said. "Just be back by eight thirty this evening."

Lasco City was a big brave name for a hamlet of about five
hundred. They told me at the sundries store to take the west
road and the Cuddard place was a half mile on the left, name
on the mailbox. It was a shacky place, chickens in the dusty yard,
fence sagging. Leo Cuddard was home from work and I found
him out in back, unloading cinder block from an ancient pickup.
He was stripped to the waist, a lean, shallow man who looked
undernourished and exhausted. But the muscles in his spare back
writhed and knotted when he lifted the blocks. He had pale hair
and pale eyes and a narrow mouth. He would not look directly
at me. He grunted and kept on working as I introduced myself
and stated my business.

Finally he straightened and wiped his forehead with his narrow
arm. When those pale eyes stared at me, for some reason it

made me remember the grisly reputation Florida troops acquired in the Civil War. Tireless, deadly, merciless.

"That boy warn't no help to me, Mister, but he warn't no trouble neither. The onliest thing on his mind was that car. I didn't hold with it, but I didn't put down no foot. He fixed up that old shed there to work in, and he needed something, he went out and earned up the money to buy it. They was a crowd of them around most times, helpin' him, boys workin' and gals watchin'. Them tight-pants girls. Have radios on batteries set around so as they could twisty dance while them boys hammered that metal out. When I worked around and overheared 'em, I swear I couldn't make out more'n one word from seven. What he done was take that car to some national show, for prizes and such. But one day he just took off, like they do nowadays."

"Do you hear from him at all?"

He grinned. "I don't hear *from* him, but I sure God hear *about* him."

"How about brothers and sisters?"

"They's just one sister, older, up to Waycross, Georgia, married to an electrician, and me and his stepmother."

As if on cue, a girl came out onto the small back porch. She couldn't have been more than eighteen. Advanced pregnancy bulged the front of her cotton dress. Her voice was a shrill, penetrating whine. "Leo? Leo, honey, that can opener thing just now busted clean off the wall."

"Mind if I take a look at that shed?"

"You help yourself, Mister."

The shed was astonishingly neat. The boy had rigged up droplights. There was a pale blue pegboard wall hung with shining tools. On closer inspection I could see that rust was beginning to fleck the tools. On the workbench were technical journals and hot-rodder magazines. I looked at the improvised engine hoist, at the neat shelves of paint and lubricant.

The Farris place was nearer the center of the village. Some of them were having their evening meal. There were six adults as near as I could judge, and perhaps a dozen children from toddlers on up to tall, lanky boys. Clarissa May's mother came out onto the front porch to talk to me, explaining that her husband drove an interstate truck from the cooperative and he was away for the next few days. Mrs. Farris was grossly fat, but with delicate features, an indication of the beauty she must have once had. The rocking chair creaked under her weight and she fanned herself with a newspaper.

"I can tell you, it like to broke our hearts the way Clarissa May done us. If'n I told LeRoy once, I told him a thousand times, no good would ever come of her messin' with that Cuddard boy. His daddy is trashy. Ever so often they take him in for drunk and put him on the county road gang sixty or ninety days, and that Stubbins child he married, she's next door to feeble-witted. But children get to a certain size and know everything and turn their backs on you like an enemy. You write this up nice and in it put the message her momma and daddy want her home bad, and maybe she'll see it and come on in. You know what the Good Book says about sharper'n a sarpent's tooth. I pray to the good Lord they had the sense to drive that fool car up to Georgia and get married up at least. Him nineteen and her seventeen. The young ones are going clean out of hand these times. One night racing through this county the way they do, showing off, that Cuddard boy is going to kill hisself and my child too."

"Was she hard to control in other ways, Mrs. Farris?"

"No sir, she was neat and good and pretty and quiet, and she had the good marks. It was just about Joe Lee Cuddard she turned mulish. I think I would have let LeRoy whale that out of her if it hadn't been for her trouble.

"You're easier on a young one when there's no way of knowing how long she could be with you. Doc Mathis, he had us taking her over to the Miami clinic. Sometimes they kept her and sometimes they didn't, and she'd get behind in her school and then catch up fast. Many times we taken her over there. She's got the sick blood and it takes her poorly. She should be right here, where's help to care for her in the bad spells. It was October last year, we were over to the church bingo, LeRoy and me, and Clarissa May been resting up in her bed a few days, and that wild boy come in and taking her off in that snorty car, the little ones couldn't stop him. When I think of her out there . . . poorly and all . . ."

At a little after nine we were in position. I was with Sergeant Lazeer at the west end of that eighteen-mile stretch of State

Road 21. The patrol car was backed into a narrow dirt road, lights out. Gaiders and McCollum were similarly situated at the east end of the trap. We were smeared with insect repellent, and we had used spray on the backs of each other's shirts where the mosquitoes were biting through the thin fabric.

Lazeer had repeated his instructions over the radio, and we composed ourselves to wait. "Not much travel on this road this time of year," Lazeer said. "But some tourists come through at the wrong time, they could mess this up. We just got to hope that don't happen."

"Can you block the road with just one car at each end?"

"If he comes through from the other end, I move up quick and put it crosswise where he can't get past, and Frank has a place like that at the other end. Crosswise with the lights and the dome blinker on, but we both are going to stand clear because maybe he can stop it and maybe he can't. But whichever way he comes, we got to have the free car run close herd so he can't get time to turn around when he sees he's bottled."

Lazeer turned out to be a lot more talkative than I had anticipated. He had been in law enforcement for twenty years and had some violent stories. I sensed he was feeding them to me, waiting for me to suggest I write a book about him. From time to time we would get out of the car and move around a little.

"Sergeant, you're pretty sure you've picked the right time and place?"

"He runs on the nights the moon is big. Three or four nights out of the month. He doesn't run the main highways, just these back country roads—the long straight paved stretches where he can really wind that thing up. Lord God, he goes through towns like a rocket. From reports we got, he runs the whole night through, and this is one way he comes, one way or the other, maybe two, three times before moonset. We got to get him. He's got folks laughing at us."

I sat in the car half listening to Lazeer tell a tale of blood and horror. I could hear choruses of swamp toads mingling with the whine of insects close to my ears, looking for a biting place. A couple of times I had heard the bass throb of a 'gator.

Suddenly Lazeer stopped and I sensed his tenseness. He leaned forward, head cocked. And then, mingled with the wet country shrilling, and then overriding it, I heard the oncoming high-pitched snarl of high combustion.

"Hear it once and you don't forget it," Lazeer said, and unhooked the mike from the dash and got through to McCollum and Gaiders. "He's coming through this end, boys. Get yourself set."

He hung up and in the next instant the C.M. Special went by. It was a resonant howl that stirred echoes inside the inner ear. It was a tearing, bursting rush of wind that rattled fronds and turned leaves over. It was a dark shape in moonlight, slamming by, the howl diminishing as the wind of passage died.

Lazeer plunged the patrol car out onto the road in a screeching turn, and as we straightened out, gathering speed, he yelled to me, "Damn fool runs without lights when the moon is bright enough."

As had been planned, we ran without lights too, to keep Joe Lee from smelling the trap until it was too late. I tightened my seat belt and peered at the moonlit road. Lazeer had estimated we could make it to the far end in ten minutes or a little less. The world was like a photographic negative—white world and black trees and brush, and no shades of grey. As we came quickly up to speed, the heavy sedan began to feel strangely light. It toe-danced, tender and capricious, the wind roar louder than the engine sound. I kept wondering what would happen if Joe Lee stopped dead up there in darkness. I kept staring ahead for the murderous bulk of his vehicle.

Soon I could see the distant red wink of the other sedan, and then the bright cone where the headlights shone off the shoulder into the heavy brush. When my eyes adjusted to that brightness, I could no longer see the road. We came down on them with dreadful speed. Lazeer suddenly snapped our lights on, touched the siren. We were going to see Joe Lee trying to back and turn around on the narrow paved road, and we were going to block him and end the night games.

We saw nothing. Lazeer pumped the brakes. He cursed. We came to a stop ten feet from the side of the other patrol car. McCollum and Gaiders came out of the shadows. Lazeer and I undid our seat belts and got out of the car.

"We didn't see nothing and we didn't hear a thing," Frank Gaiders said.

Lazeer summed it up. "OK, then. I was running without lights too. Maybe the first glimpse he got of your flasher, he cramps it over onto the left shoulder, tucks it over as far as he dares. I could go by without seeing him. He backs around and goes back the way he came, laughing hisself sick. There's the second chance he tried that and took it too far, and he's wedged in a ditch. Then there's the third chance he lost it. He could have dropped a wheel off onto the shoulder and tripped hisself and gone flying three hundred feet into the swamp. So what we do, we go back there slow. I'll go first and keep my spotlight on the right, and you keep yours on the left. Look for that car and for places where he could have busted through."

At the speed Lazeer drove, it took over a half hour to traverse the eighteen-mile stretch. He pulled off at the road where we had waited. He seemed very depressed, yet at the same time amused.

They talked, then he drove me to the courthouse where my car was parked. He said, "We'll work out something tighter and I'll give you a call. You might as well be in at the end."

I drove sedately back to Lauderdale.

Several days later, just before noon on a bright Sunday, Lazeer phoned me at my apartment and said, "You want to be in on the finish of this thing, you better do some hustling and leave right now."

"You've got him?"

"In a manner of speaking." He sounded sad and wry. "He dumped that machine into a canal off Route 27 about twelve miles south of Okeelanta. The wrecker'll be winching it out any time now. The driver says he and the gal are still in it. It's been on the radio news. Diver read the tag, and it's his. Last year's. He didn't trouble hisself getting a new one."

I wasted no time driving to the scene. I certainly had no trouble identifying it. There were at least a hundred cars pulled off on both sides of the highway. A traffic control officer tried to wave me on by, but when I showed him my press card and told him Lazeer had phoned me, he had me turn in and park beside a patrol car near the center of activity.

I spotted Lazeer on the canal bank and went over to him. A big man in face mask, swim fins and air tank was preparing to go down with the wrecker hook.

Lazeer greeted me and said, "It pulled loose the first time, so he's going to try to get it around the rear axle this time. It's in twenty feet of water, right side up, in the black mud."

"Did he lose control?"

"Hard to say. What happened, early this morning a fellow was goofing around in a little airplane, flying low, parallel to the canal, the water like a mirror, and he seen something down in there so he came around and looked again, then he found a way to mark the spot, opposite those three trees away over there, so he came into his home field and phoned it in, and we had that diver down by nine this morning. I got here about ten."

"I guess this isn't the way you wanted it to end, Sergeant."

"It sure God isn't. It was a contest between him and me, and I wanted to get him my own way. But I guess it's a good thing he's off the night roads."

I looked around. The red and white wrecker was positioned and braced. Ambulance attendants were leaning against their vehicle, smoking and chatting. Sunday traffic slowed and was waved on by.

"I guess you could say his team showed up," Lazeer said.

Only then did I realize the strangeness of most of the waiting vehicles. The cars were from a half-dozen counties, according to the tag numbers. There were many big, gaudy, curious monsters not unlike the C.M. Special in basic layout, but quite different in design. They seemed like a visitation of Martian beasts. There were dirty fenderless sedans from the thirties with modern power plants under the hoods, and big rude racing numbers painted on the side doors. There were other cars which looked normal at first glance, but then seemed to squat oddly low, lines clean and sleek where the Detroit chrome had been taken off, the holes leaded up.

The cars and the kids were of another race. Groups of them formed, broke up and re-formed. Radios brought in a dozen stations. They drank Cokes and perched in dense flocks on open convertibles. They wandered from car to car. It had a strange carnival flavor, yet more ceremonial. From time to time somebody would start one of the car engines, rev it up to a bursting roar, and let it die away.

All the girls had long burnished hair and tidy blouses or sun tops and a stillness in their faces, a curious confidence of total acceptance which seemed at odds with the frivolous and provocative tightness of their short shorts, stretch pants, jeans. All the boys were lean, their hairdos carefully ornate, their shoulders high and square, and they moved with the lazy grace of young jungle cats. Some of the couples danced indolently, staring into each other's eyes with a frozen and formal intensity, never touching, bright hair swinging, girls' hips pumping in the stylized ceremonial twist.

Along the line I found a larger group. A boy was strumming slow chords on a guitar, a girl making sharp and erratic fill-in rhythm on a set of bongos. Another boy, in nasal and whining voice, seemed to improvise lyrics as he sang them. "C.M. Special, let it get out and *go.*/C.M. Special, let it way out and *go.*/Iron runs fast and the moon runs slow."

The circle watched and listened with a contained intensity.

Then I heard the winch whining. It seemed to grow louder as, one by one, the other sounds stopped. The kids began moving toward the wrecker. They formed a big silent semicircle. The taut woven cable, coming in very slowly, stretched down at an angle through the sun glitter on the black-brown water.

The snore of a passing truck covered the winch noise for a moment.

"Coming good now," a man said.

First you could see an underwater band of silver, close to the drop-off near the bank. Then the first edges of the big sweeping fins broke the surface, then the broad rear bumper, then the rich curves of the strawberry paint. Where it wasn't clotted with wet weed or stained with mud, the paint glowed rich and new and brilliant. There was a slow sound from the kids, a sigh, a murmur, a shifting.

As it came up further, the dark water began to spurt from it, and as the water level inside dropped, I saw, through a smeared window, the two huddled masses, the slumped boy and girl, side by side, still belted in.

I wanted to see no more. Lazeer was busy, and I got into my car and backed out and went home and mixed a drink.

I started work on it at about three thirty that afternoon. It would be a feature for the following Sunday. I worked right on through until two in the morning. It was only two thousand words, but it was very tricky and I wanted to get it just right. I had to serve two masters. I had to give lip service to the editorial bias that this sort of thing was wrong, yet at the same time I wanted to capture, for my own sake, the flavor of legend. These kids were making a special world we could not share. They were putting all their skills and dreams and energies to work composing the artifacts of a subculture, power, beauty, speed, skill and rebellion. Our culture was giving them damned little, so they were fighting for a world of their own, with its own customs, legends and feats of valor, its own music, its own ethics and morality.

I took it in Monday morning and left it on Si Walther's desk, with the hope that if it were published intact, it might become a classic. I called it "The Little War of Joe Lee Cuddard."

I didn't hear from Si until just before noon. He came out and dropped it on my desk. "Sorry," he said.

"What's the matter with it?"

"Hell, it's a very nice bit. But we don't publish fiction. You should have checked it out better, Marty, like you usually do. The examiner says those kids have been in the bottom of that canal for maybe eight months. I had Sam check her out through the clinic. She was damn near terminal eight months ago. What probably happened, the boy went to see her and found her so bad off he got scared and decided to rush her to Miami. She was still in her pajamas, with a sweater over them. That way it's a human interest bit. I had Helen do it. It's page one this afternoon, boxed."

I took my worthless story, tore it in half and dropped it into the wastebasket. Sergeant Lazeer's bad guess about the identity of his moonlight road runner had made me look like an incompetent jackass. I vowed to check all facts, get all names right, and never again indulge in glowing, strawberry flake prose.

Three weeks later I got a phone call from Sergeant Lazeer.

He said, "I guess you figured out we got some boy coming in from out of county to fun us these moonlight nights."

"Yes, I did."

"I'm right sorry about you wasting that time and effort when we were thinking we were after Joe Lee Cuddard. We're having some bright moonlight about now, and it'll run full tomorrow night. You want to come over, we can show you some fun, be-

cause I got a plan that's dead sure. We tried it last night, but
there was just one flaw, and he got away through a road we
didn't know about. Tomorrow he won't get that chance to melt
away."

I remembered the snarl of that engine, the glimpse of a dark
shape, the great wind of passage. Suddenly the backs of my hands
prickled. I remembered the emptiness of that stretch of road
when we searched it. Could there have been that much pride
and passion, labor and love and hope, that Clarissa May and Joe
Lee could forever ride the night roads of their home county,
balling through the silver moonlight? And what curious message
had assembled all those kids from six counties so quickly?

"You there? You still there?"

"Sorry, I was trying to remember my schedule. I don't think
I can make it."

"Well, we'll get him for sure this time."

"Best of luck, Sergeant."

"Six cars this time. Barricades. And a spotter plane. He hasn't
got a chance if he comes into the net."

I guess I should have gone. Maybe hearing it again, glimpsing
the dark shape, feeling the stir of the night wind, would have
convinced me of its reality. They didn't get him, of course. But
they came so close, so very close. But they left just enough
room between a heavy barricade and a live oak tree, an almost
impossibly narrow place to slam through. But thread it he did,
and rocket back onto the hard top and plunge off, leaving the
fading, dying contralto drone.

Sergeant Lazeer is grimly readying next month's trap. He says
it is the final one. Thus far, all he has captured are the two little
marks, a streak of paint on the rough edge of a timber sawhorse,
another nudge of paint on the trunk of the oak. Strawberry red.
Flecked with gold.

Cry Havoc

Davis Grubb

David Grubb (1919–1980) wrote one of the first modern serial killer novels, the highly praised *Night of the Hunter* (1953). His short fiction, some of which was dramatized on the "Alfred Hitchcock Presents" television series, has been collected into *Twelve Tales of Suspense and the Supernatural* (1964), *The Siege of 318* (1979), and *You Never Believe Me* (1989). Not included in those books is the allegorical ghost story "Cry Havoc," which reflects Grubb's flair for regional dialect and interest in Irish culture.

In 1923 the family Pollixfen migrated from Eire to settle in the small Ohio river town of Glory, West Virginia. Sean Pollixfen was a big florid boast of a man of common heritage. His wife, Deirdre, was a lady of gentle breeding; raised in a Georgian town house in Dublin's Sackville Street, she deplored Sean's harsh upbringing of their only child—ten-year-old Benjamin Michael.

The Pollixfen house was a rambling one-story structure with a great blue front door and slate flagstones set level with its threshold. Their nearest neighbor was a man named Hugger who dwelt a good three blocks up Liberty Avenue.

When the Thing began, it was an autumn night at supper. Benjy abruptly laid down his knife and fork and tilted his ear, harking. "But for what?" Sean asked him.

"I was listening for the auguries of the War that's coming, sor."

"Wisht, now, boyo!" cried Sean. " 'Tis 1932. The Great War ended fourteen years ago this November. And surely there's not another one in sight."

Sean paused, reminiscing, smiling.

"Still, somehow, I'd favor another War," he said. "I'm proud to be wearing the sleeve of this good linen jacket pinned up to me left shoulder. I lost that hook at First Ypres. Yet, despite that, it was a Glory."

Benjy made no reply, though a moment later he left the table, went to the bathroom, and threw up his supper.

Next morning at eight two men pulled up in a truck out front. Moments later they had laboriously borne a huge pine crate to the flagstone threshold and rang the bell. Sean, on his way to his Position at the Firm, answered their ring.

"Is this here the residence of Master Benjamin Michael Pollixfen?"

"It is that," Sean replied, rapping the crate with his malacca cane. " 'Tis another gift for me boy Benjy from his Uncle Liam in Kilronan. He's always sending the lad a grand present, no matter what the occasion!"

That night when they had finished supper, Sean went to Benjy's room. He stared at the great crate's contents, all ranked round the room so thick that one could scarce walk among them. There were 5000 miniature lead soldiers—Boche, French, and English. There was every manner of ammunition and instrument of warfare, from caissons and howitzers to hangars and tarmac for the landing fields of the miniature aircraft of all varieties and types—from Gotha bombers for the Boche to D.H.4's for the British and Bréguets for the French.

"Now Liam is showing good sense," Sean said. "Rocking horses were fine for you a year ago. But you're ten now, Benjy. 'Tis time you learned the lessons of Life's most glorious Game!"

Benjy stared at the little soldiers, cast and tinted down to the very wrinkle of a puttee, the drape of a trench coat. Moreover, no two soldiers wore the same facial expressions. Benjy could read in these faces Fear, Zest, Valor, Humdrum, Cravenness, Patriotism, and Sedition. And somehow each of them seemed waiting. But for what? For whom? Sean missed seeing these subtleties. Yet Benjy saw. Benjy knew. Aye, he knew all too well.

"They are green, dads," Benjy said. "Green as the turf of Saint Stephens Green park. The British officers are just days out of Sandhurst, the gun crews hardly a fortnight from the machine-gun school at Wisquies. They don't know the noise of a whizbang from a four-ten or a five-nine. Yet once they've been through a bloody baptism such as Hannescamps or the Somme they'll know. Aye, they'll know then."

"And what would *you* be knowing of Hannescamps or the Somme?" Sean chuckled.

Benjy made no reply.

And so the three strange weeks of it began. Benjy spent every waking hour working feverishly in the great black lot of nonarable ground beyond Deirdre's flower-and-kitchen garden. While about him all the world seemed filled with the sound of locusts sawing down the great green tree of summer.

Benjy carved out the laceries of trenches with his Swiss Army knife. He found strips of lath and split them to lay down as duckboards. He sandbagged the trenches well in front. Beyond this he staked, on ten-penny nails, the thin barbed wire which had come on spools in the great crate. Some distance to the rear of both sides he set up his little field hospitals, and his hangars and the tarmac fields for the little fighter, reconnaissance, and bombing planes.

At the kitchen door Sean would watch the boy and listen as Benjy chanted songs that Sean and his man had sung at Locrehof Farm or Trone Woods once they'd billeted down for a night in some daub-and-wattle stable. He could fairly smell the sweet ammoniac scent of the manure of kine, lambs, and goats, and the fragrance as well of the Gold Flake and State Express cigarettes they smoked, saving only enough to barter for a bottle or two of Pichon Longueville '89 or perhaps a liter of Paul Ruinart.

Strange to relate, it had not yet begun to trouble Sean that the boy knew of these things, that he sang songs Sean had never taught him and sometimes in French which *no one* had ever taught him. As for Benjy he soon began to show the strain. Deirdre's scale in the bathroom showed that in ten days he had lost twelve pounds. He seldom finished supper. For there was that half-hour's extra twilight to work in. Sean gloated. Deirdre grieved.

"Why in Saint Brigid's blessed name don't you put an end to it?" she would plead.

"No, woman, I shan't."

"And why not then?"

"Because me boyo shall grow up to be what I wanted for

meself—a soldier poet more glorious than Rupert Brooke or the taffy Wilfred Owen."

"And then dead of their cursed war—dead before they could come to full flower of Saint Brigid's sacred gift."

"So much the better," Sean replied icily one night. "We must all die one day or another. And no man knows the hour. Death it has no clocks. Moreover, we are Pollixfens, Kin on me father's side to Eire's glory of poets—William Butler Yeats."

"But Yeats died in no war," Deirdre protested.

"Better he had," Sean said. " 'Twould have increased his esteem a thousandfold."

Deirdre went off to bed weeping.

Next night in Benjy's room Sean spoke his dreams out plain.

" 'Tis stark truth, old man," he said. "Real War is a rough go. But there is that Glory of Glories in it."

Benjy said nothing.

"Don't you understand me, boyo? Glory!"

"I see no Glory," said the child. "I see poor fools butchering each other for reasons kept secret from them. Oh, they give reasons. King and Country. They leave out, of course, Industry. No, dads, there are no fields of Honor. There are only insane abattoirs."

Sean colored at this, got up and strode from the boy's room. Yet a minute later, unable to contain himself, he was back.

"Now, boyo!" he cried out. "Either you shed from yourself these craven, blasphemous, and treasonable speculations or I shall leave you to grow up and learn War the hard way. As did I."

"And what might that mean, sor?"

"It means that I shall go to Al Hugger's ga-rage and fetch home three ten-gallon tins of petrol and douse the length and breadth of your little No Man's Land of toys and then set a lucifer to it."

"That would be a most fearsome mistake, sor. For on the morning when the little armies came they were mine. Now I am Theirs. And so, poor dads, are you."

"That does it then! 'Tis petrol and a lucifer for all five thousand of the little perishers!"

Benjy smiled, sadly.

"But 'tis no longer a skimpy five thousand now, man dear.

'Tis close to a million. Perhaps more. Even files-on-parade could not count their hosts.''

Wisht, now! How could that be? Did Liam send you another great crate?''

"No, sor. There's been Conscription on both sides. And enlistments by the million. A fair fever of outrage infects every man and boy of the King's Realm from Land's End to Aberdeen since Lord Kitchener went down in one of his Majesty's dreadnaughts off the Dolomites. Then there's Foch and Clemenceau and Joffre. They've whipped up the zest of Frenchmen to a pitch not known since the days of Robespierre and Danton in the Terror. In Germany the Boche seethe at every word from Hindenburg or Ludendorf or Kaiser Willie.''

Benjy chuckled, despite himself.

"Willie—the English King's cousin! Willie and Georgie! Lord, 'tis more of a family squabble than a War!''

He sobered then.

"No, sor,'' Benjy said. "Cry havoc now and let loose the dogs of War!''

Sean stared, baffled.

"Tell me, boyo. If you loathe War so, why do you go at your little War game with such zest?''

"Why, because there's twins inside me, I suppose.'' Benjy replied, and press him as he might, Sean could elicit no more from the boy.

Sean's face sobered. He went off with a troubled mind to Deirdre in their goose-down bed. Lying there on his back he could hear Benjy singing an old war ditty—*The Charlie Chaplin Walk*. Sean's batman, a Nottinghamshire collier, had used to sing that before the Somme. Sean was drowsy but could not sleep. Yet soon he roused up wide-waking from the drowsiness. Was it thunder he heard out yonder in the night? And that flickering light across the sill of the back window. Was it heat lightning?

He stole from Deirdre's sound-sleeping side and stared out the rear window. A river fog lay waist deep upon the land. Among the tinted autumn trees the cold sweet light of fireflies came and went as though they were stars that could not make up their minds. Yet the flashes and flames that flickered beneath the cloak of mists on the black lot were not sweet, not cold.

Sean could hear the small smart chatter of machine guns.

There were the blasts of howitzers and whizbangs and mortars. Above the shallow sea of leprous white mists the Aviatiks and Sopwith Strutters swooped and dove and immelmaned in dogfights.

Far to the rear Sean could see Benjy in his peejays, standing and watching.The child's wild face was grievous and weeping. He had flung out his spindly arms as if transcendentally to appease the madness to which he bore such suffering witness.

Sean crept shivering back into the bed. He lay awake, again thinking of Liam's great gift that had come to life, proliferated, and had now taken possession both of himself and Benjy.

And it went on thus. For another two weeks. Then one morning all was changed. Pale, half staggering from lack of sleep and haggard-eyed from poring over the war map thumbtacked to his play table beneath the gooseneck lamp's harsh circle of illumination. Benjy—almost faint—came down to breakfast all smiles.

"What does that Chessy cat grin on your face mean, boyo?" Sean asked.

"C'est la guerre, mon vieux, c'est la guerre!" cried Benjy. "But last night news came through—"

"C'est la guerre and so on." Deirdre intervened. "And what might that alien phrase mean to these poor untutored ears?"

" 'Tis French," Sean said. "That's War, old man, that's War."

"But now—tomorrow night at midnight—it will be over!" Benjy cried brightly.

"Tomorrow night and midnight be damned!" Sean exclaimed. *"Tonight* at midnight it shall end! I am unable to endure another night of it, and so I have determined to end it all meself! Benjy, I swear now by the holy martyred names of the Insurrection of Easter '16—Pearse, Casement, John Connolly, and the O'Rahilly—that I shall not let this thing possess the two of us for even one night more! I shall end it with me petrol and me lucifer at midnight tonight!"

"Lord save us, dads, you mustn't talk so!" cried Benjy. "Word has been flashed to all forces up and down the lines that the cease-fire is set for tomorrow's midnight. Already the gunfire is only token. Already the men crawl fearlessly over sandbags and under the barbed wire and march boldly into the midst of No Man's Land to embrace each other. They barter toffees and jars of Bovrils and tins of chocs for marzipan and *fastnacht krapfen* and strudels and *himbeer kuchen*! They show each other sweat-and-muck-smeared snapshots of mothers, sweethearts, and children back home. Men who a day ago were at each other's throats!"

Deirdre watched and listened, helpless, baffled, appalled.

"No matter to all the sweet sticky treacle of your talk!" Sean cried, "I'll not let this madness take possession of our home! So 'tis petrol and a lucifer to the whole game tonight at the strike of twelve! And a fiery fitting end to it all!"

"Bloody ballocks to that!" shouted Benjy, outraged.

"Go to your room, boy," Sean said, struggling to control himself. "We have man's words to say. Not words for the hearing of your mum."

A moment later Sean was strutting the length and breadth of Benjy's bedroom like a bloated popinjay. His swagger stick was in his hand; it seemed to give him back some of his old lost Valor, some long mislaid or time-rotted Authority. As he walked he slapped it in vainglorious bellicosity against his thigh.

Benjy watched him solemnly, sadly. "They'll not let you do this thing," he said. He paused. "Nor shall I."

Sean whirled, glaring.

"Ah, so it has come to that then!" he barked out in the voice of a glory-gutted martinet. " 'Tis they shan't and I shan't and you shan't, eh? Well, we shall see about that! I am King of this house. And I am King of all its environs!"

"No," Benjy said, his face above the war map tacked to his table. "You are no King. You are a King's Fool. Though lacking in a King's Fool's traditional and customary wisdom and vision."

Sean broke then. In a stride he crossed the room and slashed the boy across the face with the swagger stick.

A thin ribbon of blood coursed down from the corner of Benjy's mouth. A droplet of it splattered like a tiny crimson starfish or a mark on the map to commemorate some dreadful battle encounter.

"King, I say! King!" Sean was shouting, pacing the room again. There was a livid stripe across the child's cheek where the leather had fallen. But there was even more change in Benjy's face. And even something newer, something darker in the mind behind that face. The boy smiled.

"Come then," Benjy said softly. "Let us sit a while and tell sad stories of the Death of Kings."

The next day neither child nor father spoke nor looked each other in the eye. When occasionally they would be forced to pass in a corridor, it was in the stiff-legged, ominous manner of pit-bulls circling in a small seat-encircled arena. Deirdre, sensing something dreadful between them, was helplessly distraught. For what did she know of any of it, dear gentle Deirdre?

Benjy did not appear for supper. Sean ate ravenously. When he was done he drove his car into town and came back moments later with the three ten-gallon tins of petrol. He ranked them neatly alongside the black lot's border.

At nine Sean and Deirdre went to bed. For three hours Sean lay staring at the bar of harvest moonlight which fell across the carpet from the window sill to the threshold of the bedroom door. Now and again halfhearted gunfire could be heard from the black lot. Soon Sean began speaking within himself a wordless colloquy. Fear had begun to steal upon him. Misgivings. He could not forget the Thing he had seen in the boy's face after the blow of the stiff, hardened leather. He could never forget the strange new timbre of the boy's voice when he spoke softly shortly after.

As the great clock in the hallway struck the chime of eleven thirty, Sean decided to forego the whole headstrong project. Let the cease-fire come in its ordained time. What could another twenty-four hours matter? There was scarcely any War waging in the black lot anyway. Cheered by his essentially craven decision he started, in his night shirt, down the hallway toward Benjy's room to inform him of his change of mind.

Within ten feet of the boy's bolted door Sean came to a standstill. He listened. It was unmistakable. The tiny quacking chatter of a voice speaking from a field telephone. And Benjy's murmurous voice giving orders back. Only one phrase caught Sean's ear. And that phrase set beads of sweat glistening on his face in the pallid gaslight of the long broad hallway. The words were in French. But Sean knew French.

"On a besoin des assassins."

Sean felt a chill seize him, shaming the manhood of him. "We now have need of the assassins."

Shamed to the core of his soul, Sean fled back to the bedroom.

With his one arm he turned the key in the door lock. With that same arm he fetched a ladder-back chair from against the wall and propped the top rung under the knob. Then he hastened to the bureau drawer where he kept the memorabilia of his old long-forgotten War and fetched out his BEF Webley.

The pistol was still well greased. It was loaded, the cartridge pins a little dark with verdigris but operable. Then Sean went and lay atop the quilt, shivering and clutching the silly, ineffectual pistol in his hand.

That was when he first heard them. Myriad feet; tiny footsteps and not those of small animals with clawed and padded paws. Boots. Tiny boots. The myriad scrape of microscopically small hobnails. Boots. By the thousands. By the thousands of thousands. And then abruptly above their measured, disciplined tread there burst forth suddenly the skirl of Royal Scots' Highlanders' bagpipes, the rattle of tiny drums, the piercing tweedle of little fifes, the brash impudence of German brass bands.

Deirdre still slept. Even the nights of the War in the black lot had never wakened her. It was to Sean's credit that he did not rouse her now. For, as never before in this life—not even in the inferno of First Ypres or the Somme—had he so craved the company of another mortal. A word. A touch. A look.

Abruptly, just beyond the door, there was a command followed by total silence. Sean chuckled. They were not out there. It had been a fantasy of his overwrought mind. A nightmare—a *cauchmare* as the French call it. But his tranquillity was short-lived. He heard a tiny voice in German crying orders to crank a howitzer to its proper angle of trajectory. Another shouted command. Sean sensed, with an old soldier's instinct, the yank of the lanyard. He heard the detonation, felt the hot Krupp steel barrel's recoil, saw flame flare as the shell blasted a ragged hole in the door where the lock had been.

The impact flung the door wide and sent the chair spinning across the moonlit carpet. And now, in undisciplined and furious anarchy, they swarmed across the door sill like a blanket of gray putrescent mud. Gone from them were the gay regimental colors, the spit-and-polish decorum of the morning of the great crate's arrival. Now they were muck-draped and gangrenous, unwashed and stinking of old deaths, old untended wounds. Some knuckled their way on legless stumps. Others hobbled savagely on make-shift crutches.

Sean sat up and emptied every bullet from the Webley into their midst. He might as well have sought to slaughter the sea with handfuls of flung seashells. All of them wore tiny gas masks. A shouted command and small steel cylinders on miniature wheeled platforms were trundled across the door sill and ranked before the bed. Another shout and gun crews of four men each wheeled in, to face the bed, behind the gas cylinders, ten Lewis and ten Maxim machine guns.

At a cry from the leader these now began a racking enfilade of Sean's body. He had but time to cross himself and begin a Hail Mary when the cocks of the little gas cylinders were screwed open and the first green cloud of gas reached his nostrils. Enveloped in a cloud of gas, the big man uttered one last choking scream and slid into the carpet and into their very midst.

In a twinkling they swarmed over him like a vast shroud of living manure. They stabbed him with the needle points of their tiny bayonets, again and again. At last one of these sought out and found the big man's jugular vein. A shouted command again. the lift and fall of a bloody saber.

"All divisions—ri' tur'!"

And to a man they obeyed.

"All divisions—'orm rank!"

Again they obeyed.

"All divisions—quick 'arch!"

And with pipers skirling, drums drubbing, fifes shrilling, and brass bands blaring they went the way they had come. The siege was a *fait accompli.*

Awakened by all the gunfire and clamor at last, and at the very moment of the door's collapse, Deirdre sat up, watching throughout. First in smiling disbelief, then in fruitless attempt to persuade herself that she was dreaming it all, then in acceptance, and, at last, in horror. Now as the first wisps of the chlorine stung her nostrils she went raving and irreversibly insane, sprang from her side of the bed, and hurtled through the side window, taking screen and all, to tumble onto the turf three feet below.

In the hushed autumn street of the night Deirdre, beneath the moon and the galaxies and the cold promiscuous fireflies, fled back into the hallucination of Youth returned. She raced up and down under the tinted trees. She twirled an imaginary pink lace parasol as if doing a turn on a small stage. She chanted the Harry Lauder and Vesta Tilley ballads from the music halls of her Dublin girlhood.

Wakened by all this daft medley of unfamiliar songs, Al Hugger, the nearest neighbor, took down his old AEF Springfield rifle and came to the house to discover what calamity had befallen it.

When, at last, he stood in the bedroom doorway, he looked first at the monstrous ruin which had been Sean, humped in his blood on the carpet by the bed. Then Hugger saw the blasé and unruffled figure of Benjy, clad only in his peejays and sitting straight as the blackthorn stick of a Connaught County squire in the ladder-back chair now back against the wall. Almost all the gas had been cleared from the room by the clean river wind which coursed steadily between the two open windows.

"No one," Hugger said presently—more to himself than to the child—"shall likely ever know what happened in this room tonight. Better they don't. Yes, I hope they don't. Never. For there is something about it all—something—"

Benjy yawned. Prodigiously. He smiled hospitably at Al Hugger. He looked at the Thing—like a great beached whale—on the carpet by the bedside. He yawned again.

"*C'est la guerre, mon vieux, c'est la guerre,*" he said.

Night-Side

To Gloria Whelan

Joyce Carol Oates

A prolific essayist, poet, and critic, Joyce Carol Oates (1938–   ) published her acclaimed first story collection, *By the North Gate* (1963), when she was only twenty-five and won the National Book Award for her novel *them* (1970). An undercurrent of the dark and grotesque runs through much of her fiction, including the gothic trilogy *Bellefleur* (1980), *A Bloodsmoor Romance* (1982), and *Mysteries of Winterthurn* (1984), and the four psychological suspense novels published under her Rosamond Smith pseudonym. "Night-Side," from her stunning collection *Night-Side: Eighteen Tales* (1977), is one of the most haunting stories ever written about man's confrontation with the Unknown.

6 February 1887. Quincy, Massachusetts. Montague House.

Disturbing experience at Mrs. A———'s home yesterday evening. Few theatrics—comfortable though rather pathetically shabby surroundings—an only mildly sinister atmosphere (especially in contrast to the Walpurgis Night presented by that shameless charlatan in Portsmouth: the Dwarf Eustace who presumed to introduce me to Swedenborg himself, under the erroneous impression that I am a member of the Church of the New Jerusalem—*I*!). Nevertheless I came away disturbed, and my conversa-

193

tion with Dr. Moore afterward, at dinner, though dispassionate
and even, at times, a bit flippant, did not settle my mind.
Perry Moore is of course a hearty materialist, an Aristotelian-
Spencerian with a love of good food and drink, and an appreciation of the more nonsensical vagaries of life; when in his company
I tend to support that general view, as I do at the University as
well—for there is a terrific pull in my nature toward the gregari-
ous that I cannot resist. (That I do not wish to resist.) Once I
am alone with my thoughts, however, I am accursed with doubts
about my own position and nothing seems more precarious than
my intellectual "convictions."

The more hardened members of our Society, like Perry Moore,
are apt to put the issue bluntly: Is Mrs. A———of Quincy a
conscious or unconscious fraud? The conscious frauds are relatively easy to deal with; once discovered, they prefer to erase
themselves from further consideration. The unconscious frauds
are not, in a sense, "frauds" at all. It would certainly be difficult
to prove criminal intention. Mrs. A———, for instance, does not
accept money or gifts so far as we have been able to determine,
and both Perry Moore and I noted her courteous but firm refusal
of the Judge's offer to send her and her husband (presumably
ailing?) on holiday to England in the spring. She is a mild, self-
effacing, rather stocky woman in her mid-fifties who wears her
hair parted in the center, like several of my maiden aunts, and
whose sole item of adornment was an old-fashioned cameo
brooch; her black dress had the appearance of having been home-
made, though it was attractive enough, and freshly ironed. According to the Society's records she has been a practicing medium
now for six years. Yet she lives, still, in an undistinguished section of Quincy, in a neighborhood of modest frame dwellings.
The A———s' house is in fairly good condition, especially considering the damage routinely done by our winters, and the only
room we saw, the parlor, is quite ordinary, with overstuffed
chairs and the usual cushions and a monstrous horsehair sofa
and, of course, the oaken table; the atmosphere would have been
so conventional as to have seemed disappointing had not Mrs.
A———made an attempt to brighten it, or perhaps to give it a
glamourously occult air, by hanging certain watercolors about the
room. (She claims that the watercolors were "done" by one of
her contact spirits, a young Iroquois girl who died in the seven-

teen seventies of smallpox. They are touchingly garish—mandalas and triangles and stylized eyeballs and even a transparent Cosmic Man with Indian-black hair.)

At last night's sitting there were only three persons in addition to Mrs. A————. Judge T————of the New York State Supreme Court (now retired); Dr. Moore; and I, Jarvis Williams. Dr. Moore and I came out from Cambridge under the aegis of the Society for Psychical Research in order to make a preliminary study of the kind of mediumship Mrs. A————affects. We did not bring a stenographer along this time though Mrs. A———— indicated her willingness to have the sitting transcribed; she struck me as being rather warmly cooperative, and even interested in our formal procedures, though Perry Moore remarked afterward at dinner that she had struck him as "noticeably reluctant." She was, however, flustered at the start of the séance and for a while it seemed as if we and the Judge might have made the trip for nothing. (She kept waving her plump hands about like an embarrassed hostess, apologizing for the fact that the spirits were evidently in a "perverse uncommunicative mood tonight.")

She did go into trance eventually, however. The four of us were seated about the heavy round table from approximately 6:50 P.M. to 9 P.M. For nearly forty-five minutes Mrs. A———— made abortive attempts to contact her Chief Communicator and then slipped abruptly into trance (dramatically, in fact: her eyes rolled back in her head in a manner that alarmed me at first), and a personality named Webley appeared. "Webley's" voice appeared to be coming from several directions during the course of the sitting. At all times it was at least three yards from Mrs. A————; despite the semi-dark of the parlor I believe I could see the woman's mouth and throat clearly enough, and I could not detect any obvious signs of ventriloquism. (Perry Moore, who is more experienced than I in psychical research, and rather more casual about the whole phenomenon, claims he has witnessed feats of ventriloquism that would make poor Mrs. A————look quite shabby in comparison.) "Webley's" voice was raw, singsong, peculiarly disturbing. At times it was shrill and at other times so faint as to be nearly inaudible. Something brattish about it. Exasperating. "Webley" took care to pronounce his

final *g*'s in a self-conscious manner, quite unlike Mrs. A———.
(Which could be, of course, a deliberate ploy.)

This Webley is one of Mrs. A———'s most frequent manifest-
ing spirits, though he is not the most reliable. Her Chief Communicator is a Scots patriarch who lived "in the time of Merlin"
and who is evidently very wise; unfortunately he did not choose
to appear yesterday evening. Instead, Webley presided. He is
supposed to have died some seventy-five years ago at the age of
nineteen in a house just up the street from the A———s'. He
was either a butcher's helper or an apprentice tailor. He died in
a fire—or by a "slow dreadful crippling disease"—or beneath a
horse's hooves, in a freakish accident; during the course of the
sitting he alluded self-pityingly to his death but seemed to have
forgotten the exact details. At the very end of the evening he
addressed me directly as Dr. Williams of Harvard University,
saying that since I had influential friends in Boston I could help
him with his career—it turned out he had written hundreds of
songs and poems and parables but none had been published;
would I please find a publisher for his work? Life had treated him
so unfairly. His talent—his genius—had been lost to humanity. I
had it within my power to help him, he claimed, was I not *obliged*
to help him . . . ? He then sang one of his songs, which sounded
to me like an old ballad; many of the words were so shrill as to be
unintelligible, but he sang it just the same, repeating the verses in
a haphazard order:

> *This ae nighte, this ae nighte,*
> *—Every nighte and alle,*
> *Fire and fleet and candle-lighte,*
> *And Christe receive thy saule.*
> *When thou from hence away art past,*
> *—Every nighte and alle,*
> *To Whinny-muir thou com'st at last:*
> *And Christie receive thy saule.*
>
> *From Brig o' Dread when thou may'st pass,*
> *—Every nighte and alle,*
> *The whinnes sall prick thee to the bare bane:*
> *And Christe receive thy saule.*

The elderly Judge T———had come up from New York City
in order, as he earnestly put it, to "speak directly to his deceased
wife as he was never able to do while she was living"; but Webley
treated the old gentleman in a high-handed, cavalier manner, as
if the occasion were not at all serious. He kept saying, "Who is
there tonight? *Who* is there? Let them introduce themselves
again—I don't *like* strangers! I tell you I don't *like* strangers!"
Though Mrs. A———had informed us beforehand that we would
witness no physical phenomena, there were, from time to time,
glimmerings of light in the darkened room, hardly more than the
tiny pulsations of light made by fireflies; and both Perry Moore
and I felt the table vibrating beneath our fingers. At about the
time when Webley gave way to the spirit of Judge T———'s
wife, the temperature in the room seemed to drop suddenly and
I remember being gripped by a sensation of panic—but it lasted
only an instant and I was soon myself again. (Dr. Moore claimed
not to have noticed any drop in temperature and Judge T———
was so rattled after the sitting that it would have been pointless
to question him.)

The séance proper was similar to others I have attended. A
spirit—or a voice—laid claim to being the late Mrs. T———;
this spirit addressed the survivor in a peculiarly intense, urgent
manner, so that it was rather embarrassing to be present. Judge
T———was soon weeping. His deeply creased face glistened with
tears like a child's.

"Why Darrie! *Darrie!* Don't cry! Oh don't cry!" the spirit said.
"No one is dead, Darrie. There is no death. No death! . . . Can
you hear me, Darrie? Why are you so frightened? So upset? No
need, Darrie, no need! Grandfather and Lucy and I are together
here—happy together. Darrie, look up! Be brave, my dear! My
poor frightened dear! We never knew each other, did we? My
poor dear! My love! . . . I saw you in a great transparent house,
a great burning house; poor Darrie, they told me you were ill,
you were weak with fever; all the rooms of the house were aflame
and the staircase was burnt to cinders, but there were figures
walking up and down, Darrie, great numbers of them, and you
were among them, dear, stumbling in your fright—so clumsy!
Look up, dear, and shade your eyes, and you will see me. Grandfather helped me—did you know? Did I call out his name at the
end? My dear, my darling, it all happened so quickly—we never

knew each other, did we? Don't be hard on Annie! Don't be cruel! Darrie? Why are you crying?" And gradually the spirit voice grew fainter; or perhaps something went wrong and the channels of communication were no longer clear. There were repetitions, garbled phrases, meaningless queries of "Dear? Dear?" that the Judge's replies did not seem to placate. The spirit spoke of her gravesite, and of a trip to Italy taken many years before, and of a dead or unborn baby, and again of Annie—evidently Judge T———'s daughter; but the jumble of words did not always make sense and it was a great relief when Mrs. A———suddenly woke from her trance.

Judge T———rose from the table, greatly agitated. He wanted to call the spirit back; he had not asked her certain crucial questions; he had been overcome by emotion and had found it difficult to speak, to interrupt the spirit's monologue. But Mrs. A———(who looked shockingly tired) told him the spirit would not return again that night and they must not make any attempt to call it back.

"The other world obeys its own laws," Mrs. A———said in her small, rather reedy voice.

We left Mrs. A———'s home shortly after 9:00 P.M. I too was exhausted; I had not realized how absorbed I had been in the proceedings.

Judge T———is also staying at Montague House, but he was too upset after the sitting to join us for dinner. He assured us, though, that the spirit was authentic—the voice had been his wife's, he was certain of it, he would stake his life on it. She had never called him "Darrie" during her lifetime, wasn't it odd that she called him "Darrie" now?—and was so concerned for him, so loving?—and concerned for their daughter as well? He was very moved. He had a great deal to think about. (Yes, he'd had a fever some weeks ago—a severe attack of bronchitis and a fever; in fact, he had not completely recovered.) What was extraordinary about the entire experience was the wisdom revealed: There is no death.

There is no death.

Dr. Moore and I dined heartily on roast crown of lamb, spring potatoes with peas, and buttered cabbage. We were served two kinds of bread—German rye and sour-cream rolls; the hotel's

butter was superb; the wine excellent; the dessert—crepes with
cream and toasted almonds—looked marvelous, though I had not
any appetite for it. Dr. Moore was ravenously hungry. He talked
as he ate, often punctuating his remarks with rich bursts of laughter. It was his opinion, of course, that the medium was a fraud—
and not a very skillful fraud, either. In his fifteen years of amateur, intermittent investigations he had encountered far more
skillful mediums. Even the notorious Eustace with his levitating
tables and hobgoblin chimes and shrieks was cleverer than Mrs.
A———; one knew of course that Eustace was a cheat, but one
was hard pressed to explain his method. Whereas Mrs. A———
was quite transparent.

Dr. Moore spoke for some time in his amiable, dogmatic way.
He ordered brandy for both of us, though it was nearly midnight
when we finished our dinner and I was anxious to get to bed. (I
hoped to rise early and work on a lecture dealing with Kant's
approach to the problem of Free Will, which I would be deliv-
ering in a few days.) But Dr. Moore enjoyed talking and seemed
to have been invigorated by our experience at Mrs. A———'s.

At the age of forty-three Perry Moore is only four years my
senior, but he has the air, in my presence at least, of being
considerably older. He is a second cousin of my mother, a very
successful physician with a bachelor's flat and office in Louisburg
Square; his failure to marry, or his refusal, is one of Boston's
perennial mysteries. Everyone agrees that he is learned, witty,
charming, and extraordinarily intelligent. Striking rather than
conventionally handsome, with a dark, lustrous beard and darkly
bright eyes, he is an excellent amateur violinist, an enthusiastic
sailor, and a lover of literature—his favorite writers are Fielding,
Shakespeare, Horace, and Dante. He is, of course, the perfect
investigator in spiritualist matters since he is detached from the
phenomena he observes and yet he is indefatigably curious; he
has a positive love, a mania, for facts. Like the true scientist he
seeks facts that, assembled, may possibly give rise to hypotheses:
he does not set out with a hypothesis in mind, like a sort of
basket into which certain facts may be tossed, helter-skelter,
while others are conventionally ignored. In all things he is an
empiricist who accepts nothing on faith.

"If the woman is a fraud, then," I say hesitantly, "you believe she is a self-deluded fraud? And her spirits' information is gained by means of telepathy?"

"Telepathy indeed. There can be no other explanation," Dr. Moore says emphatically. "By some means not yet known to science . . . by some uncanny means she suppresses her conscious personality . . . and thereby releases other, secondary personalities that have the power of seizing upon others' thoughts and memories. It's done in a way not understood by science at the present time. But it will be understood eventually. Our investigations into the unconscious powers of the human mind are just beginning; we're on the threshold, really, of a new era."

"So she simply picks out of her clients' minds whatever they want to hear," I say slowly. "And from time to time she can even tease them a little—insult them, even: she can unloose a creature like that obnoxious Webley upon a person like Judge T——without fear of being discovered. Telepathy. . . . Yes, that would explain a great deal. Very nearly everything we witnessed tonight."

"Everything, I should say," Dr. Moore says.

In the coach returning to Cambridge I set aside Kant and my lecture notes and read Sir Thomas Browne: *Light that makes all things seen, makes some things invisible. The greatest mystery of Religion is expressed by adumbration.*

19 March 1887. Cambridge, 11 P.M.

Walked ten miles this evening; must clear cobwebs from mind.

Unhealthy atmosphere. Claustrophobic. Last night's sitting in Quincy—a most unpleasant experience.

(Did not tell my wife what happened. Why is she so curious about the Spirit World?—about Perry Moore?)

My body craves more violent physical activity. In the summer, thank God, I will be able to swim in the ocean: the most strenuous and challenging of exercises.

Jotting down notes re the Quincy experience:

I. Fraud

Mrs. A——, possibly with accomplices, conspires to deceive: she does research into her clients' lives beforehand, possibly bribes servants. She is either a very skillful ventriloquist or works with someone who is. (Husband? Son? The husband is a retired cabinetmaker said to be in poor health; possibly consumptive. The son, married, lives in Waterbury.)

Her stated wish to avoid publicity and her declining of payment may simply be ploys; she may intend to make a great deal of money at some future time.

(Possibility of blackmail?—might be likely in cases similar to Perry Moore's.)

II. Non-fraud
Naturalistic
1. Telepathy. She reads minds of clients.
2. "Multiple personality" of medium. Aspects of her own buried psyche are released as her conscious personality is suppressed. These secondary beings are in mysterious rapport with the "secondary" personalities of the clients.

Spiritualistic
1. The controls are genuine communicators, intermediaries between our world and the world of the dead. These spirits give way to other spirits, who then speak through the medium; or
2. These spirits *influence* the medium, who relays their messages using her own vocabulary. Their personalities are then filtered through and limited by hers.
3. The spirits are not those of the deceased; they are perverse, willful spirits. (Perhaps demons? But there are no demons.)

III. Alternative hypothesis
Madness: the medium is mad, the clients are mad, even the detached, rationalist investigators are mad.

Yesterday evening at Mrs. A———'s home, the second sitting Perry Moore and I observed together, along with Miss Bradley, a stenographer from the Society, and two legitimate clients—a Brookline widow, Mrs. P———, and her daughter Clara, a handsome young woman in her early twenties. Mrs. A———exactly as she appeared to us in February; possibly a little stouter. Wore black dress and cameo brooch. Served Lapsang tea, tiny sandwiches, and biscuits when we arrived shortly after 6 P.M. Seemed quite friendly to Perry, Miss Bradley, and me; fussed over us,

like any hostess; chattered a bit about the cold spell. Mrs.
P——and her daughter arrived at six-thirty and the sitting
began shortly thereafter.

Jarring from the very first. A babble of spirit voices. Mrs.
A——in trance, head flung back, mouth gaping, eyes rolled
upward. Queer. Unnerving. I glanced at Dr. Moore but he
seemed unperturbed, as always. The widow and her daughter,
however, looked as frightened as I felt.

Why are we here, sitting around this table?

What do we believe we will discover?

What are the risks we face . . . ?

"Webley" appeared and disappeared in a matter of minutes.
His shrill, raw, aggrieved voice was supplanted by that of a creature of indeterminate sex who babbled in Gaelic. This creature
in turn was supplanted by a hoarse German, a man who identified himself as Felix; he spoke a curiously ungrammatical German. For some minutes he and two or three other spirits
quarreled. (Each declared himself Mrs. A——'s Chief Communicator for the evening.) Small lights flickered in the semi-dark
of the parlor and the table quivered beneath my fingers and I
felt, or believed I felt, something brushing against me, touching
the back of my head. I shuddered violently but regained my
composure at once. An unidentified voice proclaimed in English
that the Spirit of our Age was Mars: there would be a cata-
strophic war shortly and most of the world's population would
be destroyed. All atheists would be destroyed. Mrs. A——
shook her head from side to side as if trying to wake. Webley
appeared, crying "Hello? Hello? I can't see anyone! Who is
there? Who has called me?" but was again supplanted by another
spirit who shouted long strings of words in a foreign language.
[Note: I discovered a few days later that this language was Walachian, a Romanian dialect. Of course Mrs. A——, whose
ancestors are English, could not possibly have known Walachian,
and I rather doubt that the woman has even heard of the Walachian people.]

The sitting continued in this chaotic way for some minutes.
Mrs. P——must have been quite disappointed, since she had
wanted to be put in contact with her deceased husband. (She
needed advice on whether or not to sell certain pieces of property.) Spirits babbled freely in English, German, Gaelic, French,

even in Latin, and at one point Dr. Moore queried a spirit in Greek, but the spirit retreated at once as if not equal to Dr. Moore's wit. The atmosphere was alarming but at the same time rather manic; almost jocular. I found myself suppressing laughter. Something touched the back of my head and I shivered violently and broke into perspiration, but the experience was not altogether unpleasant; it would be very difficult for me to characterize it.

And then—

And then, suddenly, everything changed. There was complete calm. A spirit voice spoke gently out of a corner of the room, addressing Perry Moore by his first name in a slow, tentative, groping way. "Perry? Perry . . . ?" Dr. Moore jerked about in his seat. He was astonished; I could see by his expression that the voice belonged to someone he knew.

"Perry . . . ? This is Brandon. I've waited so long for you, Perry, how could you be so selfish? I forgave you. Long ago. You couldn't help your cruelty and I couldn't help my innocence. Perry? My glasses have been broken—I can't see. I've been afraid for so long, Perry, please have mercy on me! I can't bear it any longer. I didn't *know* what it would be like. There are crowds of people here, but we can't see one another, we don't know one another, we're strangers, there is a universe of strangers—I can't see anyone clearly—I've been lost for twenty years. Perry, I've been waiting for you for twenty years! You don't dare turn away again, Perry! Not again! Not after so long!"

Dr. Moore stumbled to his feet, knocking his chair aside.

"No— Is it— I don't believe—"

"Perry? Perry? Don't abandon me again, Perry! Not again!"

"What is this?" Dr. Moore cried.

He was on his feet now; Mrs. A————woke from her trance with a groan. The women from Brookline were very upset and I must admit that I was in a mild state of terror, my shirt and my underclothes drenched with perspiration.

The sitting was over. It was only seven-thirty.

"Brandon?" Dr. Moore cried. "Wait. Where are—? Brandon? Can you hear me? Where are you? Why did you do it, Brandon? Wait! Don't leave! Can't anyone call him back— Can't anyone help me—"

Mrs. A——rose unsteadily. She tried to take Dr. Moore's hands in hers but he was too agitated.

"I heard only the very last words," she said. "They're always that way—so confused, so broken—the poor things— Oh, what a pity! It wasn't murder, was it? Not murder! Suicide—? I believe suicide is even worse for them! The poor broken things, they wake in the other world and are utterly, utterly lost—they have no guides, you see—no help in crossing over— They are completely alone for eternity—"

"Can't you call him back?" Dr. Moore asked wildly. He was peering into a corner of the parlor, slightly stooped, his face distorted as if he were staring into the sun. "Can't someone help me? . . . Brandon? Are you here? Are you here somewhere? For God's sake can't someone help!"

"Dr. Moore, please, the spirits are gone—the sitting is over for tonight—"

"You foolish old woman, leave me alone! Can't you see I— I—I must not lose him— Call him back, will you? I insist! I insist!"

"Dr. Moore, please— You mustn't shout—"

"I said call him back! At once! *Call him back!*"

Then he burst into tears. He stumbled against the table and hid his face in his hands and wept like a child; he wept as if his heart had been broken.

And so today I have been reliving the séance. Taking notes, trying to determine what happened. A brisk windy walk of ten miles. Head buzzing with ideas. Fraud? Deceit? Telepathy? Madness?

What a spectacle! Dr. Perry Moore calling after a spirit, begging it to return—and then crying, afterward, in front of four astonished witnesses.

Dr. Perry Moore of all people.

My dilemma: whether I should report last night's incident to Dr. Rowe, the president of the Society, or whether I should say nothing about it and request that Miss Bradley say nothing. It would be tragic if Perry's professional reputation were to be damaged by a single evening's misadventure; and before long all of Boston would be talking.

In his present state, however, he is likely to tell everyone about it himself.

At Montague House the poor man was unable to sleep. He would have kept me up all night had I had the stamina to endure his excitement.

There *are* spirits! There have always been spirits!

His entire life up to the present time has been misspent!

And of course, most important of all—there is no death!

He paced about my hotel room, pulling at his beard nervously. At times there were tears in his eyes. He seemed to want a response of some kind from me but whenever I started to speak he interrupted; he was not really listening.

"Now at last I know. I can't undo my knowledge," he said in a queer hoarse voice. "Amazing, isn't it, after so many years . . . so many wasted years. . . . Ignorance has been my lot, darkness . . . and a hideous complacency. My God, when I consider my deluded smugness! I am so ashamed, so ashamed. All along people like Mrs. A——have been in contact with a world of such power . . . and people like me have been toiling in ignorance, accumulating material achievements, expending our energies in idiotic transient things. . . . But all that is changed now. Now I know. I *know*. There is no death, as the Spiritualists have always told us."

"But, Perry, don't you think— Isn't it possible that—"

"I *know*," he said quietly. "It's as clear to me as if I had crossed over into that other world myself. Poor Brandon! He's no older now than he was *then*. The poor boy, the poor tragic soul! To think that he's still living after so many years. . . . Extraordinary. . . . It makes my head spin," he said slowly. For a moment he stood without speaking. He pulled at his beard, then absently touched his lips with his fingers, then wiped at his eyes. He seemed to have forgotten me. When he spoke again his voice was hollow, rather ghastly. He sounded drugged. "I . . . I had been thinking of him as . . . as dead, you know. As dead. Twenty years. Dead. And now, tonight, to be forced to realize that . . . that he isn't dead after all. . . . It was laudanum he took. I found him. His rooms on the third floor of Weld Hall. I found him, I had no real idea, none at all, not until I read the note . . . and of course I destroyed the note . . . I had to, you see: for his sake. For his sake more than mine. It was because he realized there could be no . . . no hope. . . . Yet he called me cruel! You heard him, Jarvis, didn't you? Cruel! I suppose I was. Was I? I don't know what to think. I must talk with him again. I . . . I don't know what to . . . what to think. I. . . ."

"You look awfully tired, Perry. It might be a good idea to go to bed," I said weakly.

". . . recognized his voice at once. Oh at once: no doubt. None. What a revelation! And my life so misspent. . . . Treating people's *bodies*. Absurd. I know now that nothing matters except that other world . . . nothing matters except our dead, our beloved dead . . . who are *not dead*. What a colossal revelation. . . . ! Why, it will change the entire course of history. It will alter men's minds throughout the world. You were there, Jarvis, so you understand. You were a witness. . . ."

"But—"

"You'll bear witness to the truth of what I am saying?"

He stared at me, smiling. His eyes were bright and threaded with blood.

I tried to explain to him as courteously and sympathetically as possible that his experience at Mrs. A———'s was not substantially different from the experiences many people have had at séances. "And always in the past psychical researchers have taken the position—"

"You were *there*," he said angrily. "You heard Brandon's voice as clearly as I did. Don't deny it!"

"—Have taken the position that—that the phenomenon can be partly explained by the telepathic powers of the medium—"

"That was Brandon's *voice*," Perry said. "I felt his presence, I tell you! *His*. Mrs. A———had nothing to do with it—nothing at all. I feel as if . . . as if I could call Brandon back by myself. . . . I feel his presence even now. Close about me. He isn't dead, you see; no one is dead, there's a universe of . . . of people who are not dead. . . . Parents, grandparents, sisters, brothers, everyone . . . everyone. . . . How can you deny, Jarvis, the evidence of your own senses? You were there with me tonight and you know as well as I do. . . ."

"Perry, I don't *know*. I did hear a voice, yes, but we've heard voices before at other sittings, haven't we? There are always voices. There are always 'spirits.' The Society has taken the position that the spirits could be real, of course, but that there are other hypotheses that are perhaps more likely—"

"Other hypotheses indeed!" Perry said irritably. "You're like a man with his eyes shut tight who refuses to open them out of sheer cowardice. Like the cardinals refusing to look through Galileo's telescope! And you have pretensions of being a man of learning, of science. . . . Why, we've got to destroy all the records we've made so far; they're a slander on the world of the spirits. Thank God we didn't file a report yet on Mrs. A———! It would be so embarrassing to be forced to call it back. . . ."

"Perry, please. Don't be angry. I want only to remind you of the fact that we've been present at other sittings, haven't we?—and we've witnessed others responding emotionally to certain phenomena. Judge T———, for instance. He was convinced he'd spoken with his wife. But you must remember, don't you, that you and I were not at all convinced . . . ? It seemed to us more likely that Mrs. A———is able, through extrasensory powers we don't quite understand, to read the minds of her clients, and then to project certain voices out into the room so that it sounds as if they are coming from other people. . . . You even said, Perry, that she wasn't a very skillful ventriloquist. You said—"

"What does it matter what, in my ignorance, I said?" he cried. "Isn't it enough that I've been humiliated? That my entire life has been turned about? Must you insult me as well—sitting there so smugly and insulting *me*? I think I can make claim to being someone whom you might respect."

And so I assured him that I did respect him. And he walked about the room, wiping at his eyes, greatly agitated. He spoke again of his friend, Brandon Gould, and of his own ignorance, and of the important mission we must undertake to inform men and women of the true state of affairs. I tried to talk with him, to reason with him, but it was hopeless. He scarcely listened to me.

". . . must inform the world . . . crucial truth. . . . There is no death, you see. Never was. Changes civilization, changes the course of history. Jarvis?" he said groggily. "You see? *There is no death*."

25 March 1887. Cambridge.

Disquieting rumors re Perry Moore. Heard today at the University that one of Dr. Moore's patients (a brother-in-law of Dean Barker) was extremely offended by his behavior during a consultation last week. Talk of his having been drunk—which I find incredible. If the poor man appeared to be excitable and not his customary self, it was not because he was *drunk,* surely.

Another far-fetched tale told me by my wife, who heard it from her sister Maude: Perry Moore went to church (St. Aidan's Episcopal Church on Mount Street) for the first time in a decade, sat alone, began muttering and laughing during the sermon, and finally got to his feet and walked out, creating quite a stir. *What delusions! What delusions!*—he was said to have muttered.

I fear for the poor man's sanity.

31 March 1887. Cambridge. 4 A.M.

Sleepless night. Dreamed of swimming . . . swimming in the ocean . . . enjoying myself as usual when suddenly the water turns thick . . . turns to mud. Hideous! Indescribably awful. I was swimming nude in the ocean, by moonlight, I believe, ecstatically happy, entirely alone, when the water turned to mud. . . . Vile, disgusting mud; faintly warm; sucking at my body. Legs, thighs, torso, arms. Horrible. Woke in terror. Drenched with perspiration: pajamas wet. One of the most frightening nightmares of my adulthood.

A message from Perry Moore came yesterday just before dinner. Would I like to join him in visiting Mrs. A——— sometime soon, in early April perhaps, on a noninvestigative basis . . . ? He is uncertain now of the morality of our "investigating" Mrs. A——— or any other medium.

4 April 1887. Cambridge.

Spent the afternoon from two to five at William James's home on Irving Street, talking with Professor James of the inexplicable phenomenon of consciousness. He is robust as always, rather irreverent, supremely confident in a way I find enviable; rather like Perry Moore before his conversion (Extraordinary eyes—so piercing, quick, playful; a graying beard liberally threaded with white; close-cropped graying hair; a large, curving, impressive forehead; a manner intelligent and graceful and at the same time rough-edged, as if he anticipates or perhaps even hopes for recalcitration in his listeners.). We both find conclusive the ideas set forth in Binét's *Alterations of Personality* . . . unsettling as these ideas may be to the rationalist position. James speaks of a *peculiarity* in the constitution of human nature: that is, the fact that we inhabit not only our ego-consciousness but a wide field of psychological experience (most clearly represented by the phenomenon of memory, which no one can adequately explain) over which we have no control whatsoever. In fact, we are not generally aware of this field of consciousness.

We inhabit a lighted sphere, then; and about us is a vast penumbra of memories, reflections, feelings, and stray uncoordinated thoughts that "belong" to us theoretically, but that do not seem to be part of our conscious identity. (I was too timid to ask Professor James whether it might be the case that we do not inevitably own these aspects of the personality—that such phenomena belong as much to the objective world as to our subjective selves.) It is quite possible that there is an element of some indeterminate kind: oceanic, timeless, and living, against which the individual being constructs temporary barriers as part of an ongoing process of unique, particularized survival; like the ocean itself, which appears to separate islands that are in fact not "islands" at all, but aspects of the earth firmly joined together below the surface of the water. Our lives, then, resemble these islands. . . . All this is no more than a possibility, Professor James and I agreed.

James is acquainted, of course, with Perry Moore. But he declined to speak on the subject of the poor man's increasingly eccentric behavior when I alluded to it. (It may be that he knows even more about the situation than I do—he enjoys a multitude of acquaintances in Cambridge and Boston.) I brought our conversation round several times to the possibility of the *naturalness* of the conversion experience in terms of the individual's evolution of self, no matter how his family, his colleagues, and society in general viewed it, and Professor James appeared to agree; at least he did not emphatically disagree. He maintains a healthy skepticism, of course, regarding Spiritualist claims, and all evangelical and enthusiastic religious movements, though he is, at the same time, a highly articulate foe of the "rationalist" position and he believes that psychical research of the kind some of us are attempting will eventually unearth riches—revealing aspects of the human psyche otherwise closed to our scrutiny.

"The fearful thing," James said, "is that we are at all times vulnerable to incursions from the 'other side' of the personality. . . . We cannot determine the nature of the total personality simply because much of it, perhaps most, is hidden from us. . . . When we are invaded, then, we are overwhelmed and surrender immediately. Emotionally charged intuitions, hunches, guesses, even ideas may be the least aggressive of these incursions; but there are visual and auditory hallucinations, and forms of automatic behavior not controlled by the conscious mind. . . . Ah, you're thinking I am simply describing insanity?"

I stared at him, quite surprised.

"No. Not at all. Not at all," I said at once.

Reading through my grandfather's journals, begun in East Anglia many years before my birth. Another world then. Another language, now lost to us. *Man is sinful by nature. God's justice takes precedence over His mercy.* The dogma of Original Sin: something brutish about the innocence of that belief. And yet consoling. . . .

Fearful of sleep since my dreams are so troubled now. The voices of impudent spirits (Immanuel Kant himself come to chide me for having made too much of his categories—!), stray shouts and whispers I cannot decipher, the faces of my own beloved dead hovering near, like carnival masks, insubstantial and possibly fraudulent. Impatient with my wife, who questions me too closely on these personal matters; annoyed from time to time, in the evenings especially, by the silliness of the children. (The eldest is twelve now and should know better.) Dreading to receive another lengthy letter—sermon, really—from Perry Moore re his "new position," and yet perversely hoping one will come soon.

I must know.

(Must know *what* . . . ?)

I must know.

10 April 1887. Boston. St. Aidan's Episcopal Church.

Funeral service this morning for Perry Moore; dead at forty-three.

17 April 1887. Seven Hills, New Hampshire.

A weekend retreat. No talk. No need to think.

Visiting with a former associate, author of numerous books. Cartesian specialist. Elderly. Partly deaf. Extraordinarily kind to me. (Did not ask about the Department or about my work.) Intensely interested in animal behavior now, in observation primarily; fascinated with the phenomenon of hibernation.

He leaves me alone for hours. He sees something in my face I cannot see myself.

The old consolations of a cruel but just God: ludicrous today.

In the nineteenth century we live free of God. We live in the illusion of freedom-of-God.

Dozing off in the guest room of this old farmhouse and then waking abruptly. *Is someone here? Is someone here?* My voice queer, hushed, childlike. *Please: is someone here?*

Silence.

Query: Is the penumbra outside consciousness all that was ever meant by "God"?

Query: Is inevitability all that was ever meant by "God"?

God—the body of fate we inhabit, then: no more and no less.

God pulled Perry down into the body of fate: into Himself.(Or Itself.) As Professor James might say, Dr. Moore was "vulnerable" to an assault from the other side.

At any rate he is dead. They buried him last Saturday.

25 April 1887. Cambridge.

Shelves of books. The sanctity of books. Kant, Plato, Schopenhauer, Descartes, Hume, Hegel, Spinoza. The others. All. Nietzsche, Spencer, Leibnitz (on whom I did a torturous Master's thesis). Plotinus. Swedenborg. *The Transactions of the American Society for Psychical Research*. Voltaire. Locke. Rousseau. And Berkeley: the good Bishop adrift in a dream.

An etching by Halbrech above my desk, The Thames 1801. Water too black. Inky-black. Thick with mud . . . ? Filthy water in any case.

Perry's essay, forty-five scribbled pages. "The Challenge of the Future." Given to me several weeks ago by Dr. Rowe, who feared rejecting it for the *Transactions* but could not, of course, accept it. I can read only a few pages at a time, then push it aside, too moved to continue. Frightened also.

The man had gone insane.

Died insane.

Personality broken: broken bits of intellect.

His argument passionate and disjointed, with no pretense of objectivity. Where some weeks ago he had taken the stand that it was immoral to investigate the Spirit World, now he took the stand that it was imperative we do so. We are on the brink of a new age . . . new knowledge of the universe . . . comparable to the stormy transitional period between the Ptolemaic and the Copernican theories of the universe. . . . More experiments required. Money. Donations. Subsidies by private institutions. All psychological research must be channeled into a systematic study of the Spirit World and the ways by which we can communicate with that world. Mediums like Mrs. A————must be brought to centers of learning like Harvard and treated with the respect their genius deserves. Their value to civilization is, after all, beyond estimation. They must be rescued from arduous and routine lives where their genius is drained off into vulgar pursuits . . . they must be rescued from a clientele that is mainly concerned with being put into contact with deceased relatives for utterly trivial, self-serving reasons. Men of learning must realize the gravity of the situation. Otherwise we will fail, we will stagger beneath the burden, we will be defeated, ignobly, and it will remain for the twentieth century to discover the existence of the Spirit Universe that surrounds the Material Universe, and to determine the exact ways by which one world is related to another.

Perry Moore died of a stroke on the eighth of April; died instantaneously on the steps of the Bedford Club shortly after 2

P.M. Passers-by saw a very excited, red-faced gentleman with an open collar push his way through a small gathering at the top of the steps—and then suddenly fall, as if shot down.

In death he looked like quite another person: his features sharp, the nose especially pointed. Hardly the handsome Perry Moore everyone had known.

He had come to a meeting of the Society, though it was suggested by Dr. Rowe and by others (including myself) that he stay away. Of course he came to argue. To present his "new position." To insult the other members. (He was contemptuous of a rather poorly organized paper on the medium Miss E——— of Salem, a young woman who works with objects like rings, articles of clothing, locks of hair, et cetera; and quite angry with the evidence presented by a young geologist that would seem to discredit, once and for all, the claims of Eustace of Portsmouth. He interrupted a third paper, calling the reader a "bigot" and an "ignorant fool.")

Fortunately the incident did not find its way into any of the papers. The press, misunderstanding (deliberately and maliciously) the Society's attitude toward Spiritualism, delights in ridiculing our efforts.

There were respectful obituaries. A fine eulogy prepared by Reverend Tyler of St. Aidan's. Other tributes. *A tragic loss. . . . Mourned by all who knew him. . . .* (I stammered and could not speak. I cannot speak of him, of it, even now. Am I mourning, am I aggrieved? Or merely shocked? Terrified?) Relatives and friends and associates glossed over his behavior these past few months and settled upon an earlier Perry Moore, eminently sane, a distinguished physician and man of letters. I did not disagree, I merely acquiesced; I could not make any claim to have really known the man.

And so he has died, and so he is dead. . . .

Shortly after the funeral I went away to New Hampshire for a few days. But I can barely remember that period of time now. I sleep poorly, I yearn for summer, for a drastic change of climate, of scene. It was unwise for me to take up the responsibility of psychical research, fascinated though I am by it; my classes and lectures at the University demand most of my energy.

How quickly he died, and so young: so relatively young.

No history of high blood pressure, it is said.

At the end he was arguing with everyone, however. His personality had completely changed. He was rude, impetuous, even rather profane; even poorly groomed. (Rising to challenge the first of the papers, he revealed a shirtfront that appeared to be stained.) Some claimed he had been drinking all along, for years. Was it possible . . . ? (He had clearly enjoyed the wine and brandy in Quincy that evening, but I would not have said he was intemperate.) Rumors, fanciful tales, outright lies, slander. . . . It is painful, the vulnerability death brings.

Bigots, he called us. Ignorant fools. Unbelievers—atheists—traitors to the Spirit World—heretics. Heretics! I believe he looked directly at me as he pushed his way out of the meeting room: his eyes glaring, his face dangerously flushed, no recognition in his stare.

After his death, it is said, books continue to arrive at his home from England and Europe. He spent a small fortune on obscure, out-of-print volumes—commentaries on the Kabbala, on Plotinus, medieval alchemical texts, books on astrology, witchcraft, the metaphysics of death. Occult cosmologies. Egyptian, Indian, and Chinese "wisdom." Blake, Swedenborg, Cozad. *The Tibetan Book of the Dead*. Datsky's *Lunar Mysteries*. His estate is in chaos because he left not one but several wills, the most recent made out only a day before his death, merely a few lines scribbled on scrap paper, without witnesses. The family will contest, of course. Since in this will he left his money and property to an obscure woman living in Quincy, Massachusetts, and since he was obviously not in his right mind at the time, they would be foolish indeed not to contest.

Days have passed since his sudden death. Days continue to pass. At times I am seized by a sort of quick, cold panic; at other times I am inclined to think the entire situation has been exaggerated. In one mood I vow to myself that I will never again pursue psychical research because it is simply too dangerous. In another mood I vow I will never again pursue it because it is a waste of time and my own work, my own career, must come first.

Heretics, he called us. Looking straight at me.

Still, he was mad. And is not to be blamed for the vagaries of madness.

19 June 1887. Boston.

Luncheon with Dr. Rowe, Miss Madeleine van der Post, young Lucas Matthewson; turned over my personal records and notes re the mediums Dr. Moore and I visited. (Destroyed jottings of a private nature.) Miss van der Post and Matthewson will be taking over my responsibilities. Both are young, quick-witted, alert, with a certain ironic play about their features; rather like Dr. Moore in his prime. Matthewson is a former seminary student now teaching physics at the Boston University. They questioned me about Perry Moore, but I avoided answering frankly. Asked if we were close, I said *No*. Asked if I had heard a bizarre tale making the rounds of Boston salons—that a spirit claiming to be Perry Moore has intruded upon a number of séances in the area—I said honestly that I had not; and I did not care to hear about it.

Spinoza: *I will analyze the actions and appetites of men as if it were a question of lines, of planes, and of solids.*
It is in this direction, I believe, that we must move. Away from the phantasmal, the vaporous, the unclear; toward lines, planes, and solids.
Sanity.

8 July 1887. Mount Desert Island, Maine.

Very early this morning, before dawn, dreamed of Perry Moore: a babbling gesticulating spirit, bearded, bright-eyed, obviously mad. Jarvis? Jarvis? Don't deny me! he cried. I am so . . . so bereft. . . .
Paralyzed, I faced him: neither awake nor asleep. His words were not really *words* so much as unvoiced thoughts. I heard them in my own voice; a terrible raw itching at the back of my throat yearned to articulate the man's grief.
Perry?
You don't dare deny me! Not now!
He drew near and I could not escape. The dream shifted, lost its clarity. Someone was shouting at me. Very angry, he was, and baffled—as if drunk—or ill—or injured.

Perry? I can't hear you—

—Our dinner at Montague House, do you remember? Lamb, it was. And crepes with almond for desert. You remember! You remember! You can't deny me! We were both nonbelievers then, both abysmally ignorant—you can't deny me!

(I was mute with fear or with cunning.)

—That idiot Rowe, how humiliated he will be! All of them! All of you! The entire rationalist bias, the—the conspiracy of—of fools—bigots— In a few years— In a few short years— Jarvis, where are you? Why can't I see you? Where have you gone? — My eyes can't focus: will someone help me? I seem to have lost my way. Who is here? Who am I talking with? You remember me, don't you?

(He brushed near me, blinking helplessly. His mouth was a hole torn into his pale ravaged flesh.)

Where are you? Where is everyone? I thought it would be crowded here but—but there's no one—I am forgetting so much! My name—what was my name? Can't see. Can't remember. Something very important—something very important I must accomplish—can't remember— Why is there no God? No one here? No one in control? We drift this way and that way, we come to no rest, there are no landmarks—no way of judging—everything is confused—disjointed— Is someone listening? Would you read to me, please? Would you read to me?—anything!—that speech of Hamlet's—*To be or not*—a sonnet of Shakespeare's—any sonnet, anything—*That time of year thou may in me behold*—is that it?—is that how it begins? *Bare ruin'd choirs where the sweet birds once sang.* How does it go? Won't you tell me? I'm lost—there's nothing here to see, to touch—isn't anyone listening? I thought there was someone nearby, a friend: isn't anyone here?

(I stood paralyzed, mute with caution: he passed by.)

—*When in the chronicle of wasted time—the wide world dreaming of things to come*—is anyone listening?—can anyone help?—I am forgetting so much—my name, my life—my life's work—to penetrate the mysteries—the veil—to do justice to the universe of—of what—what had I intended?—am I in my place of repose now, have I come home? Why is it so empty here? Why is no one in control? My eyes—my head—mind broken and blown about—slivers—shards—annihilating all that's made to a—a green thought—a green shade—Shakespeare? Plato? Pascal? Will someone read me Pascal again? I seem to have lost my way—I am being blown about— Jarvis, was it? My dear young friend Jarvis? But I've forgotten your last name—I've forgotten so much—

(I wanted to reach out to touch him—but could not move, could not wake. The back of my throat ached with sorrow. Silent! Silent! I could not utter a word.)

—My papers, my journal—twenty years—a key somewhere hidden—where?—ah yes: the bottom drawer of my desk—do you hear?—my desk—house—Louisburg Square—the key is hidden there—wrapped in a linen handkerchief—the strongbox is—the locked box is—hidden—my brother Edward's house—attic—trunk—steamer trunk—initials R. W. M.—Father's trunk, you see—strongbox hidden inside—my secret journals—life's work—physical and spiritual wisdom—must not be lost—are you listening?—is anyone listening? I am forgetting so much, my mind is in shreds—but if you could locate the journal and read it to me—if you could salvage it—me—I would be so very grateful—I would forgive you anything, all of you— Is anyone there? Jarvis? Brandon? No one?—My journal, my soul: will you salvage it? Will—

(He stumbled away and I was alone again.)

Perry—?

But it was too late: I awoke drenched with perspiration.

Nightmare.
Must forget.

Best to rise early, before the others. Mount Desert Island lovely in July. Our lodge on a hill above the beach. No spirits here: wind from the northeast, perpetual fresh air, perpetual waves. Best to rise early and run along the beach and plunge into the chilly water.

Clear the cobwebs from one's mind.

How beautiful the sky, the ocean, the sunrise!

No spirits here on Mount Desert Island. Swimming: skillful exertion of arms and legs. Head turned this way, that way. Eyes half shut. The surprise of the cold rough waves. One yearns almost to slip out of one's human skin at such times . . . ! Crude blatant beauty of Maine. Ocean. Muscular exertion of body. How alive I am, how living, how invulnerable; what a triumph in my every breath. . . .

Everything slips from my mind except the present moment. I am living, I am alive, I am immortal. Must not weaken: must not sink. Drowning? No. Impossible. Life is the only reality. It is not extinction that awaits but a hideous dreamlike state, a perpetual groping, blundering—far worse than extinction—incomprehensible: so it is life we must cling to, arm over arm, swimming, conquering the element that sustains us.

Jarvis? someone cried. *Please hear me—*

How exquisite life is, the turbulent joy of life contained in flesh! I heard nothing except the triumphant waves splashing about me. I swam for nearly an hour. Was reluctant to come ashore for breakfast, though our breakfasts are always pleasant rowdy sessions: my wife and my brother's wife and our seven children thrown together for the month of July. Three boys, four girls: noise, bustle, health, no shadows, no spirits. No time to think. Again and again I shall emerge from the surf, face and hair and body streaming water, exhausted but jubilant, triumphant. Again and again the children will call out to me, excited, from the day-side of the world that they inhabit.

I will not investigate Dr. Moore's strongbox and his secret journal; I will not even think about doing so. The wind blows words away. The surf is hypnotic. I will not remember this morning's dream once I sit down to breakfast with the family. I will not clutch my wife's wrist and say *We must not die! We dare not die!*—for that would only frighten and offend her.

Jarvis? she is calling at this very moment.

And I say *Yes—? Yes, I'll be there at once.*

This Is Death

Donald E. Westlake

Donald Westlake (1933–   ) established his unique credentials
as a hard-boiled humorist through the creation of inept burglar
John Francis Dortmunder, hero of *The Hot Rock* (1970), *Bank
Shot* (1972), *Drowned Hopes* (1990), and other novels. His few
ventures into the fantastic can be found in *Curious Facts Preceding My Execution and Other Fictions* (1968), *Tomorrow's Crimes*
(1989), and the comic apocalypse novel *Humans* (1992). "This
Is Death" bristles with the sort of sardonic wit for which Westlake
is best known.

It's hard not to believe in ghosts when you are one. I hanged
myself in a fit of truculence—stronger than pique, but not so
dignified as despair—and regretted it before the thing was well
begun. The instant I kicked the chair away, I wanted it back,
but gravity was turning my former wish to its present command;
the chair would not right itself from where it lay on the floor,
and my 193 pounds would not cease to urge downward from the
rope thick around my neck.

There was pain, of course, quite horrible pain centered in my
throat, but the most astounding thing was the way my cheeks
seemed to swell. I could barely see over their round red hills,
my eye staring in agony at the door, *willing* someone to come in
and rescue me, though I knew there was no one in the house,
and in any event the door was carefully locked. My kicking legs
caused me to twist and turn, so that sometimes I faced the door
and sometimes the window, and my shivering hands struggled
with the rope so deep in my flesh I could barely find it and most
certainly could not pull it loose.

I was frantic and terrified, yet at the same time my brain possessed a cold corner of aloof observation. I seemed now to be everywhere in the room at once, within my writhing body but also without, seeing my frenzied spasms, the thick rope, the heavy beam, the mismatched pair of lit bedside lamps throwing my convulsive double shadow on the walls, the closed locked door, the white-curtained window with its shade drawn all the way down. *This is death,* I thought, and I no longer wanted it, now that the choice was gone forever.

My name is—was—Edward Thornburn, and my dates are 1938–1977. I killed myself just a month before my fortieth birthday, though I don't believe the well-known pangs of that milestone had much if anything to do with my action. I blame it all (as I blamed most of the errors and failures of my life) on my sterility. Had I been able to father children my marriage would have remained strong, Emily would not have been unfaithful to me, and I would not have taken my own life in a final fit of truculence.

The setting was the guest room in our house in Barnstaple, Connecticut, and the time was just after seven P.M.; deep twilight, at this time of year. I had come home from the office—I was a realtor, a fairly lucrative occupation in Connecticut, though my income had been falling off recently—shortly before six, to find the note on the kitchen table: "Antiquing with Greg. Afraid you'll have to make your own dinner. Sorry. Love, Emily."

Greg was the one; Emily's lover. He owned an antique shop out on the main road toward New York, and Emily filled a part of her days as his ill-paid assistant. I knew what they did together in the back of the shop on those long midweek afternoons when there were no tourists, no antique collectors to disturb them. I knew, and I'd known for more than three years, but I had never decided how to deal with my knowledge. The fact was, I blamed myself, and therefore I had no way to *behave* if the ugly subject were ever to come into the open.

So I remained silent, but not content. I was discontent, unhappy, angry, resentful—truculent.

I'd tried to kill myself before. At first with the car, by steering it into an oncoming truck (I swerved at the last second, amid howling horns) and by driving it off a cliff into the Connecticut River (I slammed on the brakes at the very brink, and sat cov-

ered in perspiration for half an hour before backing away) and
finally by stopping athwart one of the few level crossings left in
this neighborhood. But no train came for twenty minutes, and
my truculence wore off, and I drove home.

Later I tried to slit my wrists, but found it impossible to push
sharp metal into my own skin. Impossible. The vision of my
naked wrist and that shining steel so close together washed my
truculence completely out of my mind. Until the next time.

With the rope; and then I succeeded. Oh, totally, oh, fully I
succeeded. My legs kicked at air, my fingernails clawed at my
throat, my bulging eyes stared out over my swollen purple
cheeks, my tongue thickened and grew bulbous in my mouth,
my body jigged and jangled like a toy at the end of a string, and
the pain was excruciating, horrible, not to be endured. I can't
endure it, I thought, it can't be endured. Much worse than knife
slashings was the knotted strangled pain in my throat, and my
head ballooned with pain, pressure outward, my face turning
black, my eyes no longer human, the pressure in my head building and building as though I would explode. Endless horrible
pain, not to be endured, but going on and on.

My legs kicked more feebly. My arms sagged, my hands
dropped to my side, my fingers twisted uselessly against my sop-
ping trouser legs, my head hung at an angle from the rope, I
turned more slowly in the air, like a broken wind chime on a
breezeless day. The pains lessened, in my throat and head, but
never entirely stopped.

And now I saw that my distended eyes had become lusterless,
gray. The moisture had dried on the eyeballs, they were as dead
as stones. And yet I could see them, my own eyes, and when I
widened my vision I could *see* my entire body, turning, hanging,
no longer twitching, and with horror I realized I was dead.

But *present.* Dead, but still present, with the scraping ache still
in my throat and the bulging pressure still in my head. Present,
but no longer in that used-up clay, that hanging meat; I was
suffused through the room, like indirect lighting, everywhere
present but without a source. What happens now? I wondered,
dulled by fear and strangeness and the continuing pains, and I
waited, like a hovering mist, for whatever would happen next.

But nothing happened. I waited; the body became utterly still;
the double shadow on the wall showed no vibration; the bedside

lamps continued to burn; the door remained shut and the window shade drawn; and nothing happened.

What *now?* I craved to scream the question aloud, but I could not. My throat ached, but I had no throat. My mouth burned, but I had no mouth. Every final strain and struggle of my body remained imprinted in my mind, but I had no body and no brain and no *self,* no substance. No power to speak, no power to move myself, no power to *re*move myself from this room and this suspended corpse. I could only wait here, and wonder, and go on waiting.

There was a digital clock on the dresser opposite the bed, and when it first occurred to me to look at it the numbers were 7:21—perhaps twenty minutes after I'd kicked the chair away, perhaps fifteen minutes since I'd died. Shouldn't something happen, shouldn't some *change* take place?

The clock read 9:11 when I heard Emily's Volkswagen drive around to the back of the house. I had left no note, having nothing I wanted to say to anyone and in any event believing my own dead body would be eloquent enough, but I hadn't thought I would be *present* when Emily found me. I was justified in my action, however much I now regretted having taken it, I was justified, I knew I was justified, but I didn't want to see her face when she came through that door. She had wronged me, she was the cause of it, she would have to know that as well as I, but I didn't want to see her face.

The pains increased, in what had been my throat, in what had been my head. I heard the back door slam, far away downstairs, and I stirred like air currents in the room, but I didn't leave, I couldn't leave.

"Ed? Ed? It's me, hon!"

I know it's you. I must go away now, I can't stay here, I must go away. Is there a God? Is this my soul, this hovering presence? *Hell* would be better than this, take me away to Hell or wherever I'm to go, don't leave me here!

She came up the stairs, calling again, walking past the closed guest room door. I heard her go into our bedroom, heard her call my name, heard the beginnings of apprehension in her voice. She went by again, out there in the hall, went downstairs, became quiet.

What was she doing? Searching for a note perhaps, some message from me. Looking out the window, seeing again my Chevrolet, knowing I must be home. Moving through the rooms of this old house, the original structure a barn nearly 200 years old, converted by some previous owner just after the Second World War, bought by me twelve years ago, furnished by Emily—and Greg—from their interminable, damnable, awful antiques. Shaker furniture, Colonial furniture, hooked rugs and quilts, the old yellow pine tables, the faint sense always of being in some slightly shabby minor museum, this house that I had bought but never loved. I'd bought it for Emily, I did everything for Emily, because I knew I could never do the one thing for Emily that mattered. I could never give her a child.

She was good about it, of course. Emily *is* good, I never blamed her, never completely blamed *her* instead of myself. In the early days of our marriage she made a few wistful references, but I suppose she saw the effect they had on me, and for a long time she has said nothing. But I have known.

The beam from which I had hanged myself was a part of the original building, a thick hand-hewed length of aged timber eleven inches square, chevroned with the marks of the hatchet that had shaped it. A strong beam, it would support my weight forever. It would support my weight until I was found and cut down. Until I was found.

The clock read 9:23 and Emily had been in the house twelve minutes when she came upstairs again, her steps quick and light on the old wood, approaching, pausing, stopping. "Ed?"

The doorknob turned.

The door was locked, of course, with the key on the inside. She'd have to break it down, have to call someone else to break it down, perhaps she wouldn't be the one to find me after all. Hope rose in me, and the pains receded.

"Ed? Are you in there?" She knocked at the door, rattled the knob, called my name several times more, then abruptly turned and ran away downstairs again, and after a moment I heard her voice, murmuring and unclear. She had called someone, on the phone.

Greg, I thought, and the throat-rasp filled me, and I wanted this to be the end. I wanted to be taken away, dead body and living soul, taken away. I wanted everything to be finished.

She stayed downstairs, waiting for him, and I stayed upstairs, waiting for them both. Perhaps she already knew what she'd find up here, and that's why she waited below.

I didn't mind about Greg, about being present when he came in. I didn't mind about *him*. It was Emily I minded.

The clock read 9:44 when I heard tires on the gravel at the side of the house. He entered, I heard them talking down there, the deeper male voice slow and reassuring, the lighter female voice quick and frightened, and then they came up together, neither speaking. The doorknob turned, jiggled, rattled, and Greg's voice called, "Ed?"

After a little silence Emily said, "He wouldn't— He wouldn't *do* anything, would he?"

"Do anything?" Greg sounded almost annoyed at the question. "What do you mean, do anything?"

"He's been so depressed, he's— Ed!" And forcibly the door was rattled, the door was shaken in its frame.

"Emily, don't. Take it easy."

"I shouldn't have called you," she said. "Ed, *please!*"

"Why not? For heaven's sake, Emily—"

"Ed, *please* come out, don't scare me like this!"

"*Why shouldn't* you call me, Emily?"

"Ed isn't stupid, Greg. He's—"

There was then a brief silence, pregnant with the hint of murmuring. They thought me still alive in here, they didn't want me to hear Emily say, "He *knows,* Greg, he knows about us."

The murmurings sifted and shifted, and then Greg spoke loudly, "That's ridiculous. Ed? Come out, Ed, let's talk this over." And the doorknob rattled and clattered, and he sounded annoyed when he said, "We must get in, that's all. Is there another key?"

"I think all the locks up here are the same. Just a minute."

They were. A simple skeleton key would open any interior door in the house. I waited, listening, knowing Emily had gone off to find another key, knowing they would soon come in together, and I felt such terror and revulsion for Emily's entrance that I could feel myself shimmer in the room, like a reflection in a warped mirror. Oh, can I at least stop seeing? In life I had eyes, but also eyelids, I could shut out the intolerable, but now I was only a presence, a total presence, I *could not* stop my awareness.

The rasp of key in lock was like rough metal edges in my throat; my memory of a throat. The pain flared in me, and through it I heard Emily asking what was wrong, and Greg answering. "The key's in it, on the other side."

"Oh, dear God! Oh, Greg, what has he done?"

"We'll have to take the door off its hinges," he told her. "Call Tony. Tell him to bring the toolbox."

"Can't you push the key through?"

Of course he could, but he said, quite determinedly, "Go *on*, Emily," and I realized then he had no intention of taking the door down. He simply wanted her away when the door was first opened. Oh, very good, *very* good!

"All right," she said doubtfully, and I heard her go away to phone Tony. A beetle-browed young man with great masses of black hair and olive complexion, Tony lived in Greg's house and was a kind of handyman. He did work around the house and was also (according to Emily) very good at restoration of antique furniture; stripping paint, reassembling broken parts, that sort of thing.

There was now a renewed scraping and rasping at the lock, as Greg struggled to get the door open before Emily's return. I found myself feeling unexpected warmth and liking toward Greg. He wasn't a bad person. Would he marry her now? They could live in this house, he'd had more to do with its furnishing than I. Or would this room hold too grim a memory, would Emily have to sell the house, live elsewhere? She might have to sell at a low price; as a realtor, I knew the difficulty in selling a house where a suicide has taken place. No matter how much they may joke about it, people are still afraid of the supernatural. Many of them would believe this room was haunted.

It was then I finally realized the room *was* haunted. With me! *I'm a ghost,* I thought, thinking the word for the first time, in utter blank astonishment. I'm a ghost.

Oh, how dismal! To hover here, to be a boneless fleshless aching *presence* here, to be a kind of ectoplasmic mildew seeping through the days and nights, alone, unending, a stupid pain-racked misery-filled observer of the comings and goings of strangers—she *would* sell the house, she'd have to, I was sure of that. Was this my punishment? The punishment of the suicide, the solitary hell of him who takes his own life. To remain forever a sentient nothing, bound by a force greater than gravity itself to the place of one's finish.

I was distracted from this misery by a sudden agitation in the key on this side of the lock. I saw it quiver and jiggle like something alive, and then it popped out—it seemed to *leap* out, itself a suicide leaping from a cliff—and clattered to the floor, and an instant later the door was pushed open and Greg's ashen face stared at my own purple face, and after the astonishment and horror, his expression shifted to revulsion—and contempt?—and he backed out, slamming the door. Once more the key turned in the lock, and I heard him hurry away downstairs.

The clock read 9:58. *Now* he was telling her. *Now* he was giving her a drink to calm her. *Now* he was phoning the police. *Now* he was talking to her about whether or not to admit their affair to the police; what would they decide?

"Noooooooooo!"

The clock read 10:07. What had taken so long? Hadn't he even called the police yet?

She was coming up the stairs, stumbling and rushing, she was pounding on the door, screaming my name. I shrank into the corners of the room, I *felt* the thuds of her fists against the door, I cowered from her. She can't come in, dear God don't let her in! I don't care what she's done, I don't care about anything, just don't let her see me! *Don't let me see her!*

Greg joined her. She screamed at him, he persuaded her, she raved, he argued, she demanded, he denied. "Give me the key. Give me the key."

Surely he'll hold out, surely he'll take her away, surely he's stronger, more forceful.

He gave her the key.

No. *This* cannot be endured. *This* is the horror beyond all else. She came in, she walked into the room, and the sound she made will always live inside me. That cry wasn't human; it was the howl of every creature that has ever despaired. *Now* I know what despair is, and why I called my own state mere truculence.

Now that it was too late, Greg tried to restrain her, tried to hold her shoulders and draw her from the room, but she pulled away and crossed the room toward—not toward *me*. I was everywhere in the room, driven by pain and remorse, and Emily walked toward the carcass. She looked at it almost tenderly, she even reached up and touched its swollen cheek. "Oh, Ed," she murmured.

The pains were as violent now as in the moments before my death. The slashing torment in my throat, the awful distension in my head, they made me squirm in agony all over again; but I *could not* feel her hand on my cheek.

Greg followed her, touched her shoulder again, spoke her name, and immediately her face dissolved, she cried out once more and wrapped her arms around the corpse's legs and clung to it, weeping and gasping and uttering words too quick and broken to understand. Thank *God* they were too quick and broken to understand!

Greg, that fool, did finally force her away, though he had great trouble breaking her clasp on the body. But he succeeded, and pulled her out of the room and slammed the door, and for a little while the body swayed and turned, until it became still once more.

That was the worst. Nothing could be worse than that. The long days and nights here—how long must a stupid creature like myself *haunt* his death-place before release?—would be horrible, I knew that, but not so bad as this. Emily would survive, would sell the house, would slowly forget. (Even I would slowly forget.) She and Greg could marry. She was only 36, she could still be a mother.

For the rest of the night I heard her wailing, elsewhere in the house. The police did come at last, and a pair of grim silent white-coated men from the morgue entered the room to cut me—it—down. They bundled it like a broken toy into a large oval wicker basket with long wooden handles, and they carried it away.

I had thought I might be forced to stay with the body, I had feared the possibility of being buried with it, of spending eternity as a thinking nothingness in the black dark of a casket, but the body left the room and I remained behind.

A doctor was called. When the body was carried away the room door was left open, and now I could plainly hear the voices from downstairs. Tony was among them now, his characteristic surly monosyllable occasionally rumbling, but the main thing for a while was the doctor. He was trying to give Emily a sedative, but she kept wailing, she kept speaking high hurried frantic sen-

tences as though she had too little time to say it all. "I did it!"
she cried, over and over. "I did it! I'm to blame!"

Yes. That was the reaction I'd wanted, and expected, and here
it was, and it was horrible. Everything I had desired in the last
moments of my life had been granted to me, and they were all
ghastly beyond belief. I *didn't* want to die! I *didn't* want to give
Emily such misery! And more than all the rest I didn't want to
be here, seeing and hearing it all.

They did quiet her at last, and then a policeman in a rumpled
blue suit came into the room with Greg, and listened while Greg
described everything that had happened. While Greg talked, the
policeman rather grumpily stared at the remaining length of rope
still knotted around the beam, and when Greg had finished the
policeman said, "You're a close friend of his?"

"More of his wife. She works for me. I own The Bibelot, an
antique shop out on the New York road."

"Mmm. Why on earth did you let her in here?"

Greg smiled; a sheepish embarrassed expression. "She's
stronger than I am," he said. "A more forceful personality.
That's always been true."

It was with some surprise I realized it *was* true. Greg was
something of a weakling, and Emily was very strong. (*I* had been
something of a weakling, hadn't I? Emily was the strongest of
us all.)

The policeman was saying, "Any idea why he'd do it?"

"I think he suspected his wife was having an affair with me."
Clearly Greg had rehearsed this sentence, he'd much earlier
come to the decision to say it and had braced himself for the
moment. He blinked all the way through the statement, as
though standing in a harsh glare.

The policeman gave him a quick shrewd look. "Were you?"

"Yes."

"She was getting a divorce?"

"No. She doesn't love me, she loved her husband."

"Then why sleep around?"

"Emily wasn't sleeping *around,*" Greg said, showing offense
only with that emphasized word. "From time to time, and not
very often, she was sleeping with me."

"Why?"

"For comfort." Greg too looked at the rope around the beam,

as though it had become me and he was awkward speaking in its presence. "Ed wasn't an easy man to get along with," he said carefully. "He was moody. It was getting worse."

"Cheerful people don't kill themselves," the policeman said.

"Exactly. Ed was depressed most of the time, obscurely angry now and then. It was affecting his business, costing him clients. He made Emily miserable but she wouldn't leave him, she loved him. I don't know what she'll do now."

"You two won't marry?"

"Oh, no." Greg smiled, a bit sadly. "Do you think we murdered him, made it look like suicide so we could marry?"

"Not at all," the policeman said. "But what's the problem? You already married?"

"I am homosexual."

The policeman was no more astonished than I. He said, "I don't get it."

"I live with my friend; that young man downstairs. I am—capable—of a wider range, but my preferences are set. I am very fond of Emily, I felt sorry for her, the life she had with Ed. I told you our physical relationship was infrequent. And often not very successful."

Oh, Emily. Oh, poor Emily.

The policeman said, "Did Thornburn know you were, uh, that way?"

"I have no idea. I don't make a public point of it."

"All right." The policeman gave one more half-angry look around the room, then said, "Let's go."

They left. The door remained open, and I heard them continue to talk as they went downstairs, first the policeman asking, "Is there somebody to stay the night? Mrs. Thornburn shouldn't be alone."

"She has relatives in Great Barrington. I phoned them earlier. Somebody should be arriving within the hour."

"You'll stay until then? The doctor says she'll probably sleep, but just in case—"

"Of course."

That was all I heard. Male voices murmured a while longer from below, and then stopped. I heard cars drive away.

How complicated men and women are. How stupid are simple actions. I had never understood anyone, least of all myself.

The room was visited once more that night, by Greg, shortly after the police left. He entered, looking as offended and repelled as though the body were still here, stood the chair up on its legs, climbed on it, and with some difficulty untied the remnant of rope. This he stuffed partway into his pocket as he stepped down again to the floor, then returned the chair to its usual spot in the corner of the room, picked the key off the floor and put it in the lock, switched off both bedside lamps and left the room, shutting the door behind him.

Now I was in darkness, except for the faint line of light under the door, and the illuminated numerals of the clock. How long one minute is! That clock was my enemy, it dragged out every minute, it paused and waited and paused and waited till I could stand it no more, and then it waited longer, and *then* the next number dropped into place. Sixty times an hour, hour after hour, all night long. I couldn't stand one night of this, how could I stand eternity?

And how could I stand the torment and torture inside my brain? That was much worse now than the physical pain, which never entirely left me. I had been right about Emily and Greg, but at the same time I had been hopelessly brainlessly wrong. I had been right about my life, but wrong; right about my death, but wrong. How *much* I wanted to make amends, and how impossible it was to do anything anymore, anything at all. My actions had all tended to this, and ended with this: black remorse, the most dreadful pain of all.

I had all night to think, and to feel the pains, and to wait without knowing what I was waiting for or when—or if—my waiting would ever end. Faintly I heard the arrival of Emily's sister and brother-in-law, the murmured conversation, then the departure of Tony and Greg. Not long afterward the guest room door opened, but almost immediately closed again, no one having entered, and a bit after that the hall light went out, and now only the illuminated clock broke the darkness.

When next would I see Emily? Would she ever enter this room again? It wouldn't be as horrible as the first time, but it would surely be horror enough.

Dawn grayed the window shade, and gradually the room appeared out of the darkness, dim and silent and morose. Apparently it was a sunless day, which never got very bright. The day went on and on, featureless, each protracted minute marked by the clock. At times I dreaded someone's entering this room, at other times I prayed for something, anything—even the presence of Emily herself—to break this unending boring *absence*. But the day went on with no event, no sound, no activity anywhere— they must be keeping Emily sedated through this first day—and it wasn't until twilight, with the digital clock reading 6:52, that the door again opened and a person entered.

At first I didn't recognize him. An angry-looking man, blunt and determined, he came in with quick ragged steps, switched on both bedside lamps, then shut the door with rather more force than necessary, and turned the key in the lock. Truculent, his manner was, and when he turned from the door I saw with incredulity that he was *me*. Me! I wasn't dead, I was alive! But how could that be?

And what was that he was carrying? He picked up the chair from the corner, carried it to the middle of the room, stood on it—

No! No!

He tied the rope around the beam. The noose was already in the other end, which he slipped over his head and tightened around his neck.

Good God, *don't*!

He kicked the chair away.

The instant I kicked the chair away I wanted it back, but gravity was turning my former wish to its present command; the chair would not right itself from where it lay on the floor, and my 193 pounds would not cease to urge downward from the rope thick around my neck.

There was pain, of course, quite horrible pain centered in my throat, but the most astounding thing was the way my cheeks seemed to swell. I could barely see over their round red hills, my eyes staring in agony at the door, *willing* someone to come in and rescue me, though I knew there was no one in the house, and in any event the door was carefully locked. My kicking legs caused me to twist and turn, so that sometimes I faced the door and sometimes the window, and my shivering hands struggled with the rope so deep in my flesh I could barely find it and most certainly could not pull it loose.

I was frantic and horrified, yet at the same time my brain

possessed a cold corner of aloof observation. I seemed now to be everywhere in the room at once, within my writhing body but also without, seeing my frenzied spasms, the thick rope, the heavy beam, the mismatched pair of lit bedside lamps throwing my convulsive double shadow on the walls, the closed locked door, the white-curtained window with its shade drawn all the way down. *This is death.*

The Making of Revelation, Part I

Philip José Farmer

Philip José Farmer (1918–) made a name for himself in science fiction and fantasy with such sexually daring works as *The Lovers* (1952), *Flesh* (1960), *Image of the Beast* (1968), and *Blown* (1969). He also has shown an interest in the interface between the mythic and historical in his "autobiography" of pulp fiction hero Doc Savage in *Doc Savage: His Apocalyptic Life* (1973), and his mingling of famous and imaginary people in the Riverworld novels *To Your Scattered Bodies Go, The Fabulous Riverboat, The Dark Design,* and *The Magic Labyrinth.* In the satirical "The Making of Revelation, Part I," Farmer imagines a meeting of real and imagined minds in an afterlife one hopes never to experience.

G od said, "Bring me Cecil B. DeMille."
"Dead or alive?" the angel Gabriel said.
"I want to make him an offer he can't refuse. Can even I do this to a dead man?"
"Oh, I see," said Gabriel, who didn't. "It will be done."
And it was.
Cecil Blount DeMille, confused, stood in front of the desk. He didn't like it. He was used to sitting behind the desk while others stood. Considering the circumstances, he wasn't about to protest. The giant, divinely handsome, bearded, pipe-smoking man behind the desk was not one you'd screw around with. However, the gray eyes, though steely, weren't quite those of a Wall Street banker. They held a hint of compassion.

Unable to meet those eyes, DeMille looked at the angel by his side. He'd always thought angels had wings. This one didn't, though he could certainly fly. He'd carried DeMille in his arms up through the stratosphere to a city of gold somewhere between the Earth and the moon. Without a space suit, too.

God, like all great entities, came right to the point.

"This is 1980 A.D. In twenty years it'll be time for The Millennium. The day of judgment. The events as depicted in the Book of Revelation or the Apocalypse by St. John the Divine. You know, the seven seals, the four horsemen, the moon dripping blood, Armageddon, and all that."

DeMille wished he'd be invited to sit down. Being dead for twenty-one years, during which he'd not moved a muscle, had tended to weaken him.

"Take a chair," God said. "Gabe, bring the man a brandy." He puffed on his pipe; tiny lightning crackled through the clouds of smoke.

"Here you are, Mr. DeMille," Gabriel said, handing him the liqueur in a cut quartz goblet. "Napoleon 1880."

DeMille knew there wasn't any such thing as a one-hundred-year-old brandy, but he didn't argue. Anyway, the stuff certainly tasted like it was. They really lived up here.

God sighed, and he said, "The main trouble is that not many people really believe in Me anymore. So My powers are not what they once were. The old gods, Zeus, Odin, all that bunch, lost their strength and just faded away, like old soldiers, when their worshippers ceased to believe in them.

"So, I just can't handle the end of the world by Myself any more. I need someone with experience, know-how, connections, and a reputation. Somebody people know really existed. You. Unless you know of somebody who's made more biblical epics than you have."

"That'll be the day," DeMille said. "But what about the unions? They really gave me a hard time, the commie bas . . . uh, so-and-so's. Are they as strong as ever?"

"You wouldn't believe their clout nowadays."

DeMille bit his lip, then said, "I want them dissolved. If I only got twenty years to produce this film, I can't be held up by a bunch of gold-brickers."

"No way," God said. "They'd all strike, and we can't afford any delays."

He looked at his big railroad watch. "We're going to be on a very tight schedule."

"Well, I don't know," DeMille said. "You can't get anything done with all their regulations, interunion jealousies, and the featherbedding. And the wages! It's no wonder it's so hard to show a profit. It's too much of a hassle!"

"I can always get D. W. Griffith."

DeMille's face turned red. "You want a grade-B production? No, no, that's all right! I'll do it, do it!"

God smiled and leaned back. "I thought so. By the way, you're not the producer, too; I am. My angels will be the executive producers. They haven't had much to do for several millennia, and the devil makes work for idle hands, you know. Haw, haw! You'll be the chief director, of course. But this is going to be quite a job. You'll have to have at least a hundred thousand assistant directors."

"But . . . that means training about 99,000 directors!"

"That's the least of our problems. Now you can see why I want to get things going immediately."

DeMille gripped the arms of the chair and said, weakly, "Who's going to finance this?"

God frowned. "That's another problem. My Antagonist has control of all the banks. If worse comes to worse, I could melt down the heavenly city and sell it. But the bottom of the gold market would drop all the way to hell. And I'd have to move to Beverly Hills. You wouldn't believe the smog there or the prices they're asking for houses.

"However, I think I can get the money. Leave that to Me."

The men who really owned the American banks sat at a long mahogany table in a huge room in a Manhattan skyscraper. The Chairman of the Board sat at the head. He didn't have the horns, tail, and hooves which legend gave him. Nor did he have an odor of brimstone. More like Brut. He was devilishly handsome and the biggest and best-built man in the room. He looked like he could have been the chief of the angels and in fact once had been. His eyes *were* evil but no more so than the others at the table, bar one.

The exception, Raphael, sat the other end of the table. The only detractions from his angelic appearance were his bloodshot eyes. His apartment on the West Side had paper-thin walls, and the swingers' party next door had kept him awake most of the night. Despite his fatigue, he'd been quite effective in presenting the offer from above.

Don Francisco "The Fixer" Fica drank a sixth glass of wine to up his courage, made the sign of the cross, most offensive to the Chairman, gulped, and spoke.

"I'm sorry, Signor, but that's the way the vote went. One hundred percent. It's a purely business proposition, legal, too, and there's no way we won't make a huge profit from it. We're gonna finance the movie, come hell or high water!"

Satan reared up from his chair and slammed a huge but well-manicured fist onto the table. Glasses of vino crashed over; plates half-filled with pasta and spaghetti rattled. All but Raphael paled.

"Dio motarello! Lecaculi! Cacasotti! Non romperci i coglioni! I'm the Chairman, and I say no, no, no!"

Fica looked at the other heads of the families. Mignotta, Fregna, Stronza, Loffa, Recchione, and Bocchino seemed scared, but each nodded the go-ahead at Fica.

"I'm indeed sorry that you don't see it our way," Fica said. "But I must ask for your resignation."

Only Raphael could meet The Big One's eyes, but business was business. Satan cursed and threatened. Nevertheless, he was stripped of all his shares of stock. He'd walked in the richest man in the world, and he stormed out penniless and an ex-member of the Organization.

Raphael caught up with him as he strode mumbling up Park Avenue.

"You're the father of lies," Raphael said, "so you can easily be a great success as an actor or politician. There's money in both fields. Fame, too. I suggest acting. You've got more friends in Hollywood than anywhere else."

"Are you nuts?" Satan snarled.

"No. Listen. I'm authorized to sign you up for the film on the end of the world. You'll be a lead, get top billing. You'll have to share it with The Son, but we can guarantee you a bigger dressing room than His. You'll be playing yourself, so it ought to be easy work."

Satan laughed so loudly that he cleared the sidewalks for two blocks. The Empire State Building swayed more than it should have in the wind.

"You and your Boss must think I'm pretty dumb! Without me the film's a flop. You're up a creek without a paddle. Why should I help you? If I do I end up at the bottom of a flaming pit forever. Bug off!"

Raphael shouted after him, "We can always get Roman Polanski!"

Raphael reported to God, who was taking His ease on His jasper and carnelian throne above which glowed a rainbow.

"He's right, Your Divinity. If he refuses to co-operate, the whole deal's off. No real Satan, no real Apocalypse."

God smiled. "We'll see."

Raphael wanted to ask Him what He had in mind. But an angel appeared with a request that God come to the special effects department. Its technicians were having trouble with the roll-up-the-sky-like-a-scroll machine.

"Schmucks!" God growled. "Do I have to do everything?"

Satan moved into a tenement on 121st Street and went on welfare. It wasn't a bad life, not for one who was used to hell. But two months later, his checks quit coming. There was no unemployment anymore. Anyone who was capable of working but wouldn't was out of luck. What had happened was that Central Casting had hired everybody in the world as production workers, stars, bit players, or extras.

Meanwhile, all the advertising agencies in the world had spread the word, good or bad depending upon the viewpoint, that the Bible was true. If you weren't a Christian, and, what was worse, a sincere Christian, you were doomed to perdition.

Raphael shot up to Heaven again.

"My God, You wouldn't believe what's happening! The Christians are repenting of their sins and promising to be good forever and ever, amen! The Jews, Moslems, Hindus, Buddhists, scientologists, animists, you name them, are lining up at the baptismal fonts! What a mess! The atheists have converted, too, and all the communist and Marxian socialist governments have been overthrown!"

"That's nice," God said. "But I'll really believe in the sincerity of the Christian nations when they kick out their present administrations. Down to the local dogcatcher."

"They're doing it!" Raphael shouted. "But maybe You don't understand! This isn't the way things go in the Book of Revelation! We'll have to do some very extensive rewriting of the script! Unless You straighten things out!"

God seemed very calm. "The script? How's Ellison coming along with it?"

Of course, God knew everything that was happening, but He pretended sometimes that He didn't. It was His excuse for talking. Just issuing a command every once in a while made for long silences, sometimes lasting for centuries.

He had hired only science fiction writers to work on the script since they were the only ones with imaginations big enough to handle the job. Besides, they weren't bothered by scientific impossibilities. God loved Ellison, the head writer, because he was the only human he'd met so far who wasn't afraid to argue with Him. Ellison was severely handicapped, however, because he wasn't allowed to use obscenities while in His presence.

"Ellison's going to have a hemorrhage when he finds out about the rewrites," Raphael said. "He gets screaming mad if anyone messes around with his scripts."

"I'll have him up for dinner," God said. "If he gets too obstreperous, I'll toss around a few lightning bolts. If he thinks he was burned before . . . Well!"

Raphael wanted to question God about the tampering with the book, but just then the head of Budgets came in. The angel beat it. God got very upset when He had to deal with money matters.

The head assistant director said, "We got a big problem now, Mr. DeMille. We can't have any Armageddon. Israel's willing to rent the site to us, but where are we going to get the forces of Gog and Magog to fight against the good guys? Everybody's converted. Nobody's willing to fight on the side of Antichrist and Satan. That means we've got to change the script again. I don't want to be the one to tell Ellison. . . ."

"Do I have to think of everything?" DeMille said. "It's no problem. Just hire actors to play the villains."

"I already thought of that. But they want a bonus. They say they might be persecuted just for *playing* the guys in the black hats. They call it the social-stigma bonus. But the guilds and the unions won't go for it. Equal pay for all extras or no movie and that's that."

DeMille sighed. "It won't make any difference anyway as long as we can't get Satan to play himself."

The assistant nodded. So far, they'd been shooting around the devil's scenes. But they couldn't put it off much longer.

DeMille stood up. "I have to watch the auditions for The Great Whore of Babylon."

The field of 100,000 candidates for the role had been narrowed to a hundred, but from what he'd heard none of these could play the part. They were all good Christians now, no matter what they'd been before, and they just didn't have their hearts in the role. DeMille had intended to cast his brand-new mistress, a starlet, a hot little number—if promises meant anything—100 percent right for the part. But just before they went to bed for the first time, he'd gotten a phone call.

"None of this hankypanky, C.B.," God had said. "You're now a devout worshipper of Me, one of the lost sheep that's found its way back to the fold. So get with it. Otherwise, back to Forest Lawn for you, and I use Griffith."

"But—but I'm Cecil B. DeMille! The rules are O.K. for the common people, but—"

"Throw that scarlet woman out! Shape up or ship out! If you marry her, fine! But remember, there'll be no more divorces!"

DeMille was glum. Eternity was going to be like living forever next door to the Board of Censors.

The next day, his secretary, very excited, buzzed him.

"Mr. DeMille! Satan's here! I don't have him for an appointment, but he says he's always had a long-standing one with you!"

Demoniac laughter bellowed through the intercom.

"C.B., my boy! I've changed my mind! I tried out anonymously for the part, but your shithead assistant said I wasn't the type for the role! So I've come to you! I can start work as soon as we sign the contract!"

The contract, however, was not the one the great director had in mind. Satan, smoking a big cigar, chuckling, cavorting, read the terms.

"And don't worry about signing in your blood. It's unsanitary. Just ink in your John Henry, and all's well that ends in hell."

"You get my soul," DeMille said weakly.

"It's not much of a bargain for me. But if you don't sign it, you won't get me. Without me, the movie's a bomb. Ask The Producer, He'll tell you how it is."

"I'll call Him now."

"No! Sign now, this very second, or I walk out forever!"

DeMille bowed his head, more in pain than in prayer.

"Now!"

DeMille wrote on the dotted line. There had never been any genuine indecision. After all, he was a film director.

After snickering Satan had left, DeMille punched a phone number. The circuits transmitted this to a station which beamed the pulses up to a satellite which transmitted these directly to the heavenly city. Somehow, he got a wrong number. He hung up quickly when Israel, the angel of death, answered. The second attempt, he got through.

"Your Divinity, I suppose. You know what I just did? It *was* the only way we could get him to play himself. You understand that, don't You?"

"Yes, but if you're thinking of breaking the contract or getting me to do it for you, forget it. What kind of an image would I have if I did something unethical like that? But not to worry. He can't get his hooks into your soul until I say so."

Not to worry? DeMille thought. I'm the one who's going to hell, not Him.

"Speaking of hooks, let Me remind you of a clause in your contract with The Studio. If you ever fall from grace, and I'm not talking about that little bimbo you were going to make your mistress, you'll die. The Mafia isn't the only one that puts out a contract. *Capice?*"

DeMille, sweating and cold, hung up. In a sense, he was already in hell. All his life with no women except for one wife? It was bad enough to have no variety, but what if whoever he married cut him off, like one of his wives—what was her name?—had done?

Moreover, he couldn't get loaded out of his skull even to forget his marital woes. God, though not prohibiting booze in His Book, had said that moderation in strong liquor was required and no excuses. Well, maybe he could drink beer, however disgustingly plebeian that was.

He wasn't even happy with his work now. He just didn't get the respect he had in the old days. When he chewed out the camerapeople, the grips, the gaffers, the actors, they stormed back at him that he didn't have the proper Christian humility, he was too high and mighty, too arrogant. God would get him if he didn't watch his big fucking mouth.

This left him speechless and quivering. He'd always thought, and acted accordingly, that the director, not God, was God. He remembered telling Charlton Heston that when Heston, who after all was *only* Moses, had thrown a temper tantrum when he'd stepped in a pile of camel shit during the filming of *The Ten Commandments.*

Was there more to the making of the end-of-the-world than appeared on the surface? Had God seemingly forgiven everybody their sins and lack of faith but was subtly, even insidiously, making everybody pay by suffering? Had He forgiven but not forgotten? Or vice versa?

God marked even the fall of a sparrow, though why the sparrow, a notoriously obnoxious and dirty bird, should be significant in God's eye was beyond DeMille.

He had the uneasy feeling that everything wasn't as simple and as obvious as he'd thought when he'd been untimely ripped from the grave in a sort of Caesarean section and carried off like a nursing baby in Gabriel's arms to the office of The Ultimate Producer.

From the *Playboy* Interview feature, December, 1990.

Playboy: Mr. Satan, why did you decide to play yourself after all?

Satan: Damned if I know.

Playboy: The rumors are that you'll be required to wear clothes in the latter-day scenes but that you steadfastly refuse. Are these rumors true?

Satan: Yes indeed. Everybody knows I never wear clothes except when I want to appear among humans without attracting undue attention. If I wear clothes it'd be unrealistic. It'd be phony, though God knows there are enough fake things in this movie. The Producer says this is going to be a PG picture, not an X-rated. That's why I walked off the set the other day. My lawyers are negotiating with The Studio now about his. But you can bet your ass that I won't go back unless things go my way, the right way. After all, I am an artist, and I have my integrity. Tell me, if you had a prong this size, would you hide it?

Playboy: The Chicago cops would arrest me before I got a block from my pad. I don't know, though, if they'd charge me with indecent exposure or being careless with a natural resource.

Satan: They wouldn't dare arrest me. I got too much on the city administration.

Playboy: That's *some* whopper. But I thought angels were sexless. You are a fallen angel, aren't you?

Satan: You jerk! What kind of researcher are you? Right there in the Bible, Genesis 6:2, it says that the sons of God, that is, the angels, took the daughters of men as wives and had children by them. You think the kids were test tube babies? Also, you dunce, I refer you to Jude 7 where it's said that the angels, like the Sodomites, committed fornications and followed unnatural lusts.

Playboy: Whew! That brimstone! There's no need getting so hot under the collar, Mr. Satan. I only converted a few years ago. I haven't had much chance to read the Bible.

Satan: I read the Bible every day. All of it. I'm a speed-reader, you know.

Playboy: You read the Bible? (Pause). Hee, hee! Do you read it for the same reason W. C. Fields did when he was dying?

Satan: What's that?

Playboy: Looking for loopholes.

DeMille was in a satellite and supervising the camerapeople while they shot the takes from ten miles up. He didn't like at all the terrific pressure he was working under. There was no chance to shoot every scene three or four times to get the best angle. Or to reshoot if the actors blew their lines. And, oh, sweet Jesus, they were blowing them all over the world!

He mopped his bald head. "I don't care what The Producer says! We have to retake at least a thousand scenes. And we've a million miles of film to go yet!"

They were getting close to the end of the breaking-of-the-seven-seals sequences. The Lamb, played by The Producer's Son, had just broken the sixth seal. The violent worldwide earthquake had gone well. The sun-turning-black-as-a-funeral-pall had been a breeze. But the moon-all-red-as-blood had had some color problems. The rushes looked more like Colonel Sanders' orange juice than hemoglobin. In DeMille's opinion the stars-falling-to-earth-like-figs-shaken-down-by-a-gale scenes had been excellent, visually speaking. But everybody knew that the stars were not little blazing stones set in the sky but were colossal balls of atomic fires each of which was many times bigger than Earth. Even one of them, a million miles from Earth, would destroy it. So where was the credibility factor?

"I don't understand you, Boss," DeMille's assistant said. "You didn't worry about credibility when you made *The Ten Commandments*. When Heston, I mean, Moses, parted the Red Sea, it was the fakiest thing I ever saw. It must've made unbelievers out of millions of Christians. But the film was a box-office success."

"It was the dancing girls that brought off the whole thing!" DeMille screamed. "Who cares about all that other bullshit when they can see all those beautiful long-legged snatches twirling their veils!"

His secretary floated from her chair. "I quit, you male chauvinistic pig! So me and my sisters are just snatches to you, you bald-headed cunt?"

His hotline to the heavenly city rang. He picked up the phone.

"Watch your language!" The Producer thundered. "If you step out of line too many times, I'll send you back to the grave! And Satan gets you right then and there!"

Chastened but boiling near the danger point, DeMille got back to business, called Art in Hollywood. The sweep of the satellite around Earth included the sky-vanishing-as-a-scroll-is-rolled-up scenes, where every-mountain-and-island-is-removed-from-its-place. If the script had called for a literal removing, the tectonics problem would have been terrific and perhaps impossible. But in this case the special effects departments only had to simulate the scenes.

Even so, the budget was strained. However, The Producer, through his unique abilities, was able to carry these off. Whereas, in the original script, genuine displacements of Greenland, England, Ireland, Japan, and Madagascar had been called for, not to mention thousands of smaller islands, these were only faked.

"Your Divinity, I have some bad news," Raphael said.

The Producer was too busy to indulge in talking about something he already knew. Millions of the faithful had backslid and taken up their old sinful ways. They believed that since so many events of the Apocalypse were being faked, God must not be capable of making any really big catastrophes. So, they didn't have anything to worry about.

The Producer, however, had decided that it would not only be good to wipe out some of the wicked but it would strengthen the faithful if they saw that God still had some muscle.

"They'll get the real thing next time," He said. "But we have to give DeMille time to set up his cameras at the right places. And we'll have to have the script rewritten, of course."

Raphael groaned. "Couldn't somebody else tell Ellison? He'll carry on something awful."

"I'll tell him. You look pretty pooped, Rafe. You need a little R&R. Take two weeks off. But don't do it on Earth. Things are going to be very unsettling there for a while."

Raphael, who had a tender heart, said, "Thanks, Boss. I'd just as soon not be around to see it."

The seal was stamped on the foreheads of the faithful, marking them safe from the burning of a third of Earth, the burning of a third of the sea to blood along with the sinking of a third of the ships at sea (which also included the crashing of a third of the airplanes in the air, something St. John had overlooked), the turning of a third of all water to wormwood (a superfluous measure since a third was already thoroughly polluted), the failure of a third of daylight, the release of giant mutant locusts from the abyss, and the release of poison-gas-breathing mutant horses, which slew a third of mankind.

DeMille was delighted. Never had such terrifying scenes been filmed. And these were nothing to the plagues which followed. He had enough film from the cutting room to make a hundred documentaries after the movie was shown. And then he got a call from The Producer.

"It's back to the special effects, my boy."

"But why, Your Divinity? We still have to shoot the-Great-Whore-of-Babylon sequences, the two-Beasts-and-the-marking-of-the-wicked, the Mount-Zion-and-The-Lamb-with-His-one-hundred - and - forty - thousand - good - men - who - haven't - defiled - themselves-with-women, the—"

"Because there aren't any wicked left by now, you dolt! And not too many of the good, either!"

"That couldn't be helped," DeMille said. "Those gas-breathing, scorpion-tailed horses kind of got out of hand. But we just *have* to have the scenes where the rest of mankind that survives the plagues still doesn't abjure its worship of idols and doesn't repent of its murders, sorcery, fornications, and robberies."

"Rewrite the script."

"Ellison will quit for sure this time."

"That's all right. I already have some hack from Peoria lined up to take his place. And cheaper, too."

DeMille took his outfit, one hundred thousand strong, to the heavenly city. Here they shot the war between Satan and his demons and Michael and his angels. This was not in the chronological sequence as written by St. John. But the logistics problems were so tremendous that it was thought best to film these out of order.

Per the rewritten script, Satan and his host were defeated, but a lot of nonbelligerents were casualties, including DeMille's best cameraperson. Moreover, there was a delay in production when Satan insisted that a stuntperson do the part where he was hurled from heaven to earth.

"Or use a dummy!" he yelled. "Twenty thousand miles is a hell of a long way to fall! If I'm hurt badly I might not be able to finish the movie!"

The screaming match between the director and Satan took place on the edge of the city. The Producer, unnoticed, came up behind Satan and kicked him from the city for the second time in their relationship with utter ruin and furious combustion.

Shrieking, "I'll sue! I'll sue!" Satan fell towards the planet below. He made a fine spectacle in his blazing entrance into the atmosphere, but the people on Earth paid it little attention. They were used to fiery portents in the sky. In fact, they were getting fed up with them.

DeMille screamed and danced around and jumped up and down. Only the presence of The Producer kept him from using foul and abusive language.

"We didn't get it on camera! Now we'll have to shoot it over!"

"His contract calls for only one fall," God said. "You'd better shoot the War-between-The-Faithful-and-True-Rider-against-the-beast-and-the-false-prophet while he recovers."

"What'll I do about the fall?" DeMille moaned.

"Fake it," the Producer said, and He went back to His office.

Per the script, an angel came down from heaven and bound up the badly injured and burned and groaning Satan with a chain and threw him into the abyss, the Grand Canyon. Then he shut and sealed it over him (what a terrific sequence that was!) so that Satan might seduce the nations no more until a thousand years had passed.

A few years later the devil's writhings caused a volcano to form above him, and the Environmental Protection Agency filed suit against Celestial Productions, Inc., because of the resultant pollution of the atmosphere.

Then God, very powerful now that only believers existed on Earth, performed the first resurrection. In this, only the martyrs were raised. And Earth, which had had much elbow room because of the recent wars and plagues, was suddenly crowded again.

Part I was finished except for the reshooting of some scenes, the dubbing in of voice and background noise, and the synchronization of the music, which was done by the cherubim and seraphim (all now unionized).

The great night of the premiere in a newly built theater in Hollywood, six million capacity, arrived. DeMille got a standing ovation after it was over. But *Time* and *Newsweek* and *The Manchester Guardian* panned the movie.

"There are some people who may go to hell after all," God growled.

DeMille didn't care about that. The film was a box-office success, grossing ten billion dollars in the first six months. And when he considered the reruns in theaters and the TV rights . . . well, had anyone ever done better?

He had a thousand more years to live. That seemed like a

long time. Now. But . . . what would happen to him when Satan was released to seduce the nations again? According to John the Divine's book, there'd be another worldwide battle. Then Satan, defeated, would be cast into the lake of fire and sulphur in the abyss.

(He'd be allowed to keep his Oscar, however.)

Would God let Satan, per the contract DeMille had signed with the devil, take DeMille with him into the abyss? Or would He keep him safe long enough to finish directing Part II? After Satan was buried for good, there'd be a second resurrection and a judging of those raised from the dead. The goats, the bad guys, would be hurled into the pit to keep Satan company. DeMille should be with the saved, the sheep, because he had been born again. But there was that contract with The Tempter.

DeMille arranged a conference with The Producer. Ostensibly, it was about Part II, but DeMille managed to bring up the subject which really interested him.

"I can't break your contract with him," God said.

"But I only signed it so that You'd be sure to get Satan for the role. It was a self-sacrifice. Greater love hath no man and all that. Doesn't that count for anything?"

"Let's discuss the shooting of the new heaven and the new Earth sequences."

At last I'm not going to be put into hell until the movie is done, DeMille thought. But after that? He couldn't endure thinking about it.

"It's going to be a terrible technical problem," God said, interrupting DeMille's gloomy thoughts. "When the second resurrection takes place, there won't be even Standing Room Only on Earth. That's why I'm dissolving the old Earth and making a new one. But I can't just duplicate the old Earth. The problem of Lebensraum would still remain. Now, what I'm contemplating is a Dyson sphere."

"What's that?"

"A scheme by a 20th-century mathematician to break up the giant planet Jupiter into large pieces and set them in orbit at the distance of Earth from the sun. The surfaces of the pieces would provide room for a population enormously larger than Earth's. It's a Godlike concept."

"What a documentary its filming would be!" DeMille said.

"Of course, if we could write some love interest in it, we could make a he . . . pardon me, a heaven of a good story!"

God looked at his big railroad watch.

"I have another appointment, C.B. The conference is over."

DeMille said good-by and walked dejectedly towards the door. He still hadn't gotten an answer about his ultimate fate. God was stringing him along. He felt that he wouldn't know until the last minute what was going to happen to him. He'd be suffering a thousand years of uncertainty, of mental torture. His life would be a cliff-hanger. Will God relent? Or will he save the hero at the very last second?

"C.B.," God said.

DeMille spun around, his heart thudding, his knees turned to water. Was this it? The fatal finale? Had God, in His mysterious and subtle way, decided for some reason that there'd be no Continued in Next Chapter for him? It didn't seem likely, but then The Producer had never promised that He'd use him as the director of Part II nor had He signed a contract with him. Maybe, like so many temperamental producers, He'd suddenly concluded that DeMille wasn't the right one for the job. Which meant that He could arrange it so that his ex-director would be thrown now, right this minute, into the lake of fire.

God said, "I can't break your contract with Satan. So. . . ."

"Yes?"

DeMille's voice sounded to him as if he were speaking very far away.

"Satan can't have your soul until you die."

"Yes?"

His voice was only a trickle of sound, a last few drops of water from a clogged drainpipe.

"So, if you don't die, and that, of course, depends upon your behavior, Satan can't ever have your soul."

God smiled and said, "See you in eternity."

But at My Back
I Will Always Hear

David Morrell

First Blood (1972), David Morrell's (1943–   ) searing portrait of
a Vietnam veteran's painful readjustment to American society,
became a cultural icon through its film adaptation and block-
buster sequel, *Rambo: First Blood, Part 2.* In addition to writing
the horror novel *The Totem* (1979), he has established a name
for himself as an espionage writer through the loosely connected
trilogy, *The Brotherhood of the Rose* (1985), *The Fraternity of
the Stone* (1985), and *The League of Night and Fog* (1987).
"But at My Back I Will Always Hear" (1983) expresses a theme
that recurs throughout Morrell's short fiction: the potentially de-
structive power of love when carried to obsessive extremes.

She phoned again last night. At 3 A.M. the way she always
does. I'm scared to death. I can't keep running. On the hotel's register downstairs, I lied about my name, address, and
occupation, hoping to hide from her. My real name's Charles
Ingram. Though I'm here in Johnstown, Pennsylvania, I'm from
Iowa City, Iowa. I teach—or used to teach until three days ago—
creative writing at the University. I can't risk going back there.
But I don't think I can hide much longer. Each night, she comes
closer.

From the start, she scared me. I came to school at eight to
prepare my classes. Through the side door of the English building
I went up a stairwell to my third-floor office, which was isolated
by a fire door from all the other offices. My colleagues used to
joke that I'd been banished, but I didn't care, for in my far-off

corner I could concentrate. Few students interrupted me. Regardless of the busy noises past the fire door, I sometimes felt there was no one else inside the building. And indeed at 8 A.M. I often *was* the only person in the building.

That day I was wrong, however, Clutching my heavy briefcase, I trudged up the stairwell. My scraping footsteps echoed off the walls of the pale-red cinderblock, the stairs of pale-green imitation marble. First floor. Second floor. The neon lights glowed coldly. Then the stairwell angled toward the third floor, and I saw her waiting on a chair outside my office. Pausing, I frowned up at her. I felt uneasy.

Eight A.M., for you, is probably not early. You've been up for quite a while so you can get to work on time or get your children off to school. But 8 A.M., for college students, is the middle of the night. They don't like morning classes. When their schedules force them to attend one, they don't crawl from bed until they absolutely have to, and they don't come stumbling into class until I'm just about to start my lecture.

I felt startled, then, to find her waiting ninety minutes early. She sat tensely: lifeless dull brown hair, a shapeless dingy sweater, baggy faded jeans with patches on the knees and frays around the cuffs. Her eyes seemed haunted, wild, and deep and dark.

I climbed the last few steps and, puzzled, stopped before her. "Do you want an early conference?"

Instead of answering, she nodded bleakly.

"You're concerned about a grade I gave you?"

This time, though, in pain she shook her head from side to side.

Confused, I fumbled with my key and opened the office, stepping in. The room was small and narrow: a desk, two chairs, a wall of bookshelves, and a window. As I sat behind the desk, I watched her slowly come inside. She glanced around uncertainly. Distraught, she shut the door.

That made me nervous. When a female student shuts the door, I start to worry that a colleague or a student might walk up the stairs and hear a female voice and wonder what's so private I want to keep the door closed. Though I should have told her to reopen it, her frantic eyes aroused such pity in me that I sacrificed my principle, deciding her torment was so personal she could talk about it only in strict secrecy.

"Sit down." I smiled and tried to make her feel at ease, though I myself was not at ease. "What seems to be the difficulty, Miss . . . ? I'm sorry, but I don't recall your name."

"Samantha Perry. I don't like 'Samantha,' though." She fidgeted. "I've shortened it to—"

"Yes? To what?"

"To 'Sam.' I'm in your Tuesday-Thursday class." She bit her lip. "You spoke to me."

I frowned, not understanding. "You mean what I taught seemed vivid to you? I inspired you to write a better story?"

"Mr. Ingram, no. I mean you *spoke* to me. You stared at me while you were teaching. You ignored the other students. You directed what you said to *me*. When you talked about Hemingway, how Frederic Henry wants to go to bed with Catherine"—She swallowed.—"you were asking me to go to bed with you."

I gaped. To disguise my shock, I quickly lit a cigarette. "You're mistaken."

"But I *heard* you. You kept staring straight at *me*. I felt all the other students knew what you were doing."

"I was only lecturing. I often look at students' faces to make sure they pay attention. You received the wrong impression."

"You weren't asking me to go to bed with you?" Her voice sounded anguished.

"No. I don't trade sex for grades."

"But I don't care about a grade!"

"I'm married. Happily. I've got two children. Anyway, suppose I did intend to proposition you. Would I do it in the middle of a class? I'd be foolish."

"Then you never meant to—" She kept biting her lip.

"I'm sorry."

"But you speak to me! Outside class I hear your voice! When I'm in my room or walking down the street! You talk to me when I'm asleep! You say you want to go to bed with me!"

My skin prickled. I felt frozen. "You're mistaken. Your imagination's playing tricks."

"But I hear your voice so clearly! When I'm studying or—"

"How? If I'm not there."

"You send your thoughts! You concentrate and put your voice inside my mind!"

Adrenaline scalded my stomach. I frantically sought an argument to disillusion her. "Telepathy? I don't believe in it. I've never tried to send my thoughts to you."

"Unconsciously?"

I shook my head from side to side. I couldn't bring myself to tell her: of all the female students in her class, she looked so plain, even if I wasn't married I'd never have wanted sex with her.

"You're studying too hard. You want to do so well you're preoccupied with me. That's why you think you hear my voice when I'm not there. I try to make my lectures vivid. As a consequence, you think I'm speaking totally to you."

"Then you shouldn't teach that way!" she shouted. "It's not fair! It's cruel! It's teasing!" Tears streamed down her face. "You made a fool of me!"

"I didn't mean to."

"But you did! You tricked me! You misled me!"

"No."

She stood so quickly I flinched, afraid she'd lunge at me or scream for help and claim I'd tried to rape her. That damned door. I cursed myself for not insisting she leave it open.

She rushed sobbing toward it. She pawed the knob and stumbled out, hysterically retreating down the stairwell.

Shaken, I stubbed out my cigarette, grabbing another. My chest tightened as I heard the dwindling echo of her wracking sobs, the awkward scuffle of her dimming footsteps, then the low deep rumble of the outside door.

The silence settled over me.

An hour later I found her waiting in class. She'd wiped her tears. The only signs of what had happened were her red and puffy eyes. She sat alertly, pen to paper. I carefully didn't face her as I spoke. She seldom glanced up from her notes.

After class I asked my graduate assistant if he knew her.

"You mean Sam? Sure, I know her. She's been getting Ds. She had a conference with me. Instead of asking how to get a better grade, though, all she did was talk about you, pumping me for information. She's got quite a thing for you. Too bad about her."

"Why?"

"Well, she's so plain, she doesn't have many friends. I doubt she goes out much. There's a problem with her father. She was vague about it, but I had the sense her three sisters are so beautiful that Daddy treats her as the ugly duckling. She wants very much to please him. He ignores her, though. He's practically disowned her. You remind her of him."

"Who? Of her father?"

"She admits you're ten years younger than him, but she says you look exactly like him."

I felt heartsick.

Two days later, I found her waiting for me—again at 8 A.M.—outside my office.

Tense, I unlocked the door. As if she heard my thought, she didn't shut it this time. Sitting before my desk, she didn't fidget. She just stared at me.

"It happened again," she said.

"In class I didn't even look at you."

"No, afterward, when I went to the library." She drew an anguished breath. "And later—I ate supper in the dorm. I heard your voice so clearly, I was sure you were in the room."

"What time was that?"

"Five-thirty."

"I was having cocktails with the Dean. Believe me, Sam, I wasn't sending messages to you. I didn't even *think* of you."

"I couldn't have imagined it! You wanted me to go to bed with you!"

"I wanted research money from the Dean. I thought of nothing else. My mind was totally involved in trying to convince him. When I didn't get the money, I was too annoyed to concentrate on anything but getting drunk."

"Your voice—"

"It isn't real. If I sent thoughts to you, wouldn't I admit what I was doing? When you asked me, wouldn't I confirm the message? Why would I deny it?"

"I'm afraid."

"You're troubled by your father."

"What?"

"My graduate assistant says you identify me with your father."

She went ashen. "That's supposed to be a secret!"

"Sam, I asked him. He won't lie to me."

"If you remind me of my father, if I want to go to bed with you, then I must want to go to bed with—"

"Sam—"

"—my father! You must think I'm disgusting!"

"No, I think you're confused. You ought to find some help. You ought to see a—"

But she never let me finish. Weeping again, ashamed, hysterical, she bolted from the room.

And that's the last I ever saw of her. An hour later, when I started lecturing, she wasn't in class. A few days later I received a drop-slip from the registrar, informing me she'd canceled all her classes.

I forgot her.

Summer came. Then fall arrived. November. On a rainy Tuesday night, my wife and I stayed up to watch the close results of the election, worried for our presidential candidate.

At 3 A.M. the phone rang. No one calls that late unless . . .

The jangle of the phone made me bang my head as I searched for a beer in the fridge. I rubbed my throbbing skull and swung alarmed as Jean, my wife, came from the living room and squinted toward the kitchen phone.

"It might be just a friend," I said. "Election gossip."

But I worried about our parents. Maybe one of them was sick or . . .

I watched uneasily as Jean picked up the phone.

"Hello?" She listened apprehensively. Frowning, she put her hand across the mouthpiece. "It's for you. A woman."

"What?"

"She's young. She asked for Mr. Ingram."

"Damn, a student."

"At 3 A.M.?"

I almost didn't think to shut the fridge. Annoyed, I yanked the pop-tab off the can of beer. My marriage is successful. I'll admit we've had our troubles. So has every couple. But we've faced those troubles, and we're happy. Jean is thirty-five, attractive, smart, and patient. But her trust in me was clearly tested at that moment. A woman had to know me awfully well to call at 3 A.M.

"Let's find out." I grabbed the phone. To prove my innocence to Jean, I roughly said, "Yeah, what?"

"I heard you." The female voice was frail and plaintive, trembling.

"Who *is* this?" I said angrily.

"It's me."

I heard a low-pitched crackle on the line.

"Who the hell is *me*? Just tell me what your name is."

"Sam."

My knees went weak. I slumped against the wall.

Jean stared. "What's wrong?" Her eyes narrowed with suspicion.

"Sam, it's 3 A.M. What's so damn important you can't wait to call me during office hours?"

"Three? It can't be. No, it's one."

"It's three. For God's sake, Sam, I know what time it is."

"Please, don't get angry. On my radio the news announcer said it was one o'clock."

"Where *are* you, Sam?"

"At Berkeley."

"California? Sam, the time-zone difference. In the Midwest it's two hours later. Here it's three o'clock."

". . . I guess I just forgot."

"But that's absurd. Have you been drinking? Are you drunk?"

"No, not exactly."

"What the hell does *that* mean?"

"Well, I took some pills. I'm not sure what they were."

"Oh, Jesus."

"Then I heard you. You were speaking to me."

"No. I told you your mind's playing tricks. The voice isn't real. You're imagining—"

"You called to me. You said you wanted me to go to bed with you. You wanted me to come to you."

"To Iowa? No. You've got to understand. Don't do it. I'm not sending thoughts to you."

"You're lying! Tell me why you're lying!"

"I don't want to go to bed with you. I'm glad you're in Berke-

ley. Stay there. Get some help. Lord, don't you realize? Those
pills. They make you hear my voice. They make you hallucinate."

"I . . ."

"Trust me, Sam. Believe me. I'm not sending thoughts to you.
I didn't even know you'd gone to Berkeley. You're two thousand
miles away from me. What you're suggesting is impossible."

She didn't answer. All I heard was low-pitched static.

"Sam—"

The dial tone abruptly droned. My stomach sank. Appalled, I
kept the phone against my ear. I swallowed dryly, shaking as I
set the phone back on its cradle.

Jean glared. "Who was that? She wasn't any 'Sam.' She wants
to go to bed with you? At 3 A.M.? What games have you been
playing?"

"None." I gulped my beer, but my throat stayed dry. "You'd
better sit. I'll get a beer for you."

Jean clutched her stomach.

"It's not what you think. I promise I'm not screwing anybody.
But it's bad. I'm scared."

I handed Jean a beer.

"I don't know why it happened. But last spring, at 8 A.M., I
went to school and . . ."

Jean listened, troubled. Afterward she asked for Sam's description, somewhat mollified to learn she was plain and pitiful.

"The truth?" Jean asked.

"I promise you."

Jean studied me. "You did nothing to encourage her?"

"I guarantee it. I wasn't aware of her until I found her waiting
for me."

"But unconsciously?"

"Sam asked me that as well. I was only lecturing the best way
I know how."

Jean kept her eyes on me. She nodded, glancing toward her
beer. "Then she's disturbed. There's nothing you can do for her.
I'm glad she moved to Berkeley. In your place, I'd have been
afraid."

"I *am* afraid. She spooks me."

*   *   *

At a dinner party the next Saturday, I told our host and hostess what had happened, motivated more than just by need to share my fear with someone else, for while the host was both a friend and a colleague, he was married to a clinical psychologist. I needed professional advice.

Diane, the hostess, listened with slim interest until halfway through my story, when she suddenly sat straight and peered at me.

I faltered. "What's the matter?"

"Don't stop. What else?"

I frowned and finished, waiting for Diane's reaction. Instead she poured more wine. She offered more lasagna.

"Something bothered you."

She tucked her long black hair behind her ears. "It could be nothing."

"I need to know."

She nodded grimly. "I can't make a diagnosis merely on the basis of your story. I'd be irresponsible."

"But hypothetically . . ."

"And *only* hypothetically. She hears your voice. That's symptomatic of a severe disturbance. Paranoia, for example. Schizophrenia. The man who shot John Lennon heard a voice. And so did Manson. So did Son of Sam."

"My God," Jean said. "Her name." She set her fork down loudly.

"The parallel occurred to me," Diane said. "Chuck, if she identifies you with her father, she might be dangerous to Jean and to the children."

"Why?"

"Jealousy. To hurt the equivalent of her mother and her rival sisters."

I felt sick; the wine turned sour in my stomach.

"There's another possibility. No more encouraging. If you continue to reject her, she could be dangerous to you. Instead of dealing with her father, she might redirect her rage and jealousy toward you. By killing you, she'd be venting her frustration toward her father."

I felt panicked. "For the *good* news."

"Understood, I'm speaking hypothetically. Possibly she's lying to you, and she doesn't hear your voice. Or, as you guessed, the drugs she takes might make her hallucinate. There could be many explanations. Without seeing her, without the proper tests, I wouldn't dare to judge her symptoms. You're a friend, so I'm compromising. Possibly she's homicidal."

"Tell me what to do."

"For openers, I'd stay away from her."

"I'm *trying*. She called from California. She's threatening to come back here to see me."

"Talk her out of it."

"I'm no psychologist. I don't know what to say to her."

"Suggest she get professional advice."

"I tried that."

"Try again. But if you find her at your office, don't go in the room with her. Find other people. Crowds protect you."

"But at 8 A.M. there's no one in the building."

"Think of some excuse to leave her. Jean, if she comes to the house, don't let her in."

Jean paled. "I've never seen her. How could I identify her?"

"Chuck described her. Don't take chances. Don't trust anyone who might resemble her, and keep a close watch on the children."

"*How?* Rebecca's twelve. Sue's nine. I can't insist they stay around the house."

Diane turned her wineglass, saying nothing.

". . . Oh, dear Lord," Jean said.

The next few weeks were hellish. Every time the phone rang, Jean and I jerked, startled, staring at it. But the calls were from our friends or from our children's friends or from some insulation/magazine/home-siding salesman. Every day I mustered courage as I climbed the stairwell to my office. Silent prayers were answered. Sam was never there. My tension dissipated. I began to feel she no longer was obsessed with me.

Thanksgiving came—the last day of peace I've known. We went to church. Our parents live too far away for us to share the feast with them. But we invited friends to dinner. We watched football. I helped Jean make the dressing for the turkey. I made both the pumpkin pies. The friends we'd invited were my colleague and his wife, the clinical psychologist. She asked if my student had continued to harass me. Shaking my head from side to side, I grinned and raised my glass in special thanks.

The guests stayed late to watch a movie with us. Jean and I felt pleasantly exhausted, mellowed by good food, good drink, good friends, when after midnight we washed all the dishes, went to bed, made love, and drifted wearily to sleep.

The phone rang, shocking me awake. I fumbled toward the bedside lamp. Jean's eyes went wide with fright. She clutched my arm and pointed toward the clock. It was 3 A.M.

The phone kept ringing.

"Don't," Jean said.

"Suppose it's someone else."

"You know it isn't."

"If it's Sam and I don't answer, she might come to the house instead of phoning."

"For God's sake, make her stop."

I grabbed the phone, but my throat wouldn't work.

"I'm coming to you," the voice wailed.

"Sam?"

"I heard you. I won't disappoint you. I'll be there soon."

"No. Wait. Listen."

"I've been listening. I hear you all the time. The anguish in your voice. You're begging me to come to you, to hold you, to make love to you."

"That isn't true."

"You say your wife's jealous of me. I'll convince her she isn't being fair. I'll make her let you go. Then we'll be happy."

"Sam, where are you? Still at Berkeley?"

"Yes. I spent Thanksgiving by myself. My father didn't want me to come home."

"You have to stay there, Sam. I didn't send my voice. You need advice. You need to see a doctor. Will you do that for me? As a favor?"

"I already did. But Dr. Campbell doesn't understand. He thinks I'm imagining what I hear. He humors me. He doesn't realize how much you love me."

"Sam, you have to talk to him again. You have to tell him what you plan to do."

"I can't wait any longer. I'll be there soon. I'll be with you."

My heart pounded frantically. I heard a roar in my head. I flinched as the phone was yanked away from me.

Jean shouted to the mouthpiece, "Stay away from us! Don't call again! Stop terrorizing—"

Jean stared wildly at me. "No one's there. The line went dead. I hear just the dial tone."

I'm writing this as quickly as I can. I don't have much more time. It's almost three o'clock.

That night, we didn't try to go back to sleep. We couldn't. We got dressed and want downstairs where, drinking coffee, we decided what to do. At eight, as soon as we'd sent the kids to school, we drove to the police.

They listened sympathetically, but there was no way they could help us. After all, Sam hadn't broken any law. Her calls weren't obscene; it was difficult to prove harassment; she'd made no overt threats. Unless she harmed us, there was nothing the police could do.

"Protect us," I insisted.

"How?" the sergeant said.

"Assign an officer to guard the house."

"How long? A day, a week, a month? That woman might not even bother you again. We're overworked and understaffed. I'm sorry—I can't spare an officer whose only duty is to watch you. I can send a car to check the house from time to time. No more than that. But if this woman does show up and bother you, then call us. We'll take care of her."

"But that might be too late."

We took the children home from school. Sam couldn't have arrived from California yet, but what else could we do? I don't own any guns. If all of us stayed together, we had some chance for protection.

That was Friday. I slept lightly. Three A.M., the phone rang. It was Sam, of course.

"I'm coming."

"Sam, where are you?"

"Reno."

"You're not flying."

"No, I can't."

"Turn back, Sam. Go to Berkeley. See that doctor."

"I can't wait to see you."

"Please—"

The dial tone was droning.

I phoned Berkeley information. Sam had mentioned Dr. Campbell. But the operator couldn't find him in the yellow pages.

"Try the University," I blurted. "Student Counseling."

I was right. A Dr. Campbell was a university psychiatrist. On Saturday I couldn't reach him at his office, but a woman answered his home. He wouldn't be available until the afternoon. At four o'clock I finally got through to him.

"You've got a patient named Samantha Perry," I began.

"I did. Not anymore."

"I know. She's left for Iowa. She wants to see me. I'm afraid. I think she might be dangerous."

"Well, you don't have to worry."

"She's not dangerous?"

"Potentially she was."

"But tell me what to do when she arrives. You're treating her. You'll know what I should do."

"No, Mr. Ingram, she won't come to see you. On Thanksgiving night, at 1 A.M., she killed herself. An overdose of drugs."

My vision failed. I clutched the kitchen table to prevent myself from falling. "That's impossible."

"I saw the body. I identified it."

"But she called that night."

"What time?"

"At 3 A.M. Midwestern time."

"Or one o'clock in California. No doubt after or before she took the drugs. She didn't leave a note, but she called you."

"She gave no indication—"

"She mentioned you quite often. She was morbidly attracted to you. She had an extreme, unhealthy certainty that she was telepathic, that you put your voice inside her mind."

"I know that! Was she paranoid or homicidal?"

"Mr. Ingram, I've already said too much. Although she's dead, I can't violate her confidence."

"But I don't think she's dead."

"I beg your pardon?"

"If she died on Thursday night, then tell me how she called again on *Friday* night."

The line hummed. I sensed the doctor's hesitation. "Mr. Ingram, you're upset. You don't know what you're saying. You've confused the nights."

"I'm telling you she called again on Friday!"

"And I'm telling she died on *Thursday*. Either someone's tricking you, or else . . ." The doctor swallowed with discomfort.

"Or?" I trembled. "*I'm* the one who's hearing voices?"

"Mr. Ingram, don't upset yourself. You're honestly confused."

I slowly put the phone down, terrified. "I'm sure I heard her voice."

That night, Sam called again. At 3 A.M. From Salt Lake City. When I handed Jean the phone she heard just the dial tone.

"But you know the goddamn phone rang!" I insisted.

"Maybe a short circuit. Chuck, I'm telling you there was no one on the line."

Then Sunday. Three A.M. Cheyenne, Wyoming. Coming closer.

But she couldn't be if she was dead.

The student paper at the University subscribes to all the other major student papers. Monday, Jean and I left the children with friends and drove to its office. Friday's copy of the Berkeley campus paper had arrived. In desperation I searched its pages. "There!" A two-inch item. Sudden student death. Samantha Perry. Tactfully, no cause was given.

Outside in the parking lot, Jean said, "Now do you believe she's dead?"

"Then tell me why I hear her voice! I've got to be crazy if I think I hear a corpse!"

"You're feeling guilty that she killed herself because of you. You shouldn't. There was nothing you could do to stop her. You've been losing too much sleep. Your imagination's taking over."

"You admit you heard the phone ring!"

"Yes, it's true. I can't explain that. If the phone's broken, we'll have it fixed. To put your mind at rest, we'll get a new, unlisted number."

I felt better. After several drinks, I even got some sleep.

But Monday night, again the phone rang. Three A.M. I jerked awake. Cringing, I insisted Jean answer it. But she heard just the dial tone. I grabbed the phone. Of course, I heard Sam's voice.

"I'm almost there. I'll hurry. I'm in Omaha."

"This number isn't listed!"

"But you told me the new one. Your wife's the one who changed it. She's trying to keep us apart. I'll make her sorry. Darling, I can't wait to be with you."

I screamed. Jean jerked away from me.

"Sam, you've got to stop! I spoke to Dr. Campbell!"

"No. He wouldn't dare. He wouldn't violate my trust."

"He said you were dead!"

"I couldn't live without you. Soon we'll be together."

Shrieking, I woke the children, so hysterical Jean had to call an ambulance. Two interns struggled to sedate me.

Omaha was one day's drive from where we live. Jean came to visit me in the hospital on Tuesday.

"Are you feeling better?" Jean frowned, troubled.

"Please, you have to humor me," I said. "All right? Suspect I've gone crazy, but for God sake, humor me. I can't prove what I'm thinking, but I know you're in danger. I am too. You have to get the children and leave town. You have to hide somewhere. Tonight at 3 A.M. she'll reach the house."

Jean stared with pity.

"Promise me!" I said.

She saw the anguish on my face and nodded.

"Maybe she won't try the house," I said. "She might come here. I have to get away. I'm not sure how, but later, when you're gone, I'll find a way to leave."

Jean peered at me, distressed; her voice sounded totally discouraged. "Chuck."

"I'll check the house when I get out of here. If you're still there, you know you'll make me more upset."

"I promise. I'll take Susan and Rebecca, and we'll drive somewhere."

"I love you."

Jean began to cry. "I won't know where you are."

"If I survive this, I'll get word to you."

"But how?"

"The English department. I'll leave a message with the secretary."

Jean leaned down to kiss me, crying, certain I'd lost my mind.

I reached the house that night. As she'd promised, Jean had left with the children. I got in my sports car and raced to the Interstate.

A Chicago hotel where at 3 A.M. Sam called from Iowa. She'd heard my voice. She said I'd told her where I was, but she was hurt and angry. "Tell me why you're running."

I fled from Chicago in the middle of the night, driving until I absolutely had to rest. I checked in here at 1 A.M. In Johnstown, Pennsylvania. I can't sleep. I've got an awful feeling. Last night Sam repeated. "Soon you'll join me." In the desk I found this stationery.

God, it's 3 A.M. I pray I'll see the sun come up.

It's almost four. She didn't phone. I can't believe I escaped, but I keep staring at the phone.

It's four. Dear Christ, I hear the ringing.

Finally I've realized. Sam killed herself at one. In Iowa the time-zone difference made it three. But I'm in Pennsylvania. In the East. A different time zone. One o'clock in California would be *four* o'clock, not three, in Pennsylvania.

Now.

The ringing persists. But I've realized something else. This hotel's unusual, designed to seem like a home.

The ringing?

God help me, it's the doorbell.

Laugh Track

Harlan Ellison

Harlan Ellison (1934–) has won virtually every award possible for writing mystery, fantasy, horror, science fiction, and television scripts. He is recognized not only as a distinguished writer of genre-bending short fiction *(Deathbird Stories, Angry Candy, The Essential Ellison)*, but also as an editor *(Dangerous Visions, Again, Dangerous Visions)*, film and television critic *(The Glass Teat, The Other Glass Teat, Harlan Ellison's Watching)*, and social commentator *(With an Edge in My Voice)*. His well-known love-hate relationship with the television medium is the source of the humorous "Laugh Track."

I loved my Aunt Babe for three reasons. The first was that even though I was only ten or eleven, she flirted with me as she did with any male of any age who was lucky enough to pass through the heat of her line-of-sight. The second was her breasts—I knew them as "titties"—which left your arteries looking like the Holland Tunnel at rush hour. And the third was her laugh. Never before and never since, in the history of this planet, including every species of life-form extant or extinct, has there been a sound as joyous as my Aunt Babe's laugh which I, as a child, imagined as the sound of the Toonerville Trolley clattering downhill. If you have never seen a panel of that long-gone comic strip, and have no idea what the Toonerville Trolley looked like, forget it. It was some terrific helluva laugh. It could pucker your lips.

My Aunt Babe died of falling asleep and not waking up in 1955, when I was twelve years old.

I first recognized her laugh while watching a segment of *Leave*

It to Beaver in November of 1957. It was on the laugh track they'd dubbed in after the show had been shot, but I was only fourteen and thought those were real people laughing at Jerry Mathers's predicament. I yelled for my mother to come quickly, and she came running from the kitchen, her hands all covered with wax from putting up the preserves, and she thought I'd hurt myself or something.

"No . . . no, I'm okay . . . listen!"

She stood there, listening. "Listen to what?" she said after a minute.

"Wait . . . wait . . . *there*! You hear that? It's Aunt Babe. She isn't dead, she's at that show."

My mother looked at me just the way your mother would look at you if you said something like that, and she shook her head, and she said something in Italian my grandmother had no doubt said while shaking her head at *her*, long ago; and she went back to imprisoning boysenberries. *I* sat there and watched The Beav and Eddie Haskell and Whitey Whitney, and broke up every time my Aunt Babe laughed at their antics.

I heard my Aunt Babe's laugh on *The Real McCoys* in 1958; on *Hennessey* and *The Many Loves of Dobie Gillis* in 1959; on *The Andy Griffith Show* in 1960; on *Car 54, Where Are You?* in 1962; and in the years that followed I laughed along with her at *The Dick Van Dyke Show, The Lucy Show, My Favorite Martian, The Addams Family, I Dream of Jeannie,* and *Get Smart!*

In 1970 I heard my Aunt Babe laughing at *Green Acres*, which—though I always liked Eddie Albert and Alvy Moore—I thought was seriously lame; and it bothered me that her taste had deteriorated so drastically. Also, her laugh seemed a little thin. Not as ebulliently Toonerville Trolley going downhill any more.

By 1972 I knew something was wrong because Aunt Babe was convulsing over *Me and the Chimp* but not a sound from her for *My World . . . And Welcome to It.*

By 1972 I was almost thirty, I was working in television, and because I had lived with the sound of my Aunt Babe's laughter for so long, I never thought there was anything odd about it, and I never again mentioned it to anyone.

Then, one night, sitting with a frozen pizza and a Dr. Brown's cream soda, watching an episode of the series I was writing, a sitcom you may remember called *Misty Malone,* I heard my Aunt Babe laughing at a line that the story editor had not understood, that he had rewritten. At that moment, bang! comes the light bulb burning in my brain, comes the epiphany, comes the rude awakening, and I hear myself say, "This is crazy. Babe's been dead and buried lo these seventeen years, and there is strictly *no way* she can be laughing at this moron line that Bill Tidy rewrote from my golden prose, and this is weirder than shit, and *what the hell is going on here*!?"

Besides which, Babe's laugh was now sounding a lot like a 1971 Pinto without chains trying to rev itself out of a snowy rut into which cinders had been shoveled.

And I suppose for the first time I understood that Babe was not alive at the taping of all those shows over the years, but was merely on an old laugh track. At which point I remembered the afternoon in 1953 when she'd taken me to the Hollywood Ranch Market to go shopping, and one of those guys had been standing there handing out tickets to the filming of TV shows, and Babe had taken two tickets to *Our Miss Brooks,* and she'd gone with some passing fancy she was dating at the time, and told us later that she thought Eve Arden was funnier than Lucille Ball.

The laugh track from that 1953 show was obviously still in circulation. Had been, in fact, in circulation for twenty years. And for twenty years my Aunt Babe had been forced to laugh at the same old weary sitcom minutiae, over and over and over. She'd had to laugh at the salt instead of the sugar in Fred Mac-Murray's coffee; at Granny Clampett sending Buddy Ebsen out to shoot a possum in Beverly Hills; at Bob Cummings trying to conceal Julie Newmar's robot identity; at The Fonz *almost* running a comb through his pompadour; at all the mistaken identities, all the improbable last-minute saves of hopeless situations, all the sophomoric pratfalls from Gilligan to Gidget. And I felt just terrible for her.

Native Americans, what we used to be allowed to call Indians when I was a kid, have a belief that if someone takes their picture with a camera, the box captures their soul. So they shy away from photographers. AmerInds seldom become bank robbers; there are cameras in banks. There was no graduation picture of Cochise in his high school yearbook.

What if—I said to myself—sitting there with that awful pizza growing cold on my lap—what if my lovely Aunt Babe, who had been a Ziegfeld Girl, and who had loved my Uncle Morrie, and who had had such wonderful titties and never let on that she knew *exactly* what I was doing when I'd fall asleep in the car on the way home and snuggle up against them, *what if* my dear Aunt Babe's soul, like her laugh, had been trapped on that goddam track?

And what if she was in there, in there forever, doomed to laugh endlessly at imbecilic shit rewritten by ex-hairdressers, instead of roaming around Heaven, flirting with the angels, which I was certain should have been her proper fate, being that she was such a swell person? What if?

It was the sort of thinking that made my head hurt a lot.

And it made me feel even lower, the more I thought about it, because I didn't know what I could do about it. I just knew that that was what had happened to my Aunt Babe; and there she was in there, condemned to the stupidest hell imaginable. In some arcane way, she had been doomed to an eternity of electronic restimulation. In speech therapy they have a name for it: cataphasia: verbal repetition. But I could tell from the frequency with which I was now hearing Babe, and from the indiscriminate use to which her laugh was being put—not just on *M*A*S*H* and *Maude,* but on yawners like *The Sandy Duncan Show* and a midseason replacement with Larry Hagman called *Here We Go Again,* which didn't—and the way her laugh was starting to slur like an ice-skating elephant, that she wasn't having much fun in there. I began to believe that she was like some sort of beanfield slave, every now and then being goosed electronically to laugh. She was a video galley slave, one of the pod people, a member of some ghastly high-frequency chain gang. Cataphasia, but worse. Oh, how I wanted to save her; to drag her out of there and let her tormented soul bound free like a snow rabbit, to vanish into great white spaces where the words *Laverne and Shirley* had never trembled in the lambent mist.

Then I went to bed and didn't think about it again until 1978.

By September of 1978 I was working for Bill Tidy again. In years to come I would refer to that pox-ridden period as the Season I Stepped in a Pile of Tidy.

Each of us has one dark eminence in his or her life who somehow has the hoodoo sign on us. Persons so cosmically loathsome that we continually spend our time when in their company silently asking ourselves, *What the hell, what the bloody hell, what the everlasting Technicolor hell am I doing sitting here with this ambulatory piece of offal? This is the worst person who ever got born, and someone ought to wash out his life with a bar of Fels-Naptha.*

But there you sit, and the next time you blink, there you sit again. It was probably the way Catherine the Great felt on her dates with Rasputin.

Bill Tidy had that hold over me.

In 1973 when I'd been just a struggling sitcom writer, getting his first breaks on *Misty Malone,* Tidy had been the story editor. An authoritarian Fascist with all the creative insight of a sump pump. But now, a mere five years later, things were a great deal different: I had created a series, which meant I was a struggling sitcom writer with my name on a parking slot at the studio; and Bill Tidy, direct lineal descendant of The Blob that tried to eat Steve McQueen, had swallowed up half the television industry. He was now the heavy-breathing half of Tidy-Spellberg Productions, in partnership with another ex-hairdresser named Harvey Spellberg, whom he'd met during a metaphysical retreat to Reno, Nevada. They'd become corporate soul mates while praying over the crap tables and in just a few years had built upon their unerring sense of how much debasement the American television-viewing audience could sustain (a much higher gag-reflex level than even the experts had postulated, thereby paving the way for *Three's Company*), to emerge as "prime suppliers" of gibbering lunacy for the three networks.

Bill Tidy was to Art as Pekin, North Dakota, is to wild nightlife.

But he was the fastest money in town when it came to marketing a series idea to one of the networks, and my agent had sent over the prospectus for *Ain't It the Truth,* without my knowing it; and before I had a chance to scream, "Nay, nay, my liege! There are some things mere humans were never meant to know, Doctor Von Frankenstein!" the network had made a development deal with the Rupert Murdoch of mindlessness, and of a sudden I was—as they so aptly put it—in bed with Bill Tidy again.

This is the definition of ambivalence: to have struggled in the ditches for five years, to have created something that was guaranteed to get on the air, and to have that creation masterminded by a toad with the charm of a charnel house and the intellect of a head of lettuce. I thought seriously of moving to Pekin, North Dakota, where the words *coaxial cable* are as speaking-in-tongues to the simple, happy natives; where the blight of Jim Nabors has never manifested itself; where I could open a grain and feed store and never have to sit in the same room with Bill Tidy as he picked his nose and surreptitiously examined the findings.

But I was weak, and even if the series croaked before the season ran its course, I would have a credit that could lead to bigger things. So I pulled down the covers, plumped the pillows, straightened the rubber pishy-pad, and got into bed with Bill Tidy.

By September, I was a raving lunatic. I spent much of my time dreaming about biting the heads off chickens. The deranged wind of network babble and foaming Tidyism blew through the haunted cathedral of my brain. What little originality and invention I'd brought to the series concept—and at best what we're talking about here is primetime network situation comedy, not a PBS tour conducted by Alistair Cooke through the Library of Alexandria—was steadily and firmly leached out of the production by Bill Tidy. Any time a line or a situation with some charm or esthetic value dared to peek its head out of the *merde* of the scripts, Tidy as Grim Reaper would lurch onto the scene swinging the scythe of his demented bad taste, and intellectual decapitation instantly followed.

I developed a hiatic hernia, I couldn't hold down solid food and took to subsisting on strained mung from Gerber's inexhaustible and vomitous larder, I snapped at everyone, sex was a concept whose time had come and gone for me, and I saw my gentle little offering to the Gods of Comedy turned into something best suited for a life under mossy stones.

Had I known that on the evening of Thursday, September 14, 1978, *Ain't It the Truth* was to premiere opposite a new ABC show called *Mork & Mindy,* and that within three weeks a dervish named Robin Williams would be dining on Nielsen rating shares the way sharks devour entire continents, I might have been able to hold onto enough of my sanity to weather the Dark Ages. And I wouldn't have gotten involved with Wally Modisett, the phantom sweetener, and I wouldn't have spoken into the black box, and I wouldn't have found the salvation for my dead Aunt Babe's soul.

But early in September Williams had not yet uttered his first *Nanoo-nanoo* (except on a spinoff segment of *Happy Days* and who the hell watched *that*?) and we had taped the first three segments of *Ain't It the Truth* before a live audience at the Burbank studios, if you can call those who voluntarily go to tapings of sitcoms "living," and late one night the specter of Bill Tidy appeared in the doorway of my office, his great horse face looming down at me like the demon that emerges from the *Night on Bald Mountain* section of Disney's *Fantasia*; and his sulphurous breath reached across the room and made all the little hairs in my nostrils curl up and try to pull themselves out so they could run away and hide in the back of my head somewhere; and the two reflective puddles of Vegemite he called eyes smoldered at me, and this is what he said. First he said:

"That fuckin' fag cheese-eater director's never gonna work again. He's gonna go two days over, mark my words. I'll see the putzola never works again."

Then he said:

"I bought another condo in Phoenix. Solid gold investment. Better than Picassos."

Then he said:

"I heard it at lunch today. A cunt is just a clam that's wearin' a fright-wig. Good, huh?"

Then he said:

"I want you to stay late tonight. I can't trust anyone else. Guy'll show up here about eight. He'll find you. Just stay put till he gets here. Never mind a name. He'll make himself known to you. Take him over to the mixing studio, run the first three shows for him. Nobody else gets in, *kapeesh, paisan*?"

I was having such a time keeping my gorge from becoming buoyant that I barely heard his directive. Bill Tidy gave new meaning to the words King of the Pig People. The only groups he had failed to insult in the space of thirteen seconds were blacks, Orientals, paraplegics, and Doukhobors, and if I didn't quickly agree to his demands, he'd no doubt round on them, as well. "Got it, Bill. Yessiree, you can count on me. Uh-huh, absolutely, right-on, dead-center, I hear ya talkin', I'm your boy, I loves workin' foah ya, Massa' Tidysuh, you can bank on me!"

He gave me a look. "You know, Angelo, you are gettin' stranger and stranger, like some kind of weird insect."

And he turned and he vanished, leaving me all alone there in the encroaching darkness, just tuning my antennae and rubbing my hind legs together.

I was slumped down on my spine, eyes closed, in the darkened office with just the desk lamp doing its best to rage against the dying of the light, when I heard someone whisper huskily, "Turn off the light."

I opened my eyes. The room was empty. I looked out the window behind my desk. It was night. I was three flights up in the production building. No one was there.

"The light. Turn off the light, can you hear what I'm telling you?"

I strained forward toward the open door and the dark hallway beyond. "You talking to me?" Nothing moved out there.

"The light. Slow; you're a very slow person."

Being Catholic, I respond like a Pavlovian dog to guilt. I turned out the light.

From the deeper darkness of the hallway I saw something shadowy detach itself and glide into my office. "Can I keep my eyes open," I said, "or would a blindfold serve to palliate this unseemly paranoia of yours?"

The shadowy form snorted disdainfully. "At these prices you can use words even bigger than that and I don't give a snap." I heard fingers snap. "You care to take me over to the mixing booth?"

I stood up. Then I sat down. "Don't wanna play." I folded my arms.

The shadowy figure got a petulant tone in his voice. "Okay, c'mon now. I've got three shows to do, and I haven't got all night. The world keeps turning. Let's go."

"Not in the cards, Lamont Cranston. I've been ordered around a lot these last few days, and since I don't know you from a stubborn stain, I'm digging in my heels. Remember the Alamo. Millions for defense, not one cent for tribute. The only thing we have to fear is fear itself. Forty-four forty or fight."

"I think that's fifty-four forty or fight," he said.

We thought about that for a while. Then after a long time I said, "Who the hell are you, and what is it you do that's so illicit and unspeakable that first of all Bill Tidy would hire you to do it, which puts you right on the same level as me, which is the level of grave robbers, dogcatchers, and horse-dopers; and second, which is so furtive and vile that you have to do it in the dead of night, coming in here wearing garb fit only for a commando raid? Answer in the key of C#."

He chuckled. It was a nice chuckle. "You're okay, kid," he said. And he dropped into the chair on the other side of my desk where writers pitching ideas for stories sat; and he turned on the desk lamp.

"Wally Modisett," he said, extending a black-gloved hand. "Sound editor." I took the hand and we shook. "Free-lance," he said.

That didn't sound so ominous. "Why the Creeping Phantom routine?"

Then he said the word no one in Hollywood says. He looked intently at all of my face, particularly around the mouth, where lies come from, and he said: "Sweetening."

If I'd had a silver crucifix, I'd have thrust it at him at arm's length. *Be still my heart,* I thought.

There are many things of which one does not speak in the television industry. One does not repeat the name of the NBC executive who was making women writers give him blowjobs in his office in exchange for writing assignments, even though he's been pensioned off with a lucrative production deal at a major studio and the network paid for his psychiatric counseling for several years. One does not talk about the astonishing Digital Dance done by the royalty numbers in a major production company's ledgers, thereby fleecing several superstar participants out of their "points" in the profits, even though it made a large stink on the *World News Tonight* and everybody scampered around trying to settle out of court while *TV Guide* watched. One does not talk about how the studio frightened a buxom ingenue who had become an overnight national sensation into modifying her demands for triple salary in the second season her series was on the air, not even to hint knowingly of a kitchen chair with nails driven up through the seat from the underside.

And one never, never, no never ever talks about the phantom sweeteners.

This show was taped before a live studio audience!

If you've heard it once, you've heard it at least twice. And so when those audiences break up and fall on the floor and roll around and drum their heels and roar so hard they have to clutch their stomachs and tears of hilarity blind them and their noses swell from crying too much and they sound as if they're all genetically selected, high-profile tickleables you fall right in with them because that ain't canned laughter, it's a live audience, onaccounta *This show was taped before a live studio audience.*

While high in the fly loft of the elegant opera house, the Phantom Sweetener looks down and chuckles smugly.

They're legendary. For years there was only Charlie Douglas, a name never spoken. A laugh man. A sound technician. A sweetener. They say he still uses laughs kidnapped off radio shows from the Forties and Fifties. Golden laughs. Unduplicable originals. Special, rich laughs that blend and support and lift and build a resonance that punches your subliminal buttons. Laughs from *The Jack Benny Show,* from segments of *The Fred Allen Show* down in Allen's Alley, from *The Chase & Sanborn Hour* with Edgar Bergen and Charlie McCarthy (one of the shows on which Charlie mixed it up with W.C. Fields). The laughs that Ed Wynn got, that Goodman and Jane Ace got, that Fanny Brice got. Rich, teak-colored laughs from a time in this country when humor wasn't produced by slugs like Bill Tidy. For a long time Charlie Douglas was all alone as the man who could make even dull thuds go over boffola.

But no one knew how good he was. Except the IRS, which took note of his underground success in the industry by raking in vast amounts of his hard-earned cash.

Using the big Spotmaster cartridges—carts that looked like eight-track cassettes, with thirty cuts per cart—twelve or fourteen per job—Charlie Douglas became a hired gun of guffaws, a highwayman of hee-haws, Zorro of zaniness; a troubleshooter working extended overtime in a specialized craft where he was a secret weapon with a never-spoken code-name.

Carrying with him from studio to studio the sounds of great happy moments stolen from radio signals long since on their way to Proxima Centauri.

And for a long time Charlie Douglas had it all to himself, because it was a closely guarded secret; not one of the open secrets perhaps unknown in Kankakee or Key West, like Merv Griffin or Ida Lupino or Roger Moore; but common knowledge at the Polo Lounge and Chasen's.

But times got fat and the industry grew and there was more work, and more money, than one Phantom Sweetener could handle.

So the mother of invention called forth more audio soldiers of fortune: Carroll Pratt and Craig Porter and Tom Kafka and two silent but sensational guys from Tokyo and techs at Glen Glenn Sound and Vidtronics. And you never mention their names or the shows they've sweetened, lest you get your buns run out of the industry. It's an open secret, closely held by the community. The networks deny their existence, the production company executives would let you nail them, hands and feet, to their office doors before they'd cop to having their shows shot before a live studio audience sweetened. In the dead of night by the phantoms.

Of whom Wally Modisett is the most mysterious.

And here I sat, across from him. He wore a black turtleneck sweater, jeans, and gloves. And he placed on the desk the legendary black box. I looked at it. He chuckled.

"That's it," he said.

"I'll be damned," I said.

I felt as if I were in church.

In sound editing, the key is equalization. Bass, treble, they can isolate a single laugh, pull it off the track, make a match even twenty years later. They put them on "endless loops" and then lay the show over to a multi-track audio machine, and feed in one laugh on a separate track, meld it, blend it in, punch it up, put that special button-punch giggle right in there with the live studio audience track. They do it, they've always done it, and soon now they'll be able to do it with digital encoding. And he sat right there in front of me with the legendary black box. Legendary, because Wally Modisett was an audio genius, an electronics Machiavelli who had built himself a secret system to do it all through that little black box that he took to the studios in the dead of night when everyone was gone, right into the booth at the mixing room, and he didn't need a multi-track.

If it weren't something to be denied to the grave, the *mensches* and moguls of the television industry would have Wally Modisett's head right up there on Mount Rushmore in the empty space between Teddy Roosevelt and Abe Lincoln.

What took twenty-two tracks for a combined layering on a huge machine, Wally Modisett carried around in the palm of his hand. And looking at his long, sensitive face, with the dark circles under his eyes, I guess I saw a foreshadowing of great things to come. There was laughter in his eyes.

I sat there most of the night, running the segments of *Ain't It the Truth.* I sat down below in the screening room while the Phantom Sweetener locked himself up in the booth. *No one,* he made it clear, watched him work his magic.

And the segments played, with the live audience track, and he used his endless loops from his carts—labeled "Single Giggle 1" and "Single Giggle 2" and slightly larger "Single Giggle 3" and the dreaded "Titter/Chuckle" and the ever-popular "Rim Shot"—those loops of his own design, smaller than those made by Spotmaster, and he built and blended and sweetened the hell out of that laugh track till even I chuckled at moronic material Bill Tidy had bastardized to a level that only the Jukes and Kallikaks could have found uproarious.

And then, on the hundredth playback, after Modisett had added another increment of hilarity, I heard my dead Aunt Babe. I sat straight up in the plush screening room chair, and I slapped the switch on the console that fed into the booth, and I yelled, "Hey! That last one! That last laugh . . . what was that . . . ?"

He didn't answer for a moment. Then, tinnily, through the console intercom, he said, "I call it a wonky."

"Where'd it come from?"

Silence.

"C'mon, man, where'd you get that laugh?"

"Why do you want to know?"

I sat there for a second, then I said, "Listen, either you've got to come down here, or let me come up there. I've got to talk to you."

Silence. Then after a moment, "Is there a coffee machine around here somewhere?"

"Yeah, over near the theater."

"I'll be down in about fifteen minutes. We'll have a cup of coffee. Think you can hold out that long?"

"If you nail a duck's foot down, does he walk in circles?"

It took me almost an hour to convince him. Finally, he decided I was almost as bugfuck as he was, and the idea was so crazy it might be fun to try and work it out. I told him I was glad he'd decided to try it because if he hadn't I'd have followed him to his secret lair and found some way to blackmail him into it, and he said, "Yeah, I can see you'd do that. You're not a well person."

"Try working with Bill Tidy sometimes," I said. "It's enough to turn Mother Teresa into a hooker."

"Give me some time," he said. "I'll get back to you."

I didn't hear from him for a year and a half. *Ain't It the Truth* had gone to the boneyard to join *The Chicago Teddy Bears* and *Angie* and *The Dumplings*. Nobody missed it, not even its creator. Bill Tidy had wielded his scythe with skill.

Then just after two A.M. on a summer night in Los Angeles, my phone rang, and I fumbled the receiver off the cradle and found my face somehow, and a voice said, "I've got it. Come." And he gave me an address, and I went.

The warehouse was large, but all his shit was jammed into one corner. Multi-tracks and oscilloscopes and VCRs and huge 3-mil-thick Mylar foam speakers that looked like the rear seats of a 1933 Chevy. And right in the middle of the floor was a larger black box.

"You're kidding?" I said.

He was like a ten-year-old kid. "Would I shit you? I'm telling you, fellah, I've gone where no man has gone before. I has done did it! Jonas Salk and Marie Curie and Lee De Forest and all the rest of them have got to move over, slide aside, get to the back of the bus." And he leaped around, howling, *"I am the king!"*

When I was able to peel him off the catwalks that made a spiderweb tracery above us, he started making some sense. Not a *lot* of sense, because I didn't understand half of what he was saying, but enough sense for me to begin to believe that this peculiar obsession of mine might have some toe in the world of reality.

"The way they taped shows back in 1953, when your aunt went to that *Our Miss Brooks,* was they'd use a ¼″ machine, reel-to-reel. They'd have directional mikes above the audience, to separate individual laughs. One track for the program, and another track for the audience. Then they'd just pick up what they want, equalize, and sock it onto one track for later use. Sweetened as need be."

He went to a portable fridge and pulled out a Dr Pepper and looked in my direction. I shook my head. I was too excited for junk food. He popped the can, took a swig, and came back to me.

"The first thing I had to do was find the original tape, the master. Took me a long time. It was in storage with . . . well, you don't need to know that. It was in storage. I must have gone through a thousand old masters. But I found her. Then I had to pull her out. But not just the *sound* of her laugh. The actual laugh itself. The electronic impulses. I used an early model of this to do it." He waved a hand at the big black box.

"She'd started sounding weak to me, over the years," I said. "Slurred sometimes. Scratchy."

"Yeah, yeah, yeah." Impatient to get on with the great revelation. "That was because she was being diminished by fifth, sixth, twentieth generation re-recording. No, I got her at full strength, and I did what I call 'deconvolving.' "

"Which is?"

"Never mind."

"You going to say 'never mind' every time I ask what the hell you did to make it work?"

"As Groucho used to say to contestants, 'You bet your ass.' "

I shrugged. It was his fairy tale.

"Once I had her deconvolved, I put her on an endless loop. But not just *any* kind of normal standard endless loop. You want to know what kind of endless loop I put her on?"

I looked at him. "You going to tell me to piss off?"

"No. Go ahead and ask."

"All right already: I'm asking. What the hell kind of endless loop did you put her on?"

"A moebius loop."

He looked at me as if he'd just announced the birth of a two-headed calf. I didn't know what the hell he was talking about. That didn't stop me from whistling through my two front teeth, loud enough to cause echoes in the warehouse and I said, "No shit?!?"

He seemed pleased, and went on faster than before. "Now I feed her into the computer, digitally encode her so she never diminishes. Slick, right? Then I feed in a program that says harmonize and synthesize her, get a simulation mapping for the instrument that produced that sound; in other words, your aunt's throat and tongue and palate and teeth and larynx and alla that. Now comes the tricky part. I build a program that postulates an actual physical *situation,* a terrain, a *place* where that voice exists. And I send the computer on a search to bring me back everything that composes that place."

"Hold hold *hold* it, Lamont. Are you trying to tell me that you went in search of the Land of Oz, using that loop of Babe's voice?"

He nodded about a hundred and sixteen times.

"How'd you do *that*? I know: piss off. But that's some kind of weird metaphysical shit. It can't be done."

"Not by drones, fellah. But *I* can do it. I *did* it." He nodded at the black box.

"The TV sitcom land where my dead Aunt Babe is trapped, it's in there, in that cube?"

"Ah calls it a *simularity matrix,*" he said, with an accent that could get him killed in South Central L.A.

"You can call it rosewater if you like, Modisett, but it sounds like the foothills of Bandini Mountain to me."

His grin was the mutant offspring of a sneer and a smirk. I'd seen that kind of look only once, on the face of a failed academic at a collegiate cocktail party. Later that evening the guy used the smirk ploy once too often and a little tweety-bird of an English prof gave him high cause to go see a periodontal reconstructionist.

"I can reconstruct her like a clone, right in the machine," he said.

"How do you know? Tried it yet?"

"It's your aunt, not mine," he said. "I told you I'd get back to you. Now I'm back to you, and I'm ready to run the showboat out to the middle of the river."

So he turned on a lot of things on the big board he had, and he moved a lot of slide-switches up the gain slots, and he did this, and he did that, and a musical hum came from the Quad speakers, and he looked over his shoulder at me, across the tangle of wires and cables that disappeared into the black box, and he said, "Wake her up."

I said, "What?"

He said, "Wake her. She's been an electronic code for almost twenty-five years. She's been asleep. She's an amputated frog leg. Send the current through her."

"How?"

"Call her. She'll recognize your voice."

"How? It's been a long time. I don't sound like the kid I was when she died."

"Trust me," he said. "Call her."

I felt like a goddam fool. "Where do I speak?"

"Just speak, asshole. She'll hear you."

So I stood there in the middle of that warehouse and said, "Aunt Babe?" There was nothing.

"A little louder. Gentle, but louder. Don't startle her."

"You're outta your . . ." His look silenced me. I took a deep breath and said, a little louder, "Hey, Aunt Babe? You in there? It's me, Angelo."

I heard something. At first it sounded like a mouse running toward me across a long blackboard, a blackboard maybe a hundred miles long. Then there was something like the wind you hear in thick woods in the autumn. Then the sound of somebody unwrapping Christmas presents. Then the sound of water, like surf, pouring into a cave at the base of a cliff, and then draining out again. Then the sound of a baby crying and the sound suddenly getting very deep as if it were a three-hundred-pound killer baby that wanted to be fed parts off a freshly killed dinosaur. This kind of torrential idiocy went on for a while, and then, abruptly, out of nowhere, I heard my Aunt Babe clearing her throat, as if she were getting up in the morning. That phlegmy throat-clearing that sounds like quarts of yogurt being shoveled out of a sink.

"Angelo . . . ?"

I crossed myself about eleven times, ran off a few fast Hail Marys and Our Fathers, swallowed hard, and said, "Yeah, Aunt Babe, it's me. How are you?"

"Let me, for a moment here, let me get my bearings." It took more than a moment. She was silent for a few minutes, though she did once say, "I'll be right with you, *mia caro.*"

And finally, I heard her say, "I am really fit to be tied. Do you have any idea what they have put me through? Do you have even the *faintest* idea how many times they've made me watch *The Partridge Family*? Do you have any *idea* how much I hate that kind of music? Never Cole Porter, never Sammy Cahn, not even a little Gus Edwards; I'd settle for Sigmund Romberg after those squalling children. *Caro nipote, quanto mi sei mancato!* Angelo . . . *bello bello.* I want you to tell me everything that's happened, because as soon as I get a chance, I'm going to make a stink you're not going to believe!"

It *was* Babe. My dearest Aunt Babe. I hadn't heard that wonderful mixture of pungent English and lilting Italian with its show biz Yiddish resonances in almost thirty years. I hadn't *spoken* any Italian in nearly twenty years. But I heard myself saying to the empty air, *"Come te la sei passata?"* How've you been?

"Ti voglio bene—bambino caro. I feel just fine. A bit fuzzy, I've been asleep a while but *come sta la famiglia? Anche quelli che non posso sopportare."*

So I told her all about the family, even the ones she couldn't stand, like Uncle Nuncio with breath like a goat, and Carmine's wife, Giuletta, who'd always called Babe a floozy. And after a while she had me try to explain what had happened to her, and I did the best I could, to which she responded, *"Non mi sento come un fantasma."*

So I told her she didn't feel like a ghost because she *wasn't,* strictly speaking, a ghost. More like a random hoot in the empty night. Well, that didn't go over too terrific, because in an instant she'd grasped the truth that if she wasn't going where it is that dead people go, she'd never meet up with my Uncle Morrie again; and that made her very sad. *"Oh, dio!"* and she started crying.

So I tried to jolly her out of it by talking about all the history that had transpired since 1955, but it turned out she knew most of it anyhow. After all, hadn't she been stuck there, inside the biggest blabbermouth the world had ever known? Even though she'd been in something like an alpha state of almost-sleep, her essence had been *saturated* with news and special reports, docu-dramas and public service announcements, talk shows and panel discussions, network extra alerts and hour-by-hour live coverage of fast-breaking events.

Eventually I got around to explaining how I'd gotten in touch with her, about Modisett and the big black box, about how the Phantom Sweetener had deconvolved her, and about Bill Tidy.

She was not unfamiliar with the name.

After all, hadn't she been stuck there, inside the all-talking, all-singing, all-dancing electromagnetic pimp for Tidy's endless supply of brain-damaged, insipid persiflage?

I painted Babe a loving word-portrait of my employer and our unholy liaison. She said: *"Stronzo! Figlio di una mignotta! Mascalzone!"* She also called him *bischero*, by which I'm sure she meant the word in its meaning of goof, or simpleton, rather than literally: "man with erection."

Modisett, who spoke no Italian, stared wildly at me, seeming to bask in the unalloyed joy of having tapped a line in some Elsewhere. Yet even he could tell from the tone of revulsion in Babe's disembodied voice that she had suffered long under the exquisite tortures of swimming in a sea of Tidy product.

What Tidy had been doing to me seemed to infuriate her. She was still my loving Aunt Babe.

So I spent all that night, and the next day, and the next night—while Modisett mostly slept and emptied Dr Pepper down his neck—chatting at leisure with my dead Aunt Babe.

You'll never know how angry someone can get from prolonged exposure to Gary Coleman.

The Phantom Sweetener can't explain what followed. He says it defies the rigors of Boolean logic, whatever the hell that means. He says it transcends the parameters of Maxwell's Equation, which ought to put Maxwell in a bit of a snit. He says (and with more than a touch of the gibber in his voice) it deflowers, rapes & pillages, breaks & enters Minkowski's Covariant Tensor. He says it is enough to start Philo T. Farnsworth spinning so hard in his grave that he would carom off Vladimir K. Zworykin in his. He says it would get Marvin Minsky up at M.I.T. speaking in tongues. He says—and this one *really* turned me around and opened my eyes—he says it (wait for it), "Distorts Riemannian geometry." To which I said, "You have *got* to be shitting me! Not Riemannian gefuckingometry!?!"

This is absolute babble to me, but it's got Modisett down on all fours, foaming at the mouth and sucking at the electrical outlets.

Apparently, Babe has found pathways in the microwave comm-system. The Phantom Sweetener says it might have happened because of what he calls "print-through," that phenomenon that occurs on audio tape when one layer magnetizes the next layer, so you hear an echo of the word or sound that is next to be spoken. He says if the tape is wound "heads out" and is stored that way, then the signal will jump. The signal that is my dead Aunt Babe has jumped. And keeps jumping. She's loose in the comm-system and she ain't asking where's the beef: *she knows!* And Modisett says the reason they can't catch her and wipe her is that old tape *always* bleeds through. Which is why, when Bill Tidy's big multimillion-dollar sitcom aired last year, instead of the audience roaring with laughter, there was the voice of this woman shouting above the din, "That's stupid! Worse than stupid! That's *bore*-ing! Ka-ka! C'mon folks, let's have a good old-fashioned Bronx cheer for crapola like this! Let's show 'em what we *really* think of this flopola!"

And then, instead of augmented laughter, instead of yoks, came a raspberry that could have floated the *Titanic* off the bottom.

Well, they pulled the tape, and they tried to find her, but she was gone, skipping off across the simularity matrix like Bambi, only to turn up the next night on another Tidy-Spellberg abomination.

Well, there was no way to stop it, and the networks got very leery of Tidy and Company, because they couldn't even use the millions of billions of dollars worth of shitty rerun shows they'd paid billions and millions for syndication rights to, and they sued the hell out of Bill Tidy, who went crazy as a soup sandwich not too long ago, and I'm told he's trying to sell ocean view lots in some place like Pekin, North Dakota, and living under the name Silas Marner or some-such because half the civilized world is trying to find him to sue his ass off.

And I might have a moment of compassion for the creep, but I haven't the time. I have three hit shows running at the moment, one each on ABC, NBC, and CBS.

They are big hits because somehow, in a way that no one seems able to figure out, there are all these little subliminal buttons being pushed by my shows, and they just soar to the top of the Nielsen ratings.

And I said to Aunt Babe, "Listen, don't you want to go to Heaven, or wherever it is? I mean, don't you want out of that limbo existence?"

And with love, because she wanted to protect her *bambino caro,* because she wanted to make up for the fact that I didn't have her wonderful bosom to fall asleep on anymore, she said, "Get out of here, Angelo, my darling? What . . . and leave show business?"

Confessions of a
(Pornographer's) Shroud

Clive Barker

Clive Barker (1952–) was a distinguished playwright and artist before he burst upon the literary scene with his six-volume *Clive Barker's Books of Blood* series between 1984 and 1985. As a novelist, he has written a modern take on the Faust legend in *The Damnation Game* (1985), blended high fantasy with horror in *Weaveworld* (1987), *The Great and Secret Show* (1989), and *Imajica* (1991), and produced a self-illustrated children's book, *The Thief of Always* (1992). In short stories like "Confessions of a (Pornographer's) Shroud," which can be read as an homage to M. R. James's " 'Oh, Whistle, and I'll Come to You, my Lad,' " Barker audaciously reconceives the themes of classic horror fiction for a more drastic modern environment.

He had been flesh once. Flesh, and bone, and ambition. But that was an age ago, or so it seemed, and the memory of that blessed state was fading fast.

Some traces of his former life remained; time and exhaustion couldn't take everything from him. He could picture clearly and painfully the faces of those he'd loved and hated. They stared through at him from the past, clear and luminous. He could still see the sweet, goodnight expressions in his children's eyes. And the same look, less sweet but no less goodnight, in the eyes of the brutes he had murdered.

Some of those memories made him want to cry, except that there were no tears to be wrung out of his starched eyes. Besides, it was far too late for regret. Regret was a luxury reserved for the living, who still had the time, the breath and the energy to act.

He was beyond all that. He, his mother's little Ronnie (oh, if she could see him now), he was almost three weeks dead. Too late for regrets by a long chalk.

He'd done all he could do to correct the errors he'd made. He'd spun out his span to its limits and beyond, stealing himself precious time to sew up the loose ends of his frayed existence. Mother's little Ronnie had always been tidy: a paragon of neatness. That was one of the reasons he'd enjoyed accountancy. The pursuit of a few misplaced pence through hundreds of figures was a game he relished; and how satisfying, at the end of the day, to balance the books. Unfortunately life was not so perfectable, as now, too late in the day, he realized. Still, he'd done his best, and that, as Mother used to say, was all anybody could hope to do. There was nothing left but to confess, and having confessed, go to his Judgment empty-handed and contrite. As he sat, draped over the use-shined seat in the Confessional Box of St. Mary Magdalene's, he fretted that the shape of his usurped body would not hold out long enough for him to unburden himself of all the sins that languished in his linen heart. He concentrated, trying to keep body and soul together for these last, vital few minutes.

Soon Father Rooney would come. He would sit behind the lattice divide of the Confessional and offer words of consolation, of understanding, of forgiveness; then, in the remaining minutes of his stolen existence, Ronnie Glass would tell his story.

He would begin by denying that most terrible stain on his character: the accusation of pornographer.

Pornographer.

The thought was absurd. There wasn't a pornographer's bone in his body. Anyone who had known him in his thirty-two years would have testified to that. My Christ, he didn't even like sex very much. That was the irony. Of all the people to be accused of peddling filth, he was about the most unlikely. When it had seemed everyone about him was parading their adulteries like third legs, he had lived a blameless existence. The forbidden life of the body happened, like car accidents, to other people; not to him. Sex was simply a roller coaster ride that one might indulge in once every year or so. Twice might be tolerable; three times nauseating. Was it any surprise then, that in nine years of marriage to a good Catholic girl this good Catholic boy only fathered two children?

But he'd been a loving man in his lustless way, and his wife Bernadette had shared his indifference to sex, so his unenthusiastic member had never been a bone of contention between them. And the children were a joy. Samantha was already growing into a model of politeness and tidiness, and Imogen (though scarcely two) had her mother's smile.

Life had been fine, all in all. He had almost owned a featureless semi-detached house in the leafier suburbs of South London. He had possessed a small garden, Sunday-tended: a soul the same. It had been, as far as he could judge, a model life, unassuming and dirt-free.

And it would have remained so, had it not been for that worm of greed in his nature. Greed had undone him, no doubt.

If he hadn't been greedy, he wouldn't have looked twice at the job that Maguire had offered him. He would have trusted his instinct, taken one look around the pokey smoke-filled office above the Hungarian pastry shop in Soho, and turned tail. But his itch for wealth diverted him from the plain truth—that he was using all his skills as an accountant to give a gloss of credibility to an operation that stank of corruption. He'd known that in his heart, of course. Known that despite Maguire's ceaseless talk of Moral Rearmament, his fondness for his children, his obsession with the gentlemanly art of Bonsai, the man was a louse. The lowest of the low. But he'd successfully shut out that knowledge, and contented himself with the job in hand: balancing the books. Maguire was generous: and that made the blindness easier to induce. He even began to like the man and his associates. He'd got used to seeing the shambling bulk that was Dennis "Dork" Luzzati, a fresh cream pastry perpetually hovering at his fat lips; got used, too, to little three-fingered Henry B. Henry, with his card tricks and his patter, a new routine every day. They weren't the most sophisticated of conversationalists, and they certainly wouldn't have been welcome at the Tennis Club, but they seemed harmless enough.

It was a shock then, a terrible shock, when he eventually drew back the veil and saw Dork, Henry and Maguire for the beasts they really were.

The revelation had occurred by accident.

One night, finishing some tax work late, Ronnie had caught a cab down to the warehouse, planning to deliver his report to Maguire by hand. He'd never actually visited the warehouse, though he'd heard it mentioned between them often enough. Maguire had been stock piling his supplies of books there for some months. Mostly cookery books, from Europe, or so Ronnie had been told. That night, that last night of cleanliness, he walked into the truth, in all its full-color glory.

Maguire was there, in one of the plain brick rooms, sitting on a chair surrounded by packages and boxes. An unshaded bulb threw a halo on to his thinning scalp; it glistened, pinkly. Dork was there too, engrossed in a cake. Henry B. was playing Patience. Piled high on every side of the trio there were magazines, thousands upon thousands of them, their covers shining, virginal, and somehow fleshy.

Maguire looked up from his calculations.

"Glassy," he said. He always used that nickname.

Ronnie stared into the room, guessing, even from a distance, what these heaped treasures were.

"Come on in," said Henry B. "Good for a game?"

"Don't look so serious," soothed Maguire, "this is just merchandise."

A kind of numb horror drew Ronnie to approach one of the stacks of magazines, and open the top copy.

Climax Erotica, the cover read, *Full Color Pornography for the Discriminating Adult. Text in English, German and French.* Unable to prevent himself he began to look through the magazine, his face stinging with embarrassment, only half-hearing the barrage of jokes and threats that Maguire was shooting off.

Swarms of obscene images flew out of the pages, horribly abundant. He'd never seen anything like it in his life. Every sexual act possible between consenting adults (and a few only doped acrobats would consent to) were chronicled in glorious detail. The performers of these unspeakable acts smiled, glassy-eyed, at Ronnie as they swarmed up out of a grease of sex, neither shame nor apology on their lust-filled faces. Every slit, every slot, every pucker and pimple of their bodies was exposed, naked beyond nakedness. The pouting, panting excess of it turned Ronnie's stomach to ash.

He closed the magazine and glanced at another pile beside it. Different faces, same furious coupling. Every depravity was catered for somewhere. The titles alone testified to the delights to be found inside. *Bizarre Women in Chains,* one read. *Enslaved by Rubber,* another promised. *Labrador Lover,* a third portrayed, in perfect focus down to the last wet whisker.

Slowly Michael Maguire's cigarette-worn voice filtered through into Ronnie's reeling brain. It cajoled, or tried to; and worse it mocked him, in its subtle way, for his naiveté.

"You had to find out sooner or later," he said. "I suppose it may as well be sooner, eh? No harm in it. All a bit of fun."

Ronnie shook his head violently, trying to dislodge the images that had taken root behind his eyes. They were multiplying already, invading a territory that had been so innocent of such possibilities. In his imagination, labradors scampered around in leather, drinking from the bodies of bound whores. It was frightening the way these pictures flowed out into his eyes, each page a new abomination. He felt he'd choke on them unless he acted.

"Horrible" was all he could say. "Horrible. Horrible. Horrible."

He kicked a pile of *Bizarre Women in Chains,* and they toppled over, the repeated images of the cover sprawling across the dirty floor.

"Don't do that," said Maguire, very quietly.

"Horrible," said Ronnie. "They're all horrible."

"There's a big market for them."

"Not me!" he said, as though Maguire was suggesting he had some personal interest in them.

"All right, so you don't like them. He doesn't like them, Dork."

Dork was wiping cream off his short fingers with a dainty handkerchief.

"Why not?"

"Too dirty for him."

"Horrible," said Ronnie again.

"Well you're in this up to your neck, my son," said Maguire. His voice was the Devil's voice, wasn't it? Surely the Devil's voice. "You may as well grin and bear it."

Dork guffawed, "Grin and bare it; I like it Mick, I like it."

Ronnie looked up at Maguire. The man was forty-five, maybe

fifty; but his face had a fretted, cracked look, old before its years. The charm was gone; it was scarcely human, the face he locked eyes with. Its sweat, its bristles, its puckered mouth made it resemble, in Ronnie's mind, the proffered backside of one of the red-raw sluts in the magazines.

"We're all known villains here," the organ was saying, "and we've got nothing to lose if we're caught again."

"Nothing," said Dork.

"Whereas you, my son, you're a spit-clean professional. Way I see it, if you want to go gabbing about this dirty business, you're going to lose your reputation as a nice, honest accountant. In fact I'd venture to suggest you'll never work again. Do you take my meaning?"

Ronnie wanted to hit Maguire, so he did; hard too. There was a satisfying snap as Maguire's teeth met at speed, and blood came quickly from between his lips. It was the first time Ronnie had fought since his schooldays, and he was slow to avoid the inevitable retaliation. The blow that Maguire returned sent him sprawling, bloodied, amongst the Bizarre Women. Before he could clamber to his feet Dork had slammed his heel into Ronnie's face, grinding the gristle in his nose. While Ronnie blinked back the blood Dork hoisted him to his feet, and held him up as a captive target for Maguire. The ringed hand became a fist, and for the next five minutes Maguire used Ronnie as a punch bag, starting below the belt and working up.

Ronnie found the pain curiously reassuring; it seemed to heal his guilty psyche better than a string of Hail Marys. When the beating was over, and Dork had let him out, defaced, into the dark, there wasn't any anger left in him, only a need to finish the cleansing Maguire had begun.

He went home to Bernadette that night and told her a lie about being mugged in the street. She was so consoling, it made him sick to be deceiving her, but he had no choice. That night, and the night after, were sleepless. He lay in his own bed, just a few feet from that of his trusting spouse, and tried to make sense of his feelings. He knew in his bones the truth would sooner or later become public knowledge. Better surely to go to the police, come clean. But that took courage, and his heart had never felt weaker. So he prevaricated through the Thursday night

and the Friday, letting the bruises yellow and the confusion
settle.

Then on Sunday, the shit hit the fan.

The lowest of the Sunday filth sheets had his face on the front
cover: complete with the banner headline: "The Sex Empire of
Ronald Glass." Inside, were photographs, snatched from innocent circumstance and construed as guilt. Glass appearing to look
pursued. Glass appearing to look devious. His natural hirsuteness
made him seem ill-shaven; his neat haircut suggested the prison
aesthetic favored by some of the criminal fraternity. Being shortsighted he squinted; photographed squinting he looked like a
lustful rat.

He stood in the newsagents, staring at his own face, and knew
his personal Armageddon was on the horizon. Shaking, he read
the terrible lies inside.

Somebody, he never exactly worked out who, had told the
whole story. The pornography, the brothels, the sex shops, the
cinemas. The secret world of smut that Maguire had masterminded was here detailed in every sordid particular. Except that
Maguire's name did not appear. Neither did Dork's, nor Henry's.
It was Glass, Glass all the way: his guilt was transparent. He
had been framed, neat as anything. A corrupter of children, the
leader called him, Little Boy Blue grown fat and horny.

It was too late to deny anything. By the time he got back to
the house Bernadette had gone, with the children in tow. Somebody had got to her with the news, probably salivating down the
phone, delighting in the sheer dirt of it.

He stood in the kitchen, where the table was laid for a breakfast the family hadn't yet eaten, and would now never eat, and
he cried. Not a great deal: his supply of tears was strictly limited,
but enough to feel the duty done. Then, having finished with his
gesture of remorse, he sat down, like any decent man who has
been deeply wronged, and planned murder.

In many ways getting the gun was more difficult than anything
that followed. It required some careful thought, some soft words,
and a good deal of hard cash. It took him a day and a half to
locate the weapon he wanted, and to learn how to use it.

Then, in his own good time, he went about his business.

Henry B. died first. Ronnie shot him in his own stripped pinewood kitchen in up-and-coming Islington. He had a cup of freshly brewed coffee in his three-fingered hand and a look of almost pitiable terror on his face. The first shot struck him in the side, denting his shirt, and causing a little blood to come. Far less than Ronnie had been steeling himself for however. More confident, he fired again. The second shot hit his intended in the neck: and that seemed to be the killer. Henry B. pitched forward like a comedian in a silent movie, not relinquishing the coffee cup until the moment before he hit the floor. The cup spun in the mingled dregs of coffee and life, and rattled, at last, to a halt.

Ronnie stepped over to the body and fired a third shot straight through the back of Henry B.'s neck. This last bullet was almost casual; swift and accurate. Then he escaped easily out of the back gate, almost elated by the ease of the act. He felt as though he'd cornered and killed a rat in his cellar; an unpleasant duty that needed to be done.

The frisson lasted five minutes. Then he was profoundly sick.

Anyway, that was Henry. All out of tricks.

Dork's death was rather more sensational. He ran out of time at the Dog Track; indeed, he was showing Ronnie his winning ticket when he felt the long-bladed knife insinuate itself between his fourth and fifth ribs. He could scarcely believe he was being murdered, the expression on his pastry-fattened face was one of complete amazement. He kept looking from side to side at the punters milling around as though at any moment one of them would point, and laugh, and tell him that this was all a joke, a premature birthday game.

Then Ronnie twisted the blade in the wound (he'd read that this was surely lethal) and Dork realized that, winning ticket or not, this wasn't his lucky day.

His heavy body was carried along in the crush of the crowd for a good ten yards until it became wedged in the teeth of the turnstile. Only then did someone feel the hot gush from Dork, and scream.

By then Ronnie was well away.

Content, feeling cleaner by the hour, he went back to the house. Bernadette had been in, collecting clothes and favorite ornaments. He wanted to say to her: take everything, it means nothing to me, but she'd slipped in and gone again, like a ghost of a housewife. In the kitchen the table was still set for that final Sunday breakfast. There was dust on the cornflakes in the children's bowls; the rancid butter was beginning to grease the air. Ronnie sat through the late afternoon, through the dusk, through until the early hours of the following morning, and tasted his newfound power over life and death. Then he went to bed in his clothes, no longer caring to be tidy, and slept the sleep of the almost good.

It wasn't so hard for Maguire to guess who'd wasted Dork and Henry B. Henry, though the idea of that particular worm turning was hard to swallow. Many of the criminal community had known Ronald Glass, had laughed with Maguire over the little deception that was being played upon the innocent. But no one had believed him capable of such extreme sanctions against his enemies. In some seedier quarters he was now being saluted for his sheer bloody mindedness; others, Maguire included, felt he had gone too far to be welcomed into the fold like a strayed sheep. The general opinion was that he be dispatched, before he did any more damage to the fragile balance of power.

So Ronnie's days became numbered. They could have been counted on the three fingers of Henry B.'s hand.

They came for him on the Saturday afternoon and took him quickly, without him having time to wield a weapon in his defense. They escorted him to a Salami and Cooked Meats warehouse, and in the icy white safety of the cold storage room they hung him from a hook and tortured him. Anyone with any claim to Dork's or Henry B.'s affections was given an opportunity to work out their grief on him. With knives, with hammers, with oxyacetylene torches. They shattered his knees and his elbows. They put out his eardrums, burned the flesh off the soles of his feet.

Finally, about eleven or so, they began to lose interest. The clubs were just getting into their rhythm, the gaming tables were beginning to simmer, it was time to be done with justice and get out on the town.

That was when Micky Maguire arrived, dressed to kill in his best bib and tucker. Ronnie knew he was there somewhere in the haze, but his senses were all but out, and he only half saw the gun levelled at his head, half felt the noise of the blast bounce around the white-tiled room.

A single bullet, immaculately placed, entered his brain through the middle of his forehead. As neat as even he could have wished, like a third eye.

His body twitched on its hook a moment, and died.

Maguire took his applause like a man, kissed the ladies, thanked his dear friends who had seen this deed done with him, and went to play. The body was dumped in a black plastic bag on the edge of Epping Forest, early on Sunday morning, just as the dawn chorus was tuning up in the ash trees and the sycamores. And that, to all intents and purposes, was the end of that. Except that it was the beginning.

Ronnie's body was found by a jogger, out before seven on the following Monday. In the day between his being dumped and being found his corpse had already begun to deteriorate.

But the pathologist had seen far, far worse. He watched dispassionately while the two mortuary technicians stripped the body, folded the clothes and placed them in tagged plastic bags. He waited patiently and attentively while the wife of the deceased was ushered into his echoing domain, her face ashen, her eyes swelled to bursting with too many tears. She looked down at her husband without love, staring at the wounds and at the marks of torture quite unflinchingly. The pathologist had a whole story written behind this last confrontation between Sex-King and untroubled wife. Their loveless marriage, their arguments over his despicable way of life, her despair, his brutality, and now, her relief that the torment was finally over and she was released to start a new life without him. The pathologist made a mental note to look up the pretty widow's address. She was delicious in her indifference to mutilation; it made his mouth wet to think of her.

Ronnie knew Bernadette had come and gone; he could sense too the other faces that popped into the mortuary just to peer down at the Sex-King. He was an object of fascination, even in death, and it was a horror he hadn't predicted, buzzing around in the cool coils of his brain, like a tenant who refuses to be ousted by the bailiffs, still seeing the world hovering around him, and not being able to act upon it.

In the days since his death there had been no hint of escape from this condition. He had sat here, in his own dead skull, unable to find a way out into the living world, and unwilling, somehow, to relinquish life entirely and leave himself to Heaven. There was still a will to revenge in him. A part of his mind, unforgiving of trespasses, was prepared to postpone Paradise in order to finish the job he had started. The books needed balancing; and until Michael Maguire was dead Ronnie could not go to his atonement.

In his round bone prison he watched the curious come and go, and knotted up his will.

The pathologist did his work on Ronnie's corpse with all the respect of an efficient fish gutter, carelessly digging the bullet out of his cranium, and nosing around in the stews of smashed bone and cartilage that had formerly been his knees and elbows. Ronnie didn't like the man. He'd leered at Bernadette in a highly unprofessional way; and now, when he was playing the professional, his callousness was positively shameful. Oh for a voice; for a fist, for a body to use for a time. Then he'd show this meat merchant how bodies should be treated. The will was not enough though: it needed a focus, and a means of escape.

The pathologist finished his report and his rough sewing, flung his juice-shiny gloves and his stained instruments on to the trolley beside the swabs and the alcohol, and left the body to the assistants.

Ronnie heard the swing doors close behind him as the man departed. Water was running somewhere, splashing into the sink; the sound irritated him.

Standing beside the table on which he lay, the two technicians discussed their shoes. Of all things, shoes. The banality of it, thought Ronnie, the life-decaying banality of it.

"You know them new heels, Lenny? The ones I got to put on my brown suedes? Useless. No bleeding good at all."

"I'm not surprised."

"And the price I paid for them. Look at that; just look at that. Worn through in a month."

"Paper thin."

"They are, Lenny, they're paper thin. I'm going to take them back."

"I would."

"I am."

"I would."

This mindless conversation, after those hours of torture, of sudden death, of the postmortem that he'd so recently endured, was almost beyond endurance. Ronnie's spirit began to buzz round and round in his brain like an angry bee trapped in an upturned jam-jar, determined to get out and start stinging—

Round and round; like the conversation.

"Paper bloody thin."

"I'm not surprised."

"Bloody foreign. These soles. Made in fucking Korea."

"Korea?"

"That's why they're paper thin."

It was unforgivable: the trudging stupidity of these people. That they should live and act and *be:* while he buzzed on and on, boiling with frustration. Was that fair?

"Neat shot, eh Lenny?"

"What?"

"The stiff. Old what's his name the Sex-King. Bang in the middle of the forehead. See that? Pop goes the weasel."

Lenny's companion, it seemed, was still preoccupied with his paper thin sole. He didn't reply. Lenny inquisitively inched back the shroud from Ronnie's forehead. The lines of sawn and scalped flesh were inelegantly sewn, but the bullet hole itself was neat.

"Look at it."

The other glanced round at the dead face. The head wound had been cleaned after the probing pincers had worked at it. The edges were white and puckered.

"I thought they usually went for the heart," said the sole searcher.

"This wasn't any street fight. It was an execution; formal like," said Lenny, poking his little finger into the wound. "It's a perfect shot. Bang in the middle of the forehead. Like he had three eyes."

"Yeah . . ."

The shroud was tossed back over Ronnie's face. The bee buzzed on; round and round.

"You hear about third eyes, don't you?"

"Do you?"

"Stella read me something about it being the center of the body."

"That's your navel. How can your forehead be the center of your body?"

"Well . . ."

"That's your navel."

"No, it's more your spiritual center."

The other didn't deign to respond.

"Just about where this bullet hole is," said Lenny, still lost in admiration for Ronnie's killer.

The bee listened. The bullet hole was just one of many holes in his life. Holes where his wife and children should have been. Holes winking up at him like sightless eyes from the pages of the magazines, pink and brown and hairlipped. Holes to the right of him, holes to the left—

Could it be, at last, that he had found here a hole that he could profit by? Why not leave by the wound?

His spirit braced itself, and made for his brow, creeping through his cortex with a mixture of trepidation and excitement. Ahead, he could sense the exit door like the light at the end of a long tunnel. Beyond the hole, the warp and weft of his shroud glittered like a promised land. His sense of direction was good; the light grew as he crept, the voices became louder. Without fanfare Ronnie's spirit spat itself into the outside world: a tiny seepage of soul. The motes of fluid that carried his will and his consciousness were soaked up by his shroud like tears by tissues.

His flesh and blood body was utterly deserted now; an icy bulk fit for nothing but the flames.

Ronnie Glass existed in a new world: a white linen world like no state he had lived or dreamed before.

Ronnie Glass was his shroud.

Had Ronnie's pathologist not been forgetful he wouldn't have come back into the mortuary at that moment, trying to locate the diary he'd written the Widow Glass' number in; and, had he not come in, he would have lived. As it was—

"Haven't you started on this one yet?" he snapped at the technicians.

They murmured some apology or other. He was always testy at this time of night; they were used to his tantrums.

"Get on with it," he said, stripping the shroud off the body and flinging it to the floor in irritation, "before the fucker walks out of here in disgust. Don't want to get our little hotel a bad reputation, do we?"

"Yes, sir. I mean, no sir."

"Well don't stand there: parcel it up. There's a widow wants him dispatched as soon as possible. I've seen all I need to see of him."

Ronnie lay on the floor in a crumpled heap, slowly spreading his influence through this newfound land. It felt good to have a body, even if it was sterile and rectangular. Bringing a power of will to bear he hadn't known he possessed, Ronnie took full control of the shroud.

At first it refused life. It had always been passive: that was its condition. It wasn't use to occupation by spirits. But Ronnie wasn't to be beaten now. His will was an imperative. Against all rules of natural behavior it stretched and knotted the sullen linen into a semblance of life.

The shroud rose.

The pathologist had located his little black book, and was in the act of pocketing it when this white curtain spread itself in his path, stretching like a man who has just woken from a deep sleep.

Ronnie tried to speak; but the only voice he could find was a whisper of the cloth on the air, too light, too insubstantial to be heard over the complaints of frightened men. And frightened they were. Despite the pathologist's call for assistance, none was forthcoming. Lenny and his companion were sliding away towards the swing doors, gaping mouths babbling entreaties to any local god who would listen.

The pathologist backed off against the postmortem table, quite out of gods.

"Get out of my sight," he said.

Ronnie embraced him, tightly.

"Help," said the pathologist, almost to himself. But help was gone. It was running down the corridors, still babbling, keeping its back to the miracle that was taking place in the mortuary. The pathologist was alone, wrapped up in this starched embrace, murmuring, at the last, some apologies he had found beneath his pride.

"I'm sorry, whoever you are. Whatever you are. I'm sorry."

But there was an anger in Ronnie that would not have any

truck with late converts; no pardons or reprieves were available. This fish-eyed bastard, this son of the scalpel had cut and examined his old body as though it was a side of beef. It made Ronnie livid to think of this creep's oh-so-cool appraisal of life, death and Bernadette. The bastard would die, here, amongst his remains, and let that be an end to his callous profession.

The corners of the shroud were forming into crude arms now, as Ronnie's memory shaped them. It seemed natural to re-create his old appearance in this new medium. He made hands first: then digits: even a rudimentary thumb. He was like a morbid Adam raised out of linen.

Even as they formed, the hands had the pathologist about the neck. As yet they had no sense of touch in them, and it was difficult to judge how hard to press on the throbbing skin, so he simply used all the strength he could muster. The man's face blackened, and his tongue, the color of a plum, stuck out from his mouth like a spear head, sharp and hard. In his enthusiasm, Ronnie broke his neck. It snapped suddenly, and the head fell backwards at a horrid angle. The vain apologies had long since stopped.

Ronnie dropped him to the polished floor, and stared down at the hands he had made, with eyes that were still two pinpricks in a sheet of stained cloth.

He felt certain of himself in this body, and God, he was strong; he'd broken the bastard's neck without exerting himself at all. Occupying this strange, bloodless physique he had a new freedom from the constraints of humanity. He was alive suddenly to the life of the air, feeling it now fill and billow him. Surely he could fly, like a sheet in the wind, or if it suited him knot himself into a fist and beat the world into submission. The prospects seemed endless.

And yet . . . he sensed that this possession was at best temporary. Sooner or later the shroud would want to resume its former life as an idle piece of cloth, and its true, passive nature would be restored. This body had not been given to him, merely loaned; it was up to him to use it to the best of his vengeful abilities. He knew the priorities. First and foremost to find Michael Maguire and dispatch him. Then, if he still had the time left, he would see the children. But it wasn't wise to go visiting as a flying shroud. Better by far to work at this illusion of humanity, and see if he could sophisticate the effect.

He'd seen what freak creases could do, making faces appear in a crumpled pillow, or in the folds of a jacket hanging on the back of the door. More extraordinary still, there was the Shroud of Turin, in which the face and body of Jesus Christ had been miraculously imprinted. Bernadette had been sent a postcard of the Shroud, with every wound of lance and nail in place. Why couldn't he make the same miracle, by force of will? Wasn't he resurrected too?

He went to the sink in the morgue and turned off the running tap, then stared into the mirror to watch his will take shape. The surface of the shroud was already twitching and scurrying as he demanded new forms of it. At first there was only the primitive outline of his head, roughly shaped, like that of a snowman. Two pits for eyes: a lumpen nose. But he concentrated, willing the linen to stretch itself to the limits of its elasticity. And behold! it worked, it really worked! The threads complained, but acquiesced to his demands, forming in exquisite reproduction the nostrils, and then the eyelids; the upper lip: now the lower. He traced from memory the contours of his lost face like an adoring lover, and remade them in every detail. Now he began to make a column for the neck, filled with air, but looking deceptively solid. Below that the shroud swelled into a manly torso. The arms were already formed; the legs followed quickly on. And it was done.

He was remade, in his own image.

The illusion was not perfect. For one thing, he was pure white, except for the stains, and his flesh had the texture of cloth. The creases of his face were perhaps too severe, almost cubist in appearance, and it was impossible to coax the cloth to make a semblance of either hair or nails. But he was as ready for the world as any living shroud could hope to be.

It was time to go out and meet his public.

"Your game, Micky."

Maguire seldom lost at poker. He was too clever, and that used face too unreadable; his tired, bloodshot eyes never let anything out. Yet, despite his formidable reputation as a winner, he never cheated. That was his bond with himself. There was no life in winning if there was a cheat involved. It was just stealing then; and that was for the criminal classes. He was a business-man, pure and simple.

Tonight, in the space of two and a half hours, he'd pocketed a tidy sum. Life was good. Since the deaths of Dork, Henry B. Henry and Glass, the police had been too concerned with Murder to take much notice of the lower orders of Vice. Besides, their palms were well crossed with silver; they had nothing to complain about. Inspector Wall, a drinking companion of many years' standing, had even offered Maguire protection from the lunatic killer who was apparently on the loose. The irony of the idea pleased Maguire mightily.

It was almost three A.M. Time for bad girls and boys to be in their beds, dreaming of crimes for the morrow. Maguire rose from the table, signifying the end of the night's gambling. He buttoned up his waistcoat and carefully reknotted his lemon water-ice silk tie.

"Another game next week?" he suggested.

The defeated players agreed. They were used to losing money to their boss, but there were no hard feelings amongst the quar-ter. There was a tinge of sadness perhaps: they missed Henry B. and Dork. Saturday nights had been such joyous affairs. Now there was a muted tone over the proceedings.

Perlgut was the first to leave, stubbing out his cheroot in the brimming ashtray.

"Night, Mick."

"Night, Frank. Give the kids a kiss from their Uncle Mick, eh?"

"Will do."

Perlgut shuffled off, with his stuttering brother in tow.

"G-g-g-goodnight."

"Night, Ernest."

The brothers clattered down the stairs.

Norton was the last to go, as always.

"Shipment tomorrow?" he asked.

"Tomorrow's Sunday," said Maguire. He never worked on Sundays; it was a day for the family.

"Not, today's Sunday," said Norton, not trying to be pedantic, just letting it come naturally. "Tomorrow's Monday."

"Yes."

"Shipment Monday?"

"I hope so."

"You going to the warehouse?"

"Probably."

"I'll pick you up then: we can run down together."

"Fine."

Norton was a good man. Humorless, but reliable.

"Night then."

"Night."

His three-inch heels were steel-tipped; they sounded like a woman's stilettos on the stairs. The door slammed below.

Maguire counted his profits, drained his glass of Cointreau, and switched out the light in the gaming room. The smoke was already staling. Tomorrow he'd have to get somebody to come up and open the window, let some fresh Soho smells in there. Salami and coffee beans, commerce and sleaze. He loved it, loved it with a passion, like a babe loves a tit.

As he descended the stairs into the darkened sex shop he heard the exchange of farewells in the street outside, followed by the slamming of car doors and the purring departure of expensive cars. A good night with good friends, what more could any man reasonably ask?

At the bottom of the stairs he stopped for a moment. The blinking street sign lights opposite illuminated the shop sufficiently for him to make out the rows of magazines. Their plastic-bound faces glinted; siliconed breasts and spanked buttocks swelled from the covers like overripe fruit. Faces dripping mascara pouted at him, offering every lonely satisfaction paper could promise. But he was unmoved; the time had long since passed when he found any of that stuff of interest. It was simply currency to him; he was neither disgusted nor aroused by it. He was a happily married man after all, with a wife whose imagination barely stretched beyond page two of the *Kama Sutra,* and whose children were slapped soundly if they spoke one questionable word.

In the corner of the shop, where the Bondage and Domination material was displayed, something rose from the floor. Maguire found it hard to focus in the intermittent light. Red, blue. Red, blue. But it wasn't Norton, nor one of the Perlguts.

It was a face he knew however, smiling at him against the

background of "Roped and Raped" magazines. Now he saw: it was Glass, clear as day, and, despite the colored lights, white as a sheet.

He didn't try to reason how a dead man could be staring at him, he just dropped his coat and his jaw, and ran.

The door was locked, and the key was one of two dozen on his ring. Oh Jesus, why did he have so many keys? Keys to the warehouse, keys to the greenhouse, keys to the whorehouse. And only that twitching light to see them by. Red, blue. Red, blue.

He rummaged amongst the keys and by some magical chance the first he tried slotted easily in the lock and turned like a finger in hot grease. The door was open, the street ahead.

But Glass glided up behind him soundlessly, and before he could step over the threshold he had thrown something around Maguire's face, a cloth of some kind. It smelt of hospitals, of ether or disinfectant or both. Maguire tried to cry out but a fist of cloth was being thrust down his throat. He gagged on it, the vomit reflex making his system revolt. In response the assassin just tightened his grip.

In the street opposite a girl Maguire knew only as Natalie (Model: seeks interesting position with strict disciplinarian) was watching the struggle in the doorway of the shop with a doped look on her vapid face. She'd seen murder once or twice; she'd seen rape aplenty, and she wasn't about to get involved. Besides, it was late, and the insides of her thighs ached. Casually she turned away down the pink lit corridor, leaving the violence to take its course. Maguire made a mental note to have the girl's face carved up one of these days. If he survived; which seemed less likely by the moment. The red, blue, red, blue was unfixable now, as his airless brain went color-blind, and though he seemed to snatch a grip on his would-be assassin, the hold seemed to evaporate, leaving cloth, empty cloth, running through his sweating hands like silk.

Then someone spoke. Not behind him, not the voice of his assassin, but in front. In the street, Norton. It was Norton. He'd returned for some reason, God love him, and he was getting out of his car ten yards down the street, shouting Maguire's name.

The assassin's choke hold faltered and gravity claimed Maguire. He fell heavily, the world spinning, to the pavement, his face purple in the lurid light.

Norton ran towards his boss, fumbling for his gun amongst the bric-á-brac in his pocket. The white-suited assassin was already backing off down the street, unprepared to take on another man. He looked, thought Norton, for all the world like a failed member of the Klu Klux Klan; a hood, a robe, a cloak. Norton dropped to one knee, took a double-handed aim at the man and fired. The result was startling. The figure seemed to balloon up, his body losing its shape, becoming a flapping mass of white cloth, with a face loosely imprinted on it. There was a noise like the snapping of Monday-washed sheets on a line, a sound that was out of place in this grimy backstreet. Norton's confusion left him responseless for a moment, and the mansheet seemed to rise in the air, illusory.

At Norton's feet, Maguire was coming round, groaning. He was trying to speak but having difficulty making himself understood through his bruised larynx and throat. Norton bent closer to him. He smelt of vomit and fear.

"Glass," he seemed to be saying.

It was enough. Norton nodded, said hush. That was the face, of course, on the sheet. Glass, the imprudent accountant. He'd watched the man's feet fried, watched the whole vicious ritual; not to his taste at all.

Well, well: Ronnie Glass had some friends apparently, friends not above revenge.

Norton looked up, but the wind had lifted the ghost above the rooftops and away.

That had been a bad experience; the first taste of failure. Ronnie remembered it still, the desolation of that night. He'd lain, heaped in a rat-run corner of a derelict factory south of the river, and calmed the panic in his fibers. What good was this trick he'd mastered if he lost control of it the instant he was threatened? He must plan more carefully, and wind his will up until it would brook no resistance. Already he sensed that his energy was ebbing: and there was a hint of difficulty in restructuring his body this second time round. He had no time to waste with fumbled failures. He must corner the man where he could not possibly escape.

* * *

Police investigations at the mortuary had led round in circles for half a day; and now into the night. Inspector Wall of the Yard had tried every technique he knew. Soft words, hard words, promises, threats, seductions, surprises, even blows. Still Lenny told the same story; a ridiculous story he swore would be corroborated when his fellow technician came out of the catatonic state he'd now taken refuge in. But there was no way the Inspector could take the story seriously. A shroud that walked? How could he put that in his report? No, he wanted something concrete, even if it was a lie.

"Can I have a cigarette?" asked Lenny for the umpteenth time. Wall shook his head.

"Hey, Fresco—" Wall addressed his right-hand man, Al Kincaid. "I think it's time you searched the lad again."

Lenny knew what another search implied; it was a euphemism for a beating. Up against the wall, legs spread, hands on head: wham! His stomach jumped at the thought.

"Listen . . ." he implored.

"What, Lenny?"

"I didn't do it."

"Of course you did it," said Wall, picking his nose. "We just want to know why. Didn't you like the old fucker? Make dirty remarks about your lady friends, did he? He had a bit of a reputation for that, I understand."

Al Fresco smirked.

"Was that why you nobbled him?"

"For God's sake," said Lenny, "you think I'd tell you a fucking story like that if I didn't see it with my own fucking eyes."

"Language," chided Fresco.

"Shrouds don't fly," said Wall, with understandable conviction.

"Then where is the shroud, eh?" reasoned Lenny.

"You incinerated it, you ate it, how the fuck should I know?"

"Language," said Lenny quietly.

The phone rang before Fresco could hit him. He picked it up, spoke and handed it to Wall. Then he hit Lenny, a friendly slap that drew a little blood.

"Listen," said Fresco, breathing with lethal proximity to Lenny as if to suck the air out of his mouth, "We know you did it, see?

You were the only one in the morgue *alive* to do it, see? We just want to know why. That's all. Just why."

"Fresco." Wall had covered the receiver as he spoke to the muscleman.

"Yes, sir."

"It's Mr. Maguire."

"Mr. Maguire?"

"Micky Maguire."

Fresco nodded.

"He's very upset."

"Oh yeah? Why's that?"

"He thinks he's been attacked, by the man in the morgue. The pornographer."

"Glass," said Lenny, "Ronnie Glass."

"Ronald Glass, like the man says," said Wall, grinning at Lenny.

"That's ridiculous," said Fresco.

"Well I think we ought to do our duty to an upstanding member of the community, don't you? Duck in to the morgue will you, make sure—"

"Make sure?"

"That the bastard's still down there—"

"Oh."

Fresco exited, confused but obedient.

Lenny didn't understand any of this: but he was past caring. What the hell was it to him anyway? He started to play with his balls through a hole in his lefthand pocket. Wall watched him with disdain.

"Don't do that," he said. "You can play with yourself as much as you like once we've got you tucked up in a nice, warm cell."

Lenny shook his head slowly, and removed his hand from his pocket. Just wasn't his day.

Fresco was already back from down the hall, a little breathless.

"He's there," he said, visibly brightened by the simplicity of the task.

"Of course he is," said Wall.

"Dead as a Dodo," said Fresco.

"What's a Dodo?" asked Lenny.

Fresco looked blank.

"Turn of phrase," he said testily.

Wall of the Yard was back on the line, talking to Maguire. The man at the other end sounded well spooked; and his reassurances seemed to do little good.

"He's all present and correct, Micky. You must have been mistaken."

Maguire's fear ran back through the phone line like a mild electric charge.

"I saw him, damn you."

"Well, he's lying down there with a hole in the middle of his head, Micky. So tell me how *can* you have seen him?"

"I don't know," said Maguire.

"Well then."

"Listen . . . if you get the chance, drop by will you? Same arrangement as usual. I could put some nice work your way."

Wall didn't like talking business on the phone, it made him uneasy.

"Later, Micky."

"O.K. Call by?"

"I will."

"Promise?"

"Yes."

Wall put down the receiver and stared at the suspect. Lenny was back to pocket billiards again. Crass little animal; another search was clearly called for.

"Fresco," said Wall in dovelike tones, "will you please teach Lenny not to play with himself in front of police officers?"

In his fortress in Richmond, Maguire cried like a baby.

He'd seen Glass, no doubt of it. Whatever Wall believed about the body being at the mortuary, he knew otherwise. Glass was out, on the street, footloose and fancyfree, despite the fact that he'd blown a hole in the bastard's head.

Maguire was a God-fearing man, and he believed in life after death, though until now he'd never questioned how it would come about. This was the answer, this blank-faced son of a whore stinking of ether: this was the way the afterlife would be. It made him weep, fearing to live, and fearing to die.

It was well past dawn now; a peaceful Sunday morning. Nothing would happen to him in the safety of the "Ponderosa," and in full daylight. This was his castle, built with his hard won thievings. Norton was here, armed to the teeth. There were dogs at every gate. No one, living or dead, would dare challenge his supremacy in this territory. Here, amongst the portraits of his heroes: Louis B. Mayer, Dillinger, Churchill; amongst his family; amidst his good taste, his money, his *objets d'art,* here he was his own man. If the mad accountant came for him he'd be blasted in his tracks, ghost or no ghost. *Finis.*

After all, wasn't he Michael Roscoe Maguire, an empire builder? Born with nothing, he'd risen by virtue of his stockbroker's face and his maverick's heart. Once in a while, maybe, and only under very controlled conditions, he might let his darker appetites show; as at the execution of Glass. He'd taken genuine pleasure in that little scenario; *his* the *coup de grâce, his* the infinite compassion of the killing stroke. But his life of violence was all but behind him now. Now he was a bourgeois, secure in his fortress.

Raquel woke at eight, and busied herself with preparing breakfast.

"You want anything to eat?" she asked Maguire.

He shook his head. His throat hurt too much.

"Coffee?"

"Yes."

"You want it in here?"

He nodded. He liked sitting in front of the window that overlooked the lawn and the greenhouse. The day was brightening; fat, fleecy clouds bucked the wind, their shadows, passing over the perfect green. Maybe he'd take up painting, he thought, like Winston. Commit his favorite landscapes to canvas; maybe a view of the garden, even a nude of Raquel, immortalized in oils before her tits sagged beyond all hope of support.

She was back purring at his side, with the coffee.

"You O.K.?" she asked.

Dumb bitch. Of course he wasn't O.K.

"Sure," he said.

"You've got a visitor."

"What?" He sat up straight in the leather chair. "Who?" She was smiling at him.

"Tracy," she said. "She wants to come in and cuddle."

He expelled a hiss of air from the sides of his mouth. Dumb, dumb bitch.

"You want to see Tracy?"

"Sure."

The little accident, as he was fond of calling her, was at the door, still in her dressing gown.

"Hi, Daddy."

"Hello, sweetheart."

She sashayed across the room towards him, her mother's walk in embryo.

"Mummy says you're ill."

"I'm getting better."

"I'm glad."

"So am I."

"Shall we go out today?"

"Maybe."

"See the fair?"

"Maybe."

She pouted fetchingly, perfectly in control of the effect. Raquel's trick all over again. He just hoped to God she wasn't going to grow up as dumb as her mother.

"We'll see," he said, hoping to imply yes, but knowing he meant no.

She hoisted herself onto his knee and he indulged her tales of a five-year-old's mischiefs for a while, then sent her packing. Talking made his throat hurt, and he didn't feel too much like the loving father today.

Alone again, he watched the shadows waltz on the lawn.

The dogs began to bark after eleven. Then, after a short while, they fell silent. He got up to find Norton, who was in the kitchen doing a jigsaw with Tracy. "The Hay-Wain" in two thousand pieces. One of Raquel's favorites.

"You check the dogs, Norton?"

"No, Boss."

"Well fucking do it."

He didn't often swear in front of the child; but he felt ready to go bang. Norton snapped to it. As he opened the back door Maguire could smell the day. It was tempting to step outside the house. But the dogs barked in a way that set his head thumping and his palms prickling. Tracy had her head down to the business of the jigsaw, her body tense with anticipation of her father's anger. He said nothing, but went straight back into the lounge.

From his chair he could see Norton striding across the lawn. The dogs weren't making a sound now. Norton disappeared from sight behind the greenhouse. A long wait. Maguire was just beginning to get agitated, when Norton appeared again, and looked up at the house, shrugging at Maguire, and speaking. Maguire unlocked the sliding door, opened it and stepped on to the patio. The day met him: balmy.

"What are you saying?" he called to Norton.

"The dogs are fine," Norton returned.

Maguire felt his body relax. Of course the dogs were O.K.; why shouldn't they bark a bit, what else were they for? He was damn near making a fool of himself, pissing his pants just because the dogs barked. He nodded to Norton and stepped off the patio on to the lawn. Beautiful day, he thought. Quickening his pace he crossed the lawn to the greenhouse, where his carefully nurtured Bonsai trees bloomed. At the door of the greenhouse Norton was waiting dutifully, going through his pockets, looking for mints.

"You want me here, sir?"

"No."

"Sure?"

"Sure," he said magnanimously, "you go back up and play with the kid."

Norton nodded.

"Dogs are fine," he said again.

"Yeah."

"Must have been the wind stirred them up."

There was a wind. Warm, but strong. It stirred the line of copper beeches that bounded the garden. They shimmered, and showed the paler undersides of their leaves to the sky, their movement reassuring in its ease and gentility.

Maguire unlocked the greenhouse and stepped into his haven. Here in this artificial Eden were his true loves, nurtured on coos and cuttlefish manure. His Sargent's Juniper, that had survived the rigors of Mount Ishizuchi; his flowering quince, his Yeddo Spruce (Picea Jesoensis), his favorite dwarf, that he'd trained, after several failed attempts, to cling to a stone. All beauties: all minor miracles of winding trunk and cascading needles, worthy of his fondest attention.

Content, mindless for a while of the outside world, he pottered amongst his flora.

The dogs had fought over possession of Ronnie as though he were a plaything. They'd caught him breaching the wall and surrounded him before he could make his escape, grinning as they seized him, tore him and spat him out. He escaped only because Norton had approached, and distracted them from their fury for a moment.

His body was torn in several places after their attack. Confused, concentrating to try and keep his shape coherent, he had narrowly avoided being spotted by Norton.

Now he crept out of hiding. The fight had sapped him of energy, and the shroud gaped, so that the illusion of substance was spoiled. His belly was torn open; his left leg all but severed. The stains had multiplied; mucus and dog shit joining the blood.

But the will, the will was all. He had come so close; this was not the time to relinquish his grip and let nature take its course. He existed in mutiny against nature, that was his state; and for the first time in his life (and death) he felt an elation. To be unnatural: to be in defiance of system and sanity, was that so bad? He was shitty, bloody, dead and resurrected in a piece of stained cloth; he was a nonsense. *Yet he was.* No one could deny him being, as long as he had the will to be. The thought was delicious: like finding a new sense in a blind, deaf world.

He saw Maguire in the greenhouse and watched him awhile. The enemy was totally absorbed in his hobby; he was even whistling the National Anthem as he tended his flowering charges. Ronnie moved closer to the glass, and closer, his voice an oh-so-gentle moan in the failing weave.

Maguire didn't hear the sigh of cloth on the window, until Ronnie's face pressed flat to the glass, the features smeared and misshapen. He dropped the Yeddo Spruce. It shattered on the floor, its branches broken.

Maguire tried to yell, but all he could squeeze from his vocal cords was a strangled yelp. He broke for the door, as the face, huge with greed for revenge, broke the glass. Maguire didn't quite comprehend what happened next. The way the head and the body seemed to flow through the broken pane, defying physics, and reassembled in his sanctum, taking on the shape of a human being.

No, it wasn't quite human. It had the look of a stroke victim, its white mask and its white body sagged down the right side, and it dragged its torn leg after it as it lunged at him.

He opened the door and retreated into the garden. The thing followed, speaking now, arms extended towards him.

"Maguire . . ."

It said his name in a voice so soft he might have imagined it. But no, it spoke again.

"Recognize me, Maguire?" it said.

And of course he did, even with its stroke-stricken, billowing features it was clearly Ronnie Glass.

"Glass," he said.

"Yes," said the ghost.

"I don't want—" Maguire began, then faltered. What didn't he want? To speak with this horror, certainly. To know that it existed; that too. To die, most of all.

"I don't want to die."

"You will," said the ghost.

Maguire felt the gust of the sheet as it flew in his face, or perhaps it was the wind that caught this insubstantial monster and threw it around him.

Whichever, the embrace stank of ether, and disinfectant, and death. Arms of linen tightened around him, the gaping face was pressed on to his, as though the thing wanted to kiss him.

Instinctively Maguire reached round his attacker, and his hands found the rent the dogs had made in the shroud. His fingers gripped the open edge of the cloth, and he pulled. He was satisfied to hear the linen tearing along its weave, and the bear hug fell away from him. The shroud bucked in his hand, the liquefied mouth wide in a silent scream.

Ronnie was feeling an agony he thought he'd left behind him with flesh and bone. But here it was again: pain, pain, pain.

He fluttered away from his mutilator, letting out what cry he could, while Maguire stumbled away up the lawn, his eyes huge. The man was close to madness, surely his mind was as good as broken. But that wasn't enough. He had to kill the bastard; that was his promise to himself and he intended to keep it.

The pain didn't disappear, but he tried to ignore it, putting all his energy into pursuing Maguire up the garden towards the house. But he was so weak now: the wind almost had mastery of him; gusting through his form and catching the frayed entrails of his body. He looked like a war-torn flag, fouled so it was scarcely recognizable, and just about ready to call it a day.

Except, except . . . Maguire.

Maguire reached the house, and slammed the door. The sheet pressed itself against the window, flapping ludicrously, its linen hands raking the glass, its almost-lost face demanding vengeance.

"Let me in," it said, "I *will* come in."

Maguire stumbled backwards across the room into the hall.

"Raquel . . ."

Where was the woman?

"Raquel . . . ?"

"Raquel . . ."

She wasn't in the kitchen. From the den, the sound of Tracy's singing. He peered in. The little girl was alone. She was sitting in the middle of the floor, headphones clamped over her ears, singing along to some favorite song.

"Mummy?" he mimed at her.

"Upstairs," she replied, without taking off the headphones.

Upstairs. As he climbed the stairs he heard the dogs barking down the garden. What was it doing? What was the fucker doing?

"Raquel . . . ?" His voice was so quiet he could barely hear it himself. It was as though he'd prematurely become a ghost in his own house.

There was no noise on the landing.

He stumbled into the brown-tiled bathroom and snapped on the light. It was flattering, and he had always liked to look at himself in it. The mellow radiance dulled the edge of age. But now it refused to lie. His face was that of an old and haunted man.

He flung open the airing cupboard and fumbled amongst the warm towels. There! a gun, nestling in scented comfort, hidden away for emergencies only. The contact made him salivate. He snatched the gun and checked it. All in working order. This weapon had brought Glass down once, and it could do it again. And again. And again.

He opened the bedroom door.

"Raquel—"

She was sitting on the edge of the bed, with Norton inserted between her legs. Both still dressed, one of Raquel's sumptuous breasts teased from her bra and pressed into Norton's accommodating mouth. She looked round, dumb as ever, not knowing what she'd done.

Without thinking, he fired.

The bullet found her openmouthed, gormless as ever, and blew a sizable hole in her neck. Norton pulled himself out, no necrophiliac he, and ran towards the window. Quite what he intended wasn't clear. Flight was impossible.

The next bullet caught Norton in the middle of the back, and passed through his body, puncturing the window.

Only then, with her lover dead, did Raquel topple back across the bed, her breast spattered, her legs splayed wide. Maguire watched her fall. The domestic obscenity didn't disgust him; it was quite tolerable. Tit and blood and mouth and lost love and all; it was quite, quite tolerable. Maybe he was becoming insensitive.

He dropped the gun.

The dogs had stopped barking.

He slipped out of the room on to the landing, closing the door quietly, so as not to disturb the child.

Mustn't disturb the child. As he walked to the top of the stairs he saw his daughter's winsome face staring up at him from the bottom.

"Daddy."

He stared at her with a puzzled expression.

"There was someone at the door. I saw them passing the window."

He started to walk unsteadily down the stairs, one at a time. Slowly does it, he thought.

"I opened the door, but there was nobody there."

Wall. It must be Wall. He would know what to do for the best.

"Was it a tall man?"

"I didn't see him properly, Daddy. Just his face. He was even whiter than you."

The door! Oh Jesus, the door! If she'd left it open. Too late.

The stranger came into the hall and his face crinkled into a kind of smile, which Maguire thought was about the worst thing he'd ever seen.

It wasn't Wall.

Wall was flesh and blood: the visitor was a rag doll. Wall was a grim man; this one smiled. Wall was life and law and order. This thing wasn't.

It was Glass of course.

Maguire shook his head. The child, not seeing the thing wavering on the air behind her, misunderstood.

"What did I do wrong?" she asked.

Ronnie sailed past her up the stairs, more a shadow now than anything remotely manlike, shreds of cloth trailing behind him. Maguire had no time to resist, nor will left to do so. He opened his mouth to say something in defense of his life, and Ronnie thrust his remaining arm, wound into a rope of linen, down Maguire's throat. Maguire choked on it, but Ronnie snaked on, past his protesting epiglottis, forging a rough way down his esophagus into Maguire's stomach. Maguire felt it there, a fullness that was like overeating, except that it squirmed in the middle of his body, raking his stomach wall and catching hold of the lining. It was all so quick, Maguire had no time to die of suffocation. In the event, he might have wished to go that way, horrid as it would have been. Instead, he felt Ronnie's hand convulse in his belly, digging deeper for a decent grip on his colon, on his duodenum. And when the hand had all it could hold, the fuckhead pulled out his arm.

The exit was swift, but for Maguire the moment would seemingly have no end. He doubled up as the disembowelling began, feeling his viscera surge up his throat, turning him inside out. His lights went out through his throat in a welter of fluids, coffee, blood, acid.

Ronnie pulled on the guts and hauled Maguire, his emptied torso collapsing on itself, towards the top of the stairs. Led by a length of his own entrails Maguire reached the top stair and pitched forward. Ronnie relinquished his hold and Maguire fell, head swathed in gut, to the bottom of the stairs, where his daughter still stood.

She seemed, by her expression, not the least alarmed; but then Ronnie knew children could deceive so easily.

The job completed, he began to totter down the stairs, uncoiling his arm, and shaking his head as he tried to recover a smidgen of human appearance. The effort worked. By the time he reached the child at the bottom of the stairs he was able to offer her something very like a human touch. She didn't respond, and all he could do was leave and hope that in time she'd come to forget.

Once he'd gone, Tracy went upstairs to find her mother. Racquel was unresponsive to her questions, as was the man on the carpet by the window. But there was something about him that fascinated her. A fat, red snake pressing out from his trousers. It made her laugh, it was such a silly little thing.

The girl was still laughing when Wall of the Yard appeared, late as usual. Though viewing the death dances the house had jumped to he was, on the whole, glad he'd been a late arrival at that particular party.

In the confessional of St. Mary Magdalene's the shroud of Ronnie Glass was now corrupted beyond recognition. He had very little feeling left in him, just the desire, so strong he knew he couldn't resist for very much longer, to let go of this wounded body. It had served him well; he had no complaints to make of it. But now he was out of breath. He could animate the inanimate no longer.

He wanted to confess though, wanted to confess so very badly. To tell the Father, to tell the Son, to tell the Holy Ghost what sins he'd performed, dreamt, longed for. There was only one thing for it: if Father Rooney wouldn't come to him then he'd go to Father Rooney.

He opened the door of the Confessional. The church was almost empty. It was evening now, he guessed, and who had the time for the lighting of candles when there was food to be cooked, love to be bought, life to be had? Only a Greek florist, praying in the aisle for his sons to be acquitted, saw the shroud stagger from the Confessional towards the door of the Vestry. It looked like some damn-fool adolescent with a filthy sheet slung over his head. The florist hated that kind of Godless behavior—look where it had got his children—he wanted to beat the kid around a bit, and teach him not to play silly beggars in the House of the Lord.

"Hey, you!" he said, too loudly.

The shroud turned to look at the florist, its eyes like two holes pressed in warm dough. The face of the ghost was so woebegone it froze the words on the florist's lips.

Ronnie tried the handle of the Vestry door. The rattling got him nowhere. The door was locked.

From inside, a breathless voice said:

"Who is it?" It was Father Rooney speaking.

Ronnie tried to reply, but no words would come. All he could do was rattle, like any worthy ghost.

"Who is it?" asked the good Father again, a little impatiently.

Confess me, Ronnie wanted to say, confess me, for I have sinned.

The door stayed shut. Inside, Father Rooney was busy. He was taking photographs for his private collection; his subject a favorite lady of his by the name of Natalie. A daughter of vice somebody had told him, but he couldn't believe that. She was too obliging, too cherubic, and she wound a rosary around her pert bosom as though she was barely out of a convent.

The jiggling of the handle had stopped now. Good, thought Father Rooney. They'd come back, whoever they were. Nothing was that urgent. Father Rooney grinned at the woman. Natalie's lips pouted back.

In the church Ronnie hauled himself to the altar, and genuflected.

Three rows back the florist rose from his prayers, incensed by this desecration. The boy was obviously drunk, the way he was reeling, the man wasn't about to be frightened by a tuppenny-colored death mask. Cursing the desecrator in ripe Greek, he snatched at the ghost as it knelt in front of the altar.

There was nothing under the sheet: nothing at all.

The florist felt the living cloth twitch in his hand, and dropped it with a tiny cry. Then he backed off down the aisle, crossing himself back and forth, back and forth, like a demented widow. A few yards from the door of the church he turned tail and ran.

The shroud lay where the florist had dropped it. Ronnie, lingering in the creases, looked up from the crumpled heap at the splendor of the altar. It was radiant, even in the gloom of the candlelit interior, and moved by its beauty, he was content to put the illusion behind him. Unconfessed, but unfearful of judgment, his spirit crept away.

*   *   *

After an hour or so Father Rooney unbolted the Vestry, escorted the chaste Natalie out of the church, and locked the front door. He peered into the Confessional on his way back, to check for hiding children. Empty, the entire church was empty. St. Mary Magdalene was a forgotten woman.

As he meandered, whistling, back to the Vestry he caught sight of Ronnie Glass's shroud. It lay sprawled on the altar steps, a forlorn pile of shabby cloth. Ideal, he thought, picking it up. There were some indiscreet stains on the Vestry floor. Just the job to wipe them up.

He sniffed the cloth, he loved to sniff. It smelt of a thousand things. Ether, sweat, dogs, entrails, blood, disinfectant, empty rooms, broken hearts, flowers and loss. Fascinating. This was the thrill of the Parish of Soho, he thought. Something new every day. Mysteries on the doorstep, on the altar step. Crimes so numerous they would need an ocean of Holy Water to wash them out. Vice for sale on every corner, if you knew where to look.

He tucked the shroud under his arm.

"I bet you've got a tale to tell," he said, snuffing out the votive candles with fingers too hot to feel the flame.

The Ghost Village

Peter Straub

Peter Straub (1943–) almost single-handedly rekindled modern interest in the ghost tale with his bestselling novel *Ghost Story* (1979), a work that followed his two earlier ghost novels, *Julia* (1975) and *If You Could See Me Now* (1977) and anticipated *Mrs. God* (1991), his tribute to British ghost-story writer Robert Aickman. More recently, Straub has concentrated on the disorienting impact of the Vietnam War on American culture in *Koko* (1988), *Mystery* (1990), and several of the stories collected in *Houses Without Doors* (1991). "The Ghost Village," a self-contained excerpt from his novel *The Throat* (1993), uses the ghost theme to express the haunting power of guilt and shame.

1

In Vietnam I knew a man who went quietly and purposefully crazy because his wife wrote him that his son had been sexually abused—"messed with"—by the leader of their church choir. This man was a black six-foot-six grunt named Leonard Hamnet, from a small town in Tennessee named Archibald. Before writing, his wife had waited until she had endured the entire business of going to the police, talking to other parents, returning to the police with another accusation, and finally succeeding in having the man charged. He was up for trial in two months. Leonard Hamnet was no happier about that than he was about the original injury.

"I got to murder him, you know, but I'm seriously thinking on murdering her too," he said. He still held the letter in his hands, and he was speaking to Spanky Burrage, Michael Poole,

Conor Linklater, SP4 Cotton, Calvin Hill, Tina Pumo, the mag-
nificent M. O. Dengler, and myself. "All this is going on, my
boy needs help, this here Mr. Brewster needs to be dismantled,
needs to be *racked* and *stacked,* and she don't tell me! Makes
me want to put her *down,* man. Take her damn head off and
put it up on a stake in the yard, man. With a sign saying: *Here
is one stupid woman.*"

We were in the unofficial part of Camp Crandall known as No
Man's Land, located between the wire perimeter and a shack,
also unofficial, where a cunning little weasel named Wilson
Manly sold contraband beer and liquor. No Man's Land, so
called because the C.O. pretended it did not exist, contained a
mound of old tires, a piss tube, and a lot of dusty red ground.
Leonard Hamnet gave the letter in his hand a dispirited look,
folded it into the pocket of his fatigues, and began to roam
around the heap of tires, aiming kicks at the ones that stuck out
furthest. "One stupid woman," he repeated. Dust exploded up
from a burst, worn-down wheel of rubber.

I wanted to make sure Hamnet knew he was angry with Mr.
Brewster, not his wife, and said, "She was trying—"

Hamnet's great glistening bull's head turned toward me.

"Look at what the woman did. She nailed that bastard. She
got other people to admit that he messed with their kids too.
That must be almost impossible. And she had the guy arrested.
He's going to be put away for a long time."

"I'll put that bitch away, too," Hamnet said, and kicked an
old gray tire hard enough to push it nearly a foot back into the
heap. All the other tires shuddered and moved. For a second it
seemed that the entire mound might collapse.

"This is my *boy* I'm talking about here," Hamnet said. "This
shit has gone far enough."

"The important thing," Dengler said, "is to take care of your
boy. You have to see he gets help."

"How'm I gonna do that from here?" Hamnet shouted.

"Write him a letter," Dengler said. "Tell him you love him.
Tell him he did right to go to his mother. Tell him you think
about him all the time."

Hamnet took the letter from his pocket and stared at it. It was
already stained and wrinkled. I did not think it could survive
many more of Hamnet's readings. His face seemed to get heav-

ier, no easy trick with a face like Hamnet's. "I got to get home," he said. "I got to get back home and take *care* of these people."

Hamnet began putting in requests for compassionate leave relentlessly—one request a day. When we were out on patrol, sometimes I saw him unfold the tattered sheet of notepaper from his shirt pocket and read it two or three times, concentrating intensely. When the letter began to shred along the folds, Hamnet taped it together.

We were going out on four- and five-day patrols during that period, taking a lot of casualties. Hamnet performed well in the field, but he had retreated so far within himself that he spoke in monosyllables. He wore a dull, glazed look, and moved like a man who had just eaten a heavy dinner. I thought he looked like a man who had given up, and when people gave up they did not last long—they were already very close to death, and other people avoided them.

We were camped in a stand of trees at the edge of a paddy. That day we had lost two men so new that I had already forgotten their names. We had to eat cold C rations because heating them with C-4 would have been like putting up billboards and arc lights. We couldn't smoke, and we were not supposed to talk. Hamnet's C rations consisted of an old can of Spam that dated from an earlier war and a can of peaches. He saw Spanky staring at the peaches and tossed him the can. Then he dropped the Spam between his legs. Death was almost visible around him. He fingered the note out of his pocket and tried to read it in the damp gray twilight.

At that moment someone started shooting at us, and the Lieutenant yelled *"Shit!"*, and we dropped our food and returned fire at the invisible people trying to kill us. When they kept shooting back, we had to go through the paddy.

The warm water came up to our chests. At the dikes, we scrambled over and splashed down into the muck on the other side. A boy from Santa Cruz, California, named Thomas Blevins got a round in the back of his neck and dropped dead into the water just short of the first dike, and another boy named Tyrell Budd coughed and dropped down right beside him. The F. O. called in an artillery strike. We leaned against the backs of the last two dikes when the big shells came thudding in. The ground shook and the water rippled, and the edge of the forest went up in a series of fireballs. We could hear the monkeys screaming.

One by one we crawled over the last dike onto the damp but solid ground on the other side of the paddy. Here the trees were much sparser, and a little group of thatched huts was visible through them.

Then two things I did not understand happened, one after the other. Someone off in the forest fired a mortar round at us— just one. One mortar, one round. That was the first thing. I fell down and shoved my face in the muck, and everybody around me did the same. I considered that this might be my last second on earth, and greedily inhaled whatever life might be left to me. Whoever fired the mortar should have had an excellent idea of our location, and I experienced that endless moment of pure, terrifying helplessness—a moment in which the soul simultaneously clings to the body and readies itself to let go of it—until the shell landed on top of the last dike and blew it to bits. Dirt, mud, and water slopped down around us, and shell fragments whizzed through the air. One of the fragments sailed over us, sliced a hamburger-size wad of bark and wood from a tree, and clanged into Spanky Burrage's helmet with a sound like a brick hitting a garbage can. The fragment fell to the ground, and a little smoke drifted up from it.

We picked ourselves up. Spanky looked dead, except that he was breathing. Hamnet shouldered his pack and picked up Spanky and slung him over his shoulder. He saw me looking at him.

"I gotta take *care* of these people," he said.

The other thing I did not understand—apart from why there had been only one mortar round—came when we entered the village.

Lieutenant Harry Beevers had yet to join us, and we were nearly a year away from the events at Ia Thuc, when everything, the world and ourselves within the world, went crazy. I have to explain what happened. Lieutenant Harry Beevers killed thirty children in a cave at Ia Thuc and their bodies disappeared, but Michael Poole and I went into that cave and knew that something obscene had happened in there. We smelled evil, we touched its wings with our hands. A pitiful character named Victor Spitalny ran into the cave when he heard gunfire, and came pinwheeling out right away, screaming, covered with welts or hives that vanished almost as soon as he came out into the air. Poor Spitalny had touched it too. Because I was twenty and already writing books in my head, I thought that the cave was the place where the other *Tom Sawyer* ended, where Injun Joe raped Becky Thatcher and slit Tom's throat.

When we walked into the little village in the woods on the other side of the rice paddy, I experienced a kind of foretaste of Ia Thuc. If I can say this without setting off all the Gothic bells, the place seemed intrinsically, inherently wrong—it was too quiet, too still, completely without noise or movement. There were no chickens, dogs, or pigs; no old women came out to look us over, no old men offered conciliatory smiles. The little huts, still inhabitable, were empty—something I had never seen before in Vietnam, and never saw again. It was a ghost village, in a country where people thought the earth was sanctified by their ancestor's bodies.

Poole's map said that the place was named Bong To.

Hamnet lowered Spanky into the long grass as soon as we reached the center of the empty village. I bawled out a few words in my poor Vietnamese.

Spanky groaned. He gently touched the sides of his helmet. "I caught a head wound," he said.

"You wouldn't have a head at all, you was only wearing your liner," Hamnet said.

Spanky bit his lips and pushed the helmet up off his head. He groaned. A finger of blood ran down beside his ear. Finally the helmet passed over a lump the size of an apple that rose up from under his hair. Wincing, Spanky fingered this enormous knot. "I see double," he said. "I'll never get that helmet back on."

The medic said, "Take it easy, we'll get you out of here."

"Out of *here*?" Spanky brightened up.

"Back to Crandall," the medic said.

Spitalny sidled up, and Spanky frowned at him. "There ain't nobody here," Spitalny said. "What the fuck is going on?" He took the emptiness of the village as a personal affront.

Leonard Hamnet turned his back and spat.

"Spitalny, Tiano," the Lieutenant said. "Go into the paddy and get Tyrell and Blevins. Now."

Tattoo Tiano, who was due to die six and a half months later and was Spitalny's only friend, said, "You do it this time, Lieutenant."

Hamnet turned around and began moving toward Tiano and Spitalny. He looked as if he had grown two sizes larger, as if his hands could pick up boulders. I had forgotten how big he was. His head was lowered, and a rim of clear white showed above the irises. I wouldn't have been surprised if he had blown smoke from his nostrils.

"Hey, I'm gone, I'm already there," Tiano said. He and Spitalny began moving quickly through the sparse trees. Whoever had fired the mortar had packed up and gone. By now it was nearly dark, and the mosquitoes had found us.

"So?" Poole said.

Hamnet sat down heavily enough for me to feel the shock in my boots. He said, "I have to go home, Lieutenant. I don't mean no disrespect, but I cannot take this shit much longer."

The Lieutenant said he was working on it.

Poole, Hamnet, and I looked around at the village.

Spanky Burrage said, "Good quiet place for Ham to catch up on his reading."

"Maybe I better take a look," the Lieutenant said. He flicked the lighter a couple of times and walked off toward the nearest hut. The rest of us stood around like fools, listening to the mosquitoes and the sounds of Tiano and Spitalny pulling the dead men up over the dikes. Every now and then Spanky groaned and shook his head. Too much time passed.

The Lieutenant said something almost inaudible from inside the hut. He came back outside in a hurry, looking disturbed and puzzled even in the darkness.

"Underhill, Poole," he said, "I want you to see this."

Poole and I glanced at each other. I wondered if I looked as bad as he did. Poole seemed to be a couple of psychic inches from either taking a poke at the Lieutenant or exploding altogether. In his muddy face his eyes were the size of hen's eggs. He was wound up like a cheap watch. I thought that I probably looked pretty much the same.

"What is it, Lieutenant?" he asked.

The Lieutenant gestured for us to come to the hut, then turned around and went back inside. There was no reason for us not to follow him. The Lieutenant was a jerk, but Harry Beevers, our next Lieutenant, was a baron, an earl among jerks, and we nearly always did whatever dumb thing he told us to do. Poole was so ragged and edgy that he looked as if he felt like shooting the Lieutenant in the back. *I* felt like shooting the Lieutenant in the back, I realized a second later. I didn't have an idea in the world what was going on in Poole's mind. I grumbled something and moved toward the hut. Poole followed.

The Lieutenant was standing in the doorway, looking over his shoulder and fingering his sidearm. He frowned at us to let us know we had been slow to obey him, then flicked on the lighter. The sudden hollows and shadows in his face made him resemble one of the corpses I had opened up when I was in graves registration at Camp White Star.

"You want to know what it is, Poole? Okay, you tell me what it is."

He held the lighter before him like a torch and marched into the hut. I imagined the entire dry, flimsy structure bursting into heat and flame. This Lieutenant was not destined to get home walking and breathing, and I pitied and hated him about equally, but I did not want to turn into toast because he had found an American body inside a hut and didn't know what to do about it. I'd heard of platoons finding the mutilated corpses of American prisoners, and hoped that this was not our turn.

And then, in the instant before I smelled blood and saw the Lieutenant stoop to lift a panel on the floor, I thought that what had spooked him was not the body of an American POW but of a child who had been murdered and left behind in this empty place. The Lieutenant had probably not seen any dead children yet. Some part of the Lieutenant was still worrying about what a girl named Becky Roddenburger was getting up to back at Idaho State, and a dead child would be too much reality for him.

He pulled up the wooden panel in the floor, and I caught the smell of blood. The Zippo died, and darkness closed down on us. The Lieutenant yanked the panel back on its hinges. The smell of blood floated up from whatever was beneath the floor. The Lieutenant flicked the Zippo, and his face jumped out of the darkness. "Now. Tell me what this is."

"It's where they hide the kids when people like us show up," I said. "Smells like something went wrong. Did you take a look?"

I saw in his tight cheeks and almost lipless mouth that he had not. He wasn't about to go down there and get killed by the Minotaur while his platoon stood around outside.

"Taking a look is your job, Underhill," he said.

For a second we both looked at the ladder, made of peeled branches leashed together with rags, that led down into the pit.

"Give me the lighter," Poole said, and grabbed it away from the Lieutenant. He sat on the edge of the hole and leaned over, bringing the flame beneath the level of the floor. He grunted at whatever he saw, and surprised both the Lieutenant and myself by pushing himself off the ledge into the opening. The light went out. The Lieutenant and I looked down into the dark open rectangle in the floor.

The lighter flared again. I could see Poole's extended arm, the jittering little fire, a packed-earth floor. The top of the concealed room was less than an inch above the top of Poole's head. He moved away from the opening.

"What is it? Are there any—" The Lieutenant's voice made a creaky sound. "Any bodies?"

"Come down here, Tim," Poole called up.

I sat on the floor and swung my legs into the pit. Then I jumped down.

Beneath the floor, the smell of blood was almost sickeningly strong.

"What do you see?" the Lieutenant shouted. He was trying to sound like a leader, and his voice squeaked on the last word.

I saw an empty room shaped like a giant grave. The walls were covered by some kind of thick paper held in place by wooden struts sunk into the earth. Both the thick brown paper and two of the struts showed old bloodstains.

"Hot," Poole said, and closed the lighter.

"Come *on*, damn it," came the Lieutenant's voice. "Get out of there."

"Yes, sir," Poole said. He flicked the lighter back on. Many layers of thick paper formed an absorbent pad between the earth and the room, and the topmost, thinnest layer had been covered with vertical lines of Vietnamese writing. The writing looked like poetry, like the left-hand pages of Kenneth Rexroth's translations of Tu Fu and Li Po.

"Well, well," Poole said, and I turned to see him pointing at what first looked like intricately woven strands of rope fixed to the bloodstained wooden uprights. Poole stepped forward and the weave jumped into sharp relief. About four feet off the ground, iron chains had been screwed to the uprights. The thick pad between the two lengths of chain had been soaked with blood. The three feet of ground between the posts looked rusty. Poole moved the lighter closer to the chains, and we saw dried blood on the metal links.

"I want you guys out of there, and I mean *now,*" whined the Lieutenant.

Poole snapped the lighter shut.

"I just changed my mind," I said softly. "I'm putting twenty bucks into the Elijah fund. For two weeks from today. That's what, June twentieth?"

"Tell it to Spanky," he said. Spanky Burrage had invented the pool we called the Elijah fund, and he held the money. Michael had not put any money into the pool. He thought that a new Lieutenant might be even worse than the one we had. Of course he was right. Harry Beevers was our next Lieutenant. Elijah Joys, Lieutenant Elijah Joys of New Utrecht, Idaho, a graduate of the University of Idaho and basic training at Fort Benning, Georgia, was an inept, weak Lieutenant, not a disastrous one. If Spanky could have seen what was coming, he would have given back the money and prayed for the safety of Lieutenant Joys.

Poole and I moved back toward the opening. I felt as if I had seen a shrine to an obscene deity. The Lieutenant leaned over and stuck out his hand—uselessly, because he did not bend down far enough for us to reach him. We levered ourselves up out of the hole stiff-armed, as if we were leaving a swimming pool. The Lieutenant stepped back. He had a thin face and thick, fleshy nose, and his Adam's apple danced around in his neck like a jumping bean. He might not have been Harry Beevers, but he was no prize. "Well, how many?"

"How many what?" I asked.

"How many are there?" He wanted to go back to Camp Crandall with a good body count.

"There weren't exactly any bodies, Lieutenant," said Poole, trying to let him down easily. He described what we had seen.

"Well, what's that good for?" He meant, *How is that going to help me?*

"Interrogations, probably," Poole said. "If you questioned

someone down there, no one outside the hut would hear anything. At night, you could just drag the body into the woods."

Lieutenant Joys nodded. "Field Interrogation Post," he said,
trying out the phrase. "Torture, Use of, Highly Indicated." He
nodded again. "Right?"

"Highly," Poole said.

"Shows you what kind of enemy we're dealing with in this
conflict."

I could no longer stand being in the same three square feet of
space with Elijah Joys, and I took a step toward the door of the
hut. I did not know what Poole and I had seen, but I knew it was
not a Field Interrogation Post, Torture, Use of, Highly Indicated,
unless the Vietnamese had begun to interrogate monkeys. It occurred to me that the writing on the wall might have been names
instead of poetry—I thought that we had stumbled into a mystery
that had nothing to do with the war, a Vietnamese mystery.

For a second music from my old life, music too beautiful to
be endurable, started playing in my head. Finally I recognized
it: "The Walk to the Paradise Gardens," from *A Village Romeo
and Juliet* by Frederick Delius. Back in Berkeley, I had listened
to it hundreds of times.

If nothing else had happened, I think I could have replayed
the whole piece in my head. Tears filled my eyes, and I stepped
toward the door of the hut. Then I froze. A ragged Vietnamese
boy of seven or eight was regarding me with great seriousness
from the far corner of the hut. I knew he was not there—I knew
he was a spirit. I had no belief in spirits, but that's what he was.
Some part of my mind as detached as a crime reporter reminded
me that "The Walk to the Paradise Gardens" was about two
children who were about to die, and that in a sense the music
was their death. I wiped my eyes with my hand, and when I
lowered my arm, the boy was still there. He was beautiful, beautiful in the ordinary way, as Vietnamese children nearly always
seemed beautiful to me. Then he vanished all at once, like the
flickering light of the Zippo. I nearly groaned aloud. That child
had been murdered in the hut: he had not just died, he had been
murdered.

I said something to the other two men and went through the
door into the growing darkness. I was very dimly aware of the
Lieutenant asking Poole to repeat his description of the uprights

and the bloody chain. Hamnet and Burrage and Calvin Hill were sitting down and leaning against a tree. Victor Spitalny was wiping his hands on his filthy shirt. White smoke curled up from Hill's cigarette, and Tina Pumo exhaled a long white stream of vapor. The unhinged thought came to me with an absolute conviction that *this* was the Paradise Gardens. The men lounging in the darkness; the pattern of the cigarette smoke, and the patterns they made, sitting or standing; the in-drawing darkness, as physical as a blanket; the frame of the trees and the flat gray-green background of the paddy.

My soul had come back to life.

Then I became aware that there was something wrong about the men arranged before me, and again it took a moment for my intelligence to catch up to my intuition. Every member of a combat unit makes unconscious adjustments as members of the unit go down in the field; survival sometimes depends on the number of people you know are with you, and you keep count without being quite aware of doing it. I had registered that two men too many were in front of me. Instead of seven, there were nine, and the two men that made up the nine of us left were still behind me in the hut. M. O. Dengler was looking at me with growing curiosity, and I thought he knew exactly what I was thinking. A sick chill went through me. I saw Tom Blevins and Tyrell Budd standing together at the far right of the platoon, a little muddier than the others but otherwise different from the rest only in that, like Dengler, they were looking directly at me.

Hill tossed his cigarette away in an arc of light. Poole and Lieutenant Joys came out of the hut behind me. Leonard Hamnet patted his pocket to reassure himself that he still had his letter. I looked back at the right of the group, and the two dead men were gone.

"Let's saddle up," the Lieutenant said. "We aren't doing any good around here."

"Tim?" Dengler asked. He had not taken his eyes off me since I had come out of the hut. I shook my head.

"Well, what was it?" asked Tina Pumo. "Was it juicy?"

Spanky and Calvin Hill laughed and slapped hands.

"Aren't we gonna torch this place?" asked Spitalny.

The Lieutenant ignored him. "Juicy enough, Pumo. Interrogation Post. Field Interrogation Post."

"No shit," said Pumo.

"These people are into torture, Pumo. It's just another indication."

"Gotcha." Pumo glanced at me and his eyes grew curious. Dengler moved closer.

"I was just remembering something," I said. "Something from the world."

"You better forget about the world while you're over here, Underhill," the Lieutenant told me. "I'm trying to keep you alive, in case you hadn't noticed, but you have to cooperate with me." His Adam's apple jumped like a begging puppy.

As soon as he went ahead to lead us out of the village, I gave twenty dollars to Spanky and said, "Two weeks from today."

"My man," Spanky said.

The rest of the patrol was uneventful.

The next night we had showers, real food, alcohol, cots to sleep in. Sheets and pillows. Two new guys replaced Tyrell Budd and Thomas Blevins, whose names were never mentioned again, at least by me, until long after the war was over and Poole, Linklater, Pumo, and I looked them up, along with the rest of our dead, on the Wall in Washington. I wanted to forget the patrol, especially what I had seen and experienced inside the hut. I wanted the oblivion which came in powdered form.

I remember that it was raining. I remember the steam lifting off the ground, and the condensation dripping down the metal poles in the tents. Moisture shone on the faces around me. I was sitting in the brothers' tent, listening to the music Spanky Burrage played on the big reel-to-reel recorder he had bought on R&R in Taipei. Spanky Burrage never played Delius, but what he played was paradisal: great jazz from Armstrong to Coltrane, on reels recorded for him by his friends back in Little Rock and which he knew so well he could find individual tracks and performances without bothering to look at the counter. Spanky liked to play disc jockey during these long sessions, changing reels and speeding past thousands of feet of tape to play the same songs by different musicians, even the same song hiding under different names—"Cherokee" and "KoKo," "Indiana" and "Donna Lee"—or long series of songs connected by titles that used the same words—"I Thought About You" (Art Tatum), "You and the Night and the Music" (Sonny Rollins),

"I Love You" (Bill Evans), "If I Could Be with You" (Ike Quebec), "You Leave Me Breathless" (Milt Jackson), even, for the sake of the joke, "Thou Swell," by Glenroy Breakstone. In his single-artist mode on this day, Spanky was ranging through the work of a great trumpet player named Clifford Brown.

On this sweltering, rainy day, Clifford Brown's music sounded regal and unearthly. Clifford Brown was walking to the Paradise Gardens. Listening to him was like watching a smiling man shouldering open an enormous door to let in great dazzling rays of light. We were out of the war. The world we were in transcended pain and loss, and imagination had banished fear. Even SP4 Cotton and Calvin Hill, who preferred James Brown to Clifford Brown, lay on their bunks listening as Spanky followed his instincts from one track to another.

After he had played disc jockey for something like two hours, Spanky rewound the long tape and said, "Enough." The end of the tape slapped against the reel. I looked at Dengler, who seemed dazed, as if awakening from a long sleep. The memory of the music was still all around us: light still poured in through the crack in the great door.

"I'm gonna have a smoke *and* a drink," Cotton announced, and pushed himself up off his cot. He walked to the door of the tent and pulled the flap aside to expose the green wet drizzle. That dazzling light, the light from another world, began to fade. Cotton sighed, plopped a wide-brimmed hat on his head, and slipped outside. Before the stiff flap fell shut, I saw him jumping through the puddles on the way to Wilson Manly's shack. I felt as though I had returned from a long journey.

Spanky finished putting the Clifford Brown reel back into its cardboard box. Someone in the rear of the tent switched on Armed Forces Radio. Spanky looked at me and shrugged. Leonard Hamnet took his letter out of his pocket, unfolded it, and read it through very slowly.

"Leonard," I said, and he swung his big buffalo's head toward me. "You still putting in for compassionate leave?"

He nodded. "You know what I gotta do."

"Yes," Dengler said, in a slow quiet voice.

"They gonna let me take care of my people. They gonna send me back."

He spoke with a complete absence of nuance, like a man who

had learned to get what he wanted by parroting words without knowing what they meant.

Dengler looked at me and smiled. For a second he seemed as alien as Hamnet. "What do you think is going to happen? To us, I mean. Do you think it'll just go on like this day after day until some of us get killed and the rest of us go home, or do you think it's going to get stranger and stranger?" He did not wait for me to answer. "I think it'll always sort of look the same, but it won't be—I think the edges are starting to melt. I think that's what happens when you're out here long enough. The edges melt."

"Your edges melted a long time ago, Dengler," Spanky said, and applauded his own joke.

Dengler was still staring at me. He always resembled a serious, dark-haired child, and never looked as though he belonged in uniform. "Here's what I mean, kind of," he said. "When we were listening to that trumpet player—"

"*Brownie,* Clifford *Brown,*" Spanky whispered.

"—I could see the notes in the air. Like they were written out on a long scroll. And after he played them, they stayed in the air for a long time."

"Sweetie-*pie,*" Spanky said softly. "You pretty hip, for a little ofay square."

"When we were back in that village, last week," Dengler said. "Tell me about that."

I said that he had been there too.

"But something happened to you. Something special."

"I put twenty bucks in the Elijah fund," I said.

"Only twenty?" Cotton asked.

"What was in that hut?" Dengler asked.

I shook my head.

"All right," Dengler said. "But it's happening, isn't it? Things are changing."

I could not speak. I could not tell Dengler in front of Cotton and Spanky Burrage that I had imagined seeing the ghosts of Blevins, Budd, and a murdered child. I smiled and shook my head.

"Fine," Dengler said.

"What the fuck you sayin' is *fine*?" Cotton said. "I don't mind listening to that music, but I do draw the line at this bullshit."

He flipped himself off his bunk and pointed a finger at me. "What date you give Spanky?"

"Fifteenth."

"He last longer than that." Cotton tilted his head as the song on the radio ended. Armed Forces Radio began playing a song by Moby Grape. Disgusted, he turned back to me. "Check it out. End of August. He be so tired, he be *sleepwalkin'*. Be halfway through his tour. The fool will go to pieces, and that's when he'll get it."

Cotton had put thirty dollars on August thirty-first, exactly the midpoint of Lieutenant Joy's tour of duty. He had a long time to adjust to the loss of the money, because he himself stayed alive until a sniper killed him at the beginning of February. Then he became a member of the ghost platoon that followed us wherever we went. I think this ghost platoon, filled with men I had loved and detested, whose names I could or could not remember, disbanded only when I went to the Wall in Washington, D.C., and by then I felt that I was a member of it myself.

2

I left the tent with a vague notion of getting outside and enjoying the slight coolness that followed the rain. The packet of Si Van Vo's white powder rested at the bottom of my right front pocket, which was so deep that my fingers just brushed its top. I decided that what I needed was a beer.

Wilson Manly's shack was all the way on the other side of camp. I never liked going to the enlisted men's club, where they were rumored to serve cheap Vietnamese beer in American bottles. Certainly the bottles had often been stripped of their labels, and to a suspicious eye the caps looked dented; also, the beer there never quite tasted like the stuff Manly sold.

One other place remained, farther away than the enlisted men's club but closer than Manly's shack and somewhere between them in official status. About twenty minutes' walk from where I stood, just at the curve in the steeply descending road to the airfield and the motor pool, stood an isolated wooden structure called Billy's. Billy himself, supposedly a Green Beret Captain who had installed a handful of bar girls in an old French command post, had gone home long ago, but his club had endured. There were no more girls, if there ever had been, and the brand-name liquor was about as reliable as the enlisted men's club's beer. When it was open, a succession of slender Montagnard boys who slept in the nearly empty upstairs rooms served drinks. I visited these rooms two or three times, but I never learned where the boys went when Billy's was closed. They spoke almost no English. Billy's did not look anything like a French command post, even one that had been transformed into a bordello: it looked like a roadhouse.

A long time ago, the building had been painted brown. The wood was soft with rot. Someone had once boarded up the two front windows on the lower floor, and someone else had torn off a narrow band of boards across each of the windows, so that light entered in two flat white bands that traveled across the floor during the day. Around six thirty the light bounced off the long foxed mirror that stood behind the row of bottles. After five minutes of blinding light, the sun disappeared beneath the pine boards, and for ten or fifteen minutes a shadowy pink glow filled the barroom. There was no electricity and no ice. Fingerprints covered the glasses. When you needed a toilet, you went to a cubicle with inverted metal boot prints on either side of a hole in the floor.

The building stood in a little grove of trees in the curve of the descending road, and as I walked toward it in the diffuse reddish light of the sunset, a mud-spattered jeep painted in the colors of camouflage gradually came into view to the right of the bar, emerging from invisibility like an optical illusion. The jeep seemed to have floated out of the trees behind it, to be a part of them.

I heard low male voices, which stopped when I stepped onto the soft boards of the front porch. I glanced at the jeep, looking for insignia or identification, but the mud covered the door panels. Something white gleamed dully from the back seat. When I looked more closely, I saw in a coil of rope an oval of bone that it took me a moment to recognize as the top of a painstakingly cleaned and bleached human skull.

Before I could reach the handle, the door opened. A boy named Mike stood before me, in loose khaki shorts and a dirty white shirt much too large for him. Then he saw who I was. "Oh," he said. "Yes. Tim. Okay. You can come in." His real name was not Mike, but Mike was what it sounded like. He carried himself with an odd defensive alertness, and he shot me a tight, uncomfortable smile. "Far table, right side."

"It's okay?" I asked, because everything about him told me that it wasn't.

"Yesss." He stepped back to let me in.

I smelled cordite before I saw the other men. The bar looked empty, and the band of light coming in through the opening over the windows had already reached the long mirror, creating a bright dazzle, a white fire. I took a couple of steps inside, and Mike moved around me to return to his post.

"Oh, hell," someone said from off to my left. "We have to put up with *this*?"

I turned my head to look into the murk of that side of the bar, and saw three men sitting against the wall at a round table. None of the kerosene lamps had been lighted yet, and the dazzle from the mirror made the far reaches of the bar even less distinct.

"Is okay, is okay," said Mike. "Old customer. Old friend."

"I bet he is," the voice said. "Just don't let any women in here."

"No women," Mike said. "No problem."

I went through the tables to the furthest one on the right.

"You want whiskey, Tim?" Mike asked.

"Tim?" the man said. *"Tim?"*

"Beer," I said, and sat down.

A nearly empty bottle of Johnny Walker Black, three glasses, and about a dozen cans of beer covered the table before them. The soldier with his back against the wall shoved aside some of the beer cans so that I could see the .45 next to the Johnny Walker bottle. He leaned forward with a drunk's sloppy coordination. The sleeves had been ripped off his shirt, and dirt darkened his skin as if he had not bathed in years. His hair had been cut with a knife, and had once been blond.

"I just want to make sure about this," he said. "You're not a woman, right? You swear to that?"

"Anything you say," I said.

"No woman walks into this place." He put his hand on the gun. "No nurse. No wife. No *anything*. You got that?"

"Got it," I said. Mike hurried around the bar with my beer.

"Tim. Funny name. Tom, now—that's a name. Tim sounds

like a little guy—like him." He pointed at Mike with his left hand, the whole hand and not merely the index finger, while his right still rested on the .45. "Little fucker ought to be wearing a dress. Hell, he practically *is* wearing a dress."

"Don't you like women?" I asked. Mike put a can of Budweiser on my table and shook his head rapidly, twice. He had wanted me in the club because he was afraid the drunken soldier was going to shoot him, and now I was just making things worse.

I looked at the two men with the drunken officer. They were dirty and exhausted—whatever had happened to the drunk had also happened to them. The difference was that they were not drunk yet.

"That is a complicated question," the drunk said. "There are questions of responsibility. You can be responsible for yourself. You can be responsible for your children and your tribe. You are responsible for anyone you want to protect. But can you be responsible for women? If so, how responsible?"

Mike quietly moved behind the bar and sat on a stool with his arms out of sight. I knew he had a shotgun under there.

"You don't have any idea what I'm talking about, do you, Tim, you rear-echelon dipshit?"

"You're afraid you'll shoot any women who come in here, so you told the bartender to keep them out."

"This wise-ass sergeant is personally interfering with my state of mind," the drunk said to the burly man on his right. "Tell him to get out of here, or a certain degree of unpleasantness will ensue."

"Leave him alone," the other man said. Stripes of dried mud lay across his lean, haggard face.

The drunken officer Beret startled me by leaning toward the other man and speaking in a clear, carrying Vietnamese. It was an old-fashioned, almost literary Vietnamese, and he must have thought and dreamed in it to speak it so well. He assumed that neither I nor the Montagnard boy would understand him.

This is serious, he said, *and I am serious. If you wish to see how serious, just sit in your chair and do nothing. Do you not know of what I am capable by now? Have you learned nothing? You know what I know. I know what you know. A great heaviness is between us. Of all the people in the world at this moment, the only ones I do not despise are already dead, or should be. At this moment, murder is weightless.*

There was more, and I cannot swear that this was exactly what he said, but it's pretty close. He may have said that murder was *empty.*

Then he said, in that same flowing Vietnamese that even to my ears sounded as stilted as the language of a third-rate Victorian novel: *Recall what is in our vehicle (carriage); you should remember what we have brought with us, because I shall never forget it. Is it so easy for you to forget?*

It takes a long time and a lot of patience to clean and bleach bone. A skull would be more difficult than most of a skeleton.

Your leader requires more of this nectar, he said, and rolled back in his chair, looking at me with his hand on his gun.

"Whiskey," said the burly soldier. Mike was already pulling the bottle off the shelf. He understood that the officer was trying to knock himself out before he would find it necessary to shoot someone.

For a moment I thought that the burly soldier to his right looked familiar. His head had been shaved so close he looked bald, and his eyes were enormous above the streaks of dirt. A stainless-steel watch hung from a slot in his collar. He extended a muscular arm for the bottle Mike passed him while keeping as far from the table as he could. The soldier twisted off the cap and poured into all three glasses. The man in the center immediately drank all the whiskey in his glass and banged the glass down on the table for a refill.

The haggard soldier who had been silent until now said, "Something is gonna happen here." He looked straight at me. "Pal?"

"That man is nobody's pal," the drunk said. Before anyone could stop him, he snatched up the gun, pointed it across the room, and fired. There was a flash of fire, a huge explosion, and the reek of cordite. The bullet went straight through the soft wooden wall, about eight feet to my left. A stray bit of light slanted through the hole it made.

For a moment I was deaf. I swallowed the last of my beer and stood up. My head was ringing.

"Is it clear that I hate the necessity for this kind of shit?" said the drunk. "Is that much understood?"

The soldier who had called me pal laughed, and the burly soldier poured more whiskey into the drunk's glass. Then he stood up and started coming toward me. Beneath the exhaustion and the stripes of dirt, his face was taut with anxiety. He put himself between me and the man with the gun.

"I am not a rear-echelon dipshit," I said. "I don't want any trouble, but people like him do not own this war."

"Will you maybe let me save your ass, Sergeant?" he whispered. "Major Bachelor hasn't been anywhere near white men in three years, and he's having a little trouble readjusting. Compared to him, we're all rear-echelon dipshits."

I looked at his tattered shirt. "Are you his babysitter, Captain?"

He gave me an exasperated look and glanced over his shoulder at the Major. "Major, put down your damn weapon. The sergeant is a combat soldier. He is on his way back to camp."

I don't care what he is, the Major said in Vietnamese.

The Captain began pulling me toward the door, keeping his body between me and the other table. I motioned for Mike to come out with me.

"Don't worry, the Major won't shoot him, Major Bachelor loves the Yards," the Captain said. He gave me an impatient glance because I had refused to move at his pace. Then I saw him notice my pupils. "God damn," he said, and then he stopped moving altogether and said "God damn" again, but in a different tone of voice.

I started laughing.

"Oh, this is—" He shook his head. "This is really—"

"Where have you *been*?" I asked him.

John Ransom turned to the table. "Hey, I know this guy. He's an old football friend of mine."

Major Bachelor shrugged and put the .45 back on the table. His eyelids had nearly closed. "I don't care about football," he said, but he kept his hand off the weapon.

"Buy the sergeant a drink," said the haggard officer.

"Buy the fucking sergeant a drink," the Major chimed in.

John Ransom quickly moved to the bar and reached for a glass, which the confused Mike put into his hand. Ransom went through the tables, filled his glass and mine, and carried both back to join me.

We watched the Major's head slip down by notches toward his chest. When his chin finally reached the unbuttoned top of his ruined shirt, Ransom said, "All right, Bob," and the other man slid the .45 out from under the Major's hand. He pushed it beneath his belt.

"The man is out," Bob said.

Ransom turned back to me. "He was up three days straight with us, God knows how long before that." Ransom did not have to specify who *he* was. "Bob and I got some sleep, trading off, but he just kept on talking." He fell into one of the chairs at my table and tilted his glass to his mouth. I sat down beside him.

For a moment no one in the bar spoke. The line of light from the open space across the windows had already left the mirror, and was now approaching the place on the wall that meant it would soon disappear. Mike lifted the cover from one of the lamps and began trimming the wick.

"How come you're always fucked up when I see you?"

"You have to ask?"

He smiled. He looked very different from when I had seen him preparing to give a sales pitch to Senator Burrman at Camp White Star. His body had thickened and hardened, and his eyes had retreated far back into his head. He seemed to me to have moved a long step nearer the goal I had always seen in him that when he had given me the zealot's word about stopping the spread of Communism. This man had taken in more of the war, and that much more of the war was inside him now.

"I got you off graves registration at White Star, didn't I?"

I agreed that he had.

"What did you call it, the body squad? It wasn't even a real graves registration unit, was it?" He smiled and shook his head. "I took care of your Captain McCue, too—he was using it as a kind of dumping ground. I don't know how he got away with it as long as he did. The only one with any training was that sergeant, what's his name. Italian."

"DeMaestro."

Ransom nodded. "The whole operation was going off the rails." Mike lit a big kitchen match and touched it to the wick of the kerosene lamp. "I heard some things—" He slumped against the wall and swallowed whiskey. I wondered if he had heard about Captain Havens. He closed his eyes. "Some crazy stuff went on back there."

I asked if he was still stationed in the highlands up around the Laotian border. He almost sighed when he shook his head.

"You're not with the tribesmen anymore? What were they, Khatu?"

He opened his eyes. "You have a good memory. No, I'm not there anymore." He considered saying more, but decided not to. He had failed himself. "I'm kind of on hold until they send me up around Khe Sahn. It'll be better up there–the Bru are tremendous. But right now, all I want to do is take a bath and get into bed. Any bed. Actually, I'd settle for a dry level place on the ground."

"Where did you come from now?"

"Incountry." His face creased and he showed his teeth. The effect was so unsettling that I did not immediately realize that he was smiling. "Way incountry. We had to get the Major out."

"Looks more like you had to pull him out, like a tooth."

My ignorance made him sit up straight. "You mean you never heard of him? Franklin Bachelor?"

And then I thought I had, that someone had mentioned him to me a long time ago.

"In the bush for years. Bachelor did stuff that ordinary people don't even *dream* of—he's a legend."

A legend, I thought. Like the Green Berets Ransom had mentioned a lifetime ago at White Star.

"Ran what amounted to a private army, did a lot of good work in Darlac Province. He was out there on his own. The man was a hero. That's straight. Bachelor got to places we couldn't even get close to—he got *inside* an NVA encampment, you hear me, *inside* the encampment and *silently* killed about an entire division."

Of all the people in the world at this minute, I remembered, the only ones he did not detest were already dead. I thought I must have heard it wrong.

"He was absorbed right into Rhade life," Ransom said. I could hear the awe in his voice. "The man even got married. Rhade ceremony. His wife went with him on missions. I hear she was beautiful."

Then I knew where I had heard of Franklin Bachelor before.

He had been a captain when Ratman and his platoon had run into him after a private named Bobby Swett had been blown to pieces on a trail in Darlac Province. Ratman had thought his wife was a black-haired angel.

And then I knew whose skull lay wound in rope in the back seat of the jeep.

"I did hear of him," I said. "I knew someone who met him. The Rhade woman, too."

"His *wife*," Ransom said.

I asked him where they were taking Bachelor.

"We're stopping overnight at Crandall for some rest. Then we hop to Tan Son Nhut and bring him back to the States—Langley. I thought we might have to strap him down, but I guess we'll just keep pouring whiskey into him."

"He's going to want his gun back."

"Maybe I'll give it to him." His look told me what he thought Major Bachelor would do with his .45, if he was left alone with it long enough. "He's in for a rough time at Langley. There'll be some heat."

"Why Langley?"

"Don't ask. But don't be naïve, either. Don't you think they're . . ." He would not finish that sentence. "Why do you think we had to bring him out in the first place?"

"Because something went wrong."

"Oh, everything went wrong. Bachelor went totally out of control. He had his own war. Ran a lot of sidelines, some of which were supposed to be under shall we say tighter controls?"

He had lost me.

"Ventures into Laos. Business trips to Cambodia. Sometimes he wound up in control of airfields Air America was using, and that meant he was in control of the cargo."

When I shook my head, he said, "Don't you have a little something in your pocket? A little package?"

A secret world—inside this world, another, secret world.

"You understand, I don't care what he did any more than I care about what *you* do. I think Langley can go fuck itself. Bachelor wrote the book. In spite of his sidelines. In spite of whatever *trouble* he got into. The man was effective. He stepped over a boundary, maybe a lot of boundaries–but tell me that you can do what we're supposed to do without stepping over boundaries."

I wondered why he seemed to be defending himself, and asked
if he would have to testify at Langley.

"It's not a trial."

"A debriefing."

"Sure, a debriefing. They can ask me anything they want. All
I can tell them is what I saw. That's *my* evidence, right? What
I saw? They don't have any evidence, except maybe this, uh,
these human remains the Major insisted on bringing out."

For a second, I wished that I could see the sober shadowy
gentlemen of Langley, Virginia, the gentlemen with slicked-back
hair and pinstriped suits, question Major Bachelor. They thought
they were serious men.

"It was like Bong To, in a funny way." Ransom waited for
me to ask. When I did not, he said, "A ghost town, I mean. I
don't suppose you've ever heard of Bong To."

"My unit was just there." His head jerked up. "A mortar
round scared us into the village."

"You saw the place?"

I nodded.

"Funny story." Now he was sorry he had ever mentioned it.
"Well, think about Bachelor, now. I think he must have been in
Cambodia or someplace, doing what he does, when his village
was overrun. He comes back and finds everybody dead, his wife
included. I mean, I don't think *Bachelor* killed those people—
they weren't just dead, they'd been made to beg for it. So Bachelor wasn't there, and his assistant, a Captain Bennington, must
have just run off—we never did find him. Officially, Bennington's MIA. It's simple. You can't find the main guy, so you make
sure he can see how mad you are when he gets back. You do a
little grievous bodily harm on his people. They were not nice to
his wife, Tim, to her they were especially not nice. What does
he do? He buries all the bodies in the village graveyard, because
that's a sacred responsibility. Don't ask me what else he does,
because you don't have to know this, okay? But the bodies are
buried. Generally speaking. Captain Bennington never does
show up. We arrive and take Bachelor away. But sooner or later,
some of the people who escaped are going to come back to that
village. They're going to go on living there. The worst thing in
the world happened to them in that place, but they won't leave.
Eventually, other people in their family will join them, if they're

still alive, and the terrible thing will be a part of their lives. Because it is not thinkable to leave your dead."

"But they did in Bong To," I said.

"In Bong To, they did."

I saw the look of regret on his face again, and said that I wasn't asking him to tell me any secrets.

"It's not a secret. It's not even military."

"It's just a ghost town."

Ransom was still uncomfortable. He turned his glass around and around in his hands before he drank. "I have to get the Major into camp."

"It's a real ghost town," I said. "Complete with ghosts."

"I honestly wouldn't be surprised." He drank what was left in his glass and stood up. He had decided not to say any more about it. "Let's take care of Major Bachelor, Bob," he said.

"Right."

Ransom carried our bottle to the bar and paid Mike. I stepped toward him to do the same, and Ransom said, "Taken care of."

There was that phrase again—it seemed I had been hearing it all day, and that its meaning would not stay still.

Ransom and Bob picked up the Major between them. They were strong enough to lift him easily. Bachelor's greasy head rolled forward. Bob put the .45 into his pocket, and Ransom put the bottle into his own pocket. Together they carried the Major to the door.

I followed them outside. Artillery pounded hills a long way off. It was dark now, and light from the lanterns spilled out through the gaps in the windows.

All of us went down the rotting steps, the Major bobbing between the other two.

Ransom opened the jeep, and they took a while to maneuver the Major into the back seat. Bob squeezed in beside him and pulled him upright.

John Ransom got in behind the wheel and sighed. He had no taste for the next part of his job.

"I'll give you a ride back to camp," he said. "We don't want an MP to get a close look at you."

I took the seat beside him. Ransom started the engine and turned on the lights. He jerked the gearshift into reverse and rolled backwards. "You know why that mortar round came in,

344 THE MISTS FROM BEYOND

don't you?" he asked me. He grinned at me, and we bounced onto the road back to the main part of camp. "He was trying to chase you away from Bong To, and your fool of a Lieutenant went straight for the place instead." He was still grinning. "It must have steamed him, seeing a bunch of round-eyes going in there."

"He didn't send in any more fire."

"No. He didn't want to damage the place. It's supposed to stay the way it is. I don't think they'd use the word, but that village is supposed to be like a kind of monument." He glanced at me again. "To shame."

For some reason, all I could think of was the drunken Major in the seat behind me, who had said that you were responsible for the people you wanted to protect. Ransom said, "Did you go into any of the huts? Did you see anything unusual there?"

"I went into a hut. I saw something unusual."

"A list of names?"

"I thought that's what they were."

"Okay," Ransom said. "You know a little Vietnamese?"

"A little."

"You notice anything about those names?"

I could not remember. My Vietnamese had been picked up in bars and markets, and was almost completely oral.

"Four of them were from a family named Trang. Trang was the village chief, like his father before him, and his grandfather before him. Trang had four daughters. As each one got to the age of six or seven, he took them down into that underground room and chained them to the posts and raped them. A lot of those huts have hidden storage areas, but Trang must have modified his after his first daughter was born. The funny thing is, I think everybody in the village knew what he was doing. I'm not saying they thought it was okay, but they let it happen. They could pretend they didn't know: the girls never complained, and nobody ever heard any screams. I guess Trang was a good-enough chief. When the daughters got to sixteen, they left for the cities. Sent back money, too. So maybe they thought it was okay, but I don't think they did, myself, do you?"

"How would I know? But there's a man in my platoon, a guy from— "

"I think there's a difference between private and public shame.

Between what's acknowledged and what is not acknowledged. That's what Bachelor has to cope with, when he gets to Langley. Some things are acceptable, as long as you don't talk about them." He looked sideways at me as we began to approach the northern end of the camp proper. He wiped his face, and flakes of dried mud fell off his cheek. The exposed skin looked red, and so did his eyes. "Because the way I see it, this is a whole general issue. The issue is: what is *expressible*? This goes way beyond the tendency of people to tolerate thoughts, actions, or behavior they would otherwise find unacceptable."

I had never heard a soldier speak this way before. It was a little bit like being back in Berkeley.

"I'm talking about the difference between what is expressed and what is described," Ransom said. "A lot of experience is unacknowledged. Religion lets us handle some of the unacknowledged stuff in an acceptable way. But suppose—just suppose— that you were forced to confront extreme experience directly, without any mediation?"

"I have," I said. "You have, too."

"More extreme than combat, more extreme than terror. Something like that happened to the Major: he *encountered* God. Demands were made upon him. He had to move out of the ordinary, even as *he* defined it."

Ransom was telling me how Major Bachelor had wound up being brought to Camp Crandall with his wife's skull, but none of it was clear to me.

"I've been learning things," Ransom told me. He was almost whispering. "Think about what would make all the people of a village pick up and leave, when sacred obligation ties them to that village."

"I don't know the answer," I said.

"An even more sacred obligation, created by a really spectacular sense of shame. When a crime is too great to live with, the memory of it becomes sacred. Becomes the crime itself–"

I remembered thinking that the arrangement in the hut's basement had been a shrine to an obscene deity.

"Here we have this village and its chief. The village knows but does not know what the chief has been doing. They are used to consulting and obeying him. Then—one day, a little boy disappears."

My heart gave a thud.

"A little boy. Say: three. Old enough to talk and get into trouble, but too young to take care of himself. He's just gone—*poof*. Well, this is Vietnam, right? You turn your back, your kid wanders away, some animal gets him. He could get lost in the jungle and wander into a claymore. Someone like you might even shoot him. He could fall into a boobytrap and never be seen again. It could happen.

"A couple of months later, it happens again. Mom turns her back, where the hell did Junior go? This time they really look, not just Mom and Grandma, all their friends. They scour the village. The *villagers* scour the village, every square foot of that place, and then they do the same to the rice paddy, and then they look through the forest.

"And guess what happens next. This is the interesting part. An old woman goes out one morning to fetch water from the well, and she sees a ghost. This old lady is part of the extended family of the first lost kid, but the ghost she sees isn't the kid's—it's the ghost of a disreputable old man from another village, a drunkard, in fact. A local no-good, in fact. He's just standing near the well with his hands together, he's hungry—that's what these people know about ghosts. The skinny old bastard wants *more*. He wants to be *fed*. The old lady gives a squawk and passes out. When she comes to again, the ghost is gone.

"Well, the old lady tells everybody what she saw, and the whole village gets in a panic. Evil forces have been set loose. Next thing you know, two thirteen-year-old girls are working in the paddy, they look up and see an old woman who died when they were ten—she's about six feet away from them. Her hair is stringy and gray and her fingernails are about a foot long. She used to be a friendly old lady, but she doesn't look too friendly now. She's hungry too, like all ghosts. They start screaming and crying, but no one else can see her, and she comes closer and closer, and they try to get away but one of them falls down, and the old woman is on her like a cat. And do you know what she does? She rubs her filthy hands over the screaming girl's face, and licks the tears and slobber off her fingers.

"The next night, another little boy disappears. Two men go looking around the village latrine behind the houses, and they see two ghosts down in the pit, shoving excrement into their mouths. They rush back into the village, and then they both see half a dozen ghosts around the chief's hut. Among them are a sister who died during the war with the French and a twenty-year-old first wife who died of dengue fever. They want to eat. One of the men screeches, because not only did he see his dead wife, who looks something like what we could call a vampire, he saw her pass into the chief's hut without the benefit of the door.

"These people believe in ghosts, Underhill, they know ghosts exist, but it is extremely rare for them to see these ghosts. And these people are like psychoanalysts, because they do not believe in accidents. Every event contains meaning.

"The dead twenty-year-old wife comes back out through the wall of the chief's hut. Her hands are empty but dripping with red, and she is licking them like a starving cat.

"The former husband stands there pointing and jabbering, and the mothers and grandmothers of the missing boys come out of their huts. They are as afraid of what they're thinking as they are of all the ghosts moving around them. The ghosts are part of what they know they know, even though most of them have never seen one until now. What is going through their minds is something new: new because it was hidden.

"The mothers and grandmothers go to the chief's door and begin howling like dogs. When the chief comes out, they push past him and they take the hut apart. And you know what they find. They found the end of Bong To."

Ransom had parked the jeep near my battalion headquarters five minutes before, and now he smiled as if he had explained everything.

"But what *happened*?" I asked. "How did you hear about it?"

He shrugged. "We learned all this in interrogation. When the women found the underground room, they knew the chief had forced the boys into sex, and then killed them. They didn't know what he had done with the bodies, but they knew he had killed the boys. The next time the VC paid one of their courtesy calls, they told the cadre leader what they knew. The VC did the rest. They were disgusted—Trang had betrayed *them*, too—betrayed everything he was supposed to represent. One of the VC we captured took the chief downstairs into his underground room and chained the man to the posts, wrote the names of the dead boys and Trang's daughters on the padding that covered the walls, and then . . . then they did what they did to him. They probably carried out the pieces and threw them into the excrement pit. And over months, bit by bit, not all at once but slowly, everybody in the village moved out. By that time, they were seeing ghosts all the time. They had crossed a kind of border."

"Do you think they really saw ghosts?" I asked him. "I mean, do you think they were real ghosts?"

"If you want an expert opinion, you'd have to ask Major Bachelor. He has a lot to say about ghosts." He hesitated for a moment, and then leaned over to open my door. "But if you ask me, sure they did."

I got out of the jeep and closed the door.

Ransom peered at me through the jeep's window. "Take better care of yourself."

"Good luck with your Bru."

"The Bru are fantastic." He slammed the jeep into gear and shot away, cranking the wheel to turn the jeep around in a giant circle in front of the battalion headquarters before he jammed it into second and took off to wherever he was going.

Two weeks later Leonard Hamnet managed to get the Lutheran chaplain at Crandall to write a letter to the Tin Man for him, and two days after that he was in a clean uniform, packing up his kit for an overnight flight to an Air Force base in California. From there he was connecting to a Memphis flight, and from there the Army had booked him onto a six-passenger puddle jumper to Lookout Mountain.

When I came into Hamnet's tent he was zipping his bag shut in a zone of quiet afforded him by the other men. He did not want to talk about where he was going or the reason he was going there, and instead of answering my questions about his flights, he unzipped a pocket on the side of his bag and handed me a thick folder of airline tickets.

I looked through them and gave them back. "Hard travel," I said.

"From now on, everything is easy," Hamnet said. He seemed rigid and constrained as he zipped the precious tickets back into the bag. By this time his wife's letter was a rag held together with Scotch tape. I could picture him reading and rereading it, for the thousandth or two thousandth time, on the long flight over the Pacific.

"They need your help," I said. "I'm glad they're going to get it."

"That's right." Hamnet waited for me to leave him alone.

Because his bag seemed heavy, I asked about the length of his leave. He wanted to get the tickets back out of the bag rather than answer me directly, but he forced himself to speak. "They gave me seven days. Plus travel time."

"Good," I said, meaninglessly, and then there was nothing left to say, and we both knew it. Hamnet hoisted his bag off his bunk and turned to the door without any of the usual farewells and embraces. Some of the other men called to him, but he seemed to hear nothing but his own thoughts. I followed him outside and stood beside him in the heat. Hamnet was wearing a tie and his boots had a high polish. He was already sweating through his stiff khaki shirt. He would not meet my eyes. In a minute a jeep pulled up before us. The Lutheran chaplain had surpassed himself.

"Goodbye, Leonard," I said, and Hamnet tossed his bag in back and got into the jeep. He sat up straight as a statue. The private driving the jeep said something to him as they drove off, but Hamnet did not reply. I bet he did not say a word to the stewardesses, either, or to the cabdrivers or baggage handlers or anyone else who witnessed his long journey home.

3

On the day after Leonard Hamnet was scheduled to return, Lieutenant Joys called Michael Poole and myself into his quarters to tell us what had happened back in Tennessee. He held a sheaf of papers in his hand, and he seemed both angry and embarrassed. Hamnet would not be returning to the platoon. It was a little funny. Well, of course it wasn't funny at all. The whole thing was terrible—that was what it was. Someone was to blame, too. Irresponsible decisions had been made, and we'd all be lucky if there wasn't an investigation. We were closest to the man, hadn't we seen what was likely to happen? If not, what the hell was our excuse?

Didn't we have any inkling of what the man was planning to do?

Well, yes, at the beginning, Poole and I said. But he seemed to have adjusted.

We have stupidity and incompetence all the way down the line here, said Lieutenant Elijah Joys. Here is a man who manages to carry a semiautomatic weapon through security at three different airports, bring it into a courthouse, and carry out threats he made months before, without anybody stopping him.

I remembered the bag Hamnet had tossed into the back of the jeep; I remembered the reluctance with which he had zipped it open to show me his tickets. Hamnet had not carried his weapon through airport security. He had just shipped it home in his bag and walked straight through customs in his clean uniform and shiny boots.

As soon as the foreman had announced the guilty verdict, Leonard Hamnet had gotten to his feet, pulled the semiautomatic pistol from inside his jacket, and executed Mr. Brewster where he was sitting at the defense table. While people shouted and screamed and dove for cover, while the courthouse officer tried to unsnap his gun, Hamnet killed his wife and his son. By the time he raised the pistol to his own head, the security officer had shot him twice in the chest. He died on the operating table at Lookout Mountain Lutheran Hospital, and his mother had requested that his remains receive burial at Arlington National Cemetery.

His mother. Arlington. I ask you.

That was what the Lieutenant said. *His mother. Arlington. I ask you.*

A private from Indianapolis named E. W. Burroughs won the six hundred and twenty dollars in the Elijah Fund when Lieutenant Joys was killed by a fragmentation bomb thirty-two days before the end of his tour. After that we were delivered unsuspecting into the hands of Harry Beevers, the Lost Boss, the worst lieutenant in the world. Private Burroughs died a week later, down in Dragon Valley along with Tiano and Calvin Hill and lots of others, when Lieutenant Beevers walked us into a mined field where we spent forty-eight hours under fire between two companies of NVA. I suppose Burroughs's mother back in Indianapolis got the six hundred and twenty dollars.